PARACHUTE

PARACHUTE

HARLEIGH RAE

This is a work of fiction. Names, characters, businesses, places, events, locales, and incidents are either the products of the author's imagination or used in a fictitious manner. Any resemblance to actual persons, living or dead, or actual events is purely coincidental. The medical references and scenarios throughout this book does not replace the advice of a medical professional. Do not self-diagnose. Consult your physician before making any changes to your diet or regular health plan.

Parachute

Library of Congress Control Number: 2023902477
Hardcover: 979-8-9877385-0-4
Paperback: 979-8-9877385-1-1

First paperback edition, 2023.

Edited by SheKnowles Editing
Proofread by Hopeful Heartbreakers
Cover Image by Studio M
Cover Design by Raevin & Co.
Layout by Raevin & Co.
Author Headshot © 2022 Javon Roye

Raevin & Co.
Baltimore, MD 21206
www.xoharleighrae.com

CONTENT WARNINGS

These content notes are made available here so readers can inform themselves if they want to. They're based on the movie classification notes that you'd find before the opening credits or on the back of the DVD. Some readers might consider these as 'spoilers' and if that's you, by all means you can skip this section. However, the subject matter explored in Parachute may be triggering for some readers. More than anything, the experience you have while reading my work matters to me. Continue reading for content notes specific to this novel:

Language: vulgar, sexual, frequent

Mental Health: emotional abandonment, medical trauma, suicide ideation

Sexual content: explicit sex scene

Disabilities: detailed medical talk, comatose, medical diagnosis of invisible illness, lupus

Death: death of parents, extensive talk of afterlife

Other: abortion (mentioned), childbirth, pre-term labor, labor complications

Dedicated to the:

Black warrior woman,
fighting silent battles alone,
and shielding her heart from love.

You can let down your guard
and let him love you.

Love doesn't die,
People do.

So, when all that's left of me
Is love,

Give me away.

Merrit Malloy, Epitaph

INTRODUCTION

"Even when I have nothing left, I'll have everything I need." - Phoenix.

With her 10-year plan working out just the way she'd mapped it 6 years ago, Phoenix welcomed the life she'd crafted for herself. There seemed to be no rain threatening her sunshine, but as legend tells it, when it rains, it indeed pours.

At the peak of her professional success, she silently fights the most challenging battle she's ever been up against. But her parents were on to something when they named her Phoenix. No matter how many times she goes down, she rises. A series of unfortunate occurrences lands her in Solace Point, searching for a cure, yet, she gets a remedy by the name of Blaise instead.

Dr. Blaise Jones has acquired everything he'd planned for himself. Leaving no box unchecked, he journeys to Solace Point for the culmination of his medical accomplishments. With a corner office and a white coat, life couldn't be more perfect. But a welcome mixer sets his sights on the ideal distraction. She lit up her corner booth with enough fire to melt the ice that had subconsciously formed around his workaholic heart.

One late-night encounter at the town's premier coffee shop complicates the sole intentions of Phoenix and Blaise. Barriers are crossed, and vows are broken in this fight for life, love, and peace. A heart-warming romance that proves, one never really falls when they're in love with their soulmate.

CHAPTER ONE

7:35 A.M. MONDAY. THE FALL SUN SHINED THROUGH THE PARTIALLY OPENED blinds of the single-paned window. As she sat on the examination table, the cool breeze from the vent over the table grazed her skin. Chill bumps formed with a slight ruffling of the fine hairs on her arms. There was no need to pull her sweater tightly around her body again because the repetitive nature of these visits had let her know what was to come next. Like a vampire with heightened sound, she turned her ear to the door, listening intently for the turning of the doorknob.

Five minutes had passed since she'd sat pressing her palms into the protective covering over the semi-comfortable, faux leather gurney-style table. Her eyes and ears hadn't relinquished the door yet, and she silently wished for an escape from the deafening silence. Four seconds later, the doctor and his team of residents marched in and introduced themselves. With not much enthusiasm, she shook each hand, not even attempting to put faces to names. She'd been through this every month. Shaking new hands, learning new names; only to do it all over again with not one new remedy to cure the chronic illness that threatened her very existence. With sore fingers and purple hands, she gave a nervous smile that signaled the lead doctor to commence.

“Ms. Colleville. How’s it been going since our last check in?”

“In short, bad. Everything hurts. My pain levels are the worst, and I'm fatigued pretty much all the time. My appetite is pretty much non-existent and now my hair is falling out in chunks. My back pain has been unbearable since I last came, and the muscle relaxers and pain meds are not dulling it at all."

“Okay, we’re going to do another blood test. I want to see what your kidneys are doing. In the meantime, I’m going to increase your Prednisone to 60mg twice a day and your Plaquenil to 400mg. So instead of the 200mg once a day, I want you to either take two tablets once a day or one tablet twice a day. Whichever one doesn’t make you too nauseous. Call Kris in about two weeks to let us know if that improves your pain and inflammation.”

After Dr. Crane had examined her joints and checked her vitals a second time, he was at his computer. Sound used to soothe her heart, but the sharp tapping of the doctor’s fingers against the keyboard pierced her ears. She was in constant agony not being able to manage her pain. The fact that she couldn’t predict how she’d feel from one day to the next was the most frustrating thing about the entire ordeal. Making plans and having a schedule were now obsolete in her new normal where nothing was normal at all.

“Okay. I'll start the increased dosage today when I take my morning meds.”

“Do you need any refills?”

“Yes. On both,” Phoenix paused. With a deep breath, she finally asked the question that was burning a hole in her brain. “Dr. Crane, do you have any idea when I can get back to work? Being home is driving me crazy.”

“I don't want to release you for work until we have your treatment plan solidified. You've already gone into psychosis more than twice and had a heart scare. I'm not sure being in that hectic work environment is conducive right now. But know that I'll use all my resources and expertise to get you back in front of that camera.

Have you thought anymore about reaching out to the therapist I recommended? He can give you some resources for support groups and help you find ways to occupy your time while you're at home."

"I've seen Dr. Reveres twice. He gave me the information for a support group and prescribed me a mood stabilizer. The support group really wasn't my scene and none of the patients were my demographic. They were all much older and had lived their lives. I started the stabilizers but hated how they made me feel. So, I've just been seeing him for talk therapy. But the sooner I can get back to work full-time the better. My work keeps me grounded. I don't want to be dependent on the medicine or the support group. I just want to get better and get back to my world."

"That's one of our goals, but the most important one is that you are healthy. I know it's hard sitting still. You're young, intelligent, and bursting with ideas. You'll get back to your work. We're working diligently and carefully to get you there. But just focus on getting your strength back. We want you healthy; not just physically for work, but mentally and emotionally for yourself as well."

"Thanks, Dr. Crane... for everything."

Phoenix had been diagnosed with systemic lupus erythematosus just before officially moving to Solace Point. All through her four years of undergrad, she suffered in silence while working toward her goals. Finally, after passing out at work, she was unable to mask the pain anymore. By the time she sought help, her pleas for answers to her constant and seemingly unprovoked agony was passed off as exaggeration and paranoia. She'd given up trying to figure out why it felt like she went to sleep twenty-one and woke up feeling like she'd aged sixty years.

Once she acquired her dream job, those pains were put on the back burner. Four Aleve a day, lots of aspirin, and countless heating pads served as the conduits for her home remedy. They barely did the trick, but barely was all she could ask for in her current predicament. So, she worked tirelessly, finding, and shooting compelling stories for her hometown's local news station. It had been her dream; the one thing she always told her parents she would do.

Then, two months shy of a year ago, her brother-in-law insisted she come to Solace Point to see the renowned rheumatologist, Dr. Ian Crane. After one visit, several blood tests, and an MRI she was finally given the answer. Though not one she wanted to hear, knowing she had SLE relieved her of the looks of annoyance the doctors would give her or the many WebMD diagnosis she'd been giving herself. She was glad to finally know what changed her from vibrant and hard working to lackluster and fatigued. But the diagnosis was only a fraction of the battle. It seemed that once she knew what she was dealing with, the disease decided to just wreak havoc on her entire life. Dr. Crane had seen her through some of the worst times of her illness, and she was grateful because he was booked for months, but as a solid for his best friend, he added her to his patient list.

"Alright, Phoenix. Kris will be in shortly to get some blood from you. We'll need a urine sample too," Dr. Crane said as he rose to his feet.

Nodding in approval, she texted her big sister that her appointment was nearing its end. An exasperated sigh left her lungs the instant she was alone. Life had become predictable, and she detested every second of it. The last two years had been like living in a bubble with a 30-mile diameter. Doctors' appointments, debriefings with her sister, and dates with her tear-stained pillows had become the only remnants of the life she once lived.

Though all these things were routine every four weeks, she never got used to any of it. The hairs on her forearm still raised from the chills she felt when she rolled her sleeve up to the elbow. Her body still tensed up as Kris placed the needle point to her skin. Her breath still sat in her throat until the tourniquet was removed.

"Hey, Phoenix. How's everybody?"

"Hi, Kris. Everybody's fine. You know Big Sis is just as over-protective as she's always been."

"Meeting her at *Noir Tea x Nature* afterward?"

"You know it. Can you make sure Dr. Crane uploads my results into the patient portal? I know Travis is going to ask about them the second he sees me."

"Sure thing. Make a fist for me," Kris responded as she tightened the tourniquet around Phoenix's bicep.

Kris worked quickly to get Phoenix squared away. Phoenix stuffed her arms back inside the thin sweater that shielded her flesh from the piercing cold. No matter how many times she walked through the double doors of her doctor's office, she would never deem it her norm. It was an inconvenience that just so happened to come around every month for the past year. The second she was bandaged and handed over the urine cup; she hightailed it from the examination room. After finishing up in the bathroom and placing her cup in the designated collection basket, she stuffed her hands in the pockets of her jeans. Never even stopping at the check-out counter, she bolted through the door and commenced her scenic route to meet her sister for a quick lunch.

The rays of Solace Point's high noon sun greeted Phoenix with a warm kiss to her frigid face. Despite the somber mood caused by visits to Solace General, mornings in this picturesque town made it impossible not to smile through the angst and pain. As she walked the seven blocks it took to reach *Noir Tea x Nature,* she greeted the shop owners as they pulled out their daily specials and fresh fruit bins. This part of Solace Point was a drastic change from the cold, fast-paced city she'd left behind. Everyone was so warm and inviting. They took their time showing people that they were genuinely happy to see them. They greeted each day with gratitude, wonder, and looked for new opportunities to give a little love to whoever might need it most.

The energy in the café was high, considering it was just after 8:30 in the morning. Phoenix cocked her head to the left as her eyes and smile fell on her big sister. Married life looked good on her. Not to mention she was able to fall off her sister's radar for much of her adult life, thanks to her amazing brother-in-law and two adorable nieces. Now that they were school-aged, she had extra time on her hands, leaving her nothing but time, space and opportunity to pine over Phoenix and her disregard for her own health.

"Baby Love, I missed you," she greeted Phoenix as she approached the table.

"Rue Rabbit." Phoenix laughed as she threw her arms around her shorter, older sister.

It had been a few weeks since they were able to embrace each other. Soccer mom duties had Rue carting her children and a few of their teammates from practices to celebratory pizza parties. Worry instantly set into the pit of Rue's stomach as Phoenix pulled away from their hug. Her body language screamed that she was weary and anxious.

Motioning with her arm, she ushered her little sister into the corner booth they occupied at least once a month. Rue scooted into the booth and pushed a steaming cup of hibiscus tea with agave nectar and a twinge of lemon toward Phoenix. For a second, joy twinkled in the inner corners of Phoenix's eyes as she cupped the piping hot mug between her palms. The corners of her lips coiled into a faint smile as she took her first sip. The potent flavor of the steeped flower sent a jolt of electricity coursing through her body.

"Mmmm. Now this is just what the doctor ordered." Phoenix exhaled as she sat her mug down after one more sip.

"So, out with it. What did Ian say? I've been on pins and needles since your text. I'm already on my second chocolate square."

"Nothing really new. He upped the strength of my meds and wants to see if that improves my pain and inflammation. Did you order any breakfast?"

"Was waiting for you."

For the remainder of the morning, the sisters enjoyed each other's company. Laughing and reminiscing about the things that when happening meant so little, but now meant the most. They shared food, but above all else, they shared the burden of one sister's affliction. Neither knew the why or even what they were truly supposed to learn from the storm that rocked Phoenix's life just as it began, but they did know that through it all they would fight together. These mornings were the eye in their storm and not one second of them did they waste.

Breakfast swiftly turned into lunch as Phoenix and Rue laughed and talked in their corner nook. Many of the locals smiled upon the sisters. Though both were fairly new to the small town, everyone loved seeing them laughing like little schoolgirls. The joy that emitted from their corner was infectious, filling whoever laid eyes on them to the brim.

At five years her senior, Rue had always been a pillar to her little sister; this time was no different. Phoenix was her pride and joy before she birthed her own children. Following the unexpected death of their parents from a car accident, she was Phoenix's confidant, comforter and provider. Every triumph they celebrated together and every tragedy they cried together. SLE was by far the hardest battle they'd ever faced, and they weren't going to allow it to cloud their rose-colored lenses. Life was better when they fought it together, no matter how ugly it seemed to get for them.

"Okay, Baby Love. Your nieces will be getting out of school shortly. I need to run a few errands before then. I love you to the moon and back."

"I love you too. I'm gonna sit here for a while longer. I still haven't gotten a chance to set up an office yet. So, Forge has been letting me set up my little workspace in the sanctuary garden free of charge. She'll be in shortly to open up the space and bring me some of her kidney tea."

"Haven't had a chance or haven't had the strength to do it?" Rue's raised eyebrow and lowered eyes narrowed in on her sister as she sat staring up at her.

"Uh. A little of both, but I'll get it done eventually. It's not like I'll be going anywhere anytime soon."

"Trav and I will be over with the girls next weekend. Make a running list in our shared notes folder. Whatever you think you need or may need, whatever you need done. I want to feel my phone vibrating off the nightstand, and I mean it. You hear me?"

"Yes, Sister. Now go before you're late picking up my road dogs."

Rue gave her sister's hand a squeeze before walking off toward the counter. She knew the first thing her children would ask for once they got in the car was some of Forge's fruit and floral roll ups. Turning to wave to her sister one last time, she smiled as Phoenix mouthed '*thank you*' a split second before she was greeted by the hustling and bustling of the downtown Solace Point crowd.

Several hours had passed and Phoenix realized she spent the entire day at the café. Her gel pen lingered on the corner of her mouth as she glanced at the full pages that lie before her on the table. Work for her looked different these days. Whereas she spent her days resting her voice for the on-camera nightly news over 10,000 miles away, she was now scribbling 3,500-5,000 words for a local newspaper. Again, another kind gesture from her endearing brother-in-law. Closing her book, she stretched her aching limbs and surveyed the evening patrons of Noir.

CHAPTER TWO

Across the room, Blaise divided his attention between his group of associates and Phoenix. He was well aware of how rude it was to keep his eyes fixated on the same stranger for more than a few seconds. He also knew that choosing to direct attention to anyone other than the person that was talking to him was equally as rude. Both rules of etiquette were ingrained in him as a child and solidified during his college public speaking course. Yet, the sight of her caused him to abandon all he'd ever learned.

As the older white man went on and on about all the perks that came along with his job, Blaise studied the woman across the room. From the moment she emerged from the back of the café, he couldn't focus his attention anywhere else. His intentions were ill-guided, as he departed from his original reason for welcoming the invitation for a night cap and debriefing of his first day touring the territory of his new position. Tucked off in the corner of the café like a radiant wall flower, she'd crossed his sight briefly as her pen scurried across the notebook she pressed her face into until she gathered her things and disappeared around a corner. Now, two hours later, she was back and had become the subject of his attention for the second time around.

Blaise wanted to be anywhere but the quaint little café on the corner. Though grateful for his new position and the change of scenery it warranted, he wanted to enjoy his last two weeks of a silent pager and empty home office. When he initially had the thought of moving early to get the lay of the land before he was actually due to begin his work, he didn't factor networking into the plans this soon. Still, he was listening to future retirees gripe and moan about having fat pockets and no time to fuck it over on yacht parties and vacation homes in high flood areas. Despite the fact that many of them only had about five to six more good years in them and the remainder had their noses so far in the air he was sure their oxygen levels suffered, he graciously accepted the invite from his college friend and new boss.

His future plans required his anti-social nature to take a back seat until he had a little wiggle room. There were doors he needed opened and the men surrounding him were how he intended to get them ajar. The second he saw her, that changed. Now, he lingered long after the host had left, shifting the conversation to more pressing topics like the understaffed department that he was hired to oversee and the disparaging reality of quality healthcare.

Hours had passed and he divided his attention between the round table of doctors, nurses and medical professionals and her. She'd sat alone, nibbling, sipping, and writing for the better part of the evening. How long she'd been there was unknown to him, but how long she'd stay was all he cared to think about.

"Excuse me, does she come here often," Blaise asked Forge as she walked by with a serving tray.

"Often enough," Forge replied.

Her eyebrow raised slightly. This face was one she'd never seen before, and she pretty much knew nearly all the patrons of her corner café. The company he kept was also unknown to her and they stuck out like sore thumbs. Not too many white coats ventured into her space because of her promotion of natural remedies and cures, but he seemed to be more open. Phoenix was certain he had to be who many were gossiping about for the past few weeks. Living in a town like Solace Point made you forget just how big it was. Nothing took long to make its way through the rumor mill. From the dark corners of the hood to the well-lit courtyard of the gated community, nothing was sacred or secret. But that was a perk sometimes and knowing a little about all the inhabitants before ever meeting them came in handy. Newcomers, vacationers, or founding families; it didn't matter, your existence in Solace Point never went under anyone's radar.

"Can you send her a cup of her favorite beverage, if she has one."

"She does. It's the *Lovely Blend.* Comes in three sizes: petite, moyenne or grande. Who should I say it's from?"

"Just somebody who sees her," Blaise replied with a boyish grin.

Before Forge had a chance to walk away, he peeled off two crisp fifties and slid them in her hand. Never missing a beat, he returned to the conversation among his colleagues.

After personally brewing the cup of tea, Forge gathered the 3 satchels of specialty tea blends and headed over to Phoenix. They were fast friends. Since the first time Trav introduced the two, Forge had treated Phoenix like the younger sister she never had. She hated that Phoenix had fallen ill just at the prime of her life when everything seemed to be falling in place for her. It was a sucky situation for anybody, but she especially hated it for young black people because she knew how much medical professionals shrugged off their suffering and made it even worse.

"Alright, Phoenix. Here's a one-month supply of my special kidney fortifying blend, your lullaby blend, and this is something new I want you to try. It will give you a little energy boost and lift your spirits," Forge said as she approached the table.

One by one, she pulled the satchels from her apron and placed them on the table. A wide grin spread across her face before she sat the cup she balanced on a saucer down in front of Phoenix.

"And a piping hot cup of the one and only *Lovely Blend* courtesy of someone who sees you," Forge announced as she nodded in Blaise's direction before walking off.

Phoenix's eyes darted in the direction of Forge's all but discreet head nod. Her cheeks rose to meet the corners of her eyes as she smiled at him when he lifted his glass. Returning the gesture, she toasted the air before raising the glass to her lips.

As she pressed her lips to the side of the hot mug, it was as if lightning had struck her right in the heart. It skipped a few beats, causing her to inhale the floral notes of the tea. The flavors combined with the electricity coursing through her body formed a culminating event she hadn't had the pleasure of penciling into her schedule for the past eighteen months. Packing up her belongings, she did her due diligence and tidied up the space she'd occupied since emerging from the garden in the back.

Spending this much time away from the couch was foreign to her. She paid for it every time, but the buzzing of life that people-watching gave her was the only remedy she had for her anxiety and depression. It allowed her the opportunity to let her mind go to a place that didn't involve remembering to log her symptoms or pop the various medications that kept her barely functioning at half capacity. With one hand tightly gripping the table's edge and the other loosely on the faux leather cushion of the seat, she slid from the booth. Gathering all her belongings and the still hot ceramic mug, she proceeded to the counter.

"Forge, can you prepare this to go? It's getting late and I need to be heading back. I walked today."

"Sure thing. You need a ride? I'll be finished up in about 10 minutes."

"No. I only walked from the hospital. I'm popping in to grab some dinner from Saxon's and then just heading to my car. The stars are glorious tonight. Think I'll go eat under them. Gotta get as much use out of this body when it's acting right. Who knows when the next time I'll feel remotely close to this good."

Casually, Phoenix leaned against the counter. Her elbows and forearms pressed against the pastry display case. Softly, her fingers strummed along the top of the case as she hummed the cadence of the soft music that filled the nearly empty café. Her eyes defied her head as she diverted them to the spot where her admirer stood talking to a small group of men. Relieved that he had turned his attention back to the company he was keeping, she allowed her gaze to linger.

Stars danced in her eyes and a foreign warmth spread throughout her fingertips as she surveyed him. His stance commanded attention. It was evident in the way his companions circled him. She was convinced his conversation was captivating because as his mouth moved, no eyes left him. Like they didn't want to miss a word his lips formed.

Irritation set in the part of her chest that willed the air to reach her deflated lungs. The desire to see his face made her unable to consume the oxygen necessary to take her next breath and remain among the living. Frustrated with the inability to really watch him how she wanted to, she completely turned her body. Her back and buttocks pressed against the case holding the cold-pressed drinks as she twirled the piece of thread she pulled from her shirt between her fingers while she blatantly defied the manners her parents instilled in her. Choosing to stare at him until he felt the heat of her gaze made him turn in her direction, she smiled coyly once he flashed her a charming half smile.

"Like what you see?"

Phoenix jumped at the sound of Forge interrupting her journalistic observation. She did like what she saw. A man hadn't crossed her mind since her fiancé bolted shortly after her first extended hospital stay. Now here she was allowing herself the privilege of a lustful gaze. He was a beautiful stranger, yet the budding in the recesses of her heart caused her mind to desire his acquaintance.

As she leaned against the counter, Phoenix talked to Forge until she finished her part of the closing duties. It was settled that she'd accompany Phoenix on her walk. There weren't many people either woman allowed in their space, but they connected almost instantly. Though fast friends, they were loyal and compassionate when it came to one another. It was only six months after her diagnosis that Phoenix decided to tell Forge the extent of her illness. And like the healing woman she was, Forge genuinely studied her books to come up with natural remedies to offset the side effects of Phoenix's prescribed medications.

"You know it's 2022, right," Forge asked as she waved good night to her closing staff.

"What?" Two deep creases formed in Phoenix's brow as confusion settled in.

"If you see something...or someone you like, you should acknowledge it...or him." Her head discreetly leaned in the direction of the guy she'd spent the last twelve minutes and 32 seconds studying.

"Ummm, no. There's no way I'm walking up to that man. He sent me a drink and gave me a wink. That T-pain shit don't work on me. Besides, I was born in the nineties, but ain't much of the 90s in this woman. I like being approached, courted, and romanced. All of that. You know, show me you want all this."

Phoenix used her hands to contour the curves of her body. Even with all the weight she'd lost and gained throughout her treatments, her body was still stacked. She was blessed with sickening measurements that made both men and women do a double take whenever she walked by them.

"That man dropped $100 on your $6 cup of tea. If you knew like I knew, you'd step to him. But suit yourself, crazy girl."

"Says the chick who was about to walk away from a damn good man over some petty ass backroom land deal. You watched enough movies to know that the money-hungry mayor never wins in the end. So you, my kettle-like friend, cannot call me the pot."

“But I wised up, and you should too. He’s nice to look at, probably nice at other things too.”

Phoenix laughed as they made their way to the exit. Waving good night to the closing staff, they entered the town square. This time of year in Solace Point was always full of wonder. The extra hours of sunlight allowed stores to stay open later. There seemed to always be something or someone to celebrate. She could always count on randomly stumbling into some seasonal festival or local event during her walks.

“You were going to leave without giving me the courtesy of a thank you?” Blaise asked as he stood in the middle of the sidewalk.

Phoenix and Forge stopped in their tracks. Phoenix’s eye cut to the right as she furrowed her brows in Forge’s direction. She wasn’t pleased with the snicker that left Forge’s vocals and she made sure she knew it with a quick elbow to the side.

“Thank you,” Phoenix smiled as she turned on her heels.

Her eyes damn near bulged from their sockets as she got to take all of him in for the first time. Her gaze fell on him like he was a lost work of art. From his toes to the crown of his head, she surveyed every inch of his body. He was sexy. Beautiful even.

With abstract scars and lifelines adorning his otherwise perfectly smooth skin he was indeed worthy of a Bucksbaum award. He'd lived. It was evident in his scowl and the way his head sat high and his chest protruded a little past his shoulder. He wasn't arrogant, yet completely aware of the entrancing effect his presence had on his companions. The way words casually danced from his vocals and brushed across her ears was intoxicating. She could feel every word he spoke before they even reached her auricle.

"I wanted to leave my colleagues and join you in your little corner, but that would have been rude of me. Plus, you seemed engrossed in your alone time, didn't want to barge in on your solitude. After all, first impressions are everything," he said stepping forward.

"They are everything until they're nothing."

"Ouch." Blaise cringed as he took a step back.

Phoenix stepped forward as she held up her hand in an effort to wave the white flag. She didn't mean to come off so harsh. In all actuality, she felt out of place. Actively dating was something she hadn't done in a long while and she was evidently rusty. In her mind, she wanted him to know his gesture was appreciated and that he did make a nice first impression. She wanted to tell him that his joining her would have been a welcomed distraction from the bore of piece she was writing on the mayor's plans to build a throughway straight through 'The Junction,' Solace Point's ghetto. But instead, her words were callous, sharp and dismissive.

"I didn't mean it that way. As a woman who deals in words all day, sometimes my intent gets lost in verbal translation. Your gesture was much appreciated," she smiled as she tilted the mug in her hand.

Blaise's eyes wrinkled at the outer corners as he stared down at her. The evening sky was a bit airy, but her buttoned sweater and thin gloves still seemed over the top for the dawning spring. He easily towered over her and used it to his advantage. Looking down at the top of her head, he refrained from reaching out and smoothing down the curly fly-aways as the wind whistled around them. Like a seafarer trying to find his way home, he searched her twinkling eyes before allowing his lips to curl into a broad smile. Exposing his pristine teeth and deep dimples, he laughed at her attempt to clean up her harsh response.

"Believe me, I know how it is. Talking isn't really my strong suit either and I'll have to do it all day, every day in just two short weeks."

"I can't tell. You seemed pretty convincing in there."

Blaise chuckled. On the inside, he cockily smirked knowing she'd been watching him just as much as he watched her. Though she acted coolly, he could sense her interest was piqued and she was raging with desire to know more.

"What do you say we practice our talking skills together? Tomorrow over a cup of the Lovely Blend, the grande size this time?"

"I'm not sure about all that. I wouldn't have much to add to the conversational skills assessment. Have you been listening to our conversation?"

"Before every great teacher became as such, they were a dedicated student."

"So tell me, what would this student learn from your accelerated course?"

"For starters, she'd learn how not to let a good thing pass her by."

Phoenix shifted her weight, crossing her legs at the ankle. Her chin dropped to her chest as she tried to hide the deep berry flesh tones that covered her cheeks. She was intrigued by the captivating essence of his being. The force of his charm was magnetizing, pulling a yes from her lips before she could think to reel her acceptance back behind her vocal chords.

"Now that's a learning objective I'd like to pass with flying colors."

"Believe me, the coursework is engaging to say the least. Meet me here at 7."

"Everybody here knows the cafe closes at 7 on Tuesdays and Thursdays for the makers' workshops."

"I'm new here. Still adjusting to the way things work in a small town. I'll just grab the drinks beforehand, then we can walk and talk. I found a nice little spot a few blocks away."

"Believe me, this town is not as small as you think. And while your plan of study sounds exciting, I'm not sure it's the best option for me."

"Don't be sure, just be present. The rest will work itself out."

Phoenix pondered his request. Slowly, she enjoyed a sip of her tea. The fiery warmth of the liquid coursing down her throat knocked out the chills his smile sent up her spine. Every fiber in her now aching body told her to stand firm on her decline of his offer. She did not want to accept, but a tiny tug on the vessel that willed blood to flow through her limbs nudged her lips to open. A simple smile behind her cup and a head nod granted his request for her company the next evening.

"It's a date, Ms..." Blaise lingered, waiting for her to fill in his blank.

“Phoenix.”

“See you then, Mr...” Phoenix extended her gloved hand.

“Blaise.”

CHAPTER THREE

Blaise turned to peek at the afternoon sun that scorched his uncovered flesh as it glared through his half-opened shutters. Pushing the plush velvet comforter from the lower region of his 6-foot frame, he groggily ascended from his prostrated position on the bed. For the first time since he'd graduated high school, he finally had time to enjoy the spoils of his sacrifices. He'd spent the majority of his adult life securing his future and making sure his mother and grandmother would never have to work another day in their lives unless they wanted to. Now that he had locked down the position he'd been striving for, it was time to hone the reins and experience the life his accomplishments afforded him.

After relieving himself of what seemed like gallons of Hibiscus refreshers he'd consumed the night prior, he opted to skip his normal morning routine. He'd already slept into the late afternoon and had a laundry list of places he wanted to explore before he met up with Phoenix. As a well-traveled man, he always made sure to know the areas where his work carried him, no matter how brief his stay. Solace Point would be his forever home and learning the ways of the not-so-small town early on would help him better navigate when his days and nights ran together.

Quickly showering and dressing for his full day of sight-seeing, he grabbed his keys and dad hat as he commanded Siri to call his mother. An entire day had gone by without her ringing his phone off the hook, and as much as it relieved him, it worried him the same.

"Mama Bear, what have you been up to? I haven't heard from you in a month of Sundays," he joked when he heard her sweet voice sing through his line.

"Pinocchio, I can feel your nose poking me through the receiver," she responded quickly, pressing the button to convert their voice call to a video call.

"Uh oh! Let me find out you're reading manuals and shit now, Carolineee," Blaise sang like Andre 3000 as he locked up his house.

The cottage-style home was a change from the apartments and row homes he lived in while in undergrad at John Hopkins. It was a welcomed treat after the brownstones and 8th-floor walk-ups that he called home in San Francisco as a child. Looking back one more time, he jogged down the stairs of his wrap-around porch and hit the unlock button on his key fob. He was grateful his fraternity brother recommended he get an F-150 because the gravel driveway would have rotted his apple core every time he pulled in and out.

"I ain't reading no manual, boy. Val and the kids came by yesterday. That oldest boy showed me how to do it. Anyway, what you been up to? I ain't heard from you in a month of Sundays. Don't think because you done moved all the way out there to that reservation, I won't make a drive. If I can book a flight to Baltimore during a riot to see about my youngest baby, I shole won't squawk about a 4.5 hour drive."

"Ma, believe me, I know. You a wild one. But on the real, Ma, I was just sleeping. I sleep better out here. And stop calling it a reservation. It's just as black as where we lived in Compton, just greener and a tad bit quieter. It's urban-esque, just has a more southern, vibe. You'd like it. Reminds me of the place Pop-Pop used to always talk about or that Eatonville place J.J. always used to say she wished was real."

"Trust me, it ain't Geechee if it ain't Geechee. Ain't nothing like home."

"I hear you, Ma. But, I'm still at peace."

"I can imagine. No buzzing social sphere's keeping you awake. You just make sure you get as much rest after you start working. Have you seen the facility or your office yet?"

"I went yesterday. Roddy gave me a tour of my wing, then showed me my office. You'd love it, Ma. Beautiful skyline for you to paint when you come visit me."

"Guess this means an old lady does have an open invitation to see her hoe ass son."

Blaise threw his head back in laughter, forgetting he was driving for a second. His mother was the queen of embellishing a story and never letting you live down her version of events. Even when they were outlandish and against the character that she'd known a person to have. Smiling, he listened to her recount the time she visited during his residency and barged in on him having sex with one of the other residents. She was appalled that her handsome, educated, gloriously endowed son didn't take after his late father and give his conquests the opportunity to experience courtship.

"You'll never let that story sit on the shelf will you?"

"Nope. It scarred me for life."

"If you would let me, I plan to redeem myself tonight. I met a nice woman last night and if all goes well, she'll get to experience this courtship you and daddy have always been raving about."

"Mmmhmmm. You been out there 'bout a week. How many you done drilled before you decided to court somebody?"

"None, Ma. Not one. I imagine you don't believe me, but I've not been sampling anything. I've been unpacking and making my house a home. You'd be proud too. My décor looks picturesque enough to get a full spread in Martha Stewart magazine."

"You're making me wanna take a trip now. J.J. and the kids done been over here every day since you left. They driving me crazy. I be happy when they finish them renovations at her house."

Parking his car in the designated visitor spot, he cut the ignition and relaxed in his seat. His appointment with the horticulturist wasn't for another fifteen minutes and he knew his mother would most definitely help him pass the time. She'd been his biggest cheerleader and best friend his entire life. Though she silently wished his dreams didn't take him away from home, she was proud he was following the path that was predestined for him. No matter how old he got or how far his career took him, he never let the distance strain their closeness.

After he told his mother about the exchange he had with Phoenix that resulted in their date, he listened to her caution him. For some reason, he couldn't fathom why she felt like he needed to take his time and really get to know her. His mother always had a knowing spirit about her, and as much as she liked to pass it off as women's intuition, he knew there was a source of divination in the wells of her being. She always seemed ever-present, and the way she could sense her children's needs, desires, joys, and pains was a semblance of omniscience.

"Ard, Ma. I promise to give Phoenix all that I have, whatever that means. Now, I have to get inside this place before you be on my case about not having any life in or around my house next."

"Okay. Make sure you get a prayer plant or two. And get a few snake plants for your guest rooms. Oh, and some brown beauty magnolias for your front and back yards. You'll love the sweet vanilla scent. Love you to the moon, Son."

"Love you to infinity, Ma."

"And Beyond!" Blaise heard his big sister J.J. yell into the camera just as he ended the call.

When he booked the consultation with the horticulturist, he had no expectations. Growing up his parents always had living plants in their home no matter where they lived. He remembered how his mother went on and on about how loving plants and caring for them taught her how to appreciate life and reminded her to always shower others with love. As long as she did that, she never experienced a dry season.

According to her, plants taught people all they needed to know and gave them all they needed to sustain themselves. It was only natural for him to pick up on a few things and develop an inkling of a green thumb. He'd killed almost every plant he ever owned, except a snake plant his grandmother gifted him after he graduated from undergrad and the peace lily his mother sent him back to Baltimore with after he flew home to bury his father.

Though it was easy for him to attribute his lack of plant knowledge and patience to his busy life, that was not entirely true. While his educational and professional pursuits kept him on the go, it was clear that he just didn't want to make the time to care about much of anything else. In retrospect, he wasn't settled enough into his own life to even consider being a sanctuary for another living vessel; even if it just required water, sunlight, and the most minute bit of tender love and care.

With excitement pounding in his chest, he opened the greenhouse doors and was greeted by a scene pulled right out of Agnieszka Holland's *The Secret Garden*. The second his feet crossed the threshold, his senses went haywire. With one whiff of the glorious floral and herbal aromas in the air, he was transported to an otherworldly place.

Before anyone came into view, he allowed himself a moment to fully be present in the current state of things. He closed his eyes and felt his feet planted firmly on the packed dirt floor. He heard the melodious sounds of unknown harmonies collide with the tantalizing tastes of the greenhouse air. With a deep, intentional breath, he exhaled the last ounce of apprehension that lingered in his spirit.

Change was inevitable. He knew this his whole life. It was the only thing as sure to happen as death. Yet, no matter how well he seemed to adjust to the pervasive persistence of constant change, there was always an initial ounce of apprehension. He needed to fully dispel that trepidation from the recesses of his mind before he could tighten his bootstraps and adapt to the doggedness of ambiguity that constituted the dash between the day he was born and the day he would leave this earth.

"Welcome to King Noir Garden and Nursery." Forge smiled as she emerged from seemingly nowhere.

Blaise looked at the woman outfitted in her full bee-keeper suit. He'd never been this engrossed in an agricultural climate, but he was sure he'd encounter more cultivators as he got better acquainted with the people in his new, predominantly black home. His eyes moved rapidly, causing his head to play catch up as he took in the hanging plants above his head and along the walls on either side of him. Stepping further into the green oasis, he allowed his attention to shift back to the woman who greeted him as she stood a few feet away. getting out of her beekeeper gear.

"Hi, I'm here for a consultation with Forge King."

"That would be me," she smiled as she finished stepping out of the suit.

A dumbfounded silence washed over Blaise as he finally recognized her as the waiter from the café. It wasn't uncommon for him to see women working more than one job. There was a time when his mother worked three just to keep their house after his dad fell ill. But she didn't look like she worked that hard. Sure, all black women had this air about them to the outside world, but to their fellow black men and women, the fatigue was sensed no matter how bright-eyed and bushy-tailed they seemed. Forge didn't have that telling vibe.

"Just give me one second to get out of this suit."

"No problem."

"I know you said you were looking for fragrance trees for your exterior and air purifiers for your interiors. Are there any specifically you want or are interested in learning about today? Or do you have an idea of where you'll keep them inside? That matters when deciding on what to get."

"My thumb is pretty lime. Literally, they're only a few juicy roots from being brown. But, I'm adamant about getting them all the way green this time."

"Okay, we can start with the damn-near impossible to kill plants. I call them the Green Old Guard."

"For my front and back, I was considering magnolia trees. Honestly, I was just considering trees, my mother advised me to get magnolias, brown beauties."

Blaise watched as Forge meticulously wrote on her pad without breaking eye contact with him. He had to give it to her, she took notes better than most transcriptionists he knew. There were a million questions he wanted to ask her about her friend instead of these landscaping ones. But, like the professional he'd always been, he kept to the task at hand and continued rattling off his ideas.

"I have a wrap-around porch and a long driveway, about a quarter-mile long. I was thinking maybe something low, easy to maintain, but not simple green hedges. Maybe flowers, one with a mild scent because I don't want to overpower the vanilla from the trees. And I want them to be a nice vibrant hue," he continued.

"You're the most precise first-timer I ever had, Mr. Jones, let's start with your outside."

For the next two hours, Blaise learned about all the plant varieties and genera. He was impressed with his ability to remain attentive without the slightest hint of disinterest. His parents once told him that if he learned to truly pay attention to the signs and wonders of nature, nothing would ever be a mystery again. He'd realize the beauty in not knowing the end in the beginning and appreciate every moment. For all of his life, he'd waved them off and remained the same calculated person he'd always been. He did nothing without a plan and always had other routes lined up before he ever knew the first wouldn't happen. But after two hours, a

$6,000 deposit and a brochure for a beginner's home gardening course, Forge had made a believer out of him.

"Okay, Mr. Jones, you're all set. I'll have a team out to prepare the earth for your new babies next week. Your next payment won't be due until after that."

"Can you just go ahead and send the next invoice for the remaining 5Gs? My schedule will get hectic after next week and I will easily forget."

"Sure thing." She nodded. "In fact, I can do you one better. If you sign a pre-authorization form, I can just run the payments automatically and send your proof of payment via email."

"Sounds good."

Blaise looked around the gift shop of the nursery. From the entrance, he thought the greenhouse extended straight back, but there were several exits along the sides that led to different areas of the outside gardens. When they reached the end, they were in another building altogether. A quick peek out of the window let him know he was next door to the dwelling he entered initially. He could tell that where he stood was where the business was handled, and all money exchanged hands.

"You can just sign here, here, and here and you're officially all set."

"One more thing. I have a date tonight. What's a flower that says this is forever, but subtly?"

"Forever, huh?" Forge chuckled as she swooped her hair up into a ponytail and rounded the counter.

"Phoenix hates roses, so I can for sure tell you never get her roses."

"You remembered me," he laughed.

"How could I forget the man who dropped $100 on a $6 beverage?" She laughed. "I was just waiting for you to bring it up. My discernment is top-notch, so I knew you would."

"In that case, I was excited about it earlier. But after talking to my moms, I'm a little on ice. Her discernment makes me think she's in the lineage of a deity or something. She says Phoenix is the one I should really be serious about. And surprisingly, I didn't need her to say it, I knew it before I sent the drink."

"Your notions were right. She's an amazing woman and I'm not saying it because I'm her friend. I'm saying it because she's mine."

"She's three for three. Now, about these flowers."

"No flowers. She doesn't usually like flowers in her house because of her niece's allergies. This one will blow her away. Only problem is Phoenix loves walking, she'll probably walk to your date tonight, so she won't be able to get it back home."

Forge surveyed the four licuala grandis on the shelf and picked the one with the biggest leaves. She walked it over to the pruning table and prepared it as Blaise looked stumped.

"Then I'll just drive her home."

"That's the second problem. She won't let you drive her home. She has a thing about men knowing where she lives, and if you try to insist, she'll never call you again."

"So, what are you proposing," Blaise locked eyes with her, confused at this point. Forge's body language and her words were an oxymoron. She maneuvered like she had all the answers, yet nothing flew from her lips but problems.

"You lucked up and came into the nursery her friend owns. I'll have it delivered before the date. What do you want the card to say?"

"Some crazy lovebirds told me one time that learning to appreciate nature teaches us to appreciate the love that's standing right in front of us. Thanks for the view. Add that little squiggly dash punctuation and my name with a little heart hanging off the letter E."

Blaise smirked as he watched Forge swipe away the tear that streamed halfway down her left cheek. She'd been pecking away at the keyboard while he rattled off the two sentences. He couldn't front, the words spilled out of him effortlessly. There was no long pause after she asked the question. Like a broken levee, they burst from his lips, watering a seed he had yet to even plant in the earth.

"It's called a tilde. And how about I just print this out and you sign it by hand. I use basic word processing to make these notes, not Photoshop."

She laughed as Blaise scribbled his signature on the little card where she'd printed his note. His signature was the best in his industry. It was legible and he felt like the heart at the end sealed their fate.

"What time are you meeting her?"

"Seven."

"Cool. I'll have this at her home within the next hour or so. Enjoy yourself."

"Thanks, Oshun," Blaise joked as he carried his aloe plant and brochure with him out the door.

CHAPTER FOUR

On the east of Solace, the day had been quiet. Phoenix sat in a field of amaranths, daffodils, and zinnias as she strummed her fingers along the flowers' blooms. As the high sun beat down on her, she welcomed the sweltering heat that warmed the blood as it flowed through her tired limbs.

Mornings for her had gotten incredibly challenging and she couldn't remember the last time she was granted the opportunity to enjoy the kisses of earth's closest star. Whenever she woke up and had her body on her side, it was a blessing and never for one second did she waste it. For hours, she'd sit out in the flower field behind her house.

The vibrant flowers were symbolic with how she wanted to live the rest of her life. Though they were about a quarter of a mile from her back porch; their brilliant colors and glorious aromas after a good rain were impossible to miss. She found solace in their eternal nature and relished in the richness of the earth beneath them. With her feet buried under the topsoil where some herbivores had helped themselves to breakfast, she closed her eyes and tilted her head back.

Using her flattened palms as anchors, she slid back slightly and arched her back. For the first time, she wondered what death would give her that life hadn't. Silently, she allowed all her pondering to enter and exit her mind without the slightest hint of an answer. But they came crashing into one another as she spiraled down an endless path of queries about the afterlife.

Are the harmonies of the birds this glorious in heaven? Will the entrancing scents of amaranths, daffodils and zinnias greet her each morning? Do the sun's rays extend beyond the clouds to warm her soul, just like it warmed her heart every morning? Rarely did she let her mind wander so far from life, but this time she did, and even without knowing the answers, the poetry of her inquiries were refreshing. She didn't go to a dark place and that comforted her. It garnered her hope.

Phoenix's centered thinking was interrupted by the blaring of her cell phone. Like a child she fell to her back and flailed her arms while stomping her feet in the dirt. An agonizing groan filled the air around her as she kicked herself for not putting it on DND after she'd submitted her article. It was customary for her to completely disconnect after she got the stamp of approval from the editor of her column. Leaning up off her palms, her head snapped back from its place in the clouds and zeroed in on the marquee of Forge's number scrolling across her screen. The two lines that had formed on her forehead slowly dissipated as she smiled down at the phone.

"Hello, gorgeous one!" Forge smiled when she answered the video call. "I should have known you were back there in the flowers when you didn't answer your door."

"You're here?"

Phoenix surveyed Forge's background and recognized the lilac shutters as her own. Collecting her canvas tote bag and blanket, she stood from her seated position. She proceeded to the stone path Rue and Trav helped her put in the day after she officially moved all her stuff into the house. The piping hot graphite stepping-stone seared the flesh on her big toe, giving her a painful reminder that she had forgotten her slides. Quickly, she shuffled back to her spot and searched among the flowers for her shoes. *Ughh, shoes are such a necessary evil,* she thought as she spotted them a few feet away by the lake. She'd completely overlooked the fact that she dipped her feet there when she first wandered out into the field that morning. Once the soles of her feet were protected, she hurried up the walkaway and rounded her house.

"If I would have known you were going to stop by, I would have made some lunch or something!" She greeted Forge with a two-arm hug when she was in arm's reach.

"Oh, this isn't a social visit, but tomorrow, I'm holding you to that," Forge laughed.

"Not a social visit?" Phoenix's eyes narrowed as her left eyebrow connected with her hairline.

"I have a delivery for you." Forge could barely contain her excitement.

"A delivery?"

Phoenix was clearly stumped. She unlocked her door and tossed her belongings on the armchair that sat by the door. It was the lone piece of furniture in her vestibule and served her much relief when she'd out done herself.

"Yup. Get the door for me. I'll carry her inside."

Her? Phoenix silently questioned if her friend was finally losing her brain cells after inhaling so many different species of plants, herbs and fungi. But, as she stepped to the side with the screen door's knob tightly in her grip, those assumptions were quieted. She was barely able to contain her excitement as she looked back and her eyes landed on Forge struggling to get the massive plant up her wooden stairs. There were a few loose boards she'd been meaning to get Trav to fix and one misstep could end horrifically.

"For me? She's gorgeous! Here, let me help you."

It was obvious that Phoenix was over the moon as her cheeks rose to the corners of her eyes. She'd been ranting and raving to Forge for weeks about how much she wanted to add a licuala grandis to her parlor collection. Forge told her she hadn't grown any in years and knew that it would take quite some time to get one to grow the size that would fill the spot where she wanted to put it.

Phoenix only ever had three friends before Forge. One moved to Dubai to teach, another married her college sweetheart and followed him to Japan, and the other was a movie producer. They touched bases quarterly and vacationed together once a year. Until Forge, she never wanted to connect with anyone else. But ever since the moment they met, Phoenix knew that Forge was the kind of friend that could reciprocate the kind of loyalty and love she gave.

"I got it. I just need you to get the door so I can get her big ass inside," Forge laughed. "Besides, Rue would kick my ass if she found out I let you lift this. I know you're able but big sis is a mama hen forreal."

The women went inside and made their way towards the back of the house. Though Phoenix never imagined herself in a place like this, the down-home vibes of the house grew on her each day. She missed the smell and sounds of the city, but the quiet serenity her new place warranted was worth the trade.

"Oh, I can't wait to re-pot her."

She stood back in complete awe. Her hands covered her smile and stars twinkled in her eyes. She was in love with this 6-foot goddess that Forge had gifted her. She didn't know what she did to deserve a friend like her, but she made sure to thank God for her every day he allowed her to live. Her hand found her hip, and she nibbled on the nail of her index finger.

"Read the card first."

"Card? Why you wasting your supplies on me? You could have just told me whatever is on this card when you got here."

"That's true, if it were from me." Forge grinned.

With her interest finally piqued, Phoenix walked over to her new parlor queen and removed the clear stake from the soil. No one else would give her something like this. Forge was the only person who knew she had been looking for an adult one. Rue could barely keep up with her girls to even find a moment to research a plant, let alone think to actually order it and have it shipped to the nursery.

Hurriedly, she ripped open the lilac envelope before her curiosity decided to shift to caution. The lilac card with gold embossed script was breathtaking. As she read the two sentences over and over almost a thousand times in a minute, her smile spread like wildflowers across a vast pasture. Hot tears burned her rosy cheeks as she blushed. Pressing the card to her heart, she hugged herself before looking up at Forge, who also had tears threatening to spill from her own eyes.

"I wasn't going to go," Phoenix whispered.

"Girl! Why not?"

Forge was perplexed. She knew love when she saw it. She also knew from experience that love came like a rushing wind, sweeping you up without warning. When she stood back and watched the exchange between the two of them, she saw love. There was nothing she was more sure of in life.

Taking Phoenix's hand, she pulled them both down to the cushion in the bay window. She believed in her spirit that Phoenix and Blaise would be a couple within a matter of months, if not weeks or days. She felt it. They felt like destiny. The energy was potent around them, and she knew something that strong was impossible to snuff out. But here she was about to listen to Phoenix pass up a love she deserved.

"I hardly know what to expect from my own body from one day to the next, how can I even think about love, lust, or anything else right now?"

"With all that you've been through just this year alone, you owe it to yourself to have some fun."

"Fun leads to feelings, and I'm not trying to waste that man's time. He has his whole life ahead of him."

Phoenix had been through this before. She thought about all the time she'd devoted along with her energy and goals to her ex-fiancé.

They'd planned forever together and forever only lasted until she finally had her diagnosis.

Two months after her engagement party, he was telling her how he just couldn't stand to watch the love of his life wilt away. As he packed his bags, he told her how he'd always love her and how there was no woman who could ever hold a candle to her eternal flame. He just wasn't emotionally or mentally strong enough to watch lupus snuff out that light one blow at a time.

Though she was grateful he'd done all that and showed her that 'through sickness and health' was a vow he had no intention of honoring, even before they'd wed, she was hurt. The day he left their condo, was the day she put it up for sale. What was supposed to be one trip to get a second opinion soon turned into a second opinion and a brand new normal complete with chirping birds and trickling streams. She vowed she'd never put another man in a position to have to grapple with the reality that loving her meant ultimately losing her.

"This isn't about the uncertainty of your lupus diagnosis. This is about the uncertainty of a love that will last. You're afraid to love again because you don't know how it will be. You think you've already figured out how your lupus battle will end, so you're giving up on anything else besides death."

"Forge, I—" Phoenix started, but was cut off by Forge's objection-rendering raised hand.

"No. You don't get to do that to yourself. Life is full of uncertainty and that's what makes it worth living. You don't know what will happen with Blaise. You don't know how bad your disease will get, or even if it will get any worse than it has.

And that's why you should spend every moment living and not thinking about how people will treat you when they know what's ailing you. Or dying, please stop thinking about dying. Because neither of those things can be changed by you, so they shouldn't be your concern.

Death is eternal. But the time you were granted on this earth to be love, to receive love and to spread love is not. So, spend the time you have here to actually live the only life you were given," Forge finished.

"Forge. I'm going. I wasn't going to go. But then I spent the day in the field, thinking, reflecting, re-evaluating my life. I don't want to wither away without giving myself a fighting chance. So, I decided to meet him and just let things play out. Then I got this," she nodded toward the plant, "and this," she said as she held up the card. "And I know I'd be a fool to not at least give him a chance. I couldn't deny myself the chance to see the view, even if just this once."

"You could have told me that before I just gave you that whole speech," Forge said before allowing all 32 of her teeth to glisten as she smiled for her friend.

"I mean I tried but you barely let a sista get a word in. Now, come help me dig through these boxes and totes for something to wear besides leggings and an oversized t-shirt."

For the next two hours, Phoenix and Forge ransacked the boxes in one of the guest bedrooms, trying to find the perfect pieces to create a look for her. They sipped on the hibiscus sangria that Phoenix had prepared the day before on a whim. It was clear to everybody that though Phoenix was adamant about not getting too comfortable in Solace Point, she was doing just that. Forge teased her about clinging to an outdated fast-paced way of living and urged her to really move into her house.

The country style home was fashioned with inspiration from Eve's Bayou and The Color Purple. With its many gathering rooms, spacious upper room dwellings and wrap-around porch it was a dream home for many. Phoenix took it off the market and resided inside like it was a mere hotel room, and she was checking out as soon as the doctor gave her the all clear. Never unpacking, never fully getting comfortable in the space that she'd put down a hefty check to outbid another person who was interested. No one did that if they didn't plan to make it a home. But her friend and her sister both knew she was choosing not to allow herself the satisfaction.

Finally finding contenders in the second guest room they tore apart, box by box, they began laying different pieces together on her bedroom floor. As she tried on look after look, they finally settled on a pair of body-sculpting, high-waisted, ultra-skinny jeans that hugged every curve and sucked in every roll she wanted to hide. They paired them with a burnt orange t-shirt and Vans. Phoenix's curls were still juicy from the wash and go she'd done a day ago and she opted to pull them up in an afro puff with a few tendrils of hair coiled by her ears.

“You look good enough to bite, Boo,” Forge cooed as she made Phoenix do one final spin.

“Thanks,” Phoenix replied as she leaned in to apply a layer of gloss over her burnt orange and dark coffee ombre lips.

“You walking tonight?”

“No, I'm going to ride my bike. For some reason, I feel really good today. I'm not questioning it. I’m just gonna ride this wave ‘til it touches land.”

“For some reason my ass. We both know the reason. If the potential for love has improved your health in less than 24 hours, imagine what actually letting love in will do for you.”

“Here you go with all this love talk. It’s one date. Stop trying to send me down the aisle before I even know if this man is a contender."

“Let's see. A $100 cup of tea. A damn near $400 plant. That's half a grand on a complete stranger. Clearly he knows your worth.”

“Please. Cut the bullshit, that just means he has money to blow. And if he wants to blow it, that shit can definitely swing my way.”

“When he proposes, I won't say I told you so, just make sure y’all book the sanctuary garden for your nuptials and name your first child after me.”

"Whatever. Don’t you have to go cook up a meal or bust it open for Onyx or something?”

“Nope, he's in Fog City for the rest of the week. Which means, my match-making and prying will be unhinged and uninterrupted.”

"Ughh, I'm sending him an SOS. He needs to come bend you over the river or some shit. Get you out my hair for a few days."

"I mean he can make me climb the walls and I'm still gonna find time to be all up in your scalp. All jokes aside, just make it easy on us both and give the man an honest chance. Seriously, not just because of the gifts, because like you said, he could just have money to blow, but because you deserve to have someone love and support all of you. Don't be in your head so much."

"My head has the night off, I promise."

Phoenix decided to take the scenic route as she made her way into Downtown Solace. The town square was always brimming with this personification that she could never quite pinpoint until that moment. The buildings gathered, witnessing the hustling, and bustling of people. The wind collected whispers from private conversations had over coffee at noon. The leaves collected the discarded remnants of a first date. The seasonal changes helped her appreciate the rare moments in time she got to spend witnessing the town's transition from summer's goodnight kiss and winter's gentle song. She took in the essence of the town square as she approached it on her bike.

She'd officially experienced every season in Solace Point, and without much thought, Spring was her favorite time of year. The colorful flowers and vibrant plants were glorious to gaze upon as she looked out into the direction she was headed. They painted a visual interpretation of her present mood. Her spirits were high, and excitement coursed through every nerve-ending in her body. The turbulence of the earth beneath her mountain bike's wheels and the sloshing of water splashing up onto her knuckles lulled the tiny hint of nervousness as her fingers gripped the handle bars tighter. Her casual, every day, forced smile quickly subsided as her date slowly came into view once she made it over the hill. There he stood palming two steaming cups of her favorite tea, while he awaited her arrival. *And he is prompt, unlike that asshole who took longer to get dressed than me,"* she thought as she hopped off her bike.

Giving into the force of habit, she shook her freshly washed hair as it fell from her helmet. To rid herself of the last bit of nerves, she focused on locking up her bike. Consciously, she coached herself to keep her brain off and her heart open to the possibilities the night would bring. *Don't compare him to the coward. That man is in your past, and his actions do not reflect the actions of all men. Allow yourself to enjoy the moment. You're not dying tonight, so live like it.* The metamorphosis of the butterflies preparing to take flight in her stomach had subsided, allowing her to take a deep breath. A smile formed as her eyes met his for the first time since sharing his space.

She could feign excitement all she wanted, but the pep in her step as she approached him was evidence enough that she anticipated their date. Subtlety and awkwardness were two qualities that could never be attributed to Phoenix before she fell ill, but since the day she put a name to her pain she'd become a shell of the woman she once was. A smile and unbridled enthusiasm were all she had to give, and she prayed it would be enough. Like a fish tossed back into the ocean after washing ashore, she needed this night out. She had been dry-drowning from the time she stepped foot in Solace Point. Intimacy and romance were missing from her life, and she hated how accustomed to that truth she'd become. The hard part was conquered, she'd gotten dressed and shown up for their scheduled date. She'd kept the only thing that mattered most; her word.

"Hey, you," she greeted Blaise as she approached him.

"I was beginning to think you were standing me up," Blaise greeted with open arms.

Like opposite ends of a magnet, she gravitated to him. Without hesitation, she walked into his open arms and wrapped hers around his waist. Briefly, she let her head fall to his chest as she inhaled his scent. Whether it was his aftershave, cologne, or natural aroma, she didn't care, but her craving for more was prevalent. The aromatics of bergamot, lemongrass and whiskey soothed her. He smelled of the forest after a fresh rain, refreshing and rejuvenating.

Quickly removing herself from his frame, Phoenix stood back and took all of him in, every inch of his 6-foot-1-inch stature was magnificent. He was art in its purest form. His full-beard complimented the cruddy temp fade that covered his head and added a divine dimension to his physique. As she accepted the travel mug he extended to her, her pupils twinkled, and her cheeks burned with anticipation.

"Never. I'm a keeper of my word. I would have texted you, but I remembered I didn't get your number," Phoenix admitted.

"Open your phone," he commanded.

With two swipes, Blaise had shared his contact info with her. His email, cell, office and home address were all at her fingertips. *Total access, without even asking. God, is this my soulmate?* Phoenix chuckled as she shook away the ridiculous question she'd asked. Love at first sight, soulmates, unbreakable bonds were all elements of fairy tales she didn't have the pleasure of believing in anymore. Life was going full-speed ahead and in the clouds before she had to be was not a place she liked to pass the time visiting. Setting her phone to DND, she accepted the cup he'd extended to her.

"So, since you've been here longer than me, I was thinking you could be my tour guide. What's a fun hidden gem here? I'm gonna be a local, so I might as well get up to speed."

"What do you like to do?"

Phoenix looked down as Blaise intertwined his fingers with hers. As they walked hand-in-hand down the sidewalk she felt a heat she'd never experienced before. It was a passion for something other than her work, for someone other than her family. Being in that moment with him didn't feel foreign like she'd imagined. It felt natural, like they'd been together like this for quite some time. She took a second to mask her smile by taking a long sip of her tea.

"Nature. Quiet. Occasionally jazz and pottery. So, what do you think? Will I have to throw myself into work, or does Solace Point offer some decent distractions?"

"Look around. There's certainly no shortage of nature." Phoenix laughed. "But it depends on what you like about nature. If you want to learn about nature, Forge's cafe and nursery are the best places for edutainment. If you just like to sit and be in nature, then I've found some pretty perfect spots. Don't think I want to share them though."

"Ah, it's like that? So tell me, what do I have to do to get access to the secret spots?"

Blaise flashed that 1000 kilowatt smile again. His eyes pierced hers as she turned her eyes up to meet them. He made her uncomfortable in a way she hadn't felt since her first date with her fiancé. It warmed her body and flushed her rational thought process. As she rode her bike the twenty minutes it took to reach him, she went over thousands of scenarios in her mind and none of them ended happily. But as he stared down at her, waiting for an answer, those thoughts dissipated from her mental faculties. She disregarded the caution that consumed her and welcomed the uncertainty of dating.

"You've already earned access to this one," she announced. "We're here."

Her fingers dropped from his as she stepped back and let him take in the sight before them. The cove was one of her favorite hideouts. She'd chanced upon it while trying to map out a good walking route. Though the terrain was too uneven for everyday walking, it was a great getaway when you wanted to block out the noise of downtown Solace Point.

"This is breathtaking. How did you find this place?"

"I got lost," she laughed as she walked ahead of him.

Phoenix entered the cove as if it were her home. She reached between two rocks and pulled out a blanket and pillow wrapped tightly in a waterproof bag. As she tossed them to him, she laughed at the awe that danced in his eyes. She was a woman full of surprises, so his reaction was one she was used to experiencing.

Blaise followed in her footsteps as she carefully stepped on the uneven ground beneath them. Once they reached the other entrance to the cove, he was captivated by the picturesque scene in front of him. The waves rippled along the waters outer bank before crashing against the skyline. The sun had just begun to set. Phoenix had the same initial reaction when she found this spot, and she allowed him the moment to breathe in the beauty of it all.

Gently, she pulled the rolled blanket from under his arm and handed him her cup. As she laid it out inches away from their feet, she stole glances at him. She loved men who could appreciate the beauty that naturally occurs in the world.

"It looks even better from down here," she proclaimed as she offered him her outstretched palm.

Unhesitatingly, Blaise accepted her hand and joined her on the blanket. It was wide enough only for one, so he sat behind her, resting his legs on either side of her. Silently, the two sat talking in the gentle comfort of each other's presence. Nature and quiet were paramount to both and queries of their other shared interests proved unimportant at that moment.

After some time had passed, Phoenix allowed her back to fall against his chest. Though the warmth of a summer's day encapsulated their stroll, the chill of the ocean's waves caused bumps to form on her arms. Nuzzling into his strong arms brought her protection from the gentle winds rippling against the water. Looking out into the dark of the ocean, her mind wandered. *Sink me in the river at dawn. Send me away with the words of a love song.* As her eyes closed, she recalled the words to one of her favorite songs. She breathed in the moment. If she never got this moment back, she needed to make sure it was etched into every last one of her senses.

"I don't see how sitting in silence, listening to the waves crash against the shore is supposed to improve our public speaking," he announced, breaking the silence between them.

“Considering the fact that you'll need to put them to use much more than I'll have to, it's only right that you get the first crack at it.”

“Are you sure about that, Ms. Phoenix Colleville, lead anchor for Channel 2 action news?”

“You googled me,” she laughed as she turned her body slightly to see his face.

“I google everybody. Forced habit in this day and age. You didn't google me?”

“Now what fun would that be?”

The two shared a laugh. Though organic dating was preferred by most, it was always good to do a little pre-date investigating. Phoenix felt like she'd found her equal. Her friends and even Rue thought she was pretentious with her need to not go into anything blindly. But she saw it as a precaution. Yes, she was aware there were things a google search might not tell her, especially about the qualities that matter to her the most. But she hated going into anything not being able to have at least a baseline pulse of what to expect. She didn't get the chance to do that with Blaise. If she were being honest with herself, she was glad because it was relaxing to just sit and talk with him.

“So, tell me Ms. Third Ward, what are your aspirations in life?” Blaise quoted his sister’s favorite singer.

Phoenix’s head fell against his chest as she threw her head back in laughter. This man was full of surprises. She took a long sip of her tea before she compiled her answer. What could she say? The aspirations she had in life had all fallen apart at the seams. She was simply winging it without a plan or even an end goal. Each day was a blank slate, and she really didn’t aspire to be anything anymore. But would telling this complete stranger that be the best idea? She slowly sipped the remainder of her tea, hoping the silence between them could remain. She should have never interrupted it.

“Did I strike a nerve? Float into uncharted waters? What’s up, you just left me?”

"No, nothing like that. I just haven't thought of my aspirations in a long while."

"Can I ask you something personal?"

"That's the only kind of questions you should ask when you're getting to know someone right?"

"What brought you to Solace Point?"

"What do you mean?"

"Most people wind up at places like this when they are running from or to something or someone. From what my lil' investigative googling found, you were the next big thing. You could have had your own show in a few more years. It seems like you just ghosted your whole career. So, which is it for you?"

"A bit of both. My sister and her husband live here with their two daughters. I needed to be close to my family, they're home for me. I was at a place in life where I needed home more than anything else."

"I get it. I had several offers on the east coast, but I took this position to be close to my mother. She's in Azusa. From 18 until now, I've been on the move from place to place chasing my dream. Now that it's become my reality, I wanted to settle into a place where she was in reach, but not necessarily at my fingertips. She and my sister are my world. And my nieces and nephews. Family means the world to me too."

"My mama always used to say family was all we really had in this world that was constant. I never understood what she meant by that until these last few years."

"Your mom was right. My father told me the same. Said the only thing better than being born into a family that loves you is birthing a family that loves you."

"That's what you want? To have a family of your own."

"One day."

Phoenix turned to look up at Blaise. His dark eyes mirrored the ocean in front of them. Though she could not see through them to his soul, she was sure he could see hers. His piercing gaze told her he was searching more than the surface. Caution hurled against the wind as Phoenix rose to her knees. She leaned into Blaise and pressed her lips against his. They were soft and she fought to keep her eyes open. As much as closed eyes meant connection, she wanted to look deep into his eyes. She wanted to see herself reflected back in them. Gently, he palmed the back of her head, deepening their kiss and parting her lips with his tongue. Under the stars, with no witnesses, but the calm ocean and glowing moon, they sealed their fates with a kiss.

For the remainder of the night, she found comfort on his broad chest. The thumping of his heart calmed her worries and drowned out her fears. She had to admit she liked him, and there was no way she was about to not explore this new territory with him.

CHAPTER FIVE

Phoenix paced the foyer, waiting for any of the six elevators to ding. She was beyond confused about her test results. Though everything turned out much better than she expected, she couldn't seem to figure out why. It had only been eight weeks since her last visit, and she'd only been on the new regiment consistently for four weeks. Having near instantaneous improvement was new for her. It left an eerie feeling in the pit of her stomach like the other shoe would drop at any given moment. As much as she should have been rejoicing for a chance to take a breath, she found herself trying to figure out why things seemed to be going so perfect. Lupus had made her a bit of a pessimist and she had trouble accepting what was good for what it was. There was always a negative or looming thought tap dancing on her happiness and as much as she tried to shake the unsettling feeling she couldn't.

As she stepped onto the elevator, she frantically smashed her index finger into the lobby button. One thing she hated more than hospitals, was sharing an enclosed space with a bunch of strangers. She glanced down at her watch and realized her appointment ended much sooner than she thought. She allotted herself three hours and here she was on her way to the lab an hour early for her testing. A groan escaped her mouth as she realized she had to wait another hour for her brother-in-law to arrive with her nieces. She'd promised Rue she would take over soccer mom duties for the day while the couple enjoyed a quiet evening alone. They had been trying for baby number three since their oldest turned 10, and neither of their schedules permitted them much bump and grind time.

Phoenix strolled through the hospital with her head buried in her phone. She'd been reading over the same line of the editor's notes on her latest article for the last two stretches of hallway. The piece was scheduled to go to press that evening and she was stressing out about the last-minute changes he'd requested. It didn't help that he picked the worst day to spring this on her. Her plate was full of her appointments and stand-in nannying. She prayed that her lead editor would hurry back from vacation because her underling had been making her life a living hell for the past two weeks. He made her rework the angle of her article and now he was questioning her sources and critiquing her choice of photographs.

Pulling the first chair she spotted at the cafe, Phoenix plopped down at a table in the hospital's cafe. She pulled her iPad from her bag and set up a mini workstation. With a little under an hour to spare before her lab appointment, she decided to tackle his exhausting bubbles of notes and suggestions. It was all the time she needed to tweak the article and swap out the editorial images. Though there was a department that handled images, she loved finding them herself. It was how she made sure her targeted demographic was represented within every caveat of her stories.

As she mindlessly scrolled through the many pages of the stock site waiting to see a black person, she minimized the screen to check her email. She was sure the acting editor would have some comments on her document since it had been over half an hour. A smile obstructed her blank gaze as she noticed the red bubble over her message app icon. She knew it was going to be Blaise since he hadn't checked in since the night before.

Blaise: This whole texting thing is cool, but your presence is better. So, this is me requesting more of it.

Phoenix: What did you have in mind?

Blaise: I got tickets to a place I think you might love. Tomorrow, 2?

Phoenix: Tomorrow at 2 it is. What should I wear?

Blaise: Something warm, it involves being on the water. That's the only detail I'm giving. See you tonight.

Phoenix: Gonna have to reschedule. Promised my sister, I'd get the girls tonight. I'm on auntie duty until whenever their bedtime is.

Blaise: Just text me about 30 minutes before. Wait, will you even know 30 minutes before.

Phoenix: I'm new here. You should know Uncle B, you tell me?

Blaise: If they're pre-teens, who fucking knows. But the lil' ones, they have tells

Phoenix: How about you just FaceTime me when your shift is over. I'll be up, listening to interviews for my next article.

Blaise: Bet.

Phoenix smiled as she closed her message app and returned to her document. The last few weeks she'd spent getting to know Blaise had been such a relief. She was glad she listened to Forge and gave him an honest try. Going in with no expectations turned out perfect for her. He was all the man she ever needed. It was too early for her to consider forever, but she found her what-ifs changing from scenes of eternal rest to eternal love. Every time they were together, his conversation was captivating. She didn't understand why he was single, but she wasn't questioning it. God had a way of sending her what she needed at precisely the moment she needed it. She was beginning to feel like the time she spent with Blaise was another clear indicator of that fact.

After thirty minutes of back and forth live editing her document with her editor, she'd decided to just head to the lab early. They were usually slow around this time, and she knew she'd be able to get in and out a little quicker. Time was something she didn't have much of and wasn't keen on wasting it. Pushing the double doors, she stood back as they granted her entry into the lab she nicknamed the Rabbit hole. There were so many different areas based on the type of testing patients needed. On any given day, she'd have to visit anywhere between three to six areas and spend no less than an hour there. Today was different. She only had two areas to visit and estimated she'd spend no more than thirty minutes.

"Heyyy, Ms. Lady. Look at you coming in all smiles."

Phoenix blushed as she walked up to her favorite receptionist. He was an older, middle-aged man with a salt-and-pepper curly top and chin strap. His sunset-colored skin was always adorned with three forehead wrinkles and deep dimples. He was the highlight of her visit whenever she came in. Even on her worst days he made her feel like she was the prettiest, strongest girl in the world. No negative thoughts had a chance to enter her mind while she was in his presence. She smiled even harder as she realized Blaise had become that for her on a daily basis. When she couldn't find it in herself, she could count on him filling her up every time they talked.

"Hi, Mr. Langley. What's my wait time looking like? I got time to write a book in here," Phoenix joked.

"Depends on what the doc got in your orders for today."

"An arterial ultrasound of my legs and just a routine panel."

"I'll have to schedule you for the arterial. The tech is gone for the day. But I can have you in and out on the bloodwork if ya rollers stay put. There's no wait."

"I treated them really good today. Water all morning, so they should be too plump to even think about rolling anywhere."

Phoenix loved everything about Solace General. It was the first hospital where she saw a sea of black and brown faces in white coats. Most of the staff she encountered treated her as a human instead of an experiment. Her concerns were taken seriously, and her care team was compassionate. They allowed her to be a part of the decision making and created a partnership for her health instead of just dismissing what she was concerned about.

For the first time since she'd been a patient at Solace General, she was out of the lab in less than thirty minutes. Before anything could change, she was making a bee line for the elevator that would take her to her brother-in-law's office. She knew she'd be able to get a quick lunch and nap in there before he arrived with the girls. His office was spacious, and he always kept soups and sandwiches stocked in his mini fridge.

Just before she reached the door to his suite, she felt a strong, soft hand grip her elbow. His smell alone caused her to close her eyes and attempt to regulate her breathing. Last week, it had been hard to contain herself around him. She wanted him to fuck her six ways to Sunday every time she was in his presence.

"So, you really gon' come here and not slide by my office?"

"I didn't want to intrude. Plus, I didn't know we were on the popping-up-at-each-others'-place-of-work tip already," Phoenix confessed as she turned to face Blaise.

"You got my work, cell, and home number. Shit, you got my address. We're pretty much past the trading pleasantries phase."

Blaise cupped her chin and looked down into her face. She was glowing under the fluorescent light fixture in the hallway. Without giving a fuck who might see him, he closed the space between them. With the back of his index finger, he smoothed a loose strand of hair from her face and kissed her lips. She deepened the kiss, gripping both lapels of his white coat.

"What are you doing wandering around the hematology unit?"

"My brother-in-law's office is right there. I had my physical today, so I told him to meet me here with the girls."

Phoenix kicked herself for lying the second she said it. She didn't know why she couldn't just tell Blaise what was wrong. In the time they'd spent together, she knew he was compassionate and understanding, and given his medical background, more than capable of handling whatever she told him. But something held her back. She didn't want to taint their good thing with talk of her sordid illness. She wanted to enjoy the moments they shared without having to consider what would happen if he knew she was sick or how he'd change.

"I'm on lunch. How long before you're on nanny duty?"

"About an hour. I was about to grab a sandwich from his fridge and crash on his couch."

"You can do that in mine. C'mon."

Blaise interlocked his fingers with hers and led her back to the elevator. She rested her head on his arm as they rode the elevator down seven levels. She tried to focus on anything but the rapid beating of her heart, but the numbers weren't moving fast enough for her. This was the first time she saw him in his white coat, and it looked delectable against his midnight-hued skin. The peach shirt and navy-blue blazer underneath made her mouth water. She didn't know if it was hunger or lust, but she craved him at that moment. He looked good enough to hit the stop elevator button and gobble him up right there. But she knew there were probably cameras, and she was not about that voyeuristic life. She didn't want some security guard being the reason she made her porn debut on Tasty Blacks.

"How much farther we gotta go before we reach your office?"

Phoenix turned to face him in the elevator. Her eyes burned with desire as she stared up at him. She was hungry before she saw him, but now food was the farthest from her mind. Her stomach wasn't what she wanted filled. With no knowledge of what had gotten into her, she pressed her body into his. Her hand massaged the bulge she felt growing in his chinos. It was rare she made it this far on an elevator without having to step off and wait for the next empty one. Some higher power was most certainly granting her a moment to indulge as she let her lips lock with his again. His hand palming her ass in her ankle length body con dress caused a moan to subconsciously escape her mouth. It bounced off the walls as a sweet refrain, guiding the winding of her waist.

"You gonna have me canceling the rest of my appointments, you keep this up," he said, breaking their kiss.

"Baby, I just need a good fifteen minutes. I'll even clean you up afterwards," she whispered in his ear as she took his ear lobe in her mouth.

"Fifteen, huh?"

"Mmmhmmm," she moaned in his ear, and the elevator dinged.

"Shit."

Phoenix removed herself from his being as the door began opening. She hoped whoever was about to step on the elevator got scolded by the heat that had risen between them. They deserved to burn for intruding on their foreplay. Blaise pulled her back in front of him and turned her around. He positioned her ass right against his rock-hard dick. With both his hands wrapped around her waist, he kissed her neck just as the doors opened fully.

"Auntie!"

Phoenix's eyes nearly bulged from their sockets as Trav and her nieces stepped on the elevator. She quickly flashed them a smile and put an inch of space between her and Blaise. He discreetly pulled down the back of her dress that had begun to ride up as she grinded on his midsection.

"What's up, B," Trav dapped up Blaise as he accessed the scene. "Hey, lil' sis," he grinned as he leaned into her.

"You better not say a word to your wife," she whispered as he slung his arm over her shoulder and pulled her in for a one-armed hug.

"Y'all secret is safe with me," he laughed.

"B, she's fam. Don't fuck her over."

"And I thought you said this town wasn't small," Blaise said, pulling Phoenix back beside him in the elevator.

"I thought it wasn't," she laughed.

Trav allowed the two their time together and proceeded with his plan to take the girls for some ice cream in the food court before they were supposed to leave with Phoenix. Seeing her family on the elevator iced the fire that had been sparked between her and Blaise. They walked hand in hand to his office, in silence. *What the fuck am I doing? Am I having some kind of sick-girl-my-life's-ending-moment? This shit ain't even me forreal. Get it together, bitch. Get it together.* Phoenix plopped down in the chair across from his desk the second they were in his office. Food wasn't what she needed anymore, she needed space. She was being reckless and almost got caught with her skirt up by her family.

Blaise could feel the change in her mood instantly. He was in awe of just how in tune with her emotions and moods he was already. Whenever something was off with her, he could sense it. Everything that transpired in the last ten minutes was a shock to him. Phoenix was always direct with her words, but never with her actions the way she was earlier. It was a rare side of her, and he was there for seeing more of her on any given day. But something told him, that side probably wouldn't resurface again for a long time.

"So, Trav is your brother-in-law?"

"Yea. He's been my brother-in-law long before they ever got married. More like a second dad to me. How do y'all know each other?"

"A couple of us get together for 2-on-2 pick-up games once a week. Roddy introduced us my first week here. He's cool."

"I know."

"Don't go ice on me now, boo."

"What you mean?"

"The second he stepped on that elevator you shut me out. We are not heading down the aisle or anything. Just two people, casually dating. Don't make it seem like what we are building has to stop because I'm acquainted with your kin."

"It's nothing like that at all."

"Cool," Blaise acknowledged before pecking her lips. "I have to get back to my patients, but you can eat my lunch and crash on my sofa. I'll call you later."

Phoenix kissed Blaise one more time before he left the room. Everything about the last five minutes made her want him even more. Since meeting him there wasn't anything, he hadn't sacrificed for her. His time was what he seemed to give her so freely and without much prompting. She was beginning to love him for that alone.

Time was something she knew was precious and more valuable than even love. Love could be replaced, reshaped and replenished. Time couldn't. It was the one thing that when lost, stolen or given freely, one could never get back. There was no way to reciprocate. Opting to just take his apple chips and water, she left his lunch in the fridge and plopped down behind his desk. She leaned back in his chair and imagined for a second how good it would have been to be bent over his desk, face down on his keyboard, taking all the deep strokes he wanted to give her. Instead, she closed her eyes and slid her panties to the side. With images of him fucking her into oblivion, she massaged her clit with her thumb. Her slippery folds plumped as she inserted two fingers into her sopping pussy. It didn't take long to get her rocks off. Before leaving, she tidied up the mess she'd made on his leather chair.

One day, she thought as she prepared herself for a day in the life of Rue.

Phoenix had no idea what she was getting herself into with her nieces. As she drove them from activity to activity, she wondered where the hell Rue found the time to be wife and friend to her husband, mother to her children, and caregiver to her little sister. A sea of guilt drowned her as she thought about how Rue must feel constantly having so much to do and always finding time to fuss over her when she was battling a flare.

It was these times she hated being sick the most. Very rarely did she have to step into anyone else's shoes. Now that she had the chance to be casted in one role of Rue's busy life, she wanted to burn the script for her own even more. In the only lupus support group session she went to, she remembered a fellow lupus warrior talking about how she wished she could bear her disease alone. Phoenix never understood how someone could wish to suffer not only in silence, but alone until she was hauling a packed van of screaming nine- and ten-year-olds from soccer, to ballet, to tutoring, and then home for a whole other set of tasks.

By the time she got the girls showered, fed and tucked into bed, she was exhausted. Every limb of her body ached and all she wanted to do was crawl into the nearest bed. For an hour, she lay in bed, on her back, following the whirling ceiling fan as she considered how much easier her sister's life might be without her. She thought about how much more time she'd have to live a more fulfilling life that didn't revolve around caring for a sick relative. Pulling herself from the sunken place she was heading, she snatched her phone from the nightstand. As the bright screen illuminated the room, she closed her eyes.

"Damn, turn that shit down," she scolded herself as she slid the screen brightness bar down. Continuing her task, she navigated to the thread that had breathed new life into her since the moment it began.

Phoenix: Are you settled in yet?

Blaise: Just parked my car. Tired?

Phoenix: Exhausted.

Blaise: They gave you a run for your money?

Phoenix: That's putting it mildly. I feel like I was the one spinning on my toes.

Blaise. LOL. Get some rest. You'll need it for our date.

Phoenix: Goodnight.

Blaise: Night.

The next morning Phoenix woke before the rest of her family. She'd heard Trav and Rue come in from their date in the wee hours of the morning. Soon after she fell off into a deep sleep. As she slid on her shoes and tiptoed down the stairs, she peeked into both her nieces' rooms and saw them still fast asleep. Rue and Trav's door was closed, and she assumed they'd be sleeping in since it was the weekend. It was the perfect timing for a quick getaway before Rue begged her to hangout and she'd have to come up with a lie to decline her offer.

As she searched the living room for her purse and keys, she nearly jumped out of her skin at the sight of Trav. He sat in his armchair sipping coffee and reading the paper. A chuckle left her lips and she thought about how her father used to do the same thing every morning. Rue really did marry a man just like their father, and she found it comical because they used to butt heads so much when they were growing up.

"Morning, Bro."

"Morning, lil' sis. Why you sneaking out like some fling?"

"I gotta head back to my side of town. I have a da—meeting this afternoon and still have a good chunk of my article to read over before then."

"A meeting, huh? With B?"

Phoenix plopped down on the couch. She didn't know why she was even hiding the fact that she was dating. She wasn't some snot-nosed teenager ogling her first crush. She was 33 years old with her own house, car, and job. She honestly had no one to answer to, but still she kept whatever her and Blaise were doing to herself. Forge was the only one who knew anything before Trav caught them in the elevator.

"Yea. We're going on a date this afternoon."

"Why you hiding and sneaking around and shit? You grown as fuck tiptoeing around here like you 16 and stayed out pass curfew."

"You know how your wife is. She'd for sure make a big deal out of me dating someone. She jokes about me getting back in the dating game, but in reality, she'd lose her shit. It would be a whole new list of shit she's googling. She'd probably be trying to accompany me on every date to make sure I'm not exacerbating my symptoms," Phoenix explained.

"All true, but that ain't it, Sis."

"I don't know, Trav, I guess I just want to explore this without having to answer questions about what I'm doing, what my intentions are. You know those looming questions of forever. I just want to enjoy this. I honestly don't know who I'll be when I wake up from one day to the next. But I can say, since meeting Blaise, no matter what version of myself I am on any given day, I'm happier."

"So just tell her that. I'm sure she'll understand. Then again, maybe not. But you should still just tell her you met someone, you like him, he makes you happy, and you're just taking it day by day."

"Like that will make a difference." She side-eyed him.

"Yea, you right. This our secret," he laughed. "I love you, Sis. As long as you're happy, I'm happy for you."

After scribbling a quick note to Rue, letting her know she was heading home and would get with her on Sunday at Noir Tea, she hugged Trav and left. Once she finally made it back to her house, she kicked off her shoes and went into one of the only two furnished rooms in her home. With a press of a button, her coffee was dripping into her cup. Her shoes went flying in two different directions and she cracked her knuckles and powered on her laptop. She had about two hours to finalize her article before it was due to the editor's desk. She planned to knock it out and catch a few more hours of sleep before she had to meet Blaise at the bus station.

Sleep had come and gone. Phoenix gave herself one last glance in the mirror before grabbing her purse. She had done more driving in the last two days than she had in the last six months. Her car was probably enjoying the miles she had been putting on it. As she revved her engine, she blew a kiss at herself in the rearview mirror and mouthed 'have fun'. It was something her mother always did when Rue had a date in high school. Her eyes watered as she thought about just how much she missed out on when it came to time and moments with her parents. It had been nearly twenty years since they'd died, but there were painful reminders daily. Shaking the sad thoughts, she backed out of her driveway with unbridled excitement etched along her brow.

Just like their first date, butterflies fluttered at the deepest depths of her stomach. She brushed her sweaty palms along the sides of her dress. Blaise was the only man to make her this nervous every time she was in his presence. Partly because everything about him commanded her attention. His strong jaw line, his broad shoulders, his impeccably chiseled chest with just the right amount of body fat to serve as her throw pillow. He was perfect, and she was far from it. The other reason was because she couldn't control herself around him. She always found herself having to touch him. Her hand roamed every surface of his body, and the heat that emitted from her flesh in his presence was enough to cause her to combust. She was hot for him, and it was hell fighting the urge to just fuck on sight every single time.

Phoenix bit down on her lip as she approached him, drawing blood. He looked good enough to sop up with a biscuit in his navy blazer and tan slacks. The peach button down shirt and rose gold cufflinks made him look studious. But the rose gold bottoms in his mouth made him look super hood just like she liked them when she was in high school. A smile spread across her face as she entered his outstretched arms.

"Damn, I love when you match my fly on accident," he said, twirling her around.

Phoenix wore a navy skater dress with a deep V-neck plunge and strappy, wrap-around navy heels. Her hair was freshly washed and dyed burnt sienna. Her ears, neck, and wrist were dazzled with rose gold jewelry. She laughed at him as her palm found the back of his neck. Her left leg rose as she planted a kiss on his juicy, inviting lips. Before him, she was never one for PDA, but there was something about them that just made her want to kiss him all day, every day no matter where they were or who was watching.

"So, this place on the water, did it cost you a ton of money because the way you looking, I'm finna roll up somebody's partition."

"Nah, the partition is gonna have to stay down for this. I'm too damn excited to see your face when we get there."

"A Prince hologram concert?"

"You fucking wish," he laughed, ushering her into the car.

The pair rode in comfortable silence as Blaise gripped the steering wheel with one hand and her thigh with the other. She loved that he knew she craved touch more than anything without her having to verbalize it. From their first date until now, they always had some kind of skin-to-skin touch whenever they were in each other's space. Her hand massaged the back of his head as he drove the two hours to their destination. The second he parked the car, she started bouncing in her seat. Though she was grossly overdressed for their destination, she didn't care because he listened.

"You heard me!"

Phoenix screamed as she fumbled with the lock. She knew he'd be a little peeved she opened her own door, but she was too excited to wait for him to get out. She shut the door and just stared out to sea. The sun was just about to begin its descent from the sky, and it was beautiful. It looked just like the picture she kept in her wallet of her parents. The sky was the most bewitching blend of pinks, purples and blues. The cool breeze that bounced off the waves enveloped her in a hug.

She danced in place, extending her hand for his as he rounded the car. After he'd locked the door, intertwined his fingers with hers and proceeded to the dock. He knew this was the perfect date the second he saw the ad on Facebook. He remembered her talking about how her parents flew to San Francisco every year to celebrate their anniversary.

Phoenix raised his hand to her lips and planted a soft kiss on her knuckles while they walked. She wasn't even going to try to hide her enthusiasm. She'd never been to Alcatraz because she said it was the one trip she'd want to share with either Rue or her forever partner. She couldn't recollect if she admitted that truth to Blaise when she recounted her parents' love story, but the gesture scored him all the damn things. He was indeed the number one contender for her heart. With every date he'd carefully planned out, he was breaking down her walls, both the walls around her heart and between her legs.

"Would the beautiful couple like a picture?"

"We'd love one," Phoenix beamed as she pulled Blaise in front of the camera.

Blaise turned her around and stood behind her. With both hands intertwined with hers, he wrapped his arms around her body. Her smile widened, exposing her dimples as a tear slid down her face. He kissed it away once it reached mid-cheek while the photographer captured the shot. There wasn't anything she said that he didn't hear. When she showed him the picture on their second date, he committed it to memory so they could recreate it.

"You know you've outdone yourself, right? This is honestly the sweetest thing anyone has ever done for me. And that says a lot because my daddy did a lot of sweet things for his daughters."

"From the light that twinkles in your eye whenever you talk

about him, I know I have big shoes to fill, but I'm up for the challenge."

"Come here," Phoenix commanded as she motioned with her index finger.

She pulled him in by both sides of his lapel and slipped him her tongue. There was no more resistance on her part. While she still wasn't ready to be all out in the open around her sister, she was not dragging her feet with Blaise anymore. There was no more playing it safe. If these were her last days, like Dr. Crane told her after her second appointment with him, she was going to enjoy every moment of them with this amazing man God sent her way. She was sure she wouldn't get enough moments to make a lifetime with him, but the ones they'd share would be better than none.

"Let's get settled before the boat sets sail. I want us to have a nice spot to see the sunset. They say this tour time will have the sun setting while we're right in the middle between Alcatraz and the city."

Phoenix couldn't stop staring at him as he led her to the front of the boat. She stood right at the rail while he stood behind her. His arms gripped the rail on either side of her as she gazed out into the dark, purplish-blue sky. There was a hint, where the sun sat just a slither above the water. It was becoming less clear where the sky ended and the water began. The scene was breathtaking. As beautiful as it was, all she wanted to do was gaze into the eyes of the man that made it possible for her to be there. She turned to see him looking out into the water just like she was just a second earlier. Her excitement had rubbed off on him as they neared the island. She caressed his cheek, pulling his gaze from the picturesque scene. She traced his lips with her index thumb as she cupped his chin.

"Thank you for the view." Phoenix remembered his note from the second item he ever brought her. She gently pulled his head down to meet her lips before pressing them gently against his.

"You're welcome."

CHAPTER SIX

Something was most certainly in the air in Solace Point, but Phoenix wasn't quite sure what it was yet. She'd skipped out on lunch with her sister twice without a hint of regret. Her daily routine had been altered, and she was surprisingly open to the distractions from her problems. As she danced around her house dusting and shining everything in sight, she thought about the quaint little dates she and Blaise had shared. His sensibility to nature, openness to learning, and shockingly intuitive notions were a welcomed relief from the daily pill-popping, nap-taking lifestyle she normally led. Their late-night talks from the last three months lived rent-free in her mental rolodex. She replayed whenever she had a moment of fear, doubt, or gloom.

As she acoustically sang loudly off key with the rain serving as her only instrument, she couldn't help but smile. Life was in no way perfect, but she'd gotten to a place where she no longer dreaded waking in the morning. Facing a new day wasn't so bad. There was finally a normalcy that she wanted to get used to experiencing. Her stories for work weren't as drab anymore. Spring time in Solace meant celebrations, festivals, and an endless slew of socialite events to cover. Though she missed being on-screen, occupying the front page of the number one local newspaper week after week had her settling into a new sense of self-contentment.

Thunderous knocking on her locked screened door nearly caused her to jump from her skin. Annoyance dropped from her speech as she instructed her home system to silence her music. Armed with her feather duster, she stomped toward the back door. Lately, no one thought to call before popping up on her moments of peace. Though most days she welcomed the intrusion, that moment wasn't one of them. She was thoroughly in tune with herself, and her unsolicited visitor had completely disrupted her Zen.

"Rue, where is your key?"

Hurriedly, she rushed to unlock the door. Rue was drenched, and rain dripped from the ends of her eight stitch braids. The storm hadn't originally been in the forecast, and she was sure Rue wasn't the only one caught off guard. Tossing her a towel from the linen closet nearest the kitchen, she took the bags from her hand.

"I left my keys in the van. The girls are inside. My hands were too full to try to turn back. You really need to get Trav to build a deck out back or at least put up an awning. I had to trudge through damn near a foot of mud."

"No, I love the sound of the rain hitting the porch. Plus, I open the window and let it mist the plants in the parlor. Anyway, what is all this?"

"Just some things to hold you over until the storm passes. It's supposed to rain most of the week, and I don't want you biking or walking anywhere. Visibility is at an all-time low and you're already having vision issues."

"Thanks, Big Sis, but I was good. You should have called. I went into town a few days ago and got my necessities. Got my baby loves out in this mess for some groceries. I would have been fine ordering takeout."

"Girl, please, your baby loves got *me* out in this mess. You know soccer is rain or shine."

"Did they win? I know my celebratory canna cream better be in one of those bags."

"They didn't play yet, but I made sure to pick you up a pint. They were having a 2 for $6 sale, so I got you two of the butter pe-canna since they were out of pralines in the sky."

"Thanks. But back to this game. Why didn't they just cancel it if the visibility is so bad?"

"They scheduled a two-hour delay to prep the indoor facility. It smells good in here. You're cooking again?"

"Just a little something-something. I feel good and you know my motto. Rolled up on the side of the bed like I won..."

"Talk like a winner, my chest to that sun," Rue finished the line to the Flo Rida song as she laughed.

The aromas emitting from the stove caused Rue to deviate from her initial line of conversation. Walking further into the kitchen, she rounded the stove and lifted the lid on the pot that simmered.

"It smells yummy. What is it?"

"Mama's homemade pasta and garlic bread. I also have some apple empanadas prepped for dessert. So, thanks for the canna cream because I am all out. It's the one thing I forgot to grab when I was downtown. Gotta get my high in some form today."

"So, the cannabis has been working to offset your side effects?"

"So far, so good. I haven't had any vomiting or super long episodes of pain. Headaches don't even exist. Is it bad that I wish I would have been getting high?"

"You're silly," Rue laughed as she took off her jacket.

Phoenix watched as she walked to the door and waved her daughters inside. Since they had two hours to kill, Phoenix guessed Rue had decided to wait the storm out with her. Her anxiety kicked up several notches, instantly. She was not ready for Rue to find out she was dating someone and certainly not ready to tell her that she was seriously considering a relationship with him. Even though she'd planned for Rue to be the first person she told about Blaise, it didn't happen that way and she was not about to have her find out prematurely because of a damn thunderstorm.

Her excitement was slowly dwindling away with each step her nieces took to reach her back porch. Blaise was expected to arrive anytime within the next hour, and she wanted her house to herself. Though it wasn't much of a home yet, and she mainly lived out of boxes, it was hers. She never cared about her sister infringing on her peace because it kept her sane. But she planned to preserve her sanity in a different manner tonight. Rue and her crew were borderline cockblocking even though they didn't know it.

"Uhh, y'all staying here until the storm passes?"

"I wasn't planning on it, but if you're cooking and its mama's pasta, I figured we'd just eat with you. Trav has two surgeries today, so he wasn't going to make it home for dinner anyway."

"Ohhkay."

"I mean unless we're imposing. Lord knows I wouldn't want to do that."

"You kind of are. I planned a nice quiet evening to just be, you know, just exist, and get used to my own company again. I haven't had much of that since being here."

"If I didn't know any better, I'd think you were trying to get rid of us like me and Trav used to do to you."

"I mean, I am trying to get rid of y'all, but not for that," Phoenix laughed.

She was indeed trying to get rid of them for that, but there was no way she was about to divulge that information at that moment. She wanted them out of her hair long before he was expected. She needed to get her bread in the oven and hop in the shower. It was bad enough Blaise was coming over and she still hadn't fully moved into her house. She wanted to at least be comfortable in her skin since she wasn't comfortable in her home yet. That required at least fifteen minutes just standing under the running showerhead before she washed and moisturized her skin. If things went her way the night would end with his hands and lips running a marathon across every inch of her body.

"Why do I feel like you hiding something...or someone? You got a man up there in one of them closets? Is he dangling out the bathroom window or something?"

Rue darted up the stairs two at a time, tripping up the final one. She collapsed on the top step, laughing hysterically. Phoenix frantically ran behind her and doubled over in laughter once she saw the sight before her. Rue's flowy skirt was caught on a leaf of one of the Zaza plants that sat on every third step. Gently, she released her sister from the hold the Zaza plant had on her. Without so much as a thank you, Rue continued her mission. She first went to the bathroom to see if there was someone there she needed to help off the ledge. After coming up empty, she ran to the guest room and opened the double doors to the closet.

"Rue, you are crazy. There is no one here but me," Phoenix laughed as she stood in the doorway.

"I mean, it wouldn't be a bad thing. You broke off your engagement how long ago now? It's about time you got back up on that saddle."

"Ewww. You sound like Grammy now. Can you go before my pasta burns? I still need to shower before I eat and curl up in front of the T.V."

"Hopefully with one of those vibrators I got you. I read somewhere that masturbating is good for your immune system."

"Bye, Rue. The rain sounds like it has slowed down."

Phoenix shook her head as she and Rue descended the stairs to join the girls in the parlor. They were flipping through The Rihanna Book like they did every time they came over. Her house wasn't very inviting to children unless they were into plants and books. Luckily for her nieces, they were into fashion and music, which most of her coffee table books encompassed.

"Okay, let me go. Please call me after your appointment next week. We haven't had a chance to catch up in a while."

"I know. Work has me swamped."

"I know. I be clipping all your front-page stories."

"Ughh. You are such a mom."

"Whatever. I'm just really proud of you, Phe. You've been through so much and you're still working toward your dreams. That shit is inspiring, and I'm glad my daughters have an aunt as beautiful, brilliant, and bright as you are to look up to."

"Thanks, Rue. That means more to me than you know."

Phoenix ushered her overprotective sister and adorable nieces to the door as she hugged them all. She had exactly thirty minutes to finish tidying up her place before Blaise was due to arrive. He had proved to be more than punctual, arriving early for every date they scheduled. She stood in the doorway, waving at them once they were back inside Rue's van. She playfully kicked a pretend goal and yelled for them to kick ass at their game.

"I love you," Rue yelled through the rain.

"I love you more, drive safe."

Hurriedly, Phoenix put the finishing touches on her meal before she prepared her body for a visit from Blaise. She'd been in her house for nearly a year and had just unpacked her cookware and cutlery. Takeout and tubberware meals from Rue had sustained her since her move-in day. But for once, she felt like cooking and breaking bread at the beautifully carved dining table where she had gathered with her parents and Rue. Her parents. She hadn't thought of them much since her diagnosis. She cringed thinking about how disappointed they probably were as they watched her let everything she wanted slip away without fighting. Silently, she promised them and herself that from that moment on, fighting for the desires of her heart was all she would do, even if that meant fighting herself. Nothing, tangible or intangible, would keep her from whatever she desired to possess; career and family included.

Those proverbial butterflies returned as Phoenix gazed at her reflection in the mirror. Broadly, she smiled at the woman staring back at her. She'd missed this version of herself who never took no for an answer, even from her own lips or negative thoughts. As she fingered her head full of short, ombre lilac and purple soft waves, she winked at herself. Gently, she ran her hands across the purplish-brown splotchy rash that accented her beautiful dark skin. She'd accepted it as permanent blush. Dressed plainly in an olive green, three-piece ribbed cotton, short set and bare feet, she exited her bedroom, prepared to entertain the guest she anticipated all day.

Just as expected, Blaise lightly knocked on her stained-glass door a few minutes before he said he'd arrive. Like any other time, a beautifully hued plant adorned his right hand. Since they'd met, he'd added four plants to her indoor parlor sanctuary garden, and she prayed he'd never stop. With his free hand, he grasped her waist and closed the space between them.

"You smell like heaven on earth," he complimented as he buried his nose in her neck.

Phoenix moaned at the feel of her body wrapped in his warm frame. His breath tickled her neck as he inhaled her fragrance before planting a soft kiss on her shoulder. Instinctively, she wrapped her arms around his neck. All week, she looked forward to seeing him. They'd texted and talked during his shifts, but she wanted to be in his presence. His presence provided a sense of peace she had never experienced before him. It was addictive, and ever since their first night together at the cove, she craved his company.

“I missed you too,” she said, taking the plant from his hand. “So, what's his name?"

"I was thinking Onire. What you think?"

Blaise followed her into the parlor. The space was coming together beautifully, and it got him excited to have his own home full of fragrant greenery. Phoenix had a thumb as green as his mother's. The way she showed her plants kindness and love reassured him that she was more than capable of loving him if they made it that far.

"Like Ogun Onire, God of war and creativity?"

"Yea. It's a Baby Blue Eucalyptus. Very aromatic, but my father told me that eucalyptus branches were used to make weaponry during wartimes before we had cannons and guns."

"He was also the god of metal work, which is ironic because now almost everything used in war is crafted from metal."

"I love when you educate me."

"And I love that you don't get bored from my random facts. Where do you think I should put him?"

"Right here," Blaise motioned as he walked over to a nice sunny spot between a snake plant and monstera. "Eventually, he'll have to be transplanted outside, but the leaf shape pairs well with these two."

After they'd gotten Onire set up in his new home, they retreated to the kitchen. Blaise busied himself with setting the table and picking their wine selection for the evening. He joked about how the wine fridge and snack cabinet were the only two fully unpacked and stocked spaces in her house. She knew she needed to face the reality that she wasn't leaving Solace Point anytime soon. Meeting Forge and Blaise had her considering accepting this place as home. As much as she missed Atlanta and her dream job, the simplicity of a slower paced life was beginning to be appealing. While she plated their meals, she watched him scroll through his phone. He was a sight to see, and she couldn't see herself becoming tired of the view anytime soon.

"Bon appétit," she announced as she placed his plate on the round, water hyacinth placemat.

The second she sat down beside him; he enveloped her hand in his and blessed their food. Her smile was permanently plastered on her face as he ended his prayer by asking God to bless the person who prepared their meal. *A praying man.* She thought to herself as he released her hand. There was only a millisecond between the blessing of the meal and the sound of his fork clanking against the glass plate. Blaise's satisfying moans as the flavors exploded in his mouth let her know she hadn't lost her touch in the kitchen. It had been nearly a year since she cooked anything more than toast and grits. Without Rose Marie's, Saxon's, and Rue, she would have wilted away months ago.

After helping himself to a second serving of Bolognese pasta, they retreated to the parlor with their second bottle of wine. Blaise made himself comfortable by removing his button-down shirt, tie, and shoes. Lazily, they sat on the floor, the couch serving as their backrest. The steady fall of the heavy rain served as the only sound between them as they enjoyed each other's company. Finding a person to sit comfortably in silence with was rare and they both never wanted to penetrate the sanctity of their shared silence with small talk. They communicated on a different frequency, one where words were worth less than time spent. As she stretched out on his lap, she stared up at him. He gently rubbed her scalp as she closed her eyes.

"Really don't want this night to end," Phoenix blurted out. Her confession reverberated in the silence. It was an utterance she only meant to think, but as his eyes met hers, she knew they were in the world for him to hear. There was no taking it back.

"It doesn't have to," he replied as he lifted her head.

Gently he palmed her neck and tilted her head up to him. Bringing his forehead to hers, he used his free hand to run his thumb across her cheek before pressing his full lips to hers. Slightly, she opened her mouth, granting his tongue access. The tantalizing taste of wine on his tongue invigorated her. Soft moans escaped from her diaphragm as she leaned into his body. She rose to her knees before straddling his lap.

Phoenix abandoned caution as she gave into the innate reaction her body had to the feel of his hands roaming her bare flesh. Blaise's tongue explored her mouth as his hands got acquainted with her thighs and ass. She ground against his midsection, making his dick begin to stiffen under her. Even in his semi-erect state, she could tell he'd fill every inch of her. She anticipated it even. Her body knew pain, in fact, she'd become accustomed to the unrelenting affliction. It was time she got the immense pleasure to pair it with. His length and girth were clear-cut indicators of why he commanded attention without trying. Her hands massaged his print through his chinos.

Blaise took note of her gesture and kissed up and down her exposed collarbone and chest. His strong, soft hands massaged her braless breast through the thin crop top that served as the barrier between his flesh and hers. She moaned into his mouth from the pleasurable pressure he applied to her nipples with his thumb and index finger. Her moans, heightening his arousal.

Without another second elapsing, he bent her backward until her back was against the shag rug beneath them. He kissed her lips, harshly parting them with his tongue. The remnants of his meal and night cap on her tongue made her tingle all over. She grabbed his face on either side and pulled him on top of her. She wrapped her legs around his waist and kissed him like her life depended on it.

Blaise caressed her hips and thighs, before palming her ass. He pulled his undershirt off with one hand, while he held her in place with the other. Phoenix watched, panting, as Blaise rose to his feet and removed his pants and boxers. Her mouth watered at the sight of his erect 7.5-inch dick, its umber, dark brown-reddish shade slightly lighter than that of his sable-colored chiseled abs, creating the perfect work of art. It stood at attention, beckoning her to taste it. He stood there for a few minutes watching her admire him. He grinned cockily as he watched her grovel. He leaned down and kissed her again, before lowering himself to her panty line. He used his teeth to remove the thin cotton that formed her shorts. He blew on her clit, causing her to shiver. Burying his nose in her center, he inhaled deeply. Her scent was intoxicating. Like a vampire who smelled fresh blood for the first time, he suckled her pussy with his mouth. Sucking, biting, and licking relentlessly, he showed her pussy no mercy. Her juices coated his chin as he feasted on the best fruit he'd ever tasted. Stiffening his tongue, he double penetrated her with his tongue and thumb.

Phoenix lay in ecstasy, clawing at the rug. Her body arched as the crown of her head met to the floor. The sounds of him lapping up her juices as he ate her pussy like the last supper. She yelled out in sheer pleasure when he brought her to her peak. She'd died, left the confines of her earthly body, and watched, suspended in euphoria as he brought her to a second earth-shattering orgasm. There was no way she'd ever give him up, come hell or high water. She'd found herself completely captivated by this man who strolled casually into her life. When he finally came up for air, after causing her two more orgasms, she kissed him, eager to taste her own juices on his tongue.

Never one to be outdone, she felt it was time to show him who really could drain a python. She pushed him back enough for her to rise to her feet. She dropped to her knees in front of him and swallowed him whole in one motion. He was caught completely off guard. She handled his dick like it was curated just for her. He moaned at the feel of her stretched jaws around his 5-inch-wide dick. No woman could ever take him all in. Subconsciously, his eyes rolled to the back of his head and his toes curled nearly to the point of cramping as the tip of his dick poked her uvula. He knew at that moment that Phoenix would be his for a lifetime. When he felt himself about to explode, he pulled away from her and bent her over the empty plant stand.

With gentle but apparent force, he spread her legs and tried to fill her pussy with every inch of himself. Initially, he was met with resistance as he tapped at her opening. She yelled out in pain causing him to pull back a little. Delicately, inch-by-inch, he served her his 7.5-inches of long, hard dick in small increments until he was balls deep in her gushy shit. He stretched her to fit his manhood, imprinting on her with every stroke. Phoenix cried out from the pain and pleasure she was experiencing. As they christened the parlor with the sound of thunder and rain serving as their soundtrack, she saw her future flash before her eyes. It was a bursting scene of glorious joy and endless pleasure. It was the future she wanted to hold onto forever and ever.

As Blaise pulled all the way out and re-entered her, he trailed soft, wet kisses down her spine, sending her over the edge. Lightning lit up the sky as Blaise brought her to her fourth orgasm of the night. He hadn't even busted once and that made her heart smile. *A satisfying man, who puts my needs first.* She thought as he lifted her in the air and placed her legs around his neck. He buried his face in her center, fucking her with his tongue and teasing her clit with his thumb.

Phoenix and Blaise went at it for hours. They had completely made a mess of her parlor room. When they were finally so spent, they couldn't move, they both fell asleep on the sofa. An hour later, Blaise awoke to get some water. All the wine they consumed gave him cottonmouth and there was no way he would be able to sleep peacefully with it.

He roamed her house looking for a blanket to cover their exposed limbs. The rain had since stopped, but the chill it left behind was frigid. After searching through four boxes in her living room, and coming up empty, he woke her so they could retreat to her room. As they made their way to the second floor of her place, he took note of all the moving boxes and wrapped furniture. Once they reached her room, they fell into the bed. He laughed to himself, thinking about how he promised his mother he would focus on courting Phoenix before he made his way into her bed. It was his intention, but fate had other plans. Before falling off to sleep, he'd determined that he was spending the remainder of his weekend between her folds with her hands clawing at his tattoo-covered back.

CHAPTER SEVEN

BLAISE ROUNDED THE BACK OF HIS TRUCK AND LET THE TAILGATE DOWN. THE four months that he'd spent getting to know the brilliant, goofy, intelligent woman in his passenger seat had been refreshing. She was a welcomed escape from his hectic work life. Before her, work consumed him, but she found a way to work herself into his priorities. A giddy smile teased the corner of his mouth as he thought about just how much she'd changed him in their short time together.

He jumped up inside and opened the oversized duffle bag and began unpacking the contents. He laughed as he peered through the rear panel window and saw Phoenix straining her neck to see out of the rearview mirror. He laid the two blankets down on the truck's floor bed and placed the throw pillows down too. Taking his time, he strategically placed the string lights around the outline of the truck bed and along the top of the wheel tub.

Climbing down, he looked over his modern-day, vintage, country-inspired set up. He laughed at just how much this woman had him open. He had gone way past wooing and had officially entered the courtship his parents always reminisced about. Planning dates had become a fulfilling pastime. Finding ways to let Phoenix know he heard even what she didn't say had become his greatest challenge, one he accepted and completed with content.

Since their first date, Phoenix expressed how much she missed going to the drive-in theater. She told him so many stories about when her father and her would go once a month, just the two of them. Since her last tearful confession, he worked tirelessly with help from Roddy and his big sister to bring the drive-in theater to her. He dumped the basket of snacks in the center of the blankets.

Grabbing his tent bag, he walked a few yards away and began putting together the make-shift screen. After scouring online retailers and coming up short, he decided to DIY a screen with two-by-fours, a wooden board and a California king-sized white sheet. After everything was positioned to his liking, he hooked his phone up to the projector and determined it was time to rescue Phoenix from her curiosity. She'd never stopped straining and craning her neck to get a better look. He was sure at some point during the movie, he would be massaging the tension out of her neck and shoulders.

“Okay, so when I told you that sailing to Alcatraz was the best date I've ever been on, that was before this," Phoenix said as she breathed in the scene before her.

With his assistance, she climbed up into the truck and fell back onto the pile of various shaped pillows. Stretching her arms out, she beckoned for him to join her. Blaise wasted no time plopping down beside her. After retrieving two ice cold root beers from the cooler, he pressed play on their movie.

"Jerome! Jerome! Put on that Bobby Womack," Phoenix quoted along with the movie's opening line.

The Wood was easily among her top five favorite movies. Her back pressed against Blaise's chest as she got comfortable between his legs. Her anticipation for whatever else he had in store for her was temporarily subdued as she got ready to get into the many character roles she'd take on for the duration of the film. She planned to recite all her favorite scenes from the movie as they occurred on the big screen that sat just mere feet away from them.

Blaise couldn't keep his eyes or hands off her as she enjoyed his surprise. Phoenix's laughter soothed him after 72 hours of delivering life-altering news to critically ill patients and their families. It was a sound he wouldn't mind hearing for the rest of his life. Softly, he kissed her temple as she leaned her head back against his chest and shook a couple pieces of her Spree hard candy in her mouth. He knew he'd be asleep long before their three-movie-feature concluded. Which was also a scene from her memory with her father.

"You said it was bad timing. And I figured if I asked again, you'd say yes. If not that time, maybe the next time; until the next time became the right time," Phoenix recited as she smiled from ear to ear.

Blaise playfully placed his hand over her mouth. Phoenix laughed as she kissed his open palm before intensively giving her attention to each individual finger. His hands were beautifully sculpted with a bouquet of roses, hibiscus, peonies and eucalyptus artfully tattooed across them. She massaged his hand as they continued to watch the movie. Her doing more reciting than he did watching. He used his hands to preserve the life of others and she was grateful doctors like him and Dr. Crane existed. They worked tirelessly to give others a glimpse of hope and a chance at more time to create moments like the ones he constantly created with her since their fateful encounter.

“You just going recite this whole movie too?”

“Yes, and if the next movie is the Inkwell or Menace II Society, then you’re gonna have to deal with me as the leading role because I’m reciting them too.”

“Thank my lucky stars it’s neither of those.” He laughed as she playfully punched him in the arm.

Larenz Tate was that actor for her. The one whose career she followed from the second she finally got to watch a movie with a rating higher than PG-13. There wasn't a movie he made that she wasn't abreast of when it came to his career. Every movie, every cameo, she'd watched intently, captivated by the flexibility of his artistry. It didn't matter if he played a teenaged boy juggling summer flings or an armored truck robber or the mayor, he commanded attention and delivered a performance she wanted to experience over and over.

Blaise reminded her a lot of Larenz with his confidence that attracted everyone's attention, his intellect and ability to adapt to his environment. Nothing seemed to knock Blaise off-center. All the stories he'd told of how moments arose for him to say fuck his plan and wallow in self-despair he used to fuel his ambition and strengthen his grit. He'd been through the flood and journeyed through the wilderness and still managed to accomplish everything he said he would.

"You inspire me, you know that?"

Phoenix turned slightly so that she could see his face. Fatigue was painted all over his expression as she tried to see his eyes under his low eyelids. His beautifully thick lashes hid them from her view as she caressed the side of his face.

"That's random as hell," Blaise responded without batting an eye.

They'd made it through one and a half of the three movies he'd purchased. Though they were both probably available on streaming platforms, he had no subscriptions. With all his time being spent between the hospital and sleeping, he didn't see the need to waste money getting services he'd very rarely if ever be able to enjoy.

"I just thought you should know."

Phoenix rose up and planted a soft kiss on his lips. She hugged his neck, burying her nose into the space where his neck and shoulder joined. His seemingly natural aroma of bergamot, whiskey and lemongrass was a sensory mechanism she needed to function. He just smelled like the safe haven that she needed.

"Why?"

"Why do you need to know or why am I inspired by you?"

"The latter," Blaise answered as he pulled her back down to his chest. He wrapped his arms around her waist and rolled them both on their side.

"Your tenacity is just next level. You've experienced so much loss while you worked to have this life that you have now. It's just inspiring to know where you are now versus what you journeyed through to get here."

Blaise took a second to think about what she'd just confessed. He knew there was something else there she was trying to get at, but digging into her hidden meaning would surely interrupt how he planned to end the night, so he left it alone. Phoenix shared only the fond moments of her life with him. She had yet to share any instance that required her to exhibit vulnerability. Growing up with his mother and sister let him know that she needed to feel safe with him before divulging any of her wounds. He had every intention of making her feel his protection, not just from physical, outside sources, but also from the emotional and mental torment he saw housed behind her smile.

Even with their brief courtship, she kept so many emotional wounds covered. Her smile very rarely reached her eyes and though her eyes shone, he could feel that they'd lost a bit of their warmth. Life had hit her hard and she was taking it in stride, but he wanted desperately to carry some of that hurt with her. From the moment he bid his assistant farewell and swiped his badge to exit the hospital garage, she had quickly become his first priority. What she did while he worked. What cover story she drafted in his absence. What new secret hideaway she'd found on her walks or bike rides. He was concerned about her in a way he never thought to care about any other person who wasn't in his immediate circle. He found himself making space for her in his thoughts, prayers and even his heart.

“Thank you for noticing,” he whispered in her ear before kissing her.

"You never have to thank me for seeing you. But thank you for all this. You don't know just how much this gesture touched my heart."

Without another word, Blaise turned her around so she was completely facing him. He cupped her face at her ears and pulled her forehead to his lips. Tenderly, he kissed her forehead, then her eyelids, then her nose. Finally, his lips met hers and she moaned with pleasure. His kisses caused fireworks to ignite below her waist. Though she'd kissed her share of frogs, kissing him made her feel like Josie Geller standing in centerfield. She came undone at the seams every time his warm tongue snaked its way into hers.

Instinctively, her arms wrapped around his neck as she deepened his kiss, falling back on his chest in the process. As she straddled his lap, she broke their connection to pull her dress over her head. Instantly, the evening wind whipped around them as she pulled him up by his arms. She could tell he was tired, so she planned to make it quick, but she needed to feel him in her guts, if only for ten minutes.

"You're really going to be the death of me," he groaned as his dick sprang to life under her ass.

Her sloppy kisses trailed from his mouth to his neck to his shoulders. Softly, she trailed her nails down his chest until she was at his belt buckle. Undoing them and pulling his dick from his boxers, she spit in her hand before rubbing it up and down his shaft. Raising her hips, she positioned herself just above the tip of his fully erect pole and slid her thong to the side. She shuddered as she sat down on the tip. Slowly, she worked her way down until her ass cheeks sat on his thighs. She felt every inch of him inside her. For a few seconds she relished in that moment. She felt like he was the perfect fit for her. As she found her rhythm, she hummed Ciara's song, Body, as she rode him to oblivion.

Blaise growled as she leaned forward and sucked on his neck, biting down with just the right amount of pressure. Phoenix was a freak and used every part of her body to bring him to the top of the cliff with her. Riding an orgasm together got her extra wet and she salivated as she felt his dick pulsating against her walls, and she felt the tip in her stomach.

Unable to hold onto his nut any longer, he grabbed a hold of her waist and flipped her onto her back. He unzipped his pants and slid them down, giving himself full range of motion. In one swift motion, her thong had been ripped from her body and he smiled down at her pussy as it convulsed. She was indeed a different breed when it came to fucking, and it made him even crazier about her.

Not wanting to go another second without tasting the nectar that leaked from her contracting walls, he brought his nose to her opening and inhaled deeply. She always smelled like perfectly ripened grapefruit and tasted just as appetizing. His long, warm tongue stretched the length of her pussy as he trailed from the hood of her clit to the top of her ass crack. Before she had time to brace herself, his tongue was trailing the crack of her ass from her tail bone to her pussy. Her body writhed in pleasure as his tongue worked around her asshole. Hungrily, he lapped up the juices that trickled down from the hoisted position he had her body contorted into. She wanted to tap out but the feel of his tongue on her sensitive flesh and his index and middle fingers sloshing in her pussy felt too good.

"Ahhh. Babe, I can't take it anymore. I'm about to explode!"

Blaise didn't reply as he placed his tongue in her pussy along with his fingers. He was sending her on a trip she never could have imagined. Her mental faculties were non-existent as she clawed at Blaise's arms. As she busted in his mouth, a thousand galaxies passed behind her closed lids. With her hand palming the back of his head, she fucked his face until he replaced his tongue with his dick. Her sweet taste on his tongue coupled with the vice grip her pussy had on his dick, it wasn't long before he'd shot his seeds deep in her gut.

As she rode the wave of her orgasm, he rained sweet kissed across her collar bone and along her shoulder. Coming fully prepared for the fucking he knew she'd request; he reached above their heads and removed a warm towel from the portable towel heater and moistened it before delicately wiping her down. She nibbled on his earlobe while she massaged his head. The only thing better in the world than his dick was the aftercare he showered her with. He showed her time and time again, she was his priority.

After cleaning himself up, the couple turned their attention back to the jumbo screen. Phoenix chortled as she prepared to recite one of her favorite lines from Love Jones. But to her surprise, Blaise kissed her temple as he prepared to do just the same.

"Let me tell you something," Phoenix recited as she heard the character in the movie.

"This here, right now, at this very moment, is all that matters to me," Blaise joined in.

"I love you. That's urgent like a motherfucker," they both recited together before laughing hysterically.

"Now look at you reciting all the lines. Can't talk about me anymore."

"Oh, but I can and I will. That's just my favorite line. You don't have a favorite line, you just recite the whole damn movie."

After they'd both caught their breath, Phoenix pulled the quilt over them as they laid under the stars. She was slightly above him as he laid his head on her stomach and wrapped his arms around her waist. Being there with him was surreal. It was something not in the revised future she'd crafted for herself, but she welcomed his insertion into her plan, even if only for a little while.

"I think I might cuff you," she joked before kissing the crown of his head.

"I don't see how you can think of doing something I've already done."

"Is that so?"

"Been so since you got that note."

Phoenix didn't respond with words. Instead, she lifted his chin and kissed him. This man had done it effortlessly. He'd made her open her heart and welcome love out of the cold. She knew she loved him, but there was no way she was blurting that out. It had only been about four months since they had their first date, and she needed to make sure what they shared wasn't just a brief moment in time.

CHAPTER EIGHT

Forge beamed with joy as she leaned on the counter watching Phoenix scan the shelves in the nursery. She hadn't seen her friend in weeks. Any other time she would have been worried or angry, but she welcomed the desertion. All the texts between the two centered around Phoenix's whirlwind romance with Blaise. It was quite refreshing to see her friend so full of love and occupied with more than just press deadlines and countdowns until death.

Phoenix walked over to the counter with her arms full of medium-sized house plants. Her collection was steadily growing as each day passed. This was her third time in the nursery that week alone. Forge welcomed the business, but wondered if Phoenix planned to ever get any furniture for her house. All she ever seemed to purchase were plants or groceries. Much of her home was still in boxes and the only furniture she'd brought with her when she made the move was a hand-carved dining room set and a worn recliner that she'd since restored.

"I mean, I appreciate the business, but bitch when are we going furniture shopping? I'm tired of sitting in the damn window or on the porch every time I come visit."

"I'ont know. Something about furniture shopping just makes everything seem so permanent, you know. I don't think I'm ready for permanent thinking right now."

"Sis, you been here damn near two years now. Plus, the ink has been dry on your deed for damn near a year. What the fuck is not permanent about buying a whole ass house? A big ass house at that."

"You and Rue are on somebody's nerves about some damn furniture. Why do I gotta furnish the whole house? If we're being technical, I literally only live in like four rooms; my bedroom, the bathroom, the kitchen, and the parlor. Plus, when I die, it'll be less for y'all to sift through," Phoenix teased.

"Shut the fuck up with that death talk. I thought we were done talking tombstones and had moved on to gemstones and bridal dress colors."

Phoenix threw her head back in laughter. There was no doubt she was smitten with Blaise. His gestures melted the ice around her heart and his company calmed her fears. But she was in no way ready to be talking trips down the aisle. They'd just surpassed the sixth month mark on their courtship, and she was just enjoying herself. Aside from their time spent together, they never even said they were exclusive. For all she knew, he had other flings or at least entertained the idea of fucking around with other women.

Without dignifying Forge's comment with a response, she walked over to the other extension of the nursery. She hadn't planned to, but she wanted to get Blaise a large plant for his entry way and a fresh eucalyptus bundle for his shower. She remembered when they talked the evening before, he mentioned needing to replace the one he currently had hanging. If it was one thing she adored most about him, it was his desire to learn more about caring for plants and making his house a home. She had to give him credit because he had been there less than a year and he already had his home completely furnished and set up. He lived in his house, and it was truly a home. She felt it every time she spent the night there. His desire to get settled into his new life was endearing and a bit inspiring.

Once she'd finished picking out all she wanted to get, she returned back to the retail side. Forge was busy tagging newly potted plants from one of the nursery's many greenhouses. She knew she had struck a nerve with her comment about them clearing out her belongings after she died. It was hard for her to tiptoe around the reality of her circumstances like Forge and Rue did. She had come to terms with the reality that she might just leave this earth before everyone she loved. There was no longer fear surrounding that realization. But she sometimes didn't realize that her loved ones may not have been as ready for her physical departure from their lives.

Once her hands were free, she walked over and hugged her friend from behind. Forge very rarely retreated emotionally. She usually was very vocal about how she felt about seemingly anything. But when it came to Phoenix's health, she ran for the hills. She didn't like to think of not having her here. They'd become confidants over the year and half that they'd known each other. As an only child, she regarded Phoenix as a sister and her soul ached thinking about not having her there anymore.

"I'm sorry. I know how you feel about everything, and I should have been more careful with my words. I don't plan on going anywhere any time soon. We can start shopping for stuff next month, but only for the living room and one of the guest rooms."

"I love you, Phoenix, and a piece of my heart will surely be buried with you when you leave this earth. I know that you're at peace with everything, it's just taking me a lot longer. Honestly, as selfish as it sounds, I don't think I will ever be ready. But enough about that."

Phoenix intently listened to her friend speak her truth. She understood how Forge felt and she wished she had the chance to prepare herself her parents' demise, but she also knew life didn't work like that. She wrapped her arms around Forge and held her tightly. She felt the anguish melt from Forge's bones as she exhaled.

"How about we spend today together and forget about all my

talks of leaving this world?" Phoenix suggested as she broke their embrace.

"Sounds like a plan to me," Forge agreed.

After spending the rest of the afternoon helping Forge harvest ingredients to dry for the teas and tisanes she sold in the cafe and online shopping for furniture that fit the aesthetic of her house, Phoenix headed home to lie down. She felt like she hadn't been in her bed in weeks, and she missed it. The smell of lemongrass in her diffuser permeated her senses, instantly relaxing her and bringing Blaise to the forefront of her mind. Between working, spending time with Blaise, her family, Forge, and taking time to coordinate video chats with her best friends who worked overseas, she felt stretched to the max. All she wanted was to spend a few moments asleep in her bed without any distractions or interruptions. She hadn't told a soul, but she knew she was beginning to flare. She'd felt it a few weeks ago and opted to try to ride it out. But it was lowkey getting the best of her.

As much as her doctor told her to take it easy, she kept piling on more things to take up all her energy. She missed being a social butterfly. Before lupus crash landed in her world, she was always the life of the party and enjoyed making others come alive, but she was learning that butterflies needed to flutter a lot less when living with lupus. The moment her body connected with the bed, she sighed. Her entire body radiated pain and she'd tried to ignore it. She'd tried to conceal it behind her strong persona, but she was fighting a losing battle. Before getting too comfortable she decided she needed to shower for the next day she planned to spend never leaving her bed.

Slowly, she removed all her clothes piece by piece, tossing them in the hamper in her closet. Naked, she walked into her bathroom welcoming the cold relief the floor extended to the soles of her feet. She deliberately took each step, being sure not to put all her weight on her aching ankles. Turning the showerhead to her desired massage pressure, she stepped under the running water as the steam clouded her vision. She closed her eyes as her head fell to her chest.

The feel of the scalding water on her aching bones was a welcomed bit of pain. She let out a loud sigh as she felt the aches dispel from her limbs. After ten minutes of allowing the water to hit all her aching parts, she lathered her sponge and washed off the day's remnants.

Stepping from the shower, she hummed Snoh Aalegra's song *find someone like you*. She smiled and shook her head as she realized just how much she had really grown to like Blaise. If she were being honest with herself, she knew she probably loved him and was just scared to admit it. Admitting to love meant adding someone else to the list that had to mourn her existence once she was gone.

Dr. Crane's initial prognosis for her wasn't lengthy and not much had changed since he'd been treating her. She felt like forcing someone else into her waiting game was cruel and she would never forgive herself if she caused him that type of pain. He'd shared so much of himself with her, and she knew losing loved ones to illness was hard for him. He never got over them and though he found ways to work through the grief, she could tell he hadn't healed from the deaths of his father or grandmother. No one did actually, but he explicitly expressed how death affects him on a soul level. She never wanted to be responsible for causing him that type of irreversible pain. It'd surely leave a hole in his heart, and that was not what she wanted for them. She wanted fun with no strings attached, but she couldn't front like the strings weren't attached after the thoughtfulness of his Alcatraz Island date.

"You need some time alone. By yourself to get your head on straight. Love is for people with time. You don't have time," she coached herself as she brushed her hair down and put on her durag.

After venturing to her kitchen to reheat a bowl of her beef stew, she poured herself a glass of wine and grabbed her pill container from the counter. She usually hid it in the back of the pantry since Blaise started coming over, but forgot to put it back because she was in such a hurry that morning. She knew better than to mix her meds with alcohol, but a sudden case of the woes overtook her, and she threw caution to the wind. Tossing each pill back one by one, she washed them down with a few gulps of the Pinot Grigio in her glass. She followed it up with a glass of water before taking her soup from the microwave and retreating upstairs.

With her curtains drawn and her pillows fluffed, Phoenix laid in bed, watching episodes of *Sparks* on YouTube. Laughter bounced off the walls and ceilings as she ate her bowl of beef stew. She'd already cleared her schedule and planned to spend the next few days alone, recuperating from all that she'd been doing. A chuckle left her lips as she thought about how she'd allowed Blaise to bend her into a pretzel every chance they were alone. Most of the time the bending was initiated by her. He'd awakened something inside of her she never even knew was there. There was just something about his presence that made her pussy leak like an old faucet. Though the pleasure his dick gave her was out of this world and the next, she was surely paying the price as she winced with pain. His ears had to have been burning because just as he'd crossed her mind, he'd graced her with a text.

Blaise: hey gorgeous. wyd?

Phoenix: illegally watching tv on YouTube.

Blaise: what show you done searched the backwoods of google for this time?

Phoenix: lol. you know me so well. i'm watching sparks. wyd?

Blaise: just got done a 12-hour shift. sitting in my car trying to find the energy to start the truck and be omw home.

Phoenix: wish you were here. i miss you *sad face emoji*

Blaise: say less, on my way.

"God, I love this man. Why did you send him my way? You know

I don't have time for this right now?" Phoenix asked into the empty space.

Phoenix tossed her phone on the bed and got up to take her dishes downstairs. She pulled her robe over her cold shoulders and pushed her feet into her slippers. The night sky was filled with stars as she sat out on her porch sipping on a piping hot mug of steeped rose petals and hibiscus. It was rare that she enjoyed the view from her front yard. She loved the back so much and being close to the lake that passed through her yard made her cherish the space even more. But as she stared up at the bright moon, she admired the view. It was beautiful, almost as beautiful as the love she knew she had for Blaise.

Blaise was a breath of fresh air. He was nothing like her ex-fiancé. He was compassionate and even though he had a million and one things pulling him every which way, her gravitational pull was the strongest. In the short amount of time they'd been seeing each other, not much was put before her. Every moment he wasn't at the hospital he was either with her or asleep. She loved his attentiveness and how he seemed to listen, even when she wasn't speaking. She wished she'd had the pleasure of thanking his father for raising the perfect man.

Twenty minutes after she'd ventured to the porch, Blaise's headlights were blinding her as he pulled into her driveway. The second her eyes laid eyes on him, she saw just how tired he was. Rising to meet him at the top of her steps, she outstretched her arms for him to walk into them. She kissed his lips before grabbing his overnight bag from his hand. No, chivalry wasn't dead, and he reminded her of that fact every day, but she was just as much his peace as he was hers. However, if she could lighten his load, she would.

"How was work?"

"Long. Eventful, but very long. How was your day? Did you finish your cover story?'

"Yes. It's with the editor, which means it's above me now. But enough about that, let's get you showered and in bed. You look just like the day you had."

"Damn, tell me I'm ugly." He chuckled as he kissed her again.

"Boy, please, even at your worst you're finer than fine," she said, pulling him up the stairs and into the bathroom.

After starting the shower and setting the water temp just how he liked it, Phoenix undressed him one article of clothing at a time. She appreciated his selfless act of traveling all the way across town to lay up with her at her request, no matter how tired he was. She didn't take the gesture lightly. Everything he did showed her he was just as into her as she was him. She knew when she told Forge he could have been seeing other women it was bullshit the moment she said it. He literally had no time to see anyone else. She consumed much of his free time, and she valued every second of it.

Once Blaise was in the shower, she left the bathroom to heat a candle for his massage. As she lit the candle, she turned on her iHome to play some rain sounds. She wanted him to sleep like a baby. She felt the exhaustion the moment he wrapped her in his arms. They hadn't seen each other for the last three days and she imagined he'd probably been at work for that long.

Blaise stayed in the shower until the water turned from piping hot to freezing cold, so she knew it would be a while before he came back into the room. She fell back onto her fluffed pillows and pressed play on her show again while she waited. The silence coming from the bathroom made her lips curl up at the end. She knew he was tired, and she had every intention to let him sleep, but once his frame darkened the doorway of her master bathroom, she threw caution to the wind.

Rising from the bed, she met him at the foot of her bed. She stared up at him, her eyes lingering at his. She was transfixed by his beauty; he was art in its most natural form. The seductive grin he gave her let her know that he was on the same page. Without warning, he pulled her into his frame and traced from her neck to her sternum. She squirmed at the feel of his flesh against hers. Her temperature instantly rose fifty degrees. His hand continued its exploration, tracing her navel before trailing along her pantyline. Unable to stand the heat anymore, she leaned in and kissed his chest. Standing on her tippy toes, she trailed a string of kisses from one end of his collarbone to the next.

Gently, he grabbed her wrist and turned her around. Pressing her back to him, he tilted her head to the ceiling and dragged his left fingertips across her neck and collarbone. His right hand palmed her hand as he made her caress her own legs. She moaned as their hands massaged her clit through her silk night shorts. She could feel her heart pounding in her chest, the sound of it rapidly beating against her rib cage caused her senses to go haywire. She panted like a dog in heat as she felt her finger swipe against her clit, flesh to flesh she felt herself. It wasn't the first time and it sure wouldn't be the last, but it was by far the best.

Guiding her hand, he circled her two fingers around her center until she was soaking wet. A gasp echoed against her chest as he sunk his teeth into her exposed neck and plunged both her fingers and his inside her. Her legs widened. Her hips dropped and her knees buckled. She wanted him to take her higher than she'd ever been. Finally releasing her hands from his guided tour of her pussy, he spun her around and tongued her down like he'd just come home from war.

Standing on her tippy toes, she let her robe fall to the floor before grabbing ahold of his face on either side. He stuck his tongue out, teasing her even more. She licked his tongue before sucking on the tip of it like she planned to do his dick as soon as they made it to the bed. He palmed her ass cheeks, hoisting her in the air. Instinctively, her legs wrapped around his waist as she ground on his stomach and feasted on his lips and tongue. Her hands roamed through his hair as he walked them two feet to the bed.

Without breaking their kiss, he guided her body down to the bed. Slowly he trailed kisses down her body as he stood back and admired her. She squirmed with anticipation, waiting for whatever form of pleasure she was about to receive. Her hands explored her body, pulling and kissing on her breasts as she watched him step out of his boxers. She spread her legs as far as they could go as she instructed him to come closer with her index finger. The dim light pouring from the hanging television illuminated their frames in the darkness as he eased down between her inviting legs. He secured her thighs in the crooks of his elbows as he pulled her to the edge of the bed. Her ass hung off the edge, giving him full access to her dripping pussy.

As much as he wanted to dive in head first, his dick ached to be inside her folds. Without wasting another precious second, he positioned himself at her center. Her body quaked and shivered before he even had the tip all the way in.

"Damn, somebody missed Daddy," he whispered in her ear as he slowly slid all the way inside until he reached her g-spot.

"Ahhhhh, fuck," she replied, clawing at his back. She bit down on his chest as he delivered slow deliberate strokes in a steady succession.

She wanted to climb the walls from the immense pleasure she was experiencing. Her hands pulled at her hair, the sheets, his arms, unable to find anything that could stop the pressure from building in her gut. She was about to explode.

"I'm about to fucking cum all on my dick," she screamed as she tried to free herself from under him.

"Your dick, I love the sound of that shit falling from your lips," he said, sticking his tongue down her throat.

Pulling out, he stood and pulled her up on her wobbly legs. Grabbing the side of her sex-pleased face, he kissed her while he spun them around. As he sat down on the bed, he pulled her on top of him. Weakly, she threw her legs on either side of him, pushing him back in the process. Mounting him like a trained equestrian, she leaned down and French kissed his left nipple as she bucked on his dick. She rode with such discipline he could have sworn she had a secret profession.

"Ssssss." He gritted his teeth as she bit his bottom lip.

He wrapped the tail of her durag around his hand and pulled gently to expose her neck. He licked her neck from the base of her collar to the tip of her chin before biting her back. Low, guttural moans drowned out the voices of the television as she felt droplets of blood trickle down her chin. He licked the blood up too before devouring her lips again.

"I missed the fuck out you," he said as he gripped her waist and took control.

With deep, strong thrust, he drove up into her as she came down on his dick. Her pussy was tight, gripping his dick for dear life. He knew she was about to cum all over his shit and he was going to fill her with his seeds soon after. It was the gentleman in him that always cared more about her nut than his. He knew he would get his, but tonight was all about breaking her off. She'd expressed how much she'd missed having him around, and as he busted deep in her guts, he confessed just how much she meant to him.

"On God, I love the fuck out of you," he blurted out as her pussy milked the last of his nut from his dick.

There was no way he was ever letting her get away from him. She was too perfect in his eyes. She stayed out the way, never running down on him about his schedule. She was gorgeous, self-sufficient and could fuck him four ways to Sunday whenever, wherever.

Phoenix rolled off of him onto her back seconds after her pussy stopped pulsating. She turned her head to the side, studying his side profile. She watched him in awe as he stared up at the ceiling. Her thoughts from earlier flooded back to her as she recited his admission over in her mind. *Do I tell him I love him? I mean, does it really count if he says it while he's busting a nut? Nah, sis, you can't go out like that.* Phoenix had a full out debate with herself as her eyes roamed the room. She tried focusing on anything but the man laying next to her. Undoubtedly, her gaze fell back on him. With the little bit of energy, she caressed his cheek with the back of her hand, his beard faintly scratching her knuckles.

With a faint smile, he turned to her, placing his hand over hers.

He removed her hand from his face and placed it at his lips. Gently, he pressed his lips against her skin, causing her to release a nearly inaudible sigh.

"Thanks for tonight," she said, using her free hand to cup the side of his face.

"You ain't ever gotta thank me for sliding through," he said, standing up.

Phoenix stared at his ass until it disappeared into the bathroom. Moments later, he returned with a steaming hot hand towel and stood over her. Slightly pushing her knees open with his own, he gently wiped the remnants of their lovemaking from her pussy and thighs. After wiping his dick off, he tossed the towel in her hamper. Once they were both cum free, he joined her in the bed and pulled the blanket over them. Like second nature, her head fell to his chest and her eyes closed. She had to admit to her mind and her heart that she was better when he was there. Sleep came easier, and she was overall happier. He brought out the best parts of her without even having to pry.

The bright rays of the sun warmed her exposed flesh as she stretched in her bed. She groaned at the blaring of her cell as it rang beside her. As she snatched it up, a frown creased her brow as she stared at the empty spot next to her. Her eyes darted back and forth as she searched for any sign that Blaise hadn't left her without saying goodbye. Realizing he was indeed gone, she finally answered her phone that seemed to never stop ringing.

"Hi, Rue. What's so important you have to blow me up like this?"

"Whoa, somebody woke up as a Cranky Cathy this morning."

"Sorry, I just had a long night. What's up?" She smiled as she thought about the impromptu fuck session she had with Blaise.

"I just called to tell you that there's a screening of Jason's Lyric tonight at Maple Hill Park in The Junction and to see if you wanted to go."

"Do you even have to ask? What time? Do you want me to pick you up?"

"I'll drive. Pick up some wine and some of that cannabis strawberry jam you wanted me to try. Meet me at my house at 9."

"Oh, you tryna have a good ole time tonight, huh? Where are the girls gonna be?"

"They are going with Trav to visit Aunt Phae for the weekend."

"Oh, how is she doing these days?"

"She's good. She asks about you all the time. You should call her. I was supposed to go with them, but I feel like I haven't seen you in a month of Sundays."

"That's because you haven't. I'm sorry I keep canceling our teatime. I've just been swamped."

"It's cool. I've been swamped with this renovation of the guest house. I'm so excited about opening the massage parlor. I know you hate me asking all the time, but how have you been, you know, health wise?"

"My body has been giving me a run for my money these last few days. I feel like I'm in the ring and losing most days."

Phoenix wasn't entirely lying. While she had been feeling bad, her biggest distraction had been Blaise. He consumed her, and she didn't want to make room for anyone but him. She felt bad for lying to her sister, but she knew nothing good would come of telling her about Blaise. People thought Phoenix was the overthinker, but it was really Rue. She'd spend hours coming up with reasons why Phoenix getting in any sort of intimate relationship was bad. She had already worked overtime to stay out of her own head about what she was doing with Blaise. All she wanted to do was enjoy her time with him without anyone weighing in with their 30-page dissertation on their relationship.

"Aww. Sis, I told you you're not in Atlanta anymore. You don't have to do this alone anymore. Why haven't you called me? Every time I check in you tell me you're fine. Have you made an appointment with Patty?"

"I hate when you call him that. But I go see *Dr. Crane* in three weeks. He told me to call if things get worse before then."

"Have they gotten worse since you last talked to him?"

"A little but I'm on a deadline. I have phone interviews lined up and I'm doing an on-camera taping next week. I can hold out until next month."

"I'm coming to stay this weekend. And we can catch the next movie night in the park."

"See this is why I didn't tell you. I don't want you making a fuss over me. I'm a big girl now. I can handle things on my own. All I need is a few hours of rest, some pain meds and I'll be good as new."

Phoenix knew that her simplification of her circumstances wasn't even close to reality. She was getting worse with each day. It was as if her body had declared war and ambushed under the disguise of night. She felt weak and could barely keep food down. Every morning, it took her hours to get out of the bed. But she didn't want pity. She didn't want Rue to come over and sleep in her bed and play nurse like they were kids again. All she wanted was an ounce of normalcy.

"Phoenix, your name may mean rebirth, but you only get one life. You have to take care of yourself."

Rue cringed immediately after she finished speaking. Her heart hurt for her sister. Most days she felt like she was losing her sister to herself. Phoenix had begun to slip away from her and decided she was not okay with the choice her little sister made. Nothing she seemed to say or do could get Phoenix to see she wasn't alone in this, she never was.

"I am taking care of myself. I'm doing what's mentally best for me. I can't keep sitting around here waiting to die. I can't keep putting my life on pause for a few aches and pains."

"Sis, you don't have a few aches and pains. You are in stage three kidney failure and your body is literally in a state of constant war. You need to take it easy," Rue commanded, raising her voice a few more octaves.

"Listen, I have a meeting in twenty minutes. I'll see you tonight at 9."

"Phoenix, wait. I'm sorry for yelling. I just want you to take it just a little bit easier."

"I'm tired of taking it easy. I'm tired of tiptoeing around everyone's feelings. This is my life, and I am the only one who should have a say in how I choose to live it."

Phoenix hung up on her sister. She hated arguing, especially when it was with her. They'd always been tight, and she felt like every time they argued, it shook their foundation. She was overstimulated and all her nerve-endings tingled as she threw the blanket from her limbs and quickly stood from the bed. Her life flashed before her eyes as her legs completely gave out and she fell forward. Her head bounced off the end table, causing blood to trickle down the side of her face. Feeling defeated, she let her head fall to her arms as she laid on the cold, hardwood floor crying a river. She knew life never went according to the plans people made for their lives, but she felt like this life she was given was punishment for something she didn't even know she did.

An hour later, Phoenix had finally mustered up enough strength to get off the floor. She limped to the bathroom and flipped on the light before stepping inside. She opened her linen closet and grabbed the cane she kept folded up behind her cleaning supplies. Unfolding it, she adjusted the height and used it to make her way over to the mirror. As she pulled her growing hair back, she made a mental note to make an appointment with her barber. Pressing her finger against her wound she winced in pain. The gash wasn't big, but it was deep. Deciding she didn't need to make a trip to the E.R, she showered, popped a few aspirin and headed to the kitchen. She knew if ice wasn't in her immediate future, her head would be on swole for a few days. She could not make her Solace Point on-camera debut knotted up like Martin in the Hitman Hearns episode.

A smile spread across her face as she entered her kitchen and saw a cup from Noir Tea on the counter with a takeout container. She picked up the note Blaise wrote on one of the pages from his script pad. As much as she dreaded seeing anything resembling a prescription slip, she loved the ones that were signed B.H.J. Before preparing for her day, she sent him a quick text.

Phoenix: Thanks for breakfast. Sad I missed you this morning though. *sad face emoji*

Blaise: had early appointments and you needed the rest after last night. But I can make up for it with dinner tonight. Saxon's at 8?

Phoenix took a second to think about it. She had plans with her sister, but after the way their conversation ended, she really wasn't in the mood for more lectures. Jason's Lyric was among her Top 10 favorite movies, and she usually went to see it every time the vintage cinema in The Junction played it for throwback Thursdays. But if it meant not having to hear Rue harp on about why she needed to slow down and take it easy, she'd sacrifice a showing. It wasn't like she didn't like that her sister cared, but her idea of caring meant keeping Phoenix locked away in an ivory tower only able to come down for doctor's appointments and family dinners on Sundays.

She knew she was sick, but she didn't want to be treated like it every five seconds. She'd been taking it easy since she was diagnosed, and no amount of rest changed anything about her condition. She was tired of playing it safe. She wanted romance and mind-blowing, back-arching sex. She wanted late nights and early mornings. She wanted on-air tapings and big event coverage. She wanted that dash in between her birth and death dates to mean something when it was etched into her tombstone. She'd worked too hard to let lupus, her sister or anything else stop her from seeing at least a glimpse of her dreams come to fruition.

Phoenix: Saxon's at 8 it is. *kissy face emoji*

Blaise: *kissy face emoji*

Without a pause for consideration, Phoenix closed her text

thread with Blaise and navigated to the one with Rue. She knew at that moment her feeling for Blaise had somehow progressed. She was cancelling on her sister for him. Something they both pinky promised they'd never do when they were kids.

Phoenix: Hey, something came up. can't make it tonight.

Rue: Phe, I'm sorry, okay. Don't be like that.

Phoenix: Sis, it's water under the bridge, but really, something came up. Reschedule for next Thursday?

Rue: sure, and i'm holding you to it. This the fifth time you canceled on me, and we haven't had a sister date in months.

All day Phoenix lounged around the house nursing her head wound. She rearranged her bedroom a little after she finished the breakfast Blaise gave her. The nightstand that sat on her side of the bed had been repurposed and turned into a jewelry case. She moved it into her walk-in closet and used the two drawers to organize her bracelets, rings, watches and necklaces. The top now housed her growing perfume collection courtesy of her latest obsession with the blackgirlssmellgoods twitter feed she chanced upon, and several tubes of the new, expensive, prescriber-recommended sunblock she had to use.

After scrolling through Pinterest for date night outfit inspiration, she settled on a mid-thigh length black lace skater dress. The increased dosage of prednisone had her filling out all over. While she was grateful for what it did for her ass and titties, she found herself gravitating to peplum and skater-style clothing. Her stomach was evidence of all the pasta she'd been consuming over the last few months. It was her favorite thing to cook and eat because it allowed so much creativity and experimentation in the kitchen. But her figure showed her she needed to slow down because it was doing damage to her bank account. She found herself online shopping at least once a month because her waist size kept expanding an inch or two.

She walked into the dining room area of Saxon's and took in the scene. Since moving to Solace Point, she'd only been to the take-out side of the restaurant. Mr. Saxon was a sweet old man and his fine dining experience had aged right along with him, like fine wine. The low lighting made it hard to see, but even in a crowded room, she could make out her man's voice. *Her man.* The thought sounded nice. She realized it was time for her to take their thing to the next level. She was ready to be on his arm everywhere, no matter who might see.

Seductively, she ran her index finger along his shoulders as he talked with the waitress. She smiled as she heard him finishing up an order of her favorite bottle of red wine. It was one she usually had to have shipped, but Saxon's was one of the very few places on the west coast that ever had it. Rounding the tables, she planted a sweet kiss on his lips. He rose to pull out her chair and wait a few seconds until she was seated.

"You look breathtaking tonight," he said, sliding his fingers between hers.

"Thank you. You don't look too bad yourself, handsome." She grinned with low lids.

Phoenix loved to look at Blaise. He was just perfection to her. She gazed into those dark eyes that she loved to get lost in and felt the seat of her panties moisten. As sore as she was, she would find the strength to fuck him into the wee hours of the morning once they got back to her place or his. She bit down on her bottom lip, and thought about how he would have her legs behind her ears by the end of the night. His conversation was drowned out by her lust.

"Phoenix, are you even listening to me?" Blaise laughed.

"Honestly, nope. I was over here thinking about how I want you to put my knees behind my ears tonight."

"Baby, if that's what type of time you on, we can get this shit to go."

"No. We need a night out. The bed needs a few hours off."

Blaise laughed at her. He loved how goofy she was. She was secure in her faults and had no problem asking...or demanding what she wanted. Whenever she wanted the dick, she took it. And as long as she let him stretch her out and go balls deep, he would never turn her away. She was his for the taking, and the more he thought about it, the more he knew his mama was right. He'd found the one. The one she always said he'd find when he stopped fucking whatever woman threw him the pussy. He'd found his person.

Phoenix watched his eyes twinkle as he tilted his eyes to their intertwined hands. Her freshly painted white nails looked elegant against his deep, crimson-brown skin. Couples smiled at the smitten pair as they were escorted to their tables. The glow emitting from their corner of the restaurant was bright enough to illuminate New York City in a blackout.

"Everybody's staring at us," he laughed, "we are officially that corny couple we watch in them movies."

"Everybody stares at us, boys, girls, we can't help it baaaby," Phoenix sang off key.

Just as Blaise was about to call her a clown, the waitress brought over two glasses and their bottle of wine. She poured their first glass and sat the bottle on ice at their table. After sitting a menu down in front of each of them, she instructed them to let her know when they were ready to order. Once they were alone again, their gazes fell back on one another. They were captivated by each other presence's and nothing or no one else in the establishment mattered. They were all each other saw and everybody could tell.

"You know I kind of like the sound of that," Phoenix said, raising her glass.

She wafted the glass past her nose a few times, taking in the aromas floating from the glass. Her body tingled as she mentally prepared her palate for her favorite beverage. Her stash had depleted weeks ago, but she was so wrapped up in work and Blaise, she had never placed an order.

"What?"

"Us being that couple," she answered as she took a long sip.

"I like it too. It suits us."

"Us, I like the sound of that too."

"So, you ready to rock my chain?" He quizzed with a smirk and raised eyebrow.

Phoenix shook her head yes, as she motioned her finger for him to lean in. She planted a deep kiss on his lips. He parted her lips with his tongue, deepening the kiss. Sliding her chair beside him, he snaked the hand closest to her under the table. Roughly, he massaged her thigh, working his way up to her pussy. With his thumb, he massaged her clit through her panties, causing her to moan in his mouth. Their table was tucked off far enough from other patrons and the light was low, giving them the perfect setting for some foreplay.

"Henn Dogg, is that your ass?"

Blaise broke their kiss to see which one of his friends had interrupted him just as he was about to slide two fingers inside his woman. He chuckled as he turned to see his line brother, Triumph, and his wife Simone standing at their table. Phoenix crossed her legs under the table and fixed her eyes anywhere but on the two people standing in front of them. Their unsolicited presence was fucking up the nut she was about to get off.

"Sup, bro? Surprised y'all asses got away. Where's baby girl at tonight?"

"With her grandmother. Shit, we needed some time alone. Ever since her little ass been walking good she been a holy terror, not to mention she repeats everything we say in her toddler babbles. The terrible twos ain't got shit on the treacherous threes. "

"I can only imagine. Hey, Monie, looking beautiful as always."

"Hey, B. How are you liking Solace so far?"

"It's cool. Oh, my bad. Where the fuck are my manners? This is..."

"Phoenix..." Triumph finished.

Simone watched the light darken in Phoenix's eyes when her

husband said her name. She figured she had to have been one of his patients. It was unusual for him to out his patients like that, but she was sure the shock of seeing her with Blaise had a lot to do with his indiscretion. She watched as Phoenix visibly retreated within her own mind. She'd been there before, feeling heavily exposed with no form of cover in sight.

"Colleville," Simone chimed in. "You were the talk of the industry for a bit. Your career was budding, and you seemed to just disappear."

"I just needed a change. Something different, you know," Phoenix responded, thanking Simone with her eyes.

She did not want Blaise to find out she was seeing a therapist to cope with being diagnosed with a life-threatening, incurable disease. They were in such a good space and souring the mood with her woes was not in her plans. Eventually, she knew it was a conversation that needed to happen, but their romance was still fresh. Six months wasn't enough time to bear all the darkness. It needed to be spaced out over time.

"Perfect place to disappear to, by the way."

"You would say that because your ass did the same thing a few years ago," Triumph teased.

"Technically, it wasn't the same because I ran back home," Simone reminded her husband.

"Join us, we haven't ordered yet," Blaise insisted.

"No, you two look like you were enjoying yourself just fine," Simone countered.

"No, really. It's fine. I'd love to get to know the queen of Solace's media conglomerate," Phoenix said, motioning to the waiter to bring two more chairs and glasses.

As odd as Phoenix initially thought dining with her therapist and his wife would be, it turned out to be the opposite. She loved seeing Blaise interact with his friends. She got to learn about just how unrefined his ass was in college. Blaise was always a ball of fun, but to hear about the pranks and meetings with the dean he had during undergrad was comical. She found herself laughing all night. Simone was also a pleasure. She fangirled over Phoenix's work and even proposed that they work together in the future.

After dinner, the couple bid their dinner dates farewell and retreated back to Blaise's house for the evening. Phoenix leaned against Blaise's shoulder as he guided her up the stairs. She fell into the bed the second they made it to his room. Blaise had a consultation to prepare for, so he undressed her and tucked her into his bed, making sure to capture the essence of her drunken beauty for his memory. After snapping a picture of the moonlight shining on her closed lids, he stood in the doorway, watching her chest rise and fall. She was beauty, elegance, intelligence, goofiness, and culture all wrapped in a box and gifted to him by the universe. He didn't know what he did to deserve her, but he promised himself he would cherish it just like his mother promised him. Deciding his work could wait until the morning, he joined her. Pulling her close, he welcomed sleep as it came.

The blaring of his phone caused him to stir in his sleep. He looked down and smiled at the sight of Phoenix asleep on his chest. The warmth of her body made him feel alive inside. *God, let me wake up to this sight for the rest of my life.* He silently prayed as he grabbed his phone. No one called him early on a Sunday morning except his mother. As much as he wanted to join Phoenix back in dreamland, he knew she wouldn't stop calling until he answered. He never worked on Sundays, so she knew he wasn't dealing with any type of medical emergency.

"Good morning, Gorgeous," he sang into the camera as he answered her FaceTime call from the bed.

"Good morning, my favorite son."

"Ma, I'm your only son."

"Biologically, yes. But since I adopted all ya lil' friends, my child count has grown exponentially. How are you doing this beautiful morning?"

"I feel good, Ma. I really feel good."

Blaise's gaze fell on Phoenix as she gripped his waist tighter. She was in a deep sleep, and he knew she wasn't waking for at least another hour or two. Subconsciously, he smiled as he softly stroked her hair. He loved how she'd let it grow out. The purple, pink, and blue ombrë color looked even better now that it hung just at her shoulders. It framed her eyes perfectly. He unraveled one of her tight curls and twirled the strand of hair around his fingers while he listened to his mother talk.

"Boy, are you even listening to me?"

"Yes, Ma," Blaise laughed. "I'm listening. I think Christmas would be perfect for you to visit. I know there will be some amazing views for you to photograph and paint."

"Oh, you just want me out your hair, so you can keep hoeing around."

"Ma, how many times am I gonna have to tell you I'm not hoeing around? I will just be working."

"Save that boyish charm for them floozies you bring home."

"I'm gonna show you better than I can tell you."

"And whatever happened to the woman you met that you went on and on about courting. You know the one you said was the *one*?"

Phoenix's ears must have been burning because just as his mother asked the question, she was kissing his chest. He looked down at her as she smiled up at him. He mouthed good morning before turning his attention back to his mother.

"She's right here, Ma," Blaise panned the camera over so his mother could see Phoenix laying beside him.

Phoenix smacked his arm as she smiled at the camera. She laughed as she sat up in the bed with him. Luckily, their night didn't end in back-arching, sheet-clenching sex, so she didn't have that after sex glow.

"Good Morning, Mrs. Jones," she said as she laid her head on his shoulder.

"Why, hello, gorgeous. It's nice to finally meet you. My blabbering son talks about you all the time."

"Blabbering? Now, I wonder who I get that from."

"Shut up, B. Nice to meet you too. And thank you for teaching this one how to treat a lady." Phoenix caressed his cheek as she briefly tore her eyes from the screen to look up at him.

"It wasn't easy. It took him a few tries to master the lesson. But I'm glad he has. Maybe now he can make me a grandmother before I'm too old to spoil them."

"Ma, you got six grandkids already."

"Would you look at that conundrum. Six grands and nay one of them is yours."

Phoenix and Blaise laughed on the phone with his mother for close to an hour. She talked their heads off with reminiscent stories about her and her late husband's rollercoaster of a union. There was wisdom wrapped snugly in easily digestible jokes and satirical anecdotes. Phoenix liked his mother. She couldn't wait to meet her in person. As she listened to the two of them trade innocent insults and lighthearted banter, she knew he was the man for her. She needed to get her shit together so she could truly commit to him.

CHAPTER NINE

"Why you over here looking like you lost your damn puppy," Rue asked as she slid into their favorite booth.

The sisters shared a brief hug across the table before Rue got comfortable in her seat. This was their first sister date in months and they both were long overdue. Phoenix's head had been spinning trying to keep up with the little white lies she found herself telling Rue on demand. Her treasure trove of conceivable dishonesties had been dwindling lately, and she felt like there was no turning back. Until recent weeks, she and Blaise had been damn near inseparable aside from their work responsibilities. He'd switched shifts with another doctor and had been working back-to-back 12-hour shifts. When he had a day off, he slept it away, remembering to check-in with her before he slept and when he rose.

"Sis, I need to come clean," Phoenix said, cutting a slither of her steak and placing it to her lips.

"Lord, don't tell me you're mixing your meds and alcohol again. Or worse, skipping meds to binge drink and have watch parties with Tracy and 'em."

Phoenix laughed at her sister. She recalled living a very

dangerous and bizarre life when she was first diagnosed. Nothing mattered anymore. For her entire life, she lived on a straight and narrow path, never stepping a foot outside the route to her career goals. But after lupus came in and wreaked havoc on her plans, she met it with quite a spontaneous spirit. Before her best friends traveled to their corners of the world, they spent their days counting down the seconds until they were turning out some club. It was a time she felt defined her and allowed her to value all she had now. Though Rue never admitted it, she knew the real reason she wanted her near was to ensure she never veered that far off again. It was a considerably dark time in her life, she felt she had nothing to lose and wanted to live every moment as her last. She embodied the essence of Maurine and Mimi, from her favorite play. It ultimately landed her in a hospital for nearly a month.

"Nothing like that, but I have been lying to you, and I want to be honest with you. We've never had secrets between us until now and I don't want this to start being the bane of our existence."

"Okay, now you're scaring me. So, just spit it out," Rue said, taking a large, hard gulp of her drink. She hissed as the cognac warmed her chest.

Before she spoke again, she searched her sister's eyes. There was a glow there she hadn't realized before she sat. As Phoenix gathered her thoughts, she took the time to really look her over. She'd filled out in all the right places and seemed much more optimistic about life than she had in a long time. For the first time she realized how her verbiage had changed, and she'd begun considering the future instead of planning her demise. She giggled into her glass as she took another sip of her drink. She couldn't figure out how she didn't see it before that moment. Phoenix was dating again. The evidence was laced in her speech, her figure, her clear skin, and her outgrown hair. For her entire diagnosis, she kept it short and dyed some variation of a purple ombre. Now, she sports a low bun with laid edges or shoulder length tight curls.

"You're dating again. Ooohhh, tell me. Is it like the playing field type of dating like on some apps or something or like casual dating, meet at a bar type of thing?"

Phoenix was stunned. She replayed her actions over the last few months and dating is not what she would have guessed had the roles been reversed. Sometimes she hated how much Rue paid attention to her, she couldn't even get this past her. Laughing, she filled her mouth with steak and mashed potatoes. It was uncanny how much she just seemed to know everything.

"What you got a private investigator following me or something, how do you know that?"

"Not at all. I just took a second to consider what you could possibly be telling me. And there was no angst when you said you'd been keeping something. I remember when you used to do shit back in your teen years. Spiteful shit. You didn't even have that look of disappointment. So, the only thing I could think of was you had to be dating."

"So, you aren't mad that you're the last to know."

"Not at all. Wait, hold on, it depends on who all knows." Rue laughed, finally twirling her fork around the pasta her sister ordered prior to her late arrival.

"Just Forge, Tracy and Kellz."

"I expected as much. They are your girls."

"And Trav and the girls know."

"Wait, my husband and daughters knew before me," Rue scoffed. She faked irritation as she rolled her eyes to the heavens and waved the waiter over for another drink.

"They kind of caught us in the elevator at the hospital when I watched them on y'all date night. I swore them to secrecy. I wanted to be the one to tell you."

"Hold on, that was like three months ago now. So how long have y'all been dating."

"Seven months, yesterday."

"Seven months! Phe that's a whole damn year."

"No, it's not. It's seven months," Phoenix laughed.

Rue had always been quite the exaggerator. She laughed as she remembered how Blaise said his mother was the same way. Rue was indeed a mother hen and Phoenix couldn't do anything but love her for it. As the only parent-like figure in her life, she loved and respected Rue for always caring for her, no matter what that care entailed. Whether it was bailing her out of jail, holding her hair back while she puked her guts up after a night of underaged debauchery or sponge-bathing her when she was too weak to take care of her personal hygiene, Rue never left her to fend for herself, even in her adult years.

Phoenix always appreciated all Rue sacrificed for her growing up. She had to step up long before she was prepared to and raised her to be the strong, independent woman she'd become. They were always raised to have each other's back and Rue did not take that job lightly. She knew that her sister would stick it out with her through anything. Even when she insisted on handling some battles alone, Rue still showed up ready for war. So, thinking that Rue wouldn't have eventually figured out she was getting her back blown out on a regular basis was naive on her part. She was especially shocked to get such a chill response.

"Look, Rue, I know I should have told you this months ago, but I wanted to see how things were going to turn out. Plus, you are not the chillest berry in the peck."

"Phoenix, I'm sorry if I made you feel like you couldn't tell me this. I wouldn't have been anything other than happy for you. Your happiness really is high up on my priority list. It's all I ever wanted for you, because that's all mommy and daddy ever wanted for us."

"You're going to make me cry and I spent too long on YouTube today to perfect this natural beat. Like I'm ashamed it took me two hours and eight tries to get this brow right."

"Seriously. I know I'm not always the easiest to talk to about things because I'm always worrying and making a fuss, and I'm sorry if that overwhelms you to the point you shut me out."

Phoenix felt like Rue had just sucker-punched her in the heart.

She never wanted Rue to feel like she had an overwhelming personality because she didn't. She could be a bit overbearing at times and uber-overprotective, but Phoenix was never overwhelmed by her fretting over every little thing. It made her feel like she didn't trust her to make the right decisions, but she was never overwhelmed.

"You're not overwhelming. A little overprotective, but not overwhelming. I really just wanted to enjoy something, someone who would just let me exist without thinking I was going to break."

"So, he doesn't know?"

"Nope, and that, my sister, is why I'm over here looking like I lost my puppy as you so eloquently put it."

For the next hour, the sisters enjoyed a few cocktails and talked about Phoenix's current dilemma. She knew she couldn't go on forever without Blaise finding out she was sick. It had been far too long already, and she knew the longer she waited the worst things might get for them. Every time she thought she was ready to give him the sordid details of her diagnosis and lupus journey, her ex's words echoed in her brain. *I love you, but I can't stand to watch the love of my life wilt away. I'll always love you. There's no woman who could ever hold a candle to your eternal flame. I'm just not emotionally or mentally strong enough to watch lupus snuff out that light one blow at a time.* She wondered if lupus was loves kryptonite, snuffing out any chance she had at a forever with a man she loved. She knew she loved Blaise and she wanted to tell him, but that admission would have to come with a truth she just didn't think she was ready to divulge.

"I mean, I think you should tell him. Not telling him and wondering what he'll do or say when he finds out is doing nothing for the situation."

"Yea, I know, but what if it changes everything?"

"Then it changes everything. There is no need in prolonging the inevitable. If he's a rider, he gon' ride. If he's a folder, he gon' fold. A perfect time for him to do so really doesn't matter."

"So, I should tell him?"

"I mean, that's a choice only you can make. But I will give you two things to consider. First, what if you died tomorrow and he never knew, how do you think that will make him feel? And what's really the point in waiting? You're spending all this time with him, canceling on me," Rue threw in. "And for what if you're never going to take that leap? I can tell you really like him, maybe even love him because you're even considering telling him."

"I think I do love him. Fuck that, who am I kidding, I do love him. As crazy as it seems, I can see a future with him. Growing old, watching our kids swim in the lake out back of the house. Having y'all over for big ass family dinners and shit. The whole nine."

"So, then what's got you pumping the brakes?"

"Darrell."

"Nah, sis. I am not even finna let you do that to yourself. Real men don't fold, that nigga folded like a beach umbrella. Don't hold every man up to his measuring stick because that nigga didn't measure the fuck up at all."

"Damn, Sis. Tell him how you really feel."

Phoenix chuckled as she listened to Rue talk about her ex. They'd been together since high school and had planned an entire future together, but the second she got sick he ran for the hills. He did not pass go or collect his $200. He just packed his shit and put their condo on the market. Rue never masked her disdain for him and how he absconded with her love like a thief in the night. She hated him for how bad he caused her sister to spiral. There was never a moment she didn't blame him for Phoenix's initial choice not to fight. She felt like fighting would be for nothing because the life she'd been building was gone.

"You know I have zero cut cards when it comes to that man. I hope he choked on a chicken bone with his dog ass."

Phoenix laughed with her sister as she continued to think about what Rue had told her. She knew she could count on her for some rational advice that didn't just falter on her loving him. Because like her, Rue knew that love wasn't always enough. They had learned that the hard way and it cost them their parents. With her condition not getting any better any time in the near future she needed to start thinking about what she would do, and she honestly hadn't considered it.

She knew she should have always been considering what she'd do and how he'd feel if she were just gone. Especially since she'd been feeling more weak than usual the last few days. Phoenix hadn't told anyone or even admitted it to herself yet, but she had been feeling the effects of a lupus flare for the last few days. It started out mildly and she chalked it up to coming down with the bug that had been going around, but it had begun to get increasingly worse. She'd promised herself if she couldn't shake it on her own with rest and some time away from Blaise, then she would call Dr. Crane.

"Sister, it's been great catching up. I hope to meet this man who got you all out of sorts soon."

"How about next weekend? I'll plan dinner after we finish getting all this furniture and stuff set up."

"Next weekend is no good. We're going to see Auntie Phae. You should come, she keeps asking about you."

Phoenix rolled her eyes at the mere mention of her Aunt Phaedra. She hadn't spoken to her since her parents' funeral when she was fourteen and she didn't intend to ever speak to her again. Before their falling out, she worshiped the ground her aunt walked on. She wanted to be just like her, always chasing her dreams and defying anything that stood between her and the sky she soared toward. But she grew to resent that unbridled passion the last time her parents went to her rescue. They met fate and she lived to dance another day. It wasn't fair that she'd been the one getting arrested for a DUI and the very souls who pulled themselves out of their warm beds to get her were the ones who didn't make it home. Phaedra could go to hell for all Phoenix cared. She hadn't spoken to her since she told her such at the repast.

"I don't know why she's asking about me. What, she finally needs a liver transplant?'

"Don't be like that, Phe, she loves you. Always has, and always will. You know you were her little protege."

"Yea, well, I'm glad that shit got deaded along with mommy and daddy."

"Okay, Phe, stop. That's craziness. Why would you say that?"

Phoenix motioned for the waiter to bring over some boxes and the check. Rue had soured her mood with the mention of her aunt. She didn't know how many ways she needed to say it or how many languages she needed to say it in; she didn't now nor ever want to deal with her aunt. It was why she begged Rue to transfer colleges, so she wouldn't have to move in with the lady. She was their next of kin, and since Phoenix was still underage, she would be the legal guardian of her. She couldn't stand to look at the woman, let alone take orders from her.

Rue left well enough alone. Although she desperately wanted her mother's only sister and her only sister to mend their broken relationship, she knew Phoenix was already contemplating a lot. Though she'd never stop praying they'd get back to a place of love, she allowed Phoenix to feel how she felt about their parents' death. She couldn't invalidate them, because at times, she shared the same sentiments.

Phaedra was a wild child and disregarded every law she possibly could. Her parents were always running to bail her out because their grandparents had since written her off. Then they eventually passed mere months apart and her parents died soon after. They'd seemingly lost their immediate family in a matter of eighteen months. It was bizarre to her, and she'd somehow worked through her emotions. But she knew Phoenix held a great deal of hurt in her heart.

Phoenix thanked the universe for sending a distraction. She was not in the mood to hear Rue harping on about how she needed to forgive their aunt for the part she inadvertently played in their parents' demise. A smile crept in as she opened Blaise's message.

Blaise: I know you're out with your sister tonight but wanted to say good night before I take it in.

Phoenix: good night. I'll video call you tomorrow.

Blaise: cool. Don't get too drunk, you know how you get. Mary J Blige

Phoenix: Oh hush, you know I deserved a Grammy for that performance. We're about to call it a night. So, I'll be tucked in bed in no time.

As she placed her phone back on the table, she gave her attention back to her sister. Phoenix knew Rue was in her feelings about what she said, but she wasn't sorry. Rue knew better than to bring up her aunt. That was a no-fly zone, and she wasn't responsible for how she responded to being ambushed.

"Rue."

"Listen, Phoenix. You don't get to just say whatever you want to me and think that a sorry will fix it."

"I wasn't about to apologize. I meant what I said. Am I sorry it hurt your feelings when it wasn't intended for you, but her? Yes. But I am in no way apologetic for what I said. I want nothing to do with that lady."

"It's been damn near 20 years. You going to hold on to that forever?"

"Until the day I take my last breath and join mommy and daddy."

Phoenix signed the receipt the waiter brought over and stood to her feet. She hated how every conversation she'd had with her sister in recent months resulted in her having a sour mood after. They'd been having some tough conversations lately and she knew if they couldn't seem to get it right, she knew there was no hope for her and Blaise. The time they'd been spending away was good for them. She'd become so wrapped up in him and so in love she allowed her judgment to be clouded. Distance was what was best, and she planned to keep it that way until she could figure out how to deal with her feelings and all the anxiety she felt whenever she thought about telling him what was wrong with her.

CHAPTER TEN

PHOENIX'S ARMS LAY EXTENDED AT HER SIDE AS SHE LOOKED UP AT THE bubbling paint on her off-white ceiling. For weeks, this had been her fate. Staring at the very surface she'd been meaning to paint since the day she moved into the single-family dwelling.

Joint stiffness and chronic pain kept her from most of the work she wanted to complete around the house. For the last month, Lupus spared no second wreaking havoc on her otherwise stable life. Forge had texted her to let her know all the furniture they'd purchased would be arriving early in the afternoon. She hadn't had a free moment to consider how to make her new house feel like a home. Though not her intentions, it seemed Solace Point would be her home for quite some time, and she planned to use every ounce of her strength to make it a home she would forever remember once she ventured on.

Her eyes narrowed slowly, shutting out the tiny hint of morning sun that peeked over the rod of her room-darkening curtains. Excruciating pain soared through her limbs for most of the night. It kept her up into the wee hours of the morning, and there was no way she was letting the burning rays of sunshine and blue skies steal the few hours she was blessed with slumber once she broke down and swallowed pain relievers.

Like a toppling tree, her head fell to the left as she peeked at the clock on her nightstand. This wasn't a day she could allow lupus first dibs on her body. She had to will herself from the bed. She'd made a promise and promises were one thing she was always hellbent about keeping. Her word was precious to her and if she gave it, she made sure to make good on it. This time would be no different.

Okay Phe, you just have to swing your legs over the side of the bed. The rest will come naturally. Phoenix silently coached herself. With her eyes tightly shut, she sucked in as much air as she could and slid her left arm over to the guard rail, she'd asked her brother-in-law to install and wrapped her fingers around the cold metal. Little bumps instantly popped up all over her exposed shoulder and forearm as the fine hairs on her arm became visible. Using all the might she could muster she pulled her upper body closer to the rail, until her cheek pressed against satin-lined rubber inserts. Reversing her grip, she pushed down on the guard rail, putting as much of her weight as possible there to get herself into an upright position. Finally, opening her eyes, she allowed the gust of air she inhaled to finally escape her lungs in a ball of hot gas.

Okay, me. Getting to the upright position in less than 10 minutes. Progress. Internally, Phoenix praised herself for the feat. Though obsolete to most, it was the small victories that kept her encouraged when she'd otherwise be withering in despair and mourning the life she once knew. But, today, she sat up in bed less than ten minutes after waking and that was progress. Her body aches and debilitating stiffness usually kept her prostrated as if her king-sized bed were a luxury coffin. Stuck in place for two to three hours was how she started every day. Rue and Forge both told her to cherish that time and spend it meditating, but all she did was lie there, with tears streaming down to her ears as she watched the sun move across the sky. Yet another day she couldn't enjoy her favorite time of day.

Before she first started experiencing symptoms of lupus,

morning used to be her Zen time. She spent most of it sitting on the balcony of her 12th floor condo before she moved. The others she spent leaning against the bay window of her bedroom when rain interrupted her regularly scheduled program. Her sun greetings, journaling, and meditation had quickly been replaced with silent willpower chats that encouraged her to use all her strength to live another day.

With her right hand still gripping the guard rail and her legs dangling over the edge of her raised bed. The elevated height of the bed gave her the added space between her floor and feet to swing them into submission to her will and not that of her sickness. Humming the melody to Whitney Houston's rendition of "Jesus Loves Me" she swung her feet backward and forward, being sure they reached waist-length elevation. This wasn't recommended by any of the physical therapists she'd seen for strengthening exercises, but it's what worked best. Oblivious to the science behind it, she kept this up ever since the first time it worked for her.

After 15 minutes of humming and swinging, she scooted to the edge of the bed and anchored herself by clasping the guard rail. Tingles went up her spine as her toes connected with the cool surface of the hardwood floors. Slippers would have been ideal, and Rue had warned her over a million times to keep something on her feet, but feeling the tingling sensations shoot up her spine when she made it out of bed reminded her that she was still among the living. She was grateful for the small sensory reminder that let her know lupus hadn't won and she was still a viable contender in the battle it declared almost six years ago.

She lifted her feet and repositioned them on the floor to quiet her fear of toppling over the second she stood. Once she was sure her feet were firmly planted, she let her wrists rest on the edge of the mattress while her palms sunk into the top. With her fingers digging into the side of the bed, she put her weight on her arms and pushed off, finally standing to her feet. With her head hung low, she watched her feet as she walked, placing one foot in front of the other to the spot where she hung her plush white robe. It was one of several her sister had made for her after her first extended hospital stay. She complained so much about the gowns she had to wear and the rough blankets that protected her frail bones from the frigid hospital temperatures that Rue purchased her some custom-made gowns and robes for those occurrences that seemed to occur much more frequently than rarely.

"Morning, Baby Love!" Rue yelled as she entered Phoenix's room.

Rue was usually everything but punctual, but ever since Phoenix arrived in Solace Point, she'd become a stickler for being on time or early for everything. Phoenix was much like her, only she caught onto the value of time long before her big sister. It was the single, most important concept she learned to value more after losing their parents. Every second wasted was a second she could never get back. Time was precious to her, now more than ever. Rue's lesson came in the form of her baby sister's diagnosis. Once she had the lesson down, she packed up Phoenix and moved her all the way out west where she had been making a family with her husband. A three-hour time difference was a hindrance for her when she wanted to check in on Phoenix and surprise visits were out of the question when the drive was cross-country.

"You're early," Phoenix replied, groaning, and smashing her feet into her fuzzy slippers.

“I know. Forge, Trav and the girls will be here in about an hour. I just wanted to come over and help you with your morning routine before they all got here.”

"Rue. For the umpteenth time. I don't need a sponge bath. Really, I can dress myself."

Phoenix hated the way her sister pined over her. Though doing simple tasks like turning on the shower or buttoning her jeans had become quite challenging for her, she chose to cling to her independence. Trav and Rue were already paying a share of the mortgage and bills on her house since she wasn’t doing as much media coverage. She needed to hold onto whatever inkling of self-preservation she possibly could, and that meant spending the 15-45 minutes getting herself out of bed, struggling to handle her morning hygiene, and settling for a quick steak dinner from Miss. Rose's Jamboree because she didn't always have the strength to do any of it. Being able to care for herself was something she always prided herself on, and it had been since she got her first job at 14. Her parents gave her everything but having her own means to provide her heart's desires was always up on her priority list. Now, lupus was threatening that priority, and Rue wasn't making it any easier.

"I know that you don't need me to bathe you, Ugly. But I could help you wash your hair, iron your clothes, steep you some tea or cook you something to eat. It's okay to let people help you, Phe," Rue said as she leaned against the doorframe and watched her sister fumble with the dresser drawer.

For five minutes she stood, holding back tears as Phoenix struggled to get the top drawer open. The solid wood dresser drawer inched out slowly. With each pull, it barely budged, but her determination was unmatched. Finally, Phoenix stood back a few feet and turned to Rue with tears staining her cheeks. Swiping away at her own tears, Rue pulled her into her arms and held her as she cried. She couldn't begin to fathom how her sister was feeling. Most days, she didn't know what to do or say to her because this was new for them. No one close to them had ever been sick with anything more serious than a common cold. They were in foreign waters trying to stay afloat together. But they were both drowning in sorrow and uncertainty.

"Rue, can you help me?" Phoenix cried as she placed her head on her sister's shoulder.

"Always."

Rue knew her sister's request cloaked a double meaning. Yes, she meant to help her open the drawer where her clothes were. But the tears spilled the remnants of a broader request. Phoenix was crying out. She hadn't been functioning lately. The light that was in her eyes a few months ago, had since faded. She was giving up. Slowly, she was bowing out of the fight. *Phoenix, you have a condition called systemic lupus erythematosus.* She'd realized her sister had been fighting to keep it together even though she wore her pain well. Squeezing her shoulders, Rue let her sister know she was there for her in any capacity that she needed.

"Always," Rue whispered in her ear.

After helping Phoenix find something suitable to wear for the day's tasks, Rue left her alone to handle her hygiene needs. After the complicated birth and emergency c-section of her second daughter, she knew exactly how it felt to cling to your independence even though there was no way to do everything yourself. It filled her with sadness knowing her sister felt that way every single day and there was no remedy for it. Though she listened to her husband and supported Phoenix when she wanted to buy her own home, she wished she hadn't.

As she walked through her sister's house, she tried to get a feel for the vision Phoenix and Forge had mapped out for the furniture placement. She looked at all the boxes still stacked all over the place. She was angry with herself for letting it get this bad without calling some kind of intervention.

Releasing a breath of air, she flipped the light switch in the kitchen and began gathering the ingredients to make a light brunch spread. With all the work they had to do, she was sure they would be working through the afternoon. Painting, hanging wall art, and moving furnishings into place would consume the better part of their day.

She smiled as her baby sister entered the kitchen and took a seat at the island. She slid her a glass of water and a napkin with her medicine on it. Sadness washed over her as Phoenix frowned at the ten pills on the counter. Phoenix was tired, not just physically, but emotionally too. Rue needed her sister's breakthrough to come because she could tell she didn't have any more fight in her.

"Thanks, Sis. I appreciate you."

"You never have to thank me for doing my job. You are my baby sister. As long as there's breath in my body, I'm gonna always be there for you."

Phoenix smiled as Rue kissed her temple and left her alone. Once she was alone, a tear fell from her eye. She wanted to fight. She wanted to live a little longer. As she thought about her family and friends, she realized she wasn't ready to leave them.

A smile danced in the corner of her mouth as she closed her eyes and saw Blaise dancing in her kitchen as he made his mother's secret chili. She sighed as the tears came fast and frequent. She hated the way they ended. While she knew it was her desertion that broke their bond, she couldn't help but think about the what-ifs. What if she just told him everything? What if he wasn't like her ex? What if he was all the man that she'd ever need? What if she just stopped thinking and just let her heart influence her decisions?

While she ate, she continued to ponder how different her world might look if she got out of her way and really let Blaise love her the way she knew he was capable of. She knew she deserved love, but for some reason, she felt like it would be wasted. She'd be gone soon, and all the love she collected would go right with her. After going back and forth with herself throughout her meal, she cleaned up behind herself and went to find her sister.

Wandering through the lower level of her house, she couldn't find her anywhere. As she neared the back door, she heard laughter in the distance. As she pushed the screen open, she leaned against the doorframe looking at the beautiful scene before her. Rue, Trav, Forge and the girls were bringing in the accent pieces Forge had brought from the shop. She was grateful for them and all they did to support her even when she declined their assistance. Their love was unwavering, and she thanked God for blessing her with that kind of love because she wouldn't have even considered trying to fight if she hadn't experienced it.

"Okay, so we are getting paid in food when this is over right," Trav asked, hugging Phoenix.

"Oh, yes. Please say you'll whip up a pot of mama's pasta," Rue chimed in as she carried an end table inside.

"I would love to feed y'all, but I don't even have everything I need."

"Yes, you do. I stopped at that lil' mom and pop shop on my way over. Everything is in the pantry for you. And the seafood is in the fridge."

For the remainder of the afternoon, the family of six enjoyed each other's company as they helped Phoenix finally make her home livable. At sunset, they all joined her in the kitchen laughing and trading stories as she prepared dinner. Briefly, she took in the scene before her and smiled. It made her remember the times she and Rue sat around the kitchen with her parents and Aunt Phae while their mother prepared the same meal.

"Hey Kaleigh and Bronx, want to learn how to make homemade garlic bread?"

"Yes," they exclaimed in unison.

She was around their age when her mother first taught her how to make garlic-flavored roti. She divided the ingredients they would need up evenly and gave them both mixing bowls. Forge snapped candids of her impromptu cooking lesson with her nieces. She knew they'd want these to cherish her dear friend's memory once she was gone.

Phoenix hadn't told anyone except Forge about her worsening symptoms. Nor did she let them know she had an appointment coming up with Dr. Crane, where she would be getting another kidney biopsy because he suspected she'd moved into the near final stage of kidney failure. It was something that she felt only Forge could handle. All she wanted from her family was for them to do what they'd always done, love her for the goofy, opinionated, stubborn, intelligent and talented woman that she was. She wanted them to remember the joy she brought them, not the stinging pain of her loss.

Once the bread was hot and ready, the family sat down for what was probably one of their last meals like this. Phoenix tried her best to hold it together but as she listened to the laughs of her family serenade her, it felt like a final goodbye. A tear left her eye and fell into her glass of wine. She was overcome with emotion as her eyes darted to each person gathered around her table. She was grateful for their presence in her life. They brought her so much joy, and for the first time, she was unsure about death. She wondered if it would be lonely; if it would be cold or dark? She wondered if it were like her childhood pastor described it, with her parents meeting her and ushering her into her mansion over in glory.

Once everyone had finished their second and third helpings of pasta, they worked as a unit to clean up and put the kitchen back together the way it was before Phoenix' impromptu cooking lesson with her nieces. There was no shortage of laughter as they all told jokes and recounted stories from the week. The joyous feeling bubbling in her stomach was a feeling she never wanted to leave. She thought about proposing these joyous monthly gatherings but was unsure of just how many months she really had left. Instead, she decided to simply prolong the moment they were given.

"Hey, we should watch a movie now that the entertainment room is all set up," Rue suggested.

Phoenix gave in to the unanimous requests for movie night under the conditions that she picked the movie, and everyone agreed to a sleepover. Now that her house was completely furnished, decorated and inviting to guests, she wanted to officially make it a home. She wanted to start making memories, fond ones that her family could look back on when they missed her most. She'd realized they hadn't been making many of them lately and she was a bit angry with herself because of it.

As she thumbed through her extensive VHS and DVD collections, she smiled to herself. Family meant the world to her. Though their family was mostly on the east coast, she was grateful for the ones that kept in touch. She gave Rue a lot of slack, but she was grateful that she stuck around regardless. Pulling her movie selection off the shelf, she checked to make sure it was already rewinded. For the most part, she made sure to rewind the movies before putting them back in their boxes. But the last time she and Blaise watched that particular movie, they wound up fucking halfway through and falling asleep.

"Okay, I have to rewind the movie, so let's go make sundaes and s'mores while we wait," Phoenix announced.

The family headed out back. They all sat around the fire pit while Trav got the fire going. Kaleigh and Dallas started singing the song from Mary Kate and Ashley's *How The West Was Fun*. One thing Phoenix loved about Rue as a mom was that while she allowed her girls to experience and embrace the culture of their era, she made sure they also experienced some of the music, movies and books that they experienced and embraced growing up. She was raising two amazing children. At 11 and 13, they were certainly culture-fed.

After they'd sung around the fire and prepared canna cream sundaes, they all retreated back to the living room for the movie picture of the evening. Forge, Trav, and Rue all started slapping fives as the movie came on. *Crooklyn* was a staple when they were younger. Between that, *The Five Heartbeats* and *Meteor Man*, they didn't know which one they had to replace more from overwatching.

"TiTi, I'm sure this is available on one of those streaming services, why are we watching a VHS?" Dallas asked.

"'Cause I ain't paying $9.99 to rent a digital download for two days when I only paid $5.99 for the VHS and can watch it as much as I want."

"You tell 'em, Sis. These youngin's swear by that streaming shit. That's why every time we have a power outage, they be ready to pull their hair out from boredom," Trav laughed.

"Would y'all shush. The movie is starting," Rue commanded.

Phoenix chuckled as she recalled her childhood again. She'd been so reflective lately, and this trip down memory lane was so different. Rue always wanted the house silent when a movie played on the television. For the entirety of the movie, she remained transfixed, and it appeared nothing had changed.

The family lounged around the media room. Kaleigh and Dallas stretched out on their blanket pallet on the floor. Trav and Rue were hugged up on the couch and Forge was sprawled across the chaise. Phoenix sat in her father's worn recliner as she surveyed the room. She tried to commit their smiles to memory. In her final moments, she wanted to close her eyes and see every moment with her family that brought her joy up until she breathed her last breath.

Laughter soon turned to silence. As the family all internalized Troi's mother's funeral, they considered the fate of their aunt, sister and friend. They all tried to act like the inevitable wasn't going to happen any time soon. But reality always loomed in the back of their minds. They knew one day they'd have to say goodbye to Phoenix sooner than any of them ever expected. But for the night they chose joy. Sleep fell upon the house, and with their sweet dreams, the thoughts of goodbye's finality melted away from their mental faculties.

CHAPTER ELEVEN

SILENTLY, PHOENIX AND FORGE STARED AT EACH OTHER. THE REALITY OF DR. Crane's words still rested upon their ears, vibrating like a symbolic gong. *Pregnant.* Phoenix couldn't believe what he was saying. She had him repeat himself six times and then asked to look at the lab results herself. Carelessness was not an attribute commonly associated with her, but as she accepted what he'd said, she'd realized she'd been so careless. Getting pregnant was nowhere in her plan. Though she was grateful that pregnancy was the cause of her seemingly worsening condition, she was overcome with sadness. She hadn't even spoken to Blaise in weeks, and here she was pregnant with only three weeks to decide what she wanted to do about it.

"So, does this mean you're going to finally call or go see him?" Forge asked as they got in her car.

"I don't know. I don't even know what I am going to do."

"Do you think that's something y'all need to figure out together?"

"Yes, but seriously, what the fuck am I going to say? Sorry for ghosting you two months ago? Surprise, we're having a baby."

"I mean, that's a start," Forge snapped as she switched gears and pulled out of the parking spot.

Phoenix's muscle fatigue and weakness had progressed, preventing her from doing much of what she normally did. She'd spent the last four weeks with Rue and her family, sleeping in their guest room. As much as it pained her to ask for help, it pained her even more not being in her own home. With a shrug of her shoulders, she let Forge know she was not in the mood to even discuss the news she'd been given. *Pregnant.* It was a shocking case of events, but as she thought about how she milked Blaise's dick every time they fucked with no form of contraceptive, she couldn't say she was surprised. Unprotected sex meant she was susceptible to anything, especially a child.

"Can you take me to my house? I need to be alone for a while. I don't need Rue following me around for the next hour asking me how my appointment was. I know her intentions be in the right place, but I just need some quiet time to think."

Forge looked over at her friend. The deep worry lines that had seemed to carve themselves into her brow line made her worry. She didn't know what was going through Phoenix's head. It was because of that unknowing, she couldn't show her excitement. Though she would support any decision Phoenix made, she couldn't act like she was over the moon that Phoenix might be having a baby.

Phoenix sat in the corner of her family room for days after Forge dropped her off. Day had turned to evening several times over. Her bare feet rested atop the forest green ottoman that she'd found at a thrift shop in The Junction. It matched her father's suede armchair perfectly and she couldn't leave without securing it. As she massaged her pregnant belly, a smile crept across her face as she recalled the day she spotted it while out with Rue. Briefly, she allowed happiness to overtake her crowded brain. She was emotionally overloaded, and she knew it wasn't good for her or the precious being taking up residency inside her womb. *Oh Daddy, what am I going to do? I really got myself in a pickle. What was I thinking about letting myself fall in love? And what the hell was I thinking letting him raw dog me and nut in me like some irresponsible teenager? I knew better.*

It had been a week since she'd sat there, trying to channel his wisdom. But nothing came. She was as mentally and emotionally blocked as she was the day she found out she was expecting a child. The reality was still baffling and as she came up on the last few days before she had to make the toughest choice of her life, she contemplated life as a single, sick mother.

"Okay Dad, so if I have this baby, there's a chance they may have to grow up motherless. But then there's the possibility they might wind up sick too. Am I really capable of taking care of both of us? I can barely care for myself some days."

Phoenix leaned back, turning her attention to the stars outside her window. She watched as the moon made its way to its final point in the sky. It was full, bright and radiating with enough light to pull her from her thoughts. They had gone dark for the first time since meeting Blaise. Trying to shake the consuming path her thoughts threatened to take if she sat in silence any longer, she struggled to reach for the remote beside her feet. After scooting dangerously close to the edge of the seat, her fingers grazed the remote before it crashed to the floor.

"Dammit!"

Phoenix rose to her feet and bent down only to discover the back had popped off and the batteries had rolled under the chair. Groaning, she trudged to the kitchen to grab a fresh pair. There was no way she was getting down on all fours for any other reason than to be filled with every inch of Blaise's dick. Since that would probably never happen again, she refrained from assuming the position. After grabbing an ice-cold glass of hibiscus pomegranate juice and the batteries, she dragged her feet, listening to the scratching sound of her fuzzy slippers against the hardwood floor. As she got the batteries in the remote and reclaimed her seat, she screamed with glee at the movie her streaming service had just added.

One of her favorite teen movies of all time was a series; Sisterhood of the Traveling Pants 1 and 2. As she smashed her thumb into the play button, she considered why it was the first movie to pop up. Growing up, Phoenix never believed in coincidences, only divine alignments. As she watched the opening credits, she was certain it was definitely a divine alignment. When she started questioning her own motives, and finally transformed from an emotionally caged woman to the heart-on-my-sleeve woman, they decided to add these two movies to their lineup.

As she watched the first movie, her mind wondered even more. All the amazing, best-friend moments that she loved about this movie were amplified when she watched it at 33 years old. It spoke to her in many ways and caused many 'ah-ha' and 'that makes sense' moments. All her own friends were scattered across the globe and most of the time unreachable. Without much thought, she snatched her phone from the end table and scrolled down to the group chat she shared with her one childhood friend and two college friends. With apprehension on her fingertips, she sent the text that would rally her girls for her announcement.

Phoenix: Uh, I feel kinda silly doin' this, but uhh, this is the anchor from the news station out in Cali. You know the one with the braids?

Kellz: Ard now Alicia no keys.

Tracy: bitch! where you been, popping on the scene with your creepy ass.

Phoenix: life has been crazy in my neck of the woods. i miss you hoes.

Tracy: you must be watching sisterhood of the traveling pants

Phoenix: how the hell you know that?

Tracy: Cuz im watching it too, hoe.

Kellz: i'm jealous. my ass stuck on this excavation site and my personal laptop conked out on me.

Tracy: where are you now, Zamunda?

Kellz: bitch, i hollered. no, we're in Madagascar. be back state side in about 25 weeks if y'all hoes wanna link.

Tracy: girl, you could have just said 6 months. and i'm game. y'all hoochies can come here.

Kellz: thinking in months makes the time go slow. So i choose to think in weeks. You lucky i ain't say 182 days, because i'm counting down too.

Tracy: whatever hoe, you game or what.

Kellz: I'm in.

Phoenix: in 25 weeks my ass will be on the no fly list

Phoenix held her breath as she waited for her friends to respond. Their bubbles kept popping up and disappearing. She was sure Tracy was about to initiate a group video chat. After five minutes of radio silence, she decided to kill their curiosity and sent a picture of the sonogram she'd gotten earlier that day. She was still in shock about the whole series of events. If she had to be honest, she didn't know if she was even relieved it wasn't her kidneys worsening. That, she had prepared herself for. Hearing 'you're 14 weeks pregnant,' she had not even considered.

Two months had passed since she last saw or spoke with Blaise. Because she wasn't feeling her best, she'd been staying with Rue. Though she was feeling bad, the main reason she chose to stay there was because she knew Blaise would probably pop up at her house. She'd blocked him and avoided places where they might run into each other. She made sure her appointments were scheduled for times she knew he wasn't usually at the hospital. She'd even started going to a private lab for all her testing so she wouldn't run into him there. It was back to the pre-Blaise era of Phoenix, where she was consumed with work and going through the motions of her condition.

The incessant dinging of her phone let her know that her friends had finally got the gist of what her text message meant. The responses had her sliding from her seat in a fit of laughter.

Kellz: Bitch, I was waiting for a sike, but you dead ass serious.

Tracy: sorry i think i just flatlined. You really out their letting that man raw dog you? You ain't even let that nigga terry hit it raw.

Kellz: Ard now slim. See phe, i gotta be godmommy number 1 b/c she going have my niece or nephew out here wildin' in the streets.

Tracy: shit, just like their mama used to do.

Kellz: wait, we talking like this and didn't even ask you. What are you planning to do?

Tracy: that was fucking insensitive of us and shit. Accept our apology.

Phoenix: i don't know, but y'all will be the first to know.

After texting her friends a little longer, she felt better about everything. It was something about the free flow of emotion and one-sided conversation that they allowed her to have that just soothed her. They'd known her since high school and knew most times she just needed a sounding board. She didn't need advice, most times she just needed them to field questions her way. She had been sorting through tough decisions for much of her teenage years, and this time was no different. She had a while longer before she had to make a decision before things got complicated. She'd let Blaise know depending on what she chose to do.

This was probably the toughest choice she ever was presented with making. Even choosing her treatment care plan was easier than determining whether or not she should bring new life into the world. Her life hung in the balance countless times over every time she had a severe flare, yet she was deeply contemplative about a person who didn't even have developed organs. Life was a mystery like that. She'd already begun putting her child's needs before her.

Dr. Crane had run down all the things that could go wrong and what preventative measures they could take to ensure the probability of them happening was lessened. Carrying a baby to term while she was dealing with failing organs would not be an easy feat, but as she sat there thinking about her future, she couldn't not see her baby in it. Whether it killed her or not, she'd decided she would fight as long as she could for her child.

Being pregnant was a miracle. She honestly thought there was no way she'd ever be able to conceive with the harsh side effects coupled with the longevity of medication intake. She was taking a few that caused fertility issues and Dr. Crane had her levels regularly checked just because he knew she wanted a family one day. When he'd met her, it was all she talked about at first because she was engaged and starting a family. Though they'd split, she let him know that motherhood was in her plans at some point, and she wanted to be able to carry at least one of her children to term.

But even with the miracle of conception, there was that underlying danger of carrying a child in her condition. Phoenix didn't mind being called selfish. She thought about sacrificing herself for the uncertainty of motherhood and there was a gnawing at her core that caused her to recoil at the thought of childbirth. So much could go wrong with any pregnancy, but having lupus made things a thousand times worse in her eyes. She felt like if her family had to make the choice to save her or her baby, they'd unanimously deem her baby's life worth more than hers. She didn't want to die bringing another person into the world.

"Mommy, I know I hardly ever saw things your way as a child. I know I was probably the number one reason why your wine fridge stayed heavily stocked. But I need answers. I need to know that if I do this... If I keep this baby that I'll be able to raise them? How can I even find the strength to love someone more than I love myself to even make this type of sacrifice? I need to know that everything will be okay. Daddy, is it bad that I don't feel a connection? Do you think it's like a divine alignment? Does snatching its soul before it has time to form its flesh is supposed to make me feel less guilt and shame?"

Phoenix talked to her mother and father like they were physically sitting across from her. Her eyes were low, and she tuned out the laughter emitting from the television's speakers. She was stuck between the valley and the cliff. Suffocating from the reality that she was contemplating ending a soul's journey before it began. She was potentially rescinding a miracle from God. But her best friend's voice echoed in her ear.

No one has the right to tell you what to do with your body. People can feel however they are going to feel, and you ain't got shit to do with that. It's your body, your life and your decision. You don't owe a soul a thing.

Phoenix had made her decision. Though it was one that she knew her immediate circle would disapprove of, it was the only one that made sense for her life. While motherhood had always been a part of her distant future, she was content with that being unchecked on her goal list. Her life was precious to her, and she was hell bent on protecting not only her peace but her well-being. Death for a child was just not her idea of a fair trade. Unconditional love from a man wasn't even worth her life.

Two days after her night of self-reflection, Phoenix found herself surrounded by strangers connected by one fact: they were about to make a decision that the many deemed wrong. Her palms produced more moisture than she ever had before. It was odd because Phoenix never questioned any decision she made. But as she sat, her senses heightened right along with her emotions.

Pens gliding across paper caused her skin to crawl. The cracked pleather on the chair poked her through the black skater dress and tights she wore. She felt everything all at once and the overwhelming sensation of judgment suffocated her more than the stuffy air in the small waiting room. As she sat in the waiting room, the clock ticked behind her, and the beat of her heart vibrated her body. Her breathing slowed as she tried to control her emotions, but they kept building. Finally, she collected her belongings and bolted for the door.

Okay, Daddy. That's settled. I'm going to be somebody's mother.

The entire drive home, she held one hand against her belly. The tears flowed as she repeatedly asked her unborn child for forgiveness. She knew she'd probably never get this chance again and she wanted to be a mother. She wanted to leave a legacy behind, a tangible incarnation of the beautiful, spellbinding love she was able to experience with Blaise. Their love deserved to be tethered to this world, and their child was what would anchor her.

CHAPTER TWELVE

Phoenix was thrilled she'd decided to carry her baby to term. Every second that she wasn't working, she found herself online shopping and saving a million items to her private wishlist. Even at nearly five months, she wasn't showing as much as she thought she would be. She was sure she'd have to resort to peplum tops and ruffle dresses to hide her baby bump until the pending hoodie season commenced. But thankfully, she'd been mainly gaining boobs and thighs.

As she sat in her father's recliner rubbing her barely visible baby bump, she smiled at her favorite episode of The Originals. Klaus was reuniting with his baby after having to send her away for safety. It had always warmed her heart, but in her current condition, it tugged at her heartstrings even more.

The fear that initially plagued her head had been replaced with anticipation. Her eagerness to be a mother heightened as each day passed. With Forge, Tracy and Kellz being the only ones that knew she was expecting, she was able to relax. While she told Rue she would do better with communicating life changing events, she wanted to exist without the mother hen laying up under her until she gave birth. She knew once Rue became an aunt, she'd never know privacy again. Her sister would hover, making sure they were both healthy to a point she'd probably try to escape. Rue was a village all by herself and had been for the last 19 years of Phoenix's life. Even after she'd promised to communicate more and Rue promised to dial back her overprotective antics, neither sister had lived up to their promise as she was not as forthcoming, and Rue had not stopped smothering her.

In glimpses, she relived the moments she spent with Blaise. With all the distance she'd strategically placed between them, it became easier for her to let go of the future she'd planned for them in her head. Her nights without him were longer. Sleep came less frequently, and she knew the remedy to her world was just one phone call away. Still, she remained committed to her decision. Forcing fatherhood on him was not in her plan. They were having fun and though he'd confessed his love for her on a few occasions, she couldn't chance him walking out the second everything got tough. Loving her was a gifted curse, she came with levels of trust issues she had yet to sift through. They'd only gotten worse since her diagnosis. Aside from her family and friends, she knew deep down that no one would stick around when the tough times were all she had left. Though she shaped it as protecting them, she knew it was really about self-preservation.

Her phone pulled her from her thoughts. She kicked herself for not switching it over to DND while she spent quality time with the little human growing in her tummy.

Rue: Movies tonight? My treat.

Phoenix: I'm game. What time?

Rue: 6. Movie 10 in The Junction.

Phoenix: What, your bougie ass not dragging me back to that one in Calla Falls

Rue: I know you hate the place, so no. We're hitting your favorite theater.

A chuckle left her lips as she placed her phone down on the couch. She had a cover story to rework before she was due to meet her sister. As she looked through the pictures of Blaise her editor had sent over, a tear left her eye. She never knew she could miss anyone as much as she missed her parents, but she did. As she recalled a tweet she'd retweeted earlier that morning, she realized it really was a mystery. Mourning the loss of people who still walked the earth was an entirely different pain altogether. It left a gaping sense of longing that she knew she probably would never be able to fill. The words stopped coming as she stared at the picture.

Without thinking twice, she picked up her phone and told Siri to call him. But just as quickly as she'd made the command, she'd rescinded it. Why did Siri have to confirm every damn thing? Hearing *just to be sure, you'd like to call Blaise*, caused her to clam up. All the bravado left her fingertips as she sat her phone back down and returned to the task at hand. The love of her life was her next cover story and was the piece that made her the proudest. He'd made a real difference in bridging the equity gap for Solace Point's most underfunded and underserved community's pediatric care. Partnering with clinics, community centers and schools in the housing projects of Solace Point's east and west sides, he was making his stamp on the city. She was honored to have a front row seat to his efforts to make health care the city's number one priority. His passion shone through his fatigue every time. As she typed the last line of her story, a tear fell from her.

Two hours later, Phoenix wrapped her arms under her sister's armpits and rested her head on her shoulder. All the anguish she'd been carrying for the last sixty days seemed to dispel from her body the second Rue squeezed her. For ten minutes the sisters stood embracing each other outside the theater. Their show time was about to start, but Rue didn't care. Phoenix's heavy breathing worried her more than them missing some opening credits of a movie they'd seen probably a thousand times by now.

"Hey, Sis, how are you, really?" Rue asked with concerned etched along her brow.

"I'm okay. Really, just tired."

"Awww, baby love, we could have rescheduled this movie date if you need rest."

Rue wrapped her sister in her arms again. Though they caught stares from other movie goers, she didn't mind. Phoenix never showed much vulnerability so the fact that she admitted she was tired spoke volumes. As she held her baby sister in her arms, her heart hurt. Phoenix was like her first child, and it pained her to know there was nothing she could do to physically change Phoenix's current circumstances.

Tears burned her eyes as she tried to keep it together. She could feel her sister holding in her breath like she was afraid to break. Though not unfamiliar with Phoenix's bodily response, it was one she hadn't experienced in a while. Worry quickly set in as her sister's hot tears seared her exposed shoulder. Rue broke their embrace and scanned her sister's anguish-covered face. Something was very wrong and the reality of what it could be made her stomach knot up. This had happened before; all the events of Phoenix's last bout of steroid-induced psychosis came flooding back. It caused Phoenix to spend 36 days on the Solace General psychiatric floor and another 2 weeks being treated for a lupus flare.

Pulling a tissue from her bag, she wiped her baby sister's tears and ushered her over to the first empty bench she saw. As she sat, lightly tugging on Phoenix's arm to join her on the paint-chipped, graffiti-covered wooden bench, the light washed from her eyes. Phoenix stiffened in her grasp. Clutching her chest, she fought to get the words out.

"R-r-rue. I can't bre–" Phoenix tried to tell her sister as she tried to sit on the bench.

Rue panicked as Phoenix's legs buckled under her body. She

came crashing to the pavement, hitting the concrete with a thud. Frantically, she called out for help as her shaky hands rummaged through her purse for her phone. Two passersby rushed over to assist. She hovered as they laid her body out on the concrete.

"Honey, everything will be okay. My wife is a nurse," one of the women assured her.

The other woman positioned herself on the left side of Phoenix and began chest compressions. Rue cried uncontrollably, unable to give the 911 operator any information.

The other woman grabbed the phone and gave the operator what information she could before turning to Rue, "Honey, how old is your sister?"

"Sh-sh—. Thirty-one. She's 31," Rue pushed out in one breath as her eyes darted from her sister to the woman's hands on her chest and back to the woman with her phone.

Her mind raced as she was trying to figure out how this even happened. How couldn't she see it coming? This was not how she wanted to lose her sister. It was too soon. Phoenix had just really started living again. It wasn't time, it couldn't be time. She needed more of it. They'd wasted so much butting heads about Phoenix's lack of concern for her own condition lately that they'd forgotten to make the most of their time together.

Within seven minutes of making the nearly inaudible 911 call, Phoenix was lifted onto a gurney and hoisted into the back of an ambulance. They worked on her for a few minutes, connecting her to oxygen and IVs. Rue took that time to thank the two women who helped save her sister's life. She was sure that their willingness to jump in and administer aid to her sister was not in vain.

"Thank you for all your help," Rue acknowledged the couple as she approached them.

"Sweetie, you don't have to thank me. It's our duty to ensure the safety of our fellow black women. We'll be praying for Phoenix tonight. She's going to be alright," the nurse assured her.

"Now, go see about your sister," they instructed her.

Opting to follow behind them, Rue revved her engine, never even thinking twice about her own safety. En route, she called Trav and Forge to let them know what had happened. It all happened so fast, she honestly didn't even know what transpired. All she felt were her hot tears before she felt the crushing weight of Phoenix's body on her feet.

Gripping the steering wheel tightly, she turned into the hospital's roundabout on two wheels and slammed her foot on the brakes. She was sure she looked like a crazy woman as she dropped her keys into the valet's hand. Without waiting for her ticket, she rushed through the hospital doors and followed the signs to the emergency room. She'd been there before, many times with both her children and even her husband but she couldn't seem to remember the way. Her vision became blurred and all she heard was her own racing heartbeat as she stopped in her tracks. Phoenix wasn't breathing when she fell, at least that's what she remembered the woman who helped her say as she blew into her mouth and commenced chest compressions. But there was something about this time that made her hyperventilate. A security officer stopped her, with a gentle touch on the shoulder.

"Ma'am, are you okay?"

Snapping back to reality, Rue closed her eyes and took a deep breath. Mustering up enough strength to get the words out, she swiped away at her tears.

"Yes, can you point me toward the ER? I seemed to have gotten turned around."

"No worries. Just keep going straight down this hallway and make a left at the second opening. Cross the bridge and take the first set of elevators to the ER floor."

"Thank you."

"And ma'am, I'm praying your sister is okay. She's one of the sweetest people I've encountered in my 25 years on this job."

A smile crept across Rue's face. Phoenix would rise, she always did. The kind stranger remembering who her sister was and wishing her well served as a gentle reminder that they weren't alone. God had placed that particular guard in her path so she would know just how many prayer warriors Phoenix had. She was a kind, compassionate and loving person who decided to spread joy and light even when her world was clouded by sickness and rain. Nothing could keep her down. Whatever was happening they would get through it together because she wasn't ready to give up on her baby sister and when she made it to the ER, she'd make sure Phoenix knew that.

Once Rue had checked in at the counter, she took a seat. Her heel rapidly rose and fell against the vinyl floor. She checked her phone nearly a thousand times a minute as the seconds got the best of her. Unable to sit any longer, she paced the floor until a nurse came over to her.

"Mrs. Pratt, your sister is awake and asking for you?"

Rue took a few deep breaths and smoothed her hair down. She was sure she looked disheveled and sweaty. Phoenix didn't need to worry about her, so she did the best she could to gather her composure before they made it back to the room. As she approached the door, she stood wiping her palms down the sides of her dress. She was visibly a ball of nerves and did not want Phoenix to suspect that she did anything but hold it together. She was the oldest and keeping it together no matter the situation was always one of her greatest attributes, though her husband always told her it was a hindrance.

With a smile plastered on her face, she entered the room and looked over at her sister. Phoenix returned her smile as she stretched out her arms for a hug. IVs and cords extended from her arms and chest as her hospital gown hung off her shoulder. She turned her head as she walked over to meet her sister at her bedside. Phoenix's disdain for hospital garb was known and felt. She made a note to start keeping one of the gowns she had customized for her in both of their cars for emergencies such as these.

"Hey, my baby, how are you feeling? You scared the fuck out of me?"

"Sore as hell and tired. What happened?"

"You just started crying out of nowhere. Then when we walked to sit on the bench, you fainted. Luckily there was a nice lady who knew CPR."

"Wait, I stopped breathing?"

Rue was confused by the level of panic in her voice. It wasn't the first time Phoenix had fainted. In fact, she suffered symptoms that were mistaken as a heart attack before, but somehow this moment scared her. Her eyes were far off, she'd internalized her thinking as her eyes scanned the room. Rue watched as her sister's chest started moving more regularly. Her breathing returned to normal as they both zeroed in on the second machine. Rue's eyes widened and her chin fell to her chest as she looked down and saw the cords running from under the blanket."

"Phoenix!"

"I planned to tell you today after the movies. I knew you'd want to get sno-balls while we were on that side of town and it would have been the perfect place."

"I thought we promised the important things we had to share. Just so we are clear, pregnancy is considered an important thing," Rue smiled as she hugged her baby sister. She kissed her temple and pulled up the chair that sat by the door.

The sisters laughed and talked about Phoenix being someone's mother. Rue teased her with promises of her child giving her twice the hell Phoenix gave her. They prayed for the health and safety of both mother and child before the doctor and his team entered the room. Before he fully stepped into the room, Phoenix stiffened. Her eyes diverted to the speck of dust on the blanket as she inhaled that familiarly intoxicating scent of lemongrass and sandalwood.

"Hi Ms. Colleville, I'm Dr. Jones, you gave paramedics quite the scare today. Your bloodwork came back okay for the most part. My only concerns are your low blood pressure and blood sugar. You are also severely dehydrated. To say you and your little one were lucky today would be putting it mildly."

Phoenix clenched her eyes shut the second he mentioned the baby. As he reached out for her hand, she jumped at the initial skin-to-skin contact. She hadn't seen or talked to him in over two months, and she missed him. When he gripped her wrist, glimpses of him raising her hands above her head the last time they made love flashed across her closed lids. All the feelings she thought she'd bottled up and tucked deep in the back of her mind bubbled to the surface. She let her tears freely fall as she finally looked up at him.

For a split second, he maintained eye contact as he watched her recoil into her shell. Directing his attention back to the task at hand, he manually checked her pressure and other vitals. Lifting the blanket and the lower part of her gown, he adjusted the band around her belly to make sure the machine gave accurate readings of her baby's vitals. Phoenix watched as he stared at her belly. It seemed to grow in size the longer he stared at it. Before that moment, she kept telling herself she wasn't showing, and no one could tell. Now, it seemed like a watermelon had taken up residence in her womb.

Rue watched the interaction between the two. She could tell Phoenix was uncomfortable. Her mental battle was evident by the tension held in her shoulders. Her eyes were low, and her breathing was slow and deep. She was visibly trying to compose herself and it wasn't working. Gently, she touched her shoulder, instantly calming the racing beats of her heart.

"Phe, you okay?"

"Yea, I just need a minute alone."

Without another word, the nurse and Rue both left the room. Blaise remained at the foot of her bed. The veil of his professionalism dropped the moment the nurse closed the door. The beeping of the monitors was the only sound in the room as they both looked at her stomach. She pressed her right palm to her belly as she gripped the guard rail with her left. Sitting up in the bed, she mustered up the courage to have the conversation she knew would come eventually.

She didn't think it would happen like this, but now that it had, she had no other choice but to talk to him. Everything she tried to run from was staring her in the face and she had nowhere left to run and hide.

"Blaise..."

"Nah. Whatever you're about to say, save that shit. A fucking baby, Phoenix?"

"I'm sorry."

"Yea, you are."

Phoenix cringed as his words pierced her ears. She didn't know what to expect when she finally saw him, but she knew it wasn't this. His tone was cold, dismissive, and dripped with disdain for her. Love was replaced with disappointment, and she hated how much she'd become the thing he hated. There was no time when he showed her he wasn't down for her, but she still chose to run in the opposite direction. Her cries were silent as he finished the rest of his examination. Her body was limp as he made sure the love of his life would get to live long enough to bear their child. His anger was unmasked, and she could feel the heat emitting from his body as he invaded her space.

"Blaise, can you just stop for one second and hear me out?"

"Why? You just dropped off the face of my earth for months. And if you wouldn't have fell the fuck out today, you'd still be missing in action. So why the fuck should I give you another second of my time? You've already wasted damn near a year of it."

"Really, B? That's not fair."

"Neither is life, but here we are. I'm upping the dosage of your amlodipine from 5MG to 10MG. Your low blood sugar is probably a result of not eating enough. So, follow up with your OB in a week to see if it's still low. They may want you to take a glucose tablet if it's still low. Other than that, you can go home tonight. But, you need to sit the fuck down Phoenix, and take care of yourself. It ain't just your life at risk anymore."

Phoenix fixed her mouth to speak, but Blaise left the room. She watched as his back disappeared just as Rue entered the room. Unable to compose herself any longer, she fell apart at the seams. Her cries were loud, her eyes were clouded with tears, and her shoulders hunched. Holding her head in her hands, she released everything she'd been holding in since Dr. Crane told her that her kidneys hadn't worsened, and that she was actually pregnant, and they needed to stop her treatment immediately.

To say she was overwhelmed was an understatement. She didn't know if she was coming or going most days, and today was the tipping point. Life had come at her far faster than she could have ever imagined. Nothing her parents or sister taught her could have ever prepared her for the speed at which her life changed. In less than three years she went from a rising media star to a sick and pregnant reporter. It was depressing, unnerving, and her heart broke every time she considered the life she always had. Why couldn't things just work out for her for once? That's all she asked herself as her tears seeped through her hands and soaked the blanket.

"Oh, Phoenix, please tell me what's wrong? You've been a ball of tears all day. I'm scared. I need you to tell me something."

"That was their father," Phoenix pushed out between tears.

"Huh?"

"The doctor is my baby's father. And I didn't tell him. I feel like a fucking cliche."

"Holl-up. Holl-up. Let me get this straight. The man you've been dating for damn near a year is a doctor?"

"Was dating. As in, I ghosted him a couple weeks after you found out because I was getting sicker, and I didn't want to tell him. I didn't want to get dumped."

"Sis, you are fumbling the bag big time."

Phoenix looked at her sister incredulously before throwing her head back in laughter. She knew her sister meant exactly what she'd said. It was not some ploy to lighten the mood or make her feel good about her situation. But she also didn't need anyone to tell her how much she'd ruined a good thing. She felt it every day she woke in the morning and every night she laid in her bed alone. It was a choice she made and one she had to live with whether she wanted to or not.

Blaise wouldn't even look at her for longer than he had to, and he shut her down every time she tried to explain herself. And she didn't blame him, because if the roles were reversed, she would have probably slapped him for thinking she owed him any of her time. Explanations were for rare occasions, not patterned behavior. Since her ex, she had this rule that she'd always leave before she was ever left again. She never wanted to be the one on the wrong side of love, yet here she was staring heartbreak in the face for the second time in less than ten minutes.

"Ms. Colleville..."

"Blaise, can you drop the formalities? You basically just said fuck me two seconds ago. There's no one in here you need to keep the charade up for. Am I being discharged yet?"

Phoenix watched as he stopped in his tracks and looked at her sideways. Yes, she knew she was wrong for every action she took up until that moment. She knew she should have told him about the pregnancy as soon as she found out. She knew she should have told him she was sick when they got serious. She knew that it was her actions that had them in the emotional torment they both were currently dealing with, but his dismissive attitude was driving her crazy.

"Phoenix, I'm not doing this with you right now. I have seven other patients to care for tonight. You can go home right after the nurse gives you your discharge instructions. Get something to eat when you leave here, preferably something with fruit to give your blood sugar a boost. Don't forget to call your OB in the morning."

Rue sat back and smirked as he left the room again. She found the entire situation sheer entertainment. Her little sister had created quite the ordeal for herself, and she was on the edge of her seat seeing how she was going to level the scales. Phoenix was usually never off her game this much. Yes, she did get so into her head and made irrational decisions that she conceived as the most rational, but this situation took the medal by a landslide. There was no way Rue would have been able to make this shit up, and she couldn't wait to get home and give Trav all the updates. Holding back laughter, she helped Phoenix redress while they waited for the nurse to return.

After the sisters left the hospital, they went straight to Noir Tea for a quick dinner. Phoenix pushed her food around her plate as she thought about the evening's events. It was not the way she planned to spend the evening. What started out as a fun sisters' outing turned into a nasty lovers' quarrel. Dropping her fork on her plate, she pushed her plate away and rested her elbows on the table.

"Nope. Your baby daddy said you need to eat. You better eat up, before I call your future hubby up and request him to make house calls," Rue laughed as she sipped her fruit smoothie.

"Shut up, Rue. You make me sick. And he ain't my future nothing," Phoenix whined as she rolled her eyes.

Rue laughed as she tossed a tiny morsel of bread ad Phoenix's head. Now that her sister was okay, all she could help to do was tease her about the situation she'd landed herself in.

"Oh, baby sis, sorry to break it to you, your ass is definitely off the market. Been off the market since y'all started dating."

"How you figure that?"

"I'm sure y'all breezed through the big three?"

"What the hell is the big three?"

"The three most romantic dates. C'mon sis, you can't be out here being a hopeless romantic and not know about the big three. Beach picnic, impromptu dancing in the rain and going to the opera."

"And we never been on none of them, now look at you," Phoenix stuck her tongue out before she stuffed a fork full of her salmon and kale salad in her mouth.

"Where did y'all go on y'all first date?"

"To my favorite cove. The one you always have to check my location to find near The Junction"

"Bitch, that's beach picnic to our city living asses!" Rue laughed as she dunked her bread in the honey butter, "what was the next date?"

"He came over for dinner. I cooked pasta."

"Wait, that night it rained and I bought you groceries?"

"Yup."

"Oh, you was off the market by date one, Sis. You was cooking Mommy's recipes for that man? Plus, it's impromptu dancing in the rain," Rue laughed.

"But we didn't dance in the rain."

"You fucked that man in the parlor, with the bay windows open. Sis, that's impromptu dancing in the rain."

"OMG. Forreal, Rue. So what are you counting as the opera, since you just making this shit up as you go," Phoenix laughed heartily for the first time in a long time.

"Alcatraz. They play that opera like music during the tour. I'm telling you, boo, you done fucked around and found out with this one."

"Fuck you," Phoenix groaned as she flicked a pepper from her salad at Rue.

"How you gon' be mad at me? Be mad at yourself, baby sis. You're the one out here hiding a man, a baby, and an illness. Daddy always told us keeping secrets would come back to bite us," Rue replied as she caught the pepper in her mouth.

"You're supposed to be on my side."

"No, she's supposed to be on the right side when it's just y'all. And she's right, Sis. You owe that man a lot more than a damn explanation. You owe him a heartfelt apology and some head to top it off, no pun intended," Forge inserted as she slid into the booth beside Phoenix.

Phoenix looked around the table and rolled her eyes. She didn't necessarily expect them to be on her side. But she did expect them to at least understand why she felt like she needed to hide everything. Granted they weren't feeling her feelings or living her life, so they couldn't fathom the weight she carried every day. It was never a time '*what if*' didn't cross her mind. What ifs ruled her world since she fell ill, and it was hard to just shut them off. Her growing love for Blaise pushed her over the edge and she was barely hanging on when she found out she was pregnant. It wasn't what she wanted to hear and if she were being honest, hearing her kidneys had declined would have been easier to stomach. She had prepared herself for that bit of news, not the revelations that she and Blaise would be parents soon.

"Let me ask you this. If you gave someone almost a year of your life and they just dropped off the face of the earth, what would you do?"

"Move on."

"That's bullshit and you know it. When Darrell told you he was leaving you because you had lupus, you were devastated. So, I know you're pedaling grade A horse shit," Rue retorted.

"Okay. Okay. I was wrong, but Rue that man shut me the fuck up every time I even tried to talk to him tonight. He's not tryna hear shit from me."

"No, he's not trying to hear a bunch of bullshit from you. I bet you done told him all about your family and your childhood, but ain't said shit to him about anything that happened in your life in the last three years. You probably tell him all about growing up with Mommy, Daddy and Aunt Phae, but never mentioned how losing them sent you down a dark and delinquent path. He probably doesn't know your ass has been arrested twice or that you are terrified of jellyfish because you got stung when you were 7."

"Damn, Big Sis you ain't have to air my shit out like that."

"No, I didn't, but you should have. If you love that man as much as I know you do, then there shouldn't be a thing about you, good or bad, that he doesn't know. You should be able to trust him with your darkest secrets and your most vulnerable moments. You should be an open book to him, not a few pirated chapters."

Rue pushed Phoenix's plate back to her. She didn't want to talk about it anymore. There was nothing Phoenix needed to say to her or Forge. Everything she had to say, she needed to say to her man. She was not a child anymore and running from problems and feelings didn't fix anything. She couldn't outrun this situation because in a few months she'd be facing it all over again when the baby was born. Whatever was holding her back from living the full life God was trying to grant her, she needed to figure it out, whether she did it in solitude or on her therapist's couch.

"That's the second time I've been dismissed today, and I don't like it."

"Then get your shit together," Rue advised, "now eat up so I can get you home."

Phoenix entered her house and walked through the darkness. She retreated to her bathroom and started the bathtub. She wanted to wash away the verbal attacks to her character she'd suffered from everyone she held dear. Her armor was dented and scratched, and she needed time to regroup. There was no one in her corner. In everyone's eyes, she was the villain, and even though they had yet to really know him, they were all team Blaise. She never took the time to consider why she was the way she was, but now that she was lonely and pregnant, she had very little time to rectify the situation. Now that the truth was out, no one in her inner circle was going to let her continue to shut Blaise out of her life or her baby's. They silently showed her they would be on the right side of this mess she made, waiting for her to get her shit together.

As she leaned back on her bath pillow, she closed her eyes. With all the betrayal she felt, she wanted to cry but no tears came. Even her tear ducts were fed up with her nonsense. She knew deep down it was misplaced. No one betrayed her; in fact, they all loved her enough to call her out on her wrongdoings and force her to fix what she broke. She rehearsed what she would say to Blaise when he gave her the chance to talk. There it was, that inkling of hope. Like an epiphany, she realized that just simply changing her *ifs* to *whens* was how she could begin to pull herself out of the lamented state of existence she'd willingly ushered herself into.

CHAPTER THIRTEEN

For the umpteenth time in a seven-day span, Phoenix curled up in her father's recliner and wrapped a throw around herself. She'd assumed this position every day; it had become second nature. Shower, check sugar, eat, pop pillows and c Report to the recliner. It was her daily routine since she'd decided to start her maternity leave three months early. Every time she lifted her pill bottle and saw Blaise's name as the prescriber, she wanted to scream. He was certainly the prescriber of her current mental anguish. As much as he went after what he wanted, she was sure he would have been to her house by now. But two weeks had passed since she wound up a patient of his.

For two weeks, she sat alone watching the day turn to night without not one person checking in on her. In one day, she'd managed to piss off everyone she held dear. For the first time since moving to Solace Point, she was alone and lonely. Her mind couldn't focus on anything but confusion. She'd gotten what she thought she wanted, for everyone to stop hovering over her. But when they retreated, they took their covering with them. She felt exposed and fearful of the silence. There was no one there to pull her from her thoughts if they got too dark. There was no one to remind her that there was life at the end of her present storm. There was just the darkness and the silence that magnified it.

Before leaving work, she'd begun working on a black love in Solace Point cover story for Point Magazine. Much of her research served as a healing mechanism as she explored the multifaceted nature of love and the ways it was shown and experienced. The couples she'd interviewed had such beautiful portrayals of love's resilience and fortitude. They described the most forgiving instances of love and as she recalled them her faith grew. Hope took root in her heart, and she felt like she and Blaise would be alright. But that same article was what had her balling up on the chair crying until her ducts were dry.

For three years, she'd been in a space that for the same amount of time she didn't know how to define. She couldn't explain it. She'd tried to make sense of it from the moment she moved across the country. In any other situation, she would talk to Forge or Rue for hours trying to figure it out and other times she would sit alone, silently contemplating her next move. Either way, she never found herself without an answer because she would force whoever was with her to listen to her talk her way through whatever had her puzzled until she had the answer. Their interjections were usually never warranted, but she welcomed them when they came.

Blaise was the one who would help her sort through the clutter and find the story amid the hours and hours of written and audio interviews. Whenever she wrote around him, he gave his two cents even when she already had $5 worth of her own. Everything made her miss the time she spent with him. Any activity she tried to complete made her long for his presence. Even after he'd spent 12-hour shifts serving his patients, he still offered her whatever energy he had left. The black love cover story was their story, they'd stayed up working on it together for nearly two months. It was her proudest moment because it was her first published piece in a magazine that centered the black experience on Solace Point, and she got to share it with him.

Instead of turning on Sisterhood of the Traveling Pants for the millionth time, she reached over to the coffee table and pulled out her research. Somehow, she had to have missed the answers she was looking for. There had to be an answer among the piles of information she'd collected during her research and interviews. She couldn't understand why anyone would knowingly seek love from another person if they knew that there was an inevitable pain that had the ability to suck the soul from their lives without warning or repercussion. She needed to know why people willingly sacrificed themselves without question for a love that could change at any moment. She needed to know why this was accepted. Why was it some unwritten law? And why the hell hadn't anyone sought to bring love to justice because if others felt the way she felt or worse, love should have definitely been on trial for crimes against humanity.

For the next six hours, she burned the midnight oil like she was back in graduate school. Those hours she'd spent borrowing psychology books on Kindle Unlimited, looking up articles and scholarly journals on , and reading whatever other material she could get her hands on, was nothing compared to the deep dive she'd commenced. She searched for the answer to the unknown. It just didn't make any damn sense to her, and she was trying to make as much sense of it as she possibly could with all the research techniques and sources she'd gathered.

For the most part, she gained a bit of clarity, but like Socrates in Euthyphro, she was still not convinced. It still just did not make sense to her. But smack dab at the end of her pile was the first piece of research she had on the topic. She'd been reading and listening to so much, she had forgotten about the exploration of this idea of the triangular theory of love. She'd highlighted the part where he explained that all love was composed of three elements: intimacy, passion, and commitment. Whether it was romantic, familial, or friendly, wasn't of importance, it was simply the existence of those and how they were manifested in a relationship.

Unsatisfied with that simple, yet complex explanation, her curiosity kept her awake like that late afternoon coffee she usually enjoyed. The answer sent her down a rabbit hole and she found herself retaining much more than she had during her writing process. She read about the six types of love proposed by John Lee. Then that led her to question even more. What was intimacy? What was passion in this sense of the word? What was considered commitment and did that really look different for every relationship? Her questions seemed to pile up quicker than she could come up with answers, but her desire to get to the root of her own issues made her keep going. She wanted a deeper understanding even if she wasn't satisfied with the results.

Just as she was about to give up on her impromptu research session, one of her college associates had emailed her a link to an article. Though her research was officially over, her classmate knew she always read studies on love and how it shaped the human experience. The article outlined the three types of love we experienced in our lifetime. It said there was the young love that technically wasn't really love, but it was love because a person simply said it was love. Then there's the one that hurts the most, but it serves as the catalyst for growth. Then finally, there's that steady, last forever, love.

Of all the articles, dissertations and capstones she'd scoured, that was the answer she'd been looking for. People had simply chosen to build up a tolerance for certain pains that can come from love. People choose what they endured and who they endured it from. It wasn't about avoiding pain, it was about experiencing the hurt so that the joy would feel so much better. So that people would recognize it, acknowledge it and appreciate it when they had it.

Phoenix sat her phone down and thought about her people. She thought about the child she carried and how her love for her child would grow. She thought about Blaise and how she'd hurt him. He was dismissive because he didn't want her to see him break just as much as she had. The dismissal was a defense mechanism for the trauma she'd inadvertently caused when she left without a word. She thought about Rue and Forge and how they loved her no matter how much she tried to separate herself from them. Love really did cover a multitude and for the first time in her life, she understood what it meant. She'd figured out why she was the way she was. She'd pinpointed the exact moment when she gave up on love and it was long before her fiancé deserted her.

Glancing over at the time, she decided she'd make that call in the morning. It was clear she needed to have a heart-to-heart with her Aunt Phae. The betrayal she felt when Aunt Phae called her parents from their warm beds and ultimately to their casket broke her. She said she'd stop drinking. But she didn't and now her parents weren't here to see their grandchildren or their daughters. Phoenix knew she needed to let that hurt go.

Yes, Darrell crushed her and probably didn't even know he had as great an impact on her life going forward as he did. He practically rendered her heart immobile. It hadn't ever beat for another man the same, until Blaise warmed it with a cup of her favorite tea. He'd singlehandedly melted the ice cap and she was uncomfortable. His ever presence in her life made her realize that she had been holding on to that heartbreak for the better part of three years. It was unfathomable. Carrying around pain for all those years and not even realizing that she was in pain. The realization that her numbness to heartbreak could potentially cause her to suffer the greatest heartbreak of her life was even more debilitating than her physical condition.

Phoenix realized that she never cared to get over him because she thought death would meet her before love ever did again. Deciding against doing this alone, she called Tracy. Though she was across the world, and operating on a different time zone, she knew that her call would be answered. Tracy always answered; time and space had no rendering on their friendship, and it had been that way since they were teenagers. After having a long talk with the one person who was there through all of the craziness that was their relationship she understood that she simply didn't have the bandwidth to deal with what he'd done to her heart. She realized that she had been holding on to that heartbreak because it was probably the only love she'd ever known on this side of her life.

She was reminded that when everything finally went to shits between her and him, she was battling a horrible lupus flare. Her emotions and memories about their break up were probably suppressed from all the Zyprexa, Risperdal and Haldol she'd been prescribed to combat the steroid-induced psychosis she'd succumbed to while being treated for that severe lupus flare. That version of events made the most sense because she still didn't remember not one conversation from that time. She couldn't recall any of the events that led up to him saying he was leaving. When he told her, he had a job and apartment in another state. She knew he'd been pulling away for a while before he finally said anything. Her mind was blank for the most part. All she knew was they were friends and lovers; then they were foes. And her defense mechanism was set to Trina, 'when you see me in the street, don't speak,' levels. But she wasn't mad at him anymore. She forgave him for leaving and released herself from the hold that the anger and heartbreak associated with their ending had on her life.

With a cleared heart and mind, Phoenix massaged her belly. She felt like she could sleep peacefully knowing that the erasure of her heartbreak's last remnants were dispelled from her vessel. But, as she rocked her baby to sleep while she looked out at the stars, she realized that she'd become a shell of her existence because she chose to hide under the guise of night. She decided to keep every single conversation, date night, and companionship trapped behind the levees of her stored memory. She decided to bury her anguish and pain under her work ethic and commitment to her dreams. She chose to hinder her healing by suppressing the emotions that needed so desperately to be released. Her two most precious vessels became harboring quarters for heartbreak, pain, insecurity, fear, and regret. It was only then that she decided to completely deal and heal from that heartbreak, a heartbreak that no one on earth knew she had been harboring for so long. Hell, for a while she didn't even know. So, she decided to take the time and go through the remaining stages of grief so that she could show up fully for the people who loved her in spite of it all.

Phoenix grabbed the pen and notebook that sat beside her and decided it was time to clear the air. She didn't need a session with Triumph for this part. He'd already given her the tools she needed to heal, it was time she finally listened to him and put them into practice. When Darrell told her he was breaking off their engagement and ending their 12-year relationship she felt both rejected and dejected.

Before they were lovers, they were friends. It wasn't until the summer before they left for college they decided to date, but they'd been friends since middle school. He was in her inner circle. There was nothing about her he didn't know, although she was almost certain he would have rather not known about all the ones that came before him. But he listened anyway, gave her advice or was ready to ride out with her if she wanted to make a move on a nigga that forgot who the fuck she was. It was the same for him. They were tight like that. Which was weird to everybody who knew them because as kids, they couldn't stand each other from pre-school to sixth grade. They'd argue and exchange insults every time they were in the same space. It was pack sessions on sight from the time they became neighbors and even while they were lovers. Somewhere along the way, they'd grown to find that with aging came evolution and they didn't look at each other the same. Out of nowhere, it was like some Jojo, 'Homeboy' unofficial video played out. Suddenly, attraction came and sex came thereafter. And there she found the cliché, you can't fully love anyone else until you heal your heart.

Even as she penned him a heartfelt letter of forgiveness, she realized she wasn't heartbroken because he broke off their engagement, she was heartbroken because he chose to end their friendship too. She would have been okay not marrying him and still having him as a friend if that was what he needed to cope, but he completely abandoned her like they were never friends before the romance came. Deep down she still considered him an estranged friend. It was crazy to her but as she wrote she realized that she still regarded him as one of her best friends and she still trusted him with her secrets, her fears and her goals. She didn't know if it was because he'd literally had all of her and she felt safe even though she was overly exposed; like the kind of naked Ella Mai sings about on that amazing bonus track. There was no part of her that he hadn't met. Now that he was gone, it was hard for her to share that same nakedness with anyone else, especially a man she loved because, what if he ran for the hills just like Darrell? She didn't hate Darrell like Rue, Kellz and Tracy did, she couldn't. They'd shared too much. But she knew she needed to stand up from the place she currently occupied in grief.

Phoenix put her pen down and looked over the four-page letter she'd penned to her past lover. She'd left it all on the page. Without anything left to ponder and no desire to sleep alone for yet another night, she decided to do something she only did on the cusp of a new year. Pulling herself up from the fetal position she'd assumed after setting aside her notebook, she ventured into her room. With each step, she winced in pain. Her feet and ankles had become swollen and sore. It was literal agony to carry her child, but it was a pain she wouldn't trade for the world. Though she failed to tell him, she was proud that she got to bestow Blaise with the title he'd always deemed the most important. She touched her stomach as she felt the baby kick. Her inability to sleep had finally woken the baby from their slumber, and she sucked air through her teeth. Now that the kicking had commenced, there was no way she was going to get any sleep.

Once in her room, she walked over to her closet and pulled out a beautifully carved, antique letterbox. It had elegant gold etchings with a custom white marble rendering of her likeness as she wrote on an antique typewriter. Running her fingers over the engraving, she smiled.

"Love makes your soul crawl out from its hiding place," Phoenix spoke out loud.

It was her favorite quote from her favorite author. As she recalled how much Blaise had made her confront her demons, she nodded to the sky and shook her index finger. It was painfully clear that she indeed was madly in love with Blaise Jones, M.D. He was her person, and she knew no amount of running, ducking, and dodging would erase that fact.

"Zora, girl, you were on to something."

Plopping down on the edge of her bed, she clutched the box to her chest. The letters inside weren't intended to be seen by her eyes again until it was time to burn them. There was still 4 months left before she was supposed to have her annual holiday bonfire for one. Every year on Christmas she took the time to write her loved one's letters. Phoenix didn't know the day nor the hour when she would cease to walk with her loved ones in the flesh. She wanted to leave them a sweet reminder that would help them deal with the grief caused by her departure from her current form. She wanted to do something that would bring them comfort, encouragement, and love during their time of loss. She desired to give them one last piece of her that would let them know she felt all the love they gave, and it was enough to sustain her. In turn, she would love and watch them from her home over in glory until they met again.

Every Christmas, she'd burn the previous year's letters in a bonfire before she sat by the water and wrote their new letters for the coming year. She kept each letter filed away in the box with the recipient's name elegantly written in a thin calligraphy script. There were 7 recipients in total: Rue, Trav, Kaleigh, Bronx, Kellz, Tracy, and even her Aunt Phae, who she hadn't spoken to since her parents died. That night, she felt the sudden urge to add 3 more recipients to the collection: Blaise, Forge and her unborn baby. There was a gnawing feeling chomping away at the sheep she so desperately wanted to count. But an even more persistent feeling urged her to write the letters before she closed her eyes.

Pulling out 3 sheets of the hand-made vintage papers she'd made while binge-watching Living Single during her time confined to her sister's guest room. She smiled as she remembered the day she sat in bed with a wooden serving tray and the supplies. She made a mess of the entire bed and tried her best to clean up before they came home, but her efforts fell short. Her laughter filled the room as she recalled crying because she couldn't really help them clean up the water on the floor because her body was weak from her recent hospital stay. The deckled cotton paper had been made from old scraps of paper from her sister's pattern box. She'd aged them with RIT dye and deckled the edges with water and a wooden block from Trav's wood scraps pile. She loved that her sister and brother both had craft hobbies because during the first stages of her diagnosis when she could barely move, they made sure she had something to keep her occupied while they were away from the house. Grabbing the glass-dipped fountain pen and inkwell set from the nightstand on Blaise's side of the bed, she began writing all that she wanted to say to them. The spare key was included with her insurance documents and living will so that the letters would be located when the time came.

As she penned the closing to her baby's letter, she sat the materials on the nightstand and curled up on his side of the bed. She hugged the button up and inhaled deeply. Faint traces of lemongrass and palo santo fused with the warm, comforting scent of vanilla. The aromatic sensation of sandalwood lulled her as she begged for sleep to come. Her baby tossed and turned, before finally giving its final flutter kicks before she assumed they were asleep.

Her eyes flickered before slowly closing as a smile formed in the corn of her mouth. Sleep was finally making her acquaintance. As she drifted off to the place where dreams were had, her father's words to her after her first heartbreak echoed in her ears. She finally understood when he meant love was no respecter of person, it affected everyone. She knew what he meant when he said she needed to learn to heal from heartbreak because it would not be the last time she met it.

The thing she realized about healing was that the shit hurt before it would feel warm and wholesome. She understood why people chose not to heal because straight out the gate, it was rough. There was this misconception that healing only required a desire to improve and a few trips to the spa or gym or couch of a billed-by-the-hour therapist. But she knew firsthand that was the farthest thing from the truth. Healing wholly required grit, willpower, strength, and time.

Time was essential in healing thoroughly so that she never had to feel slighted by the situation ever again. There were no shortcuts to proper healing. It took her nearly three years to understand ignoring or working through her heartbreak was not going to heal her. She needed to do the hard work to get everything she felt out of her system. Filling those four pages was her final step. She'd spent a few hours crying 15 gallons of tears and sat in absolute darkness for what felt like days. Healing wholly required her to be completely still and shut the world out.

What she discovered on her own was that while heartbreak hurts; the depth of the hollowed-out spot was directly related to the culprit and her connection to them. It determined the intensity of her pain, the vulnerability of her existence. There were some people who cut her and hadn't even scratched the surface of her heart. She didn't feel anything besides the sting of a paper cut. Then there were those who dug a little deeper, opening her foreskin just enough for her blood to trickle a few drops. But then there was that select few who had the ability to expose her bleeding heart to the earth's elements, those were the ones that constricted the blood flow and caused her heart to stop beating for anybody else. She realized that romantic connections weren't the only ones capable of making a million cuts in the heart like the devil's star with one betrayal. True intimacy was the only criteria needed to invoke the God-forsaken ordeal and she was guilty of breaking Blaise's heart not because they were romantically involved but because he trusted her with the most intimate parts of him and she abandoned him.

Phoenix felt the tears coming as she thought about her and Blaise's thing ending. She'd always called it a thing because it wasn't ever given a proper title and honestly she didn't think a title existed for what they shared. No matter how brief, it was transcending. She'd always called it their thing and honestly wasn't sure she even cared what he called it. It was a thing, a highly intimate and overtly special thing to her, but still a thing. However, thing or not, he had a power over her emotions that she never even felt creeping in. Without a second thought, she sat up in bed and held her head in her hands. She needed to fix what she'd single-handedly broken. She needed to restore what she'd squandered.

Stretching to the left, she snatched up her phone. The bright light illuminated the darkness as she groaned at the ungodly hour displayed on the screen. He was most likely just about to end his shift at the ER. After unlocking her phone, she scrolled her call log until she found his name. Her heart sank at how far back she had to scroll, and she wanted to die a thousand deaths for letting so much time pass before she reached out. After ringing twice, he declined her FaceTime call. So, she tried again with the same result. Opting to call instead, she was met with his voicemail.

"Hey, Blaise, I get it. I'm the last person on the planet you probably want to talk to, but I've been thinking about you...about us. There's a million things I want to say, but the most important thing is that I love you, and I'm sorry."

Phoenix tossed her phone to the side and fell back onto her pillow. Her baby had just started kicking again and this time, she didn't even blame them. She'd subjected them to a whole night of unrest and discomfort. Closing her eyes, she massaged her belly until her baby calmed down. Sleep wasn't coming before the sunrise so she stopped forcing it and took the time to pray to God about what she really wanted out of the rest of her life.

CHAPTER FOURTEEN

PHOENIX'S BODY ROLLED FROM ONE SIDE OF HER BED TO THE OTHER. IT HAD been two weeks since she left Blaise a voicemail. Her days were spent writing and researching how lupus might affect the final months of her pregnancy. As she got closer to the date the doctors scheduled her C-section, she became more and more nervous. Her anxiety was high, and all she thought about was how alone she would be for the entire process.

Hugging her pillow, she cried silently. This was not how she imagined life would be for her when she had her first child. She thought she'd be the lead anchor on a cable network news outlet, married to a supportive and protective husband and in the prime of her life. Instead, she was a single, freelance journalist with a deadly disease. Where she should have been folding onesies and packing her hospital bag, she spent her time making sure her affairs were in order just in case she died during the delivery. She was terrified and there was only one person who could soothe her fears and ease her worries.

Reaching out her hand, she touched the spot where his body should have been. She was angry with herself for ruining the best relationship she'd ever had. Being in bed alone suddenly felt foreign to her. For the seven months she spent with Blaise, sleeping the night away knowing he was beside her had easily become her favorite part. Sleeping alone for so long made her forget how much more comforting a warm body was compared to the three body pillows she currently curled up with each night.

Lying flat on her back, she looked down at her protruding belly. Since finally coming to terms with what was about to happen, talking and reading to her baby became the highlight of her day. With everyone else giving her space or simply not speaking to her, she used that time to tell her baby all about her. From stories about her childhood to her rebellious teen years, she told her baby every story that made her the woman she was today.

Instead of fighting to fall asleep, she ventured downstairs. Trudging in her slippers she flicked on lights as she made her way to the kitchen. After she'd checked her sugar, she satisfied her craving for lemon-iced cookies. Taking her snack to the entertainment room, she turned on Martin for a good laugh. Finally finishing her binge, she scrolled for something else to occupy her time. Both she and the baby weren't going to sleep for at least another hour, so she kicked her feet up, got comfy, rubbed her belly, and watched another episode of *The Originals*. Like clockwork, she yawned at midnight and returned to her room. Sleep never came before then for her. Insomnia was the worst, and she knew it was because she was having separation anxiety from Blaise. She hadn't slept well since she ghosted him. The night was progressing, and she was simply watching the sky.

"I miss your Daddy, little one." She sighed as she glanced over at the clock on her table.

2:53. He's probably out cold after his shift, she thought as she grabbed her phone from the pillow beside her head. Before she could talk herself out of it, she mustered up the gull to send the message she'd wanted to send for the past month.

Phoenix: Can't sleep. Can I come over?

Blaise: ...

Blaise: No.

Without even fighting them, Phoenix sighed heavily as tears streamed down her ears and onto her pillow. Rolling to her side, she slowly extended her arm to place her phone back on the charging plate. The shakiness of her fingers caused her phone to hit the floor. Her cries grew louder when she heard the screen crash against the hardwood. The sound reverberated through the silence piercing her ears. The two-letter response was bone-chilling and unnerving. She expected him to be angry, but that text was just mean. Mean just wasn't ever a thought when it came to Blaise. She knew she'd ruined him for the next woman. How could she be so damn scary, afraid to just let a man love her. It seemed easy enough in theory, but it was difficult to put into practice when your heart took so long to recover from its last heartbreak.

Since the day they met he'd been attentive, compassionate and understanding. He took whatever she was willing to give and never pressured her for more. But his *no* pierced her in a way she couldn't recover from. The finality of it made her regret ever showing up on that breezy spring evening. She'd broken her vow and now she was stewing in misery; physically aching because she couldn't seem to get out of her own head.

Thirty minutes of massaging her belly and crying into her pillow finally lulled her enough to fall asleep. She was grateful for the time she'd taken off from her job because there was no way she'd be able to come up with a creative concept with mental and emotional anguish burning a hole in her heart. Thirty minutes of peace was all she was given. Just as she'd gotten comfortable with the two body pillows on either side of her, a steady knocking at her door jolted her from her sleep.

Groggily, she whined to her baby bump as she threw her blanket off her body. Slowly, she slid to the edge of her bed thinking the visitor would realize the error in their ways and bounce. It was about four hours before the sun was scheduled to make its appearance and every soul in Solace Point was still asleep. There was only one person she knew to be out and about at this ungodly hour. But even she knew, bothering anyone else was just tasteless. With the assistance of her guardrail, she slid into her slippers as she threw her robe over her camisole and Blaise's boxers, she left her bedroom and made her way down the long corridor that separated her bedroom from the stairs. old-fashioned house.

One step after the other, she descended the stairs thinking of all the ways to curse a soul to hell. Waking anyone from their sleep was cruel but waking a pregnant woman who had just cried her eyes out was cruel and unusual and deserved an equally cruel and unusual punishment. As she reached the door, her heart stopped. There he stood in all his glory. Sure, the frosted glass concealed his features, but she'd studied his physique long enough to spot her man even through a frosted window and the faint glow of her porch light.

Large, hail-sized droplets spilled from her tear ducts as she fumbled with the door. She could barely find the lock through the flood of tears that wouldn't let up. Taking a second to compose herself, she bent down and rested her forehead on her hand that secured the doorknob. Cupping her belly, she remained bent, crying into the sleeve of her robe. After crying all she could cry, she stood and unlocked the door.

Blaise casually leaned up against the doorpost, picking imaginary dirt from under his index finger. Gradually his low eyes cut toward her. He pushed off the wall to take all of her in as her pregnant body blocked the entryway. He'd be lying to himself if he thought she looked anything less than heavenly in her white silk robe. The moon's glow shined on her, blocking out her features, but the lamp in the vestibule created an angelic backlighting. She was perfect in all her imperfect, over-thinking glory. From the crown of her head to the soles of her feet, he eyed her. He was beyond tired and didn't know what made him jump out of his warm, lulling bed to drive 30 minutes across town to get her, but he had, and now, there was nowhere else he'd rather be.

Seven minutes of silence passed before Phoenix moved from the doorway to grant him entry. He hadn't even looked in her eyes one time and that crushed her, but she silently coached herself to keep from pouring out any more tears. She watched as he shut the door and headed toward her stairs. By the time she reached the stairs, he had disappeared to the second level of her house.

Phoenix knew he was pissed. It was evident in his silent treatment, so she opted to bypass the stairs and go to the kitchen for a glass of water. Her throat was dry from all the hard breathing she'd done trying to control her crying long enough to fall asleep. She needed a moment to think because it was on her to initiate the dialogue. After all, she had been the one who just halted what they were building without so much as a conversation.

"When you're finished, put these on, lock up, and meet me in the truck," Blaise demanded without giving her a chance to object.

Phoenix jumped at the sound of his voice as her water missed her mouth and trickled down her chin. Confusion set in as she looked up at him. He had her suitcase and carry-on bag beside him on the floor and a sweatsuit sat folded on the countertop. His scowl was damn near permanent as he stared her down. She had no idea what was going through his mind, so she slowly sat her glass down and let her unfastened robe fall to the kitchen floor. Reaching across the counter, she pulled the clothes to her and began getting dressed. Once he saw she had begun to comply with his demand, he picked up her luggage and started for the door.

"I thought you hated me," she whispered.

Stopping in his tracks, he turned in her direction. His head tilted and his eyes squinted as he surveyed the woman of his world. Shaking his head, he chuckled under his breath. She had him all over the place emotionally. He was hot with her, enraged at her inability to allow anyone to bear her life's challenges with her. But the love he felt for her overpowered all of those emotions.

As much as he wanted her to feel an ounce of what he was feeling, he loved her too much to watch her fall apart because of his silence. Her puffy, bloodshot eyes and the loud crying he listened to before she opened the door let him know she was hurting. She'd learned her lesson and had suffered enough mentally. There was no need to subject her to even more guilt.

"I could never hate you; believe me, I've tried. You disappointed me, and for that, I don't fucking like you at the moment, but I could never hate you. Now, hurry up. I'm tired as shit."

The drive to Blaise's house was uneventful. Phoenix's light snoring joined nature's chorus as Blaise enjoyed the breeze that flowed through his cracked window. He was beyond exhausted after muddling through patient appointments all day and ending the night with a benefit fundraiser for the hospital. But he was going to get his woman. She was just as much a remedy for him as he was for her. Sleep had become just as hard for him and as it had for her, and he didn't deserve insomnia. He'd been devoted to her for months and this time would be no different, no matter how consumed with disappointment she made him.

Arriving at his house in a fraction of the time it took to reach hers' he parked his truck and looked over at her as she slept. The position of the seatbelt drew his eyes to her stomach. Her six-month baby bump was a sight to see. He'd expressed to his mother how robbed he felt every time he thought about Phoenix carrying his child without him knowing. He couldn't dote on her how he imagined or tell her how appreciative he was that she was giving him the highest title he'd ever have. Here she was looking like she could pop at any moment, and he'd only found out because her desire to conceal her pregnancy from everyone who loved her was worth more than her or her baby's life.

Raising his hand, he stretched his arm across the middle console and palmed her belly. Instantly, little flutter kicks met the center of his hand, causing a single tear to fall from his eye. This was surreal. He was actually going to be someone's daddy. He was granted the opportunity to be all the man his father was for him, his mother and sister for Phoenix and their child. His eyes darted up at the feel of Phoenix's palm over his. Between his baby's kicks and her soft hand, he was emotionally spent.

Needing to put some space between them, he recoiled his hand and cut the engine on the truck. Hopping out, he rounded the vehicle and opened her door. As he helped her out, the sweet smell of vanilla calmed his anger as he felt it building in his chest all over again. Hand-in-hand, they took the short walk up to his porch and she sat in the porch swing and closed her eyes again as he fumbled with the keys. The sun was just beginning to peek over the tall trees that lined his driveway. It was beautiful and was a direct indication that they would be alright. With one arm, he swooped Phoenix from the swing and helped her inside. They made it to a guest room, and he helped her get comfortable. He couldn't sleep next to her yet, but he needed to feel her presence, just like she needed to feel his.

"Really, Blaise, the guest room?"

Smoke blared from her ears as she stood with her hand on her hip. Her eyes rolled toward the back of her head as she threw daggers in his direction.

Unfazed, he continued down the hall to his room. Once behind the door, his hands ran down the length of his face. His bedroom was his sanctuary like her parlor was hers. He never tainted it with bad vibes or sour moods. His and Phoenix's situation was full of both at the present time and his room was not the place either of them would store or unleash those feelings. After changing into his pajama bottoms, he grabbed her favorite pillow from his bed and walked down the hall.

A smile spread across his face when he returned to see her fast asleep in nothing but his night shorts. Pride entered his whirlpool of feelings knowing that just being in his midst helped her sleep better. The effect his presence had on her was endearing and boast-worthy.

Gently, he lifted her head and tucked the pillow under her horizontally so that her head, and shoulders both rested atop it. Then he slid in beside her and pulled her close.

"I love you, Blaise."

"I know. Now go to sleep." He kissed her temple and wrapped his arm under her belly.

Morning had easily come without either Blaise or Phoenix acknowledging it. Sleep hadn't been a friend to them in weeks and the calm they gave to each other was sorely missed. Blaise's alarm sounded throughout the house, causing him to finally stir. It was time for him to prepare for another afternoon at the office.

He glanced over at Phoenix who had rolled on her side hours ago. Smoothing her hair from her face, he kissed her forehead and rolled out of the bed they shared. For a few seconds, he forgot he was angry with her, but as he stood up and looked down at her frame indenting his memory foam mattress, evidence of her betrayal peeked from under the blanket.

Bending down, he planted a soft kiss on her bare baby bump and shook his head. He'd never be able to erase the initial shock of finding out she was both sick and pregnant. He wanted to feign like he didn't know the beautiful woman who had captivated every synapse of his mind, but that would be a far cry from the truth. He knew her, in fact finding out her truth made him recognize her even more. He knew her struggle and why she chose to hide her condition. It mirrored the same notion of his mother when he was ten years old, suffering through a cancer diagnosis in silence to spare everyone else.

Blaise entered his master bathroom and immediately started the multiple showerhead system he'd installed a few weeks prior. As he took his morning piss, he pressed his temple against the arm that steadied him on his feet. The feel of the cool marble under his feet and the warm steam that blanketed the bathroom soothed his raging temper.

This was love, it had to be. No other person in the world had the power to alter his demeanor the way that she had. It was exactly like his parents described it and he hated this part of it. One thing he always appreciated from his parents was their honesty about real love and the challenges that stretched and strengthened it. This was definitely a stretching phase for him. The restraint and regard he showed Phoenix was a clear indication of his ability to forgive for love's sake.

After going through his pre-shower routine—trimming his goatee, brushing his teeth, and washing his face, he stepped into the shower. The heat centered him. Turning his eyes toward the ceiling, he allowed the steady flow of water to touch each part of his body and level out his mood. After standing under the hot stream of water for nearly thirty minutes, he finally lathered his washcloth and scrubbed every inch of his 6-foot frame, rinsing and repeating before changing the scorching temperature of the water to warm. He massaged an in-shower moisturizer that Phoenix made all over his freshly washed skin before exiting the shower. Soft music flowed under the bathroom door and soothed the parts of him that the water couldn't touch. She was awake. He closed his eyes and sighed.

Blaise was greeted by Phoenix's belly before any other part of her came into his view as he rounded the corner and entered the master bedroom. She was leaning against the post at the foot of his bed. Her skin glowed under the dim lighting, and he had to admit motherhood made her even more beautiful than he could remember. Light radiated from her being and he had to admit to himself, he loved the view.

The hurt he felt behind her actions subsided a little more every time he looked at her protruding belly. But he was not granting her the privilege of knowing that. She didn't deserve his attention, not yet anyway.

Without acknowledging her presence, he turned and proceeded to his walk-in closet to find some threads to cover his limbs so he could put some more distance between them. He could feel her follow him inside. The nervousness was apparent as she took slow, deliberate steps to reach him.

"I'm sorry, B. I should have told you.

Phoenix whispered as she slid her arms around his waist. He closed his eyes, his teeth breaking the skin on the inside of his jaw. From side to side, he shook his head, releasing the hot air that built up in his chest. He ignored her voice and her touch as he continued thumbing through his three piles of chinos.

He wasn't going to dignify her admission of guilt with a response. She needed to keep talking because so far all she'd done was state the obvious. He wanted her; needed her to confess it all. He needed to hear why she felt like not telling him anything was the best thing for either of them. There was a deeper reason and the bullshit excuse of them not dating long was not cutting it for him. It was surface-level, grade A horse shit, and certainly not a perfect fertilizer for their relationship. If she expected him to forgive her or for them to grow through this, she needed to bring out the real.

"I was just angry at myself. I never thought I'd meet the one. The one person who could turn my life around. Who could make me see the light in looming darkness. Who could lift my spirits just by gazing at me. Who saw me, all of me and still loved me for all that I was...and wasn't. So, I ran and try to do it all alone. But then you came along, and I wasn't ready. I wasn't ready to experience the kind of love my mama used to tell me stories about when she tucked me in. I wasn't ready to mean the world to a man that wasn't the one who kissed my booboos and scared off the neighborhood beaus. I wasn't ready for the one, I wasn't ready for you.

Blaise stopped his wardrobe browsing as she whispered her truth into the space around them. Pride boasted in his chest knowing he'd made her believe in love. Most of what she said mirrored his own thoughts about their accidental romance. He was just as much shocked by the level of intimacy she pulled from his depths as she was about his ability to make her see a different path for her life. They were both blinded by the lives they'd planned for themselves and the steps they needed to take to make sure everything they wanted, they could obtain.

“When I moved here, I had already made a vow to myself to keep my head down, get healthy and get back to my life. And I had kept that vow without much effort. Then you, you came in and you... you watched me. You learned me, and you sent me my favorite drink. One sip. One sip was all it took for the parts of me that were locked away to be unleashed.

“Then you sent me my favorite plant and your gesture took root in my heart. That was the moment I loved you. I should have backed off then.”

Blaise closed his eyes as she paused in her confession. He knew it was hard for her to be this vulnerable, but she needed to get it out, not just because he wanted her to, but because she was holding herself back from all that life had for her. He fought the urge to turn and face her. He knew if he gazed into her eyes, there was a possibility she’d clam up and stop bearing her soul to him. He needed to hear it all. He needed to ensure she trusted him with her vulnerability and sensitivity. He needed to make sure she understood he was her refuge and her safe haven. But his love for her caused he to let those urges win. Giving her his full attention, he turned and stood frozen in place, waiting for her to finish.

“I should have returned your gift and steered clear, but for once I felt like my heart had finally got it right, so I gave us a chance. I didn't want to love you, and I tried with everything in my power not to, because I didn't want you to love and lose to love. I didn't expect to wind up pregnant, I honestly thought I couldn't get pregnant. And when I did, I was scared, confused, and unsure of what life would look like going forward.

Even still, I should have told you because you had a right to know. I should have told you because I know you love me; you've shown it every second since the day I met you. I should have trusted you enough with my heart to know you wouldn't fumble it. But I was afraid because I did trust someone enough before and he fumbled that shit so bad we lost to love. I lost to love, and I never want to feel that again."

Blaise blew out a big breath of air. All he ever asked was for her to be real with him. And it took for them to go through all this for her to tell him the truth. His silence pained her. Phoenix pressed her forehead to his chest. He felt her hot tears stream down his freshly washed skin and his heart instantly dropped to the pit of his stomach. She wrapped her arms around his waist and pressed her cheek to his shoulder. Desperately she wanted him to hug her back or say something, but he just stood there, his arms at his side. The even rising and falling of his chest let her know he wasn't angered by her admission, but she still wanted him to say it. She needed to hear him verbally reassure her that they would be okay, that they were in this together and that he wasn't going to dip on her when shit got hard.

Pulling her up by her shoulders, he lifted her chin and his heart broke. She looked defeated, like life had royally whipped her ass and she was holding onto the ropes. She'd finally let all that shit that was holding them back go. He'd wanted to fix the broken parts of her for so long, but for just as long she'd prevented him from even seeing the pieces. He never had to live with a debilitating illness, so he'd never pretend to understand what she went through every day. He'd seen patients fight every day, so he knew it was a hard road and could sometimes be an extremely lonely one. As he pulled her into his frame, he reassured her he wasn't going anywhere.

"Babe, you ain't ever gotta worry about losing love again. I'm not going anywhere. Nothing you can go through will ever make me leave you. What type of fucking man would I be if I left you at your lowest? I'm sorry you had to experience that fuck boy nature, but this is as real as it gets. I'm as real as it gets. It's going take more than an illness you never asked for to get me to leave you alone. You stuck with me. I told you that it was us since I sent you that note. I been applying pressure, and I'mma keep applying pressure when it comes to you. You're it for me, you hear me?"

Blaise wiped her eyes and cupped her face. He searched her eyes to make sure she wasn't holding onto anything else. Once he was sure she'd spilled the remnants of her reservations, he pressed his lips to hers and breathed life back into her. He watched as her eyes softened and the tears slowed up. Wrapping his arms around her neck, he deepened his kiss. It had been a few months since he got to feel up on his boo and he was three seconds from canceling his appointments for the day and laying up with her, but he refrained.

"You're staying here for a few weeks. And I'm not tryna hear any of those excuses you love to pull out your ass."

"But—"

"But shit. I'll stop by your spot on my way home to grab whatever you need for work, just text me a list."

“I’m actually on leave from work until after the baby comes. My doctors thought it was best. But I do have to...”

“I’ll water the plants and check your mail. Now what else you got because I got a counter for allum?"

"Nothing. I got nothing else. I'll see you when you get home."

"That's what I like to hear. If you plan on sleeping the rest of the day away, let me know what's up for dinner now?"

"I'll cook. Haven't done it in a while, and I love your kitchen."

"Good, then you won't mind being hauled up in here until you drop that load you've been toting around."

Blaise shot his last comment over his shoulder as he grabbed a pair of pants and made his way over to the shirts. He knew she was about to object to that. The most Phoenix ever stayed at his place was three days, but this time she had no choice. She'd denied him six months and the last three were non-negotiable. What she chose to do after she gave birth could be decided once that time came, but until then, he made the rules. There was no way he was letting her venture back to her house alone, knowing her kidneys were in piss poor shape and she was carrying his child. They both needed his medical knowledge and his help, whether she would admit it or not.

"I'm not staying here for eight weeks."

"Eight weeks? You're not due for another twelve."

"They're taking him early, you know... because of all the complications and stuff."

"What complications?"

The bass in his voice caused her to jump. He checked himself immediately because he forgave her. Forgiveness meant dealing with whatever fruit fell from that shaken tree. They'd need to have a real conversation about her pregnancy when he returned from the hospital, but for now, he needed to practice extending grace. He wasn't perfect, and at some point in their relationship, he was sure he'd require an extension of grace from her, so he did just that. With a deep breath, he closed his eyes and asked again, with less frustration in his tone.

"I apologize for yelling. I didn't mean for it to come out like that. I'm just a lil' frustrated with all this. What complications?"

"It's nothing serious," Phoenix continued before he had a chance to bombard her with any more questions.

"Phoenix, you're talking to a doctor. They don't just schedule C-sections before your due date if it's nothing serious."

Phoenix sat on the edge of the bed. There was so much they needed to discuss. Every time she thought about it, she regretted her choice to keep the baby a secret. It was stupid, juvenile, and only made everything tense with them. She blew out a breath because she knew her life was about to be turned upside down.

Blaise exited the closet and made his way over to his charging dock. Confused at the empty base, he spun in circles, his eyes darting back and forth, looking for his cell. Remembering he'd picked her up in the middle of the night, he ventured to the guest room to look there. Frustration heightened once he didn't see the phone on the dock in that room either. Grabbing his keys from the dresser, he flew down the stairs two at a time and out the front door. Once inside his truck, he snatched his cell out of the console and pressed a few buttons until he was starting a group video call with his mom, sister, and Roddy.

"Nigga, this better be serious, it's my day off and you hitting my line before noon," Roddy came through rubbing his eyes.

"Roddy, don't make me have to get in my car. You're not too old to get your ass whipped up and down one of them lil' dirt roads," Mrs. Jones chastised. "Now, Baby, why are you waking everybody up at the crack of dawn?"

"Ma, you've probably been up and to the farmer's market by now," J.J laughed.

"Heyyy, J.J. When are you coming to visit your brother so I can take your fine ass out for a night on the town," Roddy flirted with J.J., once he realized she was also on the video call.

"My very married ass is coming to visit my baby bro whenever he extends the invite and mommy volunteers to babysit."

"You haven't divorced that square yet," Roddy teased.

"Now that y'all are done with the morning report, can I get a word in? I initiated this call," Blaise asked, redirecting the conversation back to the matter at hand.

"C'mon boy, talk. It's Thursday and Janice is picking me up in twenty minutes for Thrifty Seniors Day at our favorite thrift store. We gotta be first in line to get the really good stuff."

"Phoenix is here. She said some shit about them taking the baby early. Ma, I need you. Can you get on a plane tomorrow if I get you a ticket? J.J, I just need you to promise to take care of the house for Mommy. Not sure when she'll be back yet."

"Sure, Son. I'll call Janice and tell her to go without me so I can pack some things and write your sister up some lists."

"Lists? Ma, you have been in the same house for the last 36 years. I think I know how to keep up with your day-to-day life."

"Chile—,"Vivian started.

"Roddy, I need you to get your OB fling to squeeze us in. Anytime, I'll push back my appointments if I need to. Those white boys might be on some fu—, sorry Ma. But they might not be doing the best for her, I don't trust it."

"Will do, bro. She usually doesn't take patients on Tuesday or Thursday, but she'll see her for me. Are her records at SG?"

"Yea, I think I have some prior authorization forms on my desk. I'll get her to sign them when I go back inside so she can get the records from her rheumatologist, PCP, and current OB."

The sound of Phoenix opening the passenger side door made him look up. He extended his hand and let her use it as an anchor to climb up. He made a mental note to head to the dealership on his next day off. He'd need to get running boards mounted and a handrail added on the side panel so she wouldn't be doing aerobics just to get up in his truck. Once she was safely in her seat, he turned his attention back to his group video call.

"Bro, she just hit me back. She has three speaking engagements today, but she can get y'all in before her last one. She said to be in her office at 3:15. She's in the East Wing pavilion, on the 5th floor."

"Good looking, Bro. I owe you one."

"Nah, if it's a boy, just name him after me," Roddy joked before exiting the call.

Blaise could sense Phoenix was about to start asking questions, so he shoved his phone in her face instead. She rolled her eyes before smiling at his mom and sister. They'd met her virtually and were thrilled Blaise finally found a keeper. They laughed and teased him often about how up in arms he got about her. In all the years he'd been bringing random flavors of the semester home during the holidays, they could tell she was the first one he really took seriously.

"How's my grandbaby baking in there?"

"Ma, I really hate when you say that. You act like our wombs are confectionery ovens or something."

"The way you and Charles pop them out, you'd think your womb was an easy bake oven."

Everyone in earshot laughed, including J.J's children. She and her mother always went at it about something that would be deemed cringey in today's society. This time was just like any other, light-hearted and full of laughs. Phoenix loved that Mrs.

Jones could serve pack sessions like she was still in her prime and only dreamed she'd be just as free-spirited when she reached her age.

"She's fine. She's been a little inactive since I've been up, but I'm sure as soon as I get some food, she'll be a live wire. She really gets crunk when I'm ready to take it in for the night."

"So, you're saying she; have we considered names?"

"No names. We don't know the gender yet. I just alternate the pronouns," Phoenix said. "When I'm talking to my sister or my friends I say she, and when I talk to Blaise, I say he. I don't care what I have as long as they are healthy."

"Go see about getting my baby love some food. I'll see you tomorrow."

"Tomo—"

"Okay, Ma. I'll call you later with all your flight info. Love you to infinity, J.J."

"And beyond, Booda."

Phoenix looked over at him questioningly. Handing him his phone, she shifted her weight in the seat. It was a little struggle turning to face him and after two minutes, she gave up altogether. Rolling her eyes up to the sunroof, she sighed loudly. It was unbeknownst to her what he had up his sleeve, but she was going to pry until he told her.

"So, your mom's coming to town?"

"Yea and she's staying until you're good."

"I'm good now. She really doesn't have to come to make a fuss over me. I have Rue, Forge, and you. The nursery has already been converted into a nursery."

"Phoenix listen to yourself. You haven't even moved in your house yet and your stuff has been there for damn near three years."

"Yes, I am. Rue, Trav, and the girls helped me finish everything a few months ago."

“Oh, you mean, the months you shut me out?”

“I'm not apologizing again.”

“And I’m not asking you to, but I am asking you to let me help you. You’re not in this alone and you’re not the only parent.”

“I don’t want to argue. I’m just saying I have everything under control. You don't have to take her away from her life and make her come up here and be my caregiver. If you haven’t noticed, I already have quite a few."

"She was already planning to come once the baby was born. She was there for the first few weeks of each of my nieces’ and nephews’ lives. She wasn't gonna miss our child's."

"Blaise, this is unnecessary."

"No, it's not. You are not a fucking superwoman. You don’t have to try to do all this shit by yourself. You have people who want to help you, not because you need it, but because we genuinely give a fuck about you. Just let people help you. I gotta get to work and you're coming with me."

"I am capable of being alone while you’re at work.”

"You think I don't know you can do this alone? You made that shit perfectly clear for the last six months.”

“Shit isn't about how fucking strong and resilient you are Phoenix. You have an appointment at 3:15 with a new OB."

"I'm pretty sure you going behind my back and getting me another appointment is a violation of my HIPAA rights."

"As the fucking father, no the hell it isn't. Now bring your ass on before you make me late for my first patient."

“I think you are confused. I’m carrying a child; I am not a fucking child."

“Could have fooled me,” Blaise threw over his shoulder as he hopped out of the truck.

Blaise and Phoenix moved around his bedroom in silence. She felt like he was doing the absolute most and his antics were unnecessary. She stomped as she waddled around him while he sat at his desk in the adjacent home office. Plopping down on the loveseat that sat by the window, her breathing reeked with annoyance as she expelled hot air from her lungs. Briefly looking up from the screen, he chuckled. She was sexy when she was mad, and he knew the second he got her some tea and food her feelings would mellow out.

"Sign these," he instructed while standing over her with a pen and clipboard.

"What are you involuntarily committing me to?"

"Stop being so fucking dramatic. They are prior authorizations for the new OB to get your records. She's doing me a solid by seeing you today while her office is closed. If I can get these faxed over before we head out, she'll have all your medical records before we have to see her."

"Blaise, you're taking away my rights, and it's not fair."

"Neither was you playing keep-away with my baby. Life's not fair, and when it comes to my family I don't play fair. You casually told me that them white-ass doctors want to take our baby early and think I'm not going to get a second opinion. Sign the damn forms, Phoenix. Shit isn't up for debate."

Snatching the pen, she scribbled her signature on the forms. If this was a precursor to the type of father he would be, she needed the next few weeks to mentally prepare herself for it. He took hands-on to a whole new level. She wanted to complain to her sister or Forge, but they both were not seeing eye-to-eye with her where her pregnancy was concerned. Rue made it clear she was not getting involved with anything concerning her and Blaise. She made herself perfectly clear at dinner. Phoenix needed to grow up and act like the mother she was about to be. Forge was upset she hadn't listened to her and told him when she first found out. Both only agreed to help her set up the nursery because they knew if it was up to her the baby would be living like Tarzan, wearing philodendron leaves for diapers and sleeping in a hollowed-out tree stump. Outside of plants and rattan rockers, she didn't have an interior design bone in her body.

Phoenix was perplexed that people were angry with her for not having her hand out. They were pissed that she wasn't ringing their lines every ten minutes for help with something. She had no idea why she was like that. She never figured out the exact moment that she decided independence was her only way. It was just who she had always been, even before her parents passed away a few weeks before her fifteenth birthday. Independence just worked for her. She never had to worry about being disappointed because she would always have her own back and make sure all her needs were met. But she'd painfully realized, doing it all alone may have saved her from disappointment, but it did not stop her from disappointing the ones she loved most.

"Blaise, we need to find common ground. You can't just force me to stay here until you think it's best. You can't just go around disregarding the medical care I am already receiving. If you want to be a team, I'm all for it, but this is not how I want things to be."

"You haven't shown anybody that you can be a team player, Ms. I-N-D-E-P-E-N-D-E-N-T, and until you can exhibit some team qualities I don't wanna hear shit about a team falling from those pretty lips," Blaise said, pulling her against his frame and pressing his lips against hers.

"I knew loving you was a bad idea," she laughed as she kissed him back.

"Nah, loving me was the best idea you ever had. Not thinking I would love your ass just as much is where you fucked up."

Blaise kissed her again, this time palming her ass. Standing on her toes, she cupped his face and fed him her tongue. His hands explored all the places he missed. Phoenix backed him up until he fell back in the chair. Straddling his lap, she ran her hands up his chest, taking his tank top off in the process.

"Nope. You not finna get me caught up. Go get dressed," Blaise said, kissing her one more time.

Phoenix accompanied Blaise to his office without so much as small talk. She was too focused on keeping her pressure down. She thought a quickie might do the trick, but he shot her down. The afternoon's events had worked her up and her headache was a sure indicator that she had overdone it. The last thing she needed was for her vitals to be elevated while she was at her first appointment with him. He'd be sure to have waterfalls and televisions that looped meditation music installed in his house somewhere. She loved that he was so attentive and concerned, but she was aggravated with his macho antics. His big dick energy wasn't appealing at the moment, and she thought frankly he was just being a big dick to her because he was still upset. He'd told her he forgave her, but since his acceptance of her heartfelt and vulnerable apology, he'd mentioned the omission of her pregnancy at least five times. That wasn't the behavior of someone who had forgiven a transgression.

Lunchtime finally came around and he had brought her salad, a sandwich, and peppermint tea. Laying the food out on the corner table in his office, he blessed their food and began feeding her. She was reluctant but took his display of affection as a truce. There was no denying how much she missed him, missed them together like this. So, she opened her mouth and accepted the food he offered. A moan left her mouth as she savored the peppery warmth of the turkey sandwich.

Her mother always told her love was rare, and she should try her best to hold on to it when she chanced upon it. But all she'd done since meeting Blaise was squander their love away on what-ifs and what used to be. She never really gave him a chance and now was as good a time as any to right her wrongs. Now was the time for her to let him be what he had been trying to be to and for her since they met. She knew it was now or never and she wasn't about to lose him because she had a problem relinquishing a bit of her independence.

They spent lunchtime laughing and thinking of baby names. Up until that point she honestly had no idea what she was going to do once the baby was in her arms. Rue assured her it would come naturally, but she wasn't so sure. Though she kept Blaise in the dark, she wanted nothing other than him there with her through everything. She had no intentions on raising her child without him. She just had no idea how to break the news six months ago, and after three months, it was pretty much routine to dodge his calls and hideout at her house instead of showing up at the gardening classes they signed up for together or Noir Tea by Nature.

"What time is your next appointment?"

"I am done for the day. I was supposed to cover the ER tonight, but Roddy switched with me. So, I'm all yours after your appointment?"

"Good. We can sleep the rest of the day away. I feel like I haven't slept in weeks."

"That's because you wanted to wake up having heart-to-hearts at the crack of dawn."

"I didn't want you coming in here angry. Taking your frustration out on that nice receptionist out there."

"I'd never do that. I have been frustrated for the better part of three months and she never knew the difference."

"Okay, let that be the last time you mention my departure. I already have to live with what I did. I don't need you making me pay for it for the rest of our lives."

"Why? I got about three months of responses saved up. We got a lifetime to go. I'm sure you'll do something else to make me forget about this," he laughed before kissing her forehead, "I'm just playing babe, I'm done."

Phoenix looked across the table at the man she planned to spend the rest of her life with. She was content with him. He made her feel like she was the only girl in the world. When he looked at her, her world was alright; nothing mattered. With the back of her hand, she caressed his cheek. His head remained titled as he slanted his eyes up at her. A smile teased the corner of his mouth as he grabbed her hand. Gently, he planted a small kiss on her hand.

"I love you," Phoenix confessed breathlessly.

"And I love your ole scary ass more. Now, let's go see about our baby."

Phoenix laid back on the examination table with her arms wrapped around her belly. The hard gown Blaise helped her change into scratched her skin as she tried to focus on anything but the checkup she was about to have. It had only been three days since she'd last seen her own OB/GYN and here she was about to get a second opinion she never even wanted. Her nerves were all over the place and her baby's restlessness let her know that they sensed it too. She needed to focus on something other than the humming of the vent above Blaise's head if she was going to keep her pressure down enough for the nurse to do her vitals.

Blaise massaged her thigh as she felt it slightly shaking. She'd been subconsciously bouncing it for the last fifteen minutes and he wanted her to know she was not any of it alone. He would remain by her side. As he surveyed her from head to toe, he wondered what he had to do to get her to realize that he was for her and her only. There was nothing she could say or do that would make him love her any less. She had claimed his heart from the moment he saw her typing away on her iPad in her favorite booth at her favorite coffee shop. Smitten wasn't even strong enough a word to describe how he felt about her, and he prayed his presence would show her that in a way his words couldn't tell her.

"Don't go mute on me. Let me in," Blaise instructed her as he broke the comfortable silence that rested over them.

"Babe, I'm scared. I've been putting on a brave face, but I am terrified. I don't know what to expect."

Blaise's heart broke as he saw the terror in her eyes. Her tears pooled along her lower lids threatening to flood his heart with more anguish than he could stand to carry. He wanted to carry all of it for her. He wanted to polish his armor and slay all the intangible demons that plagued her pretty little mind. He wanted to strap up and have a shoot-out with her fears, sending them all back to the dark hole they slithered from. He wanted to erase all her pain and paint her life in shades of love and light. His only desire was to make up for the time he missed. Though it was her choice to shoulder the brunt of this alone, he wanted to step in and relieve her of her plight. He wanted to shoulder this side by side and make sure she felt safe and at peace for the remainder of her life. It didn't have to be hard, and he wanted her to know that he would do everything in his power to make it as easy as God allowed.

"I'm right here. Whatever we hear today, we're in this together. I'm right here. All in. Always, in all ways. There's nothing you can call on me for. You say the word and it's heard. You got it."

"I love you," Phoenix pronounced as she lifted his hand to her lips and kissed it.

"And I love you right the fuck back," he professed, pulling her head toward him.

He planted a gentle kiss on her forehead, and she closed her eyes. Holding on his wrist, she beckoned him to keep his lips pressed in their present spot. The warmth and softness of his full lips calmed her racing heart and sprinting mind. She needed to find a quiet place in the center of the chaos she'd been calling her life. As the doctor entered with her assistant, Blaise stood to greet them. With a one-arm embrace, he thanked Dr. Ruiz for agreeing to squeeze them into her busy schedule. He knew the fragile state of her and Roddy's on-again-off-again office romance, he was taking a shot in the dark with his request.

"So, let's see how our little one is growing in there," she said after she'd finished with the new patient formalities

"I spent the ride over from the airport going over your medical records and all the results your other physician sent over. I was told you like it straight up, no chaser. Is that true?" she asked Phoenix.

"Never been put that way before, but yea, that's the truth. I'm a straight shooter. Is our baby going to be okay if I carry them full term?"

"With your current health challenges, and the fragile state of your kidneys, the risk does increase the further along you are in your pregnancy. From the tests I've seen, there isn't anything at the moment that is sounding any alarms. I do want you to take it very easy. Now, I don't like forcing mothers on bedrest, because sometimes the anxiety of that alone is even more detrimental to the baby. But in your case, I will suggest you do only what's absolutely necessary."

"Which means nothing," Blaise finally interjected.

"Babe..."

"Nah, don't babe me on this one. You do a bunch of unnecessary shit."

"Blaise, don't be like that. You still want her active to some extent. It will aid in her labor."

"Define active to some extent for her because she'll be done rode her bike to Mars otherwise."

"Stop being so dramatic," Phoenix said, punching him in the arm as everyone in the room laughed.

"No climbing. No bike riding, either." Dr. Ruiz laughed. "Absolutely no lifting, and if you exercise, keep it to chair exercises only."

"Okay. You haven't said anything I can't adhere to yet."

"What about work?" Blaise asked.

Phoenix rolled her eyes as she cut them in her direction. She'd already told him she was on leave from work. She had no idea why he insisted on making the doctor reiterate things she already knew. More and more he showed her he was going to play the overbearing hen role in this parenthood thing. She needed to find some common ground. She needed to come up with a way to show him that she was capable of taking care of their child, even before they officially met them.

"It depends on what it entails. From your report, it looks like you pretty much make your schedule. So, I'm not too concerned there."

"I'm already on leave. I'll only be writing freelance pieces until the baby comes. My work is really light right now. So, there won't be any levels of stress."

Dr. Ruiz ran down her suggested care plan for Phoenix. Everything was easy for Phoenix except the weekly blood draws and increased glucose testing. Being pregnant had her spending much more time in the hospital than she ever did since her diagnosis. Once she was left alone to redress, she sat, taking in everything said during the visit.

Blaise gathered her dress and shoes while she ripped off the itchy hospital gown. Using an antibacterial wipe, he cleaned the excess gel from her stomach, before bending and planting a kiss just below her navel. The sun-kissed colored stretched marks artfully etched across her sepia-tinted skin reminded him of his grandmother's Kintsugi collection. Each mark represented the physical, mental, and emotional stretching of her being to usher in new life. She was his queen and silently he'd planned to make sure she knew that for the rest of her life.

"Do you feel a little at ease?"

"A little. I'm still scared, but no longer terrified. Thank you for forcing me to get a second opinion. I wouldn't have considered it without you," she said as she raised her arms above her head.

She allowed him to dress her and lead her to the checkout desk for Dr. Ruiz's assistant to give her all the orders she needed for her new standing appointments at the lab. There was an inherent level of fear that lingered, but she was hopeful that her pregnancy would result in a beautiful, healthy, full-term baby. Phoenix knew it was only because of Blaise's persistent, irresistible, and genuine love. Her life indeed was no crystal stair like Langston Hughes once said, but somehow he made living easier.

CHAPTER FIFTEEN

WITH A BOWL OF WHIPPED CREAM SMOTHERED PINEAPPLES, PHOENIX SAT crisscrossed on the floor in the baby's nursery watching Blaise put together the changing table. For the life of her, she couldn't figure out why she ever took so long to let him dote on her. He was even more the perfect gentleman now that he was an expecting father. There was nothing she requested that he hadn't obliged. One day she knew she would forgive herself for denying herself this level of love for so long, but for the moment, she just soaked it in. She laughed as he scratched his head for the millionth time while looking at the directions. There were about 50 pieces and 80 screws haphazardly placed around him.

Phoenix sat her bowl down and rolled to her side. She didn't know why she insisted on sitting her ass on the floor like it wasn't hell trying to get up. Once she had finally stood to her feet, she wobbled over to where he stood contemplating his next move. Gently, she ran her hands up his back and across his shoulders. She kissed his spine, then his arm. As she walked to stand in front of him, she intertwined her fingers with his, raising his hand to her lips and kissing each finger. Longingly, she looked up at the love of her life and silently thanked God for answering a prayer she never even sent up. There had to be someone somewhere praying on her behalf because lately, her prayers consisted of two things; giving birth to a healthy baby and living long enough to see them grow. But God gave her more than she'd asked for and extended her the grace and mercy to have a man that loved even the worst parts of her.

"Why don't you take a break? You've been at this for like three hours."

"Because if I don't get it done while I have the energy, it won't get done."

"I can think of something else you can use that energy for," she grinned.

Phoenix tucked her index and middle fingers in the waistband of his sweats and pulled him closer. With her free hand, she ran her open palm up the length of his dick. Her teeth sunk into her bottom lip when she felt it jump in his pants. Hoisting herself up on her toes, she puckered her lips. Blaise met her in the middle and gave her three pecks before palming her head with both hands and feeding her his tongue. Phoenix wasted no time pushing his sweats down and freeing his dick from his boxer briefs. It had been months since he stretched her pussy, and she missed him more than she let on. Blaise lifted her in the air, hooking the crooks of her knees in the crooks of his elbows.

Sloppily they kissed like he had just returned from war. The heat between them rose instantly as he pressed her back against the wall where his mother had begun painting a mural for the baby. Her hands roamed every part of his upper body as he wrapped his arm around her waist. In one motion, he had her oversized t-shirt on the floor and her rock-hard nipple in his mouth. His hands roughly gripped her breast as he squeezed and rolled her nipple between his fingers. Her moans were deep and loud as he appreciated the weight his baby added to her.

"Babe, when's your mother coming back?" Phoenix asked as she kissed and licked on his neck and collarbone.

"She went to Forge's nursery, so for the rest of the day, I guess. And I can think of a million ways to bend you before then," he said, easing them both down on the floor.

From her widow's peak to her chin, Blaise sloppily kissed all over her face. Once he reached her lips, she latched onto his tongue like a baby to a pacifier. The salty taste of his blood heightened her arousal as she hungrily consumed his full, juicy lips. Her appetite for him was insatiable. With her palm stacked on top of each other, she palmed the crown of his head and guided him to her pussy.

Blaise licked his lips as he used two fingers to peel back her folds. Pregnancy made her pussy fatter and wetter. It pulsated as she writhed in pleasure in front of him. His mouth watered anticipating her sweet nectar on his tongue. Not wanting to waste another second, he inhaled her intoxicating pheromones. His thick tongue covered her pussy as he lapped up her juices. Steadily, his thumb circled her clit as his tongue trailed the length of her pussy to her ass crack. Phoenix's moans and screams bounced off the walls in the disheveled room as Blaise ate her pussy. Turning her on her side, he spread her ass cheeks and made figure eights around her asshole before gliding back to her pussy. His tongue stiffened as he fucked her with it.

"Ahhhh. Fuck, baby. Eat it just like that. God, ahhhh. Ssss."

Phoenix lost a little more of her sanity every time he snaked his tongue in her pussy and his thumb in her ass. He drove her mad with his vicious head game. As she gripped his head and raised her legs, he went deeper. His chin and beard were coated in her fluids as she rode his face from the side.

Blaise felt her walls tighten around his tongue and knew she was about to shower him with the sweetest honey he'd ever had the pleasure of tasting. He suckled her clit until her body went limp. Giving her a second to catch her breath, he showered her belly with kisses. Their baby kicked everywhere he kissed, causing him to pause.

"Ard, we going have to break this shit up; baby boy is woke, and I'm not fucking in front of him."

Phoenix's head popped up as she scrunched up her face. The angst of pleasure was painted over her expression as she threw her head back. Laughter soon filled the room, and she reached out her arms for him to help her sit up.

"He can't even see us."

"But he can hear us. And what if I poke him in the forehead with my dick or something?"

"Dr. Jones," Phoenix mocked, "cut the bullshit. I know you got a King Cobra swangin' between your knees and I love him about as much as I love you, but we both know the cobra is not breaking through my strong ass placenta. This shit built Phoenix tough."

"Is that so," he laughed as he helped her stand up.

Phoenix didn't answer him. Instead, she seductively dropped to her knees and licked her lips as she played with her kitty. With her free hand, she palmed his dick and French kissed the tip. It jumped in her hand like a cutlass on hydraulics. She smiled because she had him right where she wanted him. Slowly she pulled her two fingers out of her pussy and used her juices as the lubricant for a handjob. With both hands wrapped around his girth, she stroked him, rotating her wrists to twist just how she knew he loved it.

Phoenix prepared herself, opening her mouth wide enough to make room for his girth. The taste of her remnants smeared on his thick dick caused her to meddle in her gushy center. She gobbled him up like the first slice of ham on Thanksgiving. Sloppily. Hungrily. He cupped her face, spreading her cheeks wider with his pinky and index fingers. As he fucked her mouth, globs of spit coated his dick and her chin. Her eyes watered as she hummed while taking most of him down her throat before finally starting to gag. Feeling his nut build, he pulled back, ready to shoot his load all over her titties. But she grabbed the back of his thighs and held him in place, forcing him to bust down her throat.

"Damn, Bae, you really ain't have to eat me up like that. You fucking milked me," Blaise admired as he pulled her up.

Phoenix didn't respond. With a smirk, she wiped the corners of her mouth and left him standing in the middle of the nursery with a flaccid dick. As much as he wanted to pull her back into the room and finish what she started, he knew that the changing table and rocker set weren't going to assemble themselves.

For the next hour Blaise looked over the Ikea instructions, meticulously assembling his child's nursery furniture. The mind-blowing head Phoenix gave him was just what he needed to declutter his mind. Easily, she had become his remedy for everything that clouded his mental faculties. As he put the last rail on the table, he stood back and admired the handy work he'd done. Picturing his father's proud smile made him smile from ear to ear. He was going to be the best father he could be, just like his dad was to him his entire life. Tossing the screwdriver around in his hand, he looked around the room. Spontaneously, he carved *Eternal* into one of the side panels on the changing table.

Vivian stood in the doorway watching her only son. Her heart was filled with joy as she saw her husband in him. He'd grown up to be a better man than either of them expected. Before his father fell ill, Blaise was a menace. He hooked class, slang drugs in their neighborhood, and had a three-page rap sheet of petty crimes by the time he got to the ninth grade. But he eventually realized he had a bigger calling on his life and stepped up from the moment he had his first epiphany. Every move he made after that was calculated and heavily weighed against its detriment or advancement potential. Seeing him accept the unexpected role of a father made her proud. He wasn't weighing any options or thinking about how Phoenix or his child would reshape his 5- or 10-year plan. For once he was experiencing all that life and love had for him with no predilections or predictions. She loved that for him.

Silently, she walked down the hall in search of Phoenix. She knew Phoenix harbored a lot and she prayed for her to know peace and safety. She watched as Phoenix scrolled through her phone. She saw so much of herself in her son's choice for a life partner. Though he never verbally told her, she knew eventually he'd marry her. Phoenix was the keeping type. Even through her tough exterior, Mrs. Jones knew that she was delicate and needed a man who could keep her softness safe. There was no doubt in her mind that her son could be that person for Phoenix.

"Hey, Vivian, how was the nursery?"

"Chile, if I got to tell you to call me Mama Jones one more time. Everybody else does and half of them folks I can't stand. So, I don't wanna hear that me and Mrs. Jones mess no more."

"Mama Jones, how was the nursery?"

Phoenix corrected herself as she dropped her phone beside her on the bed. One thing she always prided herself on was genuinely giving a fuck about the response she got when she asked about someone's day. Too often, she felt like asking someone about their day or how they were feeling had become long form versions of hello where no one truly cared what you said next. Most times people didn't even pause long enough for anyone to reply to their feign of concern. She never wanted to become that person and made sure attention and time were given.

"It was nice. Y'all got me wanting to move on down here. I picked you up a few things. I bought you three baby plants that I thought you could put in the nursery. A Calathea Medallion, and a Lady Valentine. Your friend told me to get a prayer plant there too."

"Thank you. Your son has been in there for the last hour. I wish he comes to bed so I can go to sleep."

"He'll likely be in there all night if you don't pull him out of there."

"I'm giving him his time. I can tell he enjoys being there. Especially since everything is pretty much all ready for our little Love Jones."

"And what about you? You seem a little quieter, withdrawn a bit too the last few days."

"Just a little scared now that we are nearing the end. I can't wait to meet the person who hijacked my heart, but I won't front like I'm not shaking in my boots at the thought of being someone's mama. Being wholly responsible for how they view the world and how they accept love."

Mama Jones shook her head as she took in all that Phoenix was sharing with her. The uncertainty of motherhood was hard on every executing mother, she knew exactly how Phoenix felt. The fear of the unknown was inevitable, but she knew Phenix had all she needed to shower her child with the tender care, unconditional love, and irreplaceable wisdom that they would need to be a nurtured, whole being. As long as she and Blaise remained a unit, there was no way they would fail at parenthood. She was confident in them and knew that they would find their way together.

"It's normal to feel all that you're feeling, but while you're feeling that, I want you to also never lose sight of how much of a mother you've already been to Baby Love Jones. You already care more about her well-being than your own. You already love her with every fiber of your being. The fact that you're afraid to fail means you'd give all you have to see her happy and wholly living her life. The sacrifices you're already made for her prove your dedication. So, no matter how hard motherhood might get, hold on to everything you've already given. Sometimes we feel like we aren't doing or giving enough of ourselves to and for others, when really we are giving far-more than we really have to spare. You're going to be a great mom."

Mama Jones hugged Phoenix and kissed the crown of her head as she laid her head on her shoulder. She remembered having this same conversation with her daughter when she was nearing her delivery day. Motherhood was scary and there was no way around that fear. But like always, there was a way through it. She would make sure she equipped Phoenix with the same encouragement and support that her mother gave her, and she gave to her daughter. No woman should ever have to shoulder the weight of motherhood without a support system of other women by her side. As long as she had breath in her body she planned to support Phoenix in every way she could with this child and each one she'd birth.

Blaise entered the room just as Mama Jones stood to leave. She kissed her son on the cheek before she retreated to her own room on the other end of the long hallway. Plopping down on the bed beside Phoenix, he balanced himself on his elbow and kissed her belly. A smile slang across his face at the sound of little feet pressing against his lips. He loved how his baby reacted to his presence. It was as if they already knew he would be everything they needed him to be. After bonding with his unborn child for a few minutes, he directed his attention to the woman of his world. Her eyes were low, and his head tilted to the left. There was no guessing his mama bear was in need of cuddles and sleep. Two things he was more than happy to grant her.

"Is mama bear ready to get tucked in?" he asked as he pecked her lips with his.

"Passed ready. I was determined to wait up as long as I could. But another ten minutes and I would have been out."

"Thank you for waiting up." Blaise rested his head on her bosom and looked up at her.

He was completely enamored by the woman who seemed to have just dropped from the sky. She was the blessing he never knew he needed, the breath he never realized he inhaled. His love looked good on her. Every time he thought of her making him a father, he smiled with pride. She was indeed all he'd ever wanted in a woman, and he was hellbent on making sure he showed her how much she meant to him as long as he had breath in his lungs and blood coursing through his veins. She was the reason his heart continued to beat.

"Always," she responded, kissing his temple as he laid his head on her chest.

Blaise unfolded her favorite blanket and covered them with it. He only had a few hours before he had to be up and dressed for the first of his last six 12-hours shifts in the emergency room. He was beyond overjoyed that the hospital had finally hired a team of doctors just for the emergency room. He no longer had to juggle Phoenix, his mother, his consulting cases and the ER. With the pending arrival of his first child, the change couldn't have happened at a better time.

"I wish you could stay tonight," she pouted as he wrapped his arms around the space between her 7-month baby bump and supple breasts. They'd nearly quadrupled in size within the last month. He loved all the weight his baby gave her, and he secretly prayed the cushion lingered long after she delivered. Pulling the blanket up over them both, he got comfortable on her chest like he did every night. In a little under six weeks, he'd have to relinquish his favorite spot to his child, so he made sure every moment he got to cuddle he took advantage of it. Phoenix brought out the softness in him, just as much as he pulled it out of her.

"Three more weeks and you'll have me to yourself every weekday by 6 and all day on the weekends."

"Babe, are you serious? They finally did it?"

"Yup. They've officially staffed the emergency room with a team of doctors and residents. So, no more on-call shifts. Except for when my patients are admitted, which I requested."

Phoenix beamed with pride. One thing Blaise talked about often was filling Solace General with black and brown doctors who were passionate and knowledgeable about caring for black and brown patients. From the moment he took the position it was understood that his department would give every patient the same dignity, respect and bedside manner regardless of their demographics. He'd seen to it that Roddy made good on that stipulation of his contract. She kissed the crown of his head repeatedly as he laughed at her antics.

"I'm so proud of you, B. God, you make me the proudest woman alive."

"And you make me the best man. It's easy being your best self when you know you have someone in your corner ready to give you whatever support you might need. You let me be when I need space. You get on my ass when I'm lacking. You let me vent when I need an ear. And you handle me with tenderness when all the world sees is a strong, black man who can shoulder it all."

"Don't make me cry. You know I cry easily these days."

"Nah, don't blame that shit on my seed. You been a cry baby."

"Shut up and kiss me goodnight," she laughed with tears threatening to spill from her lids and onto his head full of waves.

CHAPTER SIXTEEN

Phoenix sat Indian style in the middle of the bed. Her blue light blocking glasses hung on the tip of her nose as she looked over the rim to read the contract she'd printed out. If anyone would have told her a year ago life would be going this good for her, she wouldn't have believed them. She was thirty-two days from meeting the little person who'd call her mommy, and just two weeks away from taping her first on-air holiday special for Solace Point.

Meeting Simone Reveres was one of the most rewarding moments she'd had for her career. Since their spontaneous double date, they'd been in communication about working together. Simone saw a grit in Phoenix that mirrored her own, and she did everything in her power to get her back on-screen. Phoenix found it easy to open up to Simone about her lupus battle and the anxiousness she'd felt as her baby's arrival neared. Expression of her innermost thoughts seemed to roll off her tongue like the chokehold on her throat chakra had been released.

She didn't know what Blaise had done to her, but his presence in her life had her peeling back layers she'd usually kept covered at all costs. She realized the power of expressing her wants, needs, and desires. She understood what genuine love, compassion, and concern felt like. There was no longer a need to retreat behind the walls she'd built up around her heart. She finally let them fall like Jericho at the behest of Blaise's unwavering love and support. She was able to decipher who was truly for her and who just wanted to be a spectator.

As she thought about the texts, phone calls and lunch dates she'd had with Simone in her sister's absence, she felt like she wasn't missing anything. Though she missed Rue, and her heart ached not having her sister by her side through one of the most important moments in her life, she couldn't harp on Rue's decision. Time wasn't on her side, and she couldn't try to make Rue see what she wanted to be blind to. She had to live for her and the little person who'd look to her for everything in just a few short weeks.

Putting the absence of her favorite person in the whole world in the back of her mind, she recalled the countless career-positioning conversations she'd had with Simone. She smiled as she recollected Simone saying she had the personality and energy that needed to be broadcast. Keeping true to her word, Simone used her connections to get Phoenix the spot as lead host anchor for the city's annual holiday telethon. As she looked at all the zeros behind the comma, she smiled. $50,000 plus a wardrobe budget was much more than she'd ever made. After blowing on the ink from her gel pen, she ran her fingers over her signature. This was really happening, and she couldn't be more excited.

Before he even reached the room, Phoenix's smile spread across her face. His new sandalwood aftershave preceded him down the hallway as he neared their bedroom. She'd missed him while he was away on business. Having Mama Jones there to keep her company was comforting, but she was beyond excited to have her man back home. He'd left her for eight days for a conference, and nightly FaceTime calls just weren't enough to dull the achiness she felt not being held by him every night. His presence calmed the anxiety that crept in more and more as they neared the arrival of their baby.

Dropping her papers and glasses on top of her laptop keyboard, she moved as fast as she could to get up. The second she was off the bed, she was colliding with his chest. Blaise looked good enough to eat two and three servings in his navy joggers and crisp, white t-shirt. His waves were deep, and his lineup was sharp. The fresh cut had him looking oceanic and her wanting to go deep sea diving. His beard had grown out since he'd been gone, and she just wanted to see it coated in all her juices.

Wrapping his arms around her waist, he pulled her in as close as he could with her belly wedging a gap between them. With one hand, he pushed her hair back out of her face. Phoenix bashfully smiled as his gaze made her nervous. She squirmed a little in his arms, unsure of his next move. His scent caused her knees to buckle slightly as she breathed him all in.

"Welcome home."

"I missed you."

"I missed you too. What have you been up to while I been away?"

Phoenix back peddled out of his arms. She was overflowing with sheer excitement. Since moving to Solace Point, her only goal had been to make it back on screen. Every move she made from the time she decided she'd come for treatment revolved around hightailing it from the town as soon as she was cleared. But God had other plans, and she was going to follow the one he laid out to perfection. There would be no deviation or delay.

Snatching the contract with her signature, she handed it to him to read over. She stood in front of him with her lips tucked between her teeth and her eyes searching his face. She watched him as he read over the document, his fingers clenching the paper tighter as his eyes scanned further and further down the page.

The stars in her eyes burned out as she saw a scowl form on his handsome face and his jaw tighten as he bit down on the inside of his cheek. It wasn't the reaction she was expecting, and it confused her. Uneasiness washed over her as her weight shifted from one foot to the next. Unable to take the silence anymore, she cut through its thickness with her soft voice.

"So, what do you think?"

"I think this is fucking irresponsible. Why would you sign this?"

"What? Why wouldn't I?"

"Phoenix. You are almost eight fucking months pregnant. What possessed you to think any of this shit was a good idea? The prep for this alone would be a bunch of unnecessary stress."

"So now my dreams and goals are unnecessary stress?"

Phoenix backed away from him until she felt her calves press against the bed frame. She was floored by his lack of excitement for her. In everything he'd ever told her about his dreams she was always uber supportive and encouraged him to go for whatever his heart desired.

To have him call her goals unnecessary and downplay them broke her to her core. She felt like the air had been vacuumed from the room as she clenched her chest. Her air was constricted, and her breath had halted mid inhale. Her brows furrowed and her lips quivered as the tears collected, weighing her lower lids down.

One by one the tears came until they flowed like a steady stream. Hitting the floor like droplets of rain on hot concrete, they steamed the room, clouding her vision. The man standing before her was different, and she didn't know what caused him to regard her with such malice in his tone. Like a wounded animal she retreated within.

"I didn't mean it like that, and you know that shit. Elena told us this would be the most crucial last few weeks, and I think taking on a project this size in this short bit of time would just add stress you don't need right now."

"Whatever, B. I don't care anymore. I'm so tired of everybody acting like I'm going to fucking break if I let the back of my foot touch any surface beside the damn shower. I am fully fucking capable of taking care of myself and this baby. I'm not going to purposefully do anything that would jeopardize either of our lives."

"That's hard to fucking believe. I almost lost both y'all once already behind your ass. Stop thinking your fucking superwoman. Stop thinking you can do every fucking thing. Because from where me, your sister and everybody else is sitting, you fucking can't."

"Fuck you, Blaise. Seriously."

The hurt had been replaced with anger and Phoenix was no longer going to sit around and listen to him tell her what she should or shouldn't be doing. This was a decision she'd made for herself and was going to see it through. It didn't matter what he or anyone else thought. If she wanted to be superwoman, she damn sure could do it without their input.

Standing, she brushed past him, causing him to stumble back at the impact of her belly against his relaxed stance. She was over the fuss everyone chose to make over her. Being handled with kid gloves had become old really fast and she wanted out. No one thought she was adult enough to run her plans by her medical team and that made her even more angry. Afterall, it was her life, and no one suffered the consequences of her actions – whether hasty or well-thought out – more than she did.

Silently, she moved around him as she packed a bag to go back to her house. Though she'd been at his home since he'd picked her up after she sent out her distress text two months ago, she knew it was time to put a little bit of space between them. She needed to be in her own space for a while without him breathing down her neck. As much as she'd missed him while he was away she knew at that moment they needed to put some more distance between them.

Everything was beginning to fall apart; she saw the signs of ruin in their future, and they were too close to forever to let it end. Time. That's what she knew they both needed. Time to assess the conversation they'd just shared. Time to process what life was about to look like for them. Time to decide if this was even what they signed up for. Time to evaluate what a love together would entail. Time where she could figure out how to compromise. These weren't things they could wait until the baby was born to figure out. These were things they needed to know about going in so that their child had the best chance they could give them.

"What are you doing," Blaise asked as he sat down on the edge of the bed.

His eyes followed her as his head shook from one side to the other. His palms ran down his face as he released a long, loud breath. Phoenix would surely be the death of him with how quickly she was prepared to run from the conversations they needed to have. Her stubbornness, though once his favorite thing about her, had become his biggest headache. She took standing firm on her choices to a whole other level, and he just didn't have the energy to deal with it. He was jet-lagged from his travels and thought he would be coming home to a back rub and blow job. But somehow the universe just didn't want to let him know peace for the night.

"I need some space. I'm going home."

"This is your fucking home. You not finna keep running every time you don't like some shit I say to you."

"And you not finna tell me what to do every time you think you fucking know what's best. You don't know shit."

"I'll tell you what I do know. I know you not leaving this fucking house."

"Oh, I'm leaving. Who gon' stop me?"

Phoenix scrunched her face up as she looked at the man sitting before her. His words dripped with venom, but his expression never changed. His body language confused her even more. Deciding that she wasn't going to exert any unnecessary energy arguing about what she was going to do, she continued with the task at hand.

As she moved around the room, he didn't move a muscle. His eyes stayed trained on her everywhere she moved. Her mind raced as she wondered what he was thinking. Feeling like this would be their final goodbye until she gave birth, she took her time gathering her necessities. It was crazy how much he'd transformed her life. She'd easily gotten comfortable in his space and as foreign as she knew her home would feel, she knew it was the best thing for her to do. She needed to breathe new air because she was suffocating under his watchful eye. He handled her like she was fragile, and it was beginning to weigh on her heavily. She felt useless.

The second she went to open their bedroom door, she felt the heat from his body as he stood behind her. His breathing was even, and as much as she didn't want to admit it, hearing how calm he was soothed her aching heart. She didn't want to leave his presence, especially after she missed him so much, but she knew it was necessary. Her worry eased a little because she knew that he was aware this wasn't goodbye forever.

"You're not leaving. You can pick any of these other rooms to stay in if it's my presence you're running from, but you're not leaving this house, Phoenix. I mean that shit."

"Blaise..."

"Blaise, shit. I mean what the fuck I said."

The base in his voice caused her to jump as her grip on the doorknob weakened. She wanted to cry, but she stood firm instead. With a deep breath, she composed herself before gripping the doorknob again. Just as it creaked, he slammed it back shut. His palm rested inches above her head on the door. Tears fell from her eyes as she let her forehead fall to the door.

"Why won't you just let me go?"

"Because I can't. I can't lose you like this. I won't lose you like this. You're your own worst enemy, and you make it seem like the world is against you. I am your world, and I'm forever rocking with you. But you gotta stop fucking running every time we not on the same page about some shit."

Slowly she lifted her head and turned to face him. He stepped back, giving her space to fully face him. He looked her over. She was visibly exhausted, and he knew she didn't want to fight him anymore. She was ready to surrender and so was he. They couldn't keep doing this same song and dance every time they disagreed about what was best for their child. The baby wasn't even in the flesh and they were already debating choices concerning their best intentions.

"I need to go home, B. I need this. I can't stay here like this. You're not losing me, I'm losing me and that's the scariest part. I'm not running from you, I'm running to myself."

The pain in the back of her eyes let him know that she was gone. He didn't want her to leave, but he knew if she stayed that she would be lost to him. She'd hate him for making her stay and he'd hate himself even more for the person he'd create. So, without another word, he slowly removed his hand from the door. As his hand traveled past her face, she pulled it toward her lips and planted the softest kiss he'd ever felt in the palm of his hand. He exhaled deeply as she pressed his palm against his chest, and the tears left her eyes.

Thirty minutes after she left, he sat in the arm chair by his window watching the last bit of light recoil from the sky. Night was officially upon him, and it was the darkest it'd ever been. There wasn't a star in the sky for as far as his eyes could see. He contemplated invading her space and pulling up on her just to be in her presence, but decided it was best he stay put.

At the sound of his door opening, he turned with hope shining in his eyes. A bit of that hope dwindled as he locked eyes with his mother. Her disapproving glare let him know he was about to get another ear full. When it came to Phoenix, his mother rode for her like she birthed her. He loved how quickly his family took to her, but in this instance he wished like hell his mother was coming to say she was on his side. Her cold stare and silence told him otherwise.

"Let me guess, you're siding with Phoenix on this too."

"I'm not siding with either of you. Your concerns are valid and so is her desire to pursue her career. Y'all need to find common ground, and that won't ever happen if you keep shaking her foundation. Let that girl do something. You try to keep her cooped up in here all the time and that's not fair."

"Ma, she literally almost died."

"And you don't think she realizes how dire her situation is? She isn't fragile."

"I know she ain't fragile. She's more than fragile to me. She's precious."

"I understand that. But, how would you feel if you worked your ass off for one thing. Then the second you get it, it slips straight through your grasp. What would you do if it came around a second time? You're walking with her, but no matter how far you two may walk together, you aren't walking in her shoes now, and you weren't when her world came crashing down either."

Blaise pondered what his mother had said. He couldn't front. From the second he saw Phoenix unconscious with a swollen belly, his whole life perspective shifted. His only goal was making sure she and his baby were safe at any cost. What he hadn't realized was his safety measures were about to pay the ultimate price because he was about to lose her. Dropping his head to his palms, he sighed. He couldn't win for losing in this situation.

"How much time you think I should give her before I apologize?"

"As much as she needs. She'll come to you. Until then, I'll keep you updated."

"Wait, so you leaving me too?"

"I know you ain't think I was staying here while my daughter-in-law is this close to birthing my grandbaby. She ain't mad at me, she's mad at you. I got an invite to her home."

"Oh, that's cold, Ma."

"No. What was cold was you calling her dreams unnecessary."

"I thought you weren't taking sides," he laughed as he threw his arms up in surrender.

"Oh, you know parents always have to say that shit, but we most certainly take sides. And this time, it wasn't yours."

Vivian looked at her son and laughed. Watching him grow into the best version of himself was one of the most rewarding journeys of her life. He'd defied what society said he'd be and made her the proudest mother walking this green earth. His level of self-reflection surpassed her own, and she admired how quickly he could admit his wrongs and apologize for the hurt he caused others. It was a rare trait, and she knew it was part of the reason he'd become so successful. Joy seemed to follow him because he acknowledged and confronted whatever threatened his joy, even if it meant confronting himself. Pulling him in, she hugged him tightly before turning to leave the room.

"Mama..."

Vivian stopped in her tracks and turned her head to face her son. She smiled, inquiry present in her eyes. This was a pivotal moment in their love story, and she knew her wisdom would only serve as the chrysalis. They needed to look within themselves and find out what mattered to them more before they could truly transform their hasty romance into a lifelong transcendent love.

"Please make sure she's okay. That's all I ever wanted."

A week had gone by since Blaise and Phoenix's separation. His world had become so routine, and he hated every moment of it. Like clockwork, he rose each morning for work and ended every evening with a steak and potato dinner from Rose Marie's. Where he used to welcome the silence that met him after a long day with patients, the silence now suffocated him. He missed being greeted by his mother and girlfriend's laughter as it filled every corner of his home. In the short time they'd been in his space, he'd grown to expect their presence. The stillness was unnerving.

Kicking off his shoes, he stripped out of his suit and headed for the shower. After the piping hot water evaporated the day's remnants from his skin, he trudged to his bedroom. Clothing himself only in a pair of pajama bottoms, he descended the stairs and trudged to the kitchen. Pulling a glass from the cabinet, he poured himself a glass of whiskey and sat down at the counter to feed his loneliness before bed. A few bites in and all he wanted to do was snatch up his cell and Facetime the love of his life. He was down bad, and the only remedy was her voice. He needed to hear it to soothe

the raging parts of him that only seemed to come alive when he wanted to lay his head down at night.

Unable to stomach another morsel of food, he scraped the nearly untouched plate into the garbage and poured another shot of whiskey. This time he made it a double. Sleep would soon follow, and he'd be thrust into yet another day where Phoenix didn't greet him in the morning with a smile and kiss to the chest. His days were long, and his nights were lonely. And the only person he had to blame was himself.

Just as he got himself wound down enough to climb into bed, the sound of his text alert drew a sigh from his lungs. Snatching the phone from the dock where he'd just placed it, he opened the message to see it was Roddy.

Roddy: Yo. You in for the night?

Blaise: I was. What's up?

Roddy: We tryna ball after shift change. You up for a pick up game?

Blaise: I'm game. Drop the location.

An hour later and Blaise was lacing up on the court. The three men around him were the brothers he never asked for but was glad God had it in his plans for their paths to cross. Their camaraderie, support, and love were what kept him going after his father passed. Their personal stories of overcoming were the reason he didn't put his life on pause after his mother's health challenges. He trusted them with his life and valued their input.

Trav, Roddy, and Triumph laughed as they took turns joking him. He looked like every bit of what he was going through, and they showed no remorse. He was the master of the madness he was currently living through, and their laughter and jokes let him know they were also Team Phoenix.

"Y'all niggas gon' laugh all night or ball out?"

"Oh, now you wanna be all about ball?" Triumph asked, holding in his laughter.

"We ain't tell you to piss your pregnant wifey off right before she pushes out your kid," Trav added.

"Ard, y'all ease up on the man. Can't y'all see he's feeling it. Look at him, waves looking more like rough seas," Roddy joked.

Blaise shook his head as he held in his laughter. Laughing was the only thing keeping him from going crazy without his lady being home. She was really standing firm on her need for space. While he could have easily gone to see her every day, he decided to take his mother's advice. If space was all she desired from him at the moment, then space was what she would get. He'd fill the hours he'd normally spend with her preparing his home for her return, his child's arrival, and kicking it with his boys.

"Nah, but forreal. Run it down to me one more time, because I'm still trying to wrap my head around it," Trav asked.

"Exactly what I told you. She got a job offer, felt like I wasn't supportive and dipped."

"And you just let her go."

"I tried to keep her there, but I couldn't bear the hurt in her eyes. Knowing I was the one causing it made me back off."

"Between you and Rue, I don't know who is going through it the most. Y'all just never learn. Phoenix is going to do what she wants and the more y'all try to restrain her, the harder she's gonna go. If you want her to take it easy, you're gonna have to release the reins some."

Blaise tucked his hands under his arms as he took in everything that Trav said to him. Phoenix had stopped talking to Rue because she felt like she wanted to make every decision for her. He'd listened to her express how she felt about people not allowing her to live, and he turned around and did the same thing. As much as he wanted to blame her for being stubborn, he had to take ownership for the part he played. It was no secret he exerted a certain level of force when folks weren't seeing things the way he felt they should see them. Usually, folks hung on his every word, taking what he suggested as commandments and adhering to how he felt things should be done to ensure their health. But Phoenix wasn't his patient, she was his woman, the mother of his child and his future wife. He couldn't expect her to do what he said because he wasn't the one charged with giving her medical care in the capacity he'd tried to enforce.

"Yea, you're right. I know I spew commands at her all the time, and for the most part, she follows my lead. I should have realized that this was something important to her because she didn't just take my lead."

"So, what you gonna do?"

"Mama said I should let her come to me when she's ready, so I'm chilling."

"Holl-up. You finna let the woman who ghosted you for nearly six months come to you when she's ready? You keep fucking around, you'll see her at y'alls kids first birthday party," Roddy advised.

"What would you have me do?"

"Shit, I'd have you go get your bitch."

"Aye, watch that shit."

"My bad, you know what I'm saying though. Just don't give her too much time. Give her a grace period, then apply pressure."

The men played three games of two on two before they decided to call it quits. They all had different situations occupying their minds and the time spent talking shit and working through their unique circumstances helped them see things clearer. Blaise left knowing what he needed to do. Phoenix was only getting one more week. If she wasn't back, he was going to get her. He understood where she was coming from. He'd considered everything she and his mother said to him and she was right. He did need to let her do whatever she wanted. She was more than capable of caring for herself and their unborn child.

The days following the spontaneous basketball games between him and his friends was just what he needed. The stress he felt prior had dissipated. While he still missed Phoenix, his mother's updates were enough to quiet his worries. Phoenix had been taking it easy, but still prepping for her special day. She'd worked hard for it, and he had to admit the pride he felt knowing he had a woman who went against everyone she loved to ensure her dreams. She knew that she was the only one who truly knew what was best for her, and she made sure she rationalized every decision she made before making it.

"Dr. Jones, you have a visitor. Should I send them back?"

Blaise looked up from the patient folder he'd been reviewing. He had a full day of appointments and not much time to spare. Taking an unexpected meeting didn't seem likely, but he knew if someone had showed up unexpectedly, then the situation was dire. It was usually just a colleague with a quick question about a patient, so he welcomed the intrusion.

"Hey."

The sound of her voice soothed him. It'd been weeks since he'd heard it, and he never wanted that much time to pass again. Dropping the folder, he pulled his reading glasses from his face and dropped them on top of the file. A smile spread across his face as he stood to meet her in the middle of her office.

"Hey. How are y'all?" Blaise asked as he palmed her stomach and kissed her lips.

"We're fine. Just came from a visit with Dr. Ruiz. Do you have a second? I'll be quick."

"I always have a second for you. Sit down."

Blaise ushered Phoenix into one of the armchairs before taking the seat across from her. Several seconds of quiet existed between them before she pulled in air. They'd spent most of their time apart and she hated it. It was a mystery how they even fell in love because she'd spent so much time running from him and the love he wanted to give her. She appreciated him for his patience, but she knew he wouldn't wait on her forever. Losing him wasn't an option, so she was ready for whatever life with him looked like.

"I don't want to fight anymore. This silent war between us has to stop. Being apart was hard, but it was what I needed to really see what I was messing up. I'm sorry I'm always running under the guise of wanting to be able to make my own decisions. I know you would never do anything that would put me, my future or my dreams in jeopardy. I miss you, and I'm ready to let you lead."

"Baby, you don't have to apologize. I'm the one who needs to apologize. I should have trusted you enough to do what you thought was best. I know you are more than capable of making the best decision. I'm proud of you and will support you in whatever you want to do."

Blaise got down on his knees and kissed her belly before leaning up and kissing her lips. He loved everything about the woman who sat before him. Her tenacity. Her firmness. Her softness. Her vulnerability. Her selflessness. But more than anything, he loved her heart and how it had the capacity to love despite everything she'd experienced. She was his, and he would do everything in his power to make sure she felt protected and supported.

CHAPTER SEVENTEEN

PHOENIX SAT UP IN BED WITH HER BLANKET HAPHAZARDLY COVERING HER lower half. Her left knee was bent under her but and her right leg dangled off the bed. Her disheveled hair and glowing skin were a result of the little human growing inside her. Their constant kicking and turning kept her awake for the majority of the night. But as sleepy as she was, she kept with her usual morning routine.

Every morning, after returning to Blaise's house, she saw him off to the office. She found joy in helping him decide what to cover his handsome limbs with and what cologne to wear as Blaise prepared for another day at the hospital. She'd kept to her promise and stayed put unless her presence was absolutely needed on set. Simone handled almost everything leading up to her Solace Point television debut and she couldn't be more grateful for the life she was making for herself. Everything seemed to be coming full circle, shaping her into a little world of miracles, signs, and wonders. God had most certainly been showing out from where she sat.

As he moved about the room, her smile widened. No one could have predicted this as the climatic scene in her story, but it was. It was the moment everything made more sense to her.

Every trial. Every hospital stay. Every rejection. Every heartbreak. Every loss. It all prepared her for this moment where she could relish in the prosperity that God had stored up for her. Pastor Mike was for sure prophesying to her when he uttered those powerful bars she sang off-key every morning in the shower. *God's gonna open the window of heaven, pour me out a blessing. I won't have room to contain it, won't even try to explain it.* Silently, she recited the words to the song that got her through the toughest moments in recent months and realized his blessings hadn't stopped pouring in yet.

Her gaze rose to meet Blaise as he joined her on the bed. Fully dressed and ready to take the day, he wrapped her in his arms. Every time he had to leave her, she felt a twinge of sadness. Even a few hours away from him was too many. She'd wasted so much time running from the one man who could love her how she desired to be loved, how she needed to be loved. Unconditionally.

His love came without prerequisites and ultimatums. When she allowed her eyes the chance to fall upon his, all she saw was her future staring back at her. Phoenix loved him so much it hurt. Being away from him pained her. Not feeling his flesh upon her flesh ached. He was her remedy and as she caressed his cheek with her knuckles, she realized there was no treatment, no cure other than him. He made all things right in her world.

"What are you over here thinking about," Blaise asked as he kissed her forehead.

His hand rested on her exposed knee as she clasped his hands with her own. It was no use trying to hide the smile that had been permanently plastered on her face since she returned to his home. Blaise made life easier for her and though it took her a long time to see just how unburdened he'd made her existence, she appreciated that he never gave up on her.

Stubbornness was ingrained in her DNA. She was almost 100% certain it was the leading cause of singleness among the younger generations in her family, starting with her Aunt Phae who she gleaned from for the majority of her formative years. But it was a trait she wanted to dispel completely. Blaise proved he could handle all of her and lead her into a place of never-ending love, light and laughter. At this stage of her life, it was all she desired and anything she committed to had to ensure those three elements would be plentiful.

"Just how lucky I am to have you."

Phoenix puckered her lips and leaned in for him to kiss her. She knew he had to be at his office for an early morning consultation before his appointments began, but she just didn't want him to go. As her due date neared, she'd become more clingy, wanting him with her every second of every day. It was unclear if excitement or fear fueled that desire, but nonetheless it was a desire she knew he would oblige if she asked. And she wasn't selfish enough to take him away from his patients. She'd been where they were, and she wouldn't want anyone brushing off her pain because of something as frivolous as their partner wanting to be held all day.

"I love you," Blaise responded as he kissed her lips three times, "and you too, Love Jones," he proclaimed, kissing her exposed belly.

Phoenix massaged his head as he talked to their baby like he did every morning before he departed their space. She chuckled as a fond memory of him chastising her for massaging his waves in the wrong direction flashed behind her closed lids. His deep, modulated voice was soothing as her eyes closed and her head met the tufted upholstered headboard.

Time and space could soar by her and she'd remain in his presence, listening to the lulling of his voice with no regard for the world that was passing them by. He was her happy space and while she could indeed find happiness elsewhere, it wouldn't be like this. It wouldn't feel like this. It never had before him, and she knew life after having him would always be dull in comparison.

"Walk me down before you fall back off to sleep."

Blaise patted her leg as he heard the change in her breathing. Groggily, she accepted his outstretched hand, allowing him to pull her to an upright position. Pushing her feet into her fluffy, plush, teddy bear slippers she dragged her feet as they walked hand-in-hand down the hallway. Phoenix hugged his arm as they made it into the main foyer. Positioning herself directly in front of him, she looked up into his smiling face. Love shined on them as the sun's rays warmed the spot where they stood. All the curtains throughout the lower level of his home were drawn, alerting them that Vivian, too, was awake.

"What do you have planned for today?"

"Not much. Lunch and some light shopping with Forge, this afternoon."

"Dinner at Saxon's tonight? I realized that we haven't officially celebrated the pending arrival of our little Love Jones."

"Only if we can visit the cove afterwards. I haven't felt the wind on my skin in a few weeks. I'm long overdue."

"It's a date," Blaise agreed before kissing her one last time before opening the door.

"Have a great day. Be the light in their storm. I love you," Phoenix said to his back as he descended the porch stairs.

"I love you back," he threw over his shoulder.

Phoenix closed the door and proceeded to the living room the second he pulled out of the driveway. She had about four hours to sleep before she needed to meet Forge. They were shopping for the nursery at her home. While it was already agreed Phoenix would spend the first six months of the baby's existence at Blaise's house, there was no future plan for her to part ways with her dream house anytime soon. She wanted to make sure her home was also baby-proofed in time. Laying across the chaise, she pulled the throw blanket over herself and was asleep in a matter of minutes.

Two hours later, she was back up with the worst heartburn she'd ever experienced. If the indicators were true, she was sure their baby would have a head full of hair the way her heartburn had worsened in less than a week. She struggled to stand up from her prostrated position and get herself a glass of water. The fragrant aromas pouring from the kitchen let her know that Vivian had prepared brunch. There wasn't a day that went by where she didn't wake to a smorgasbord of brunch food. Vivian's love for cooking and contentment with her son's kitchen was evident in how much food she made for three people. Every day they were inviting Roddy over for dinner just to make sure there was no waste.

"You're up earlier than I thought you'd be," Vivian greeted her with open arms.

"Your grandchild is causing the worst heartburn I've ever felt in my life. I couldn't sleep through it."

"I hope you know how to do hair because their daddy was the same way and he came out looking like a black panther. Big, curliest afro I ever seen on an infant."

"Oh lord, please say you're joking."

"About the afro, yes, but not the hair. He had a head full of hair and I had heartburn just like you. Sit down, I'll make you some ginger pineapple tea. That always helped me."

After an hour of laughing and talking with Vivian, Phoenix was walking into Forge's nursery looking like Oshun herself. Her beauty was undeniable as she commanded the attention of the nursery patrons.

As she perused the new additions to the shelves, she smiled and thanked everyone who complimented her on how well she carried her baby. Her baby bump was bumping to the max in her burnt orange skater dress that stopped mid-thigh. Her platform lace-up booties gave her just the right amount of ankle support not to topple over. Her thighs and titties had grown exponentially taking her up two pants sizes and three cups sizes.

Ever since she stopped stressing herself out about every little thing and running from the love of her life, pregnancy looked good on her. The way it enhanced her beauty was undeniable. Her glow was blinding as she pushed her cart through the aisles and filled it with seven new plants for Blaise's house. He'd been telling her he wanted to add more greenery throughout his living space and while it wasn't in her plan, she couldn't not grab a few that she thought complimented the common areas of his home.

"Excuse me, Ma'am. We're supposed to be going baby shopping. Why are you waltzing up to this register with all these damn plants?"

"Better question is why didn't I get the memo that you had new additions in the shop? I thought as your bestie, I always get first dibs." Phoenix pouted as she reached her arms out for a hug.

"I keep telling your ass to subscribe because I be forgetting to send you a text. Especially now. You know this is when my life gets uber hectic."

"Yea, how was Montreal?"

"It was beautiful. I really hated having to leave to come check on the shops."

"I mean, you could have called. I would have held it down for you?"

"Please! And have Blaise on my line yelling about you over-exerting yourself. I'm good on all that. I just had a few shipments to receive. Then I'm flying back out next week."

"Where to next?"

"Onyx is on his way to Dubai tomorrow. I'm going to join him there and stay until the week before Halloween."

"Why the short trip? You're usually gone until two weeks before Christmas."

"Because my favorite little crumb snatcher is set to make their debut and I don't want to miss it," Forge shrieked as she rubbed Phoenix's belly.

Phoenix talked to Forge daily, but they hadn't physically been in the same space for weeks due to Forge jet-setting with her fiancé on business trips. One season a year, she accompanied him on his travels so they could spend quality time together. Phoenix hadn't planned on being knocked-up smack dab in the middle of her friend's travel season and remorse instantly spread across her face. She already hated for anyone to make a fuss over her and now she was hearing Forge was changing her plans to coincide with her labor plans. While she would love for all three of her friends to be there when she pushed out the first baby among their circle of friends, she didn't want to infringe on anyone else's plans. She'd never ask them to sacrifice that type of time, especially when it wouldn't just cost them time, but money. None of her friends were local except Forge and she was not considered local during these months.

"You don't have to do that. Between Blaise and Mama Jones, I have enough hands on deck for the big day."

"What type of godmother would I be if I'm clean across the world when you give birth?"

"One who has a life, a man and the opportunity to give them a little god brother or sister," Phoenix laughed.

"I mean I can do that in any country. But back to you. Why are you buying all these damn plants?"

"They're not for me. Blaise has been talking about adding more and I think these will be perfect in the sunroom and guest rooms."

"Look at you, redecorating. So does this mean things have been going okay since I've been away?"

Phoenix tried to hide the giddiness she felt just thinking about how things had been with Blaise. Instead of immediately answering, she started putting her plants on the counter for Forge to ring them up. Honestly, she didn't want to answer for fear of jinxing how incredible she felt. Blaise was all the man that she'd ever need.

"They've been more than great. Seriously, Forge, thanks for pushing me to accept his date?"

"Don't thank me. You are the one who got out of your own way."

"He's so damn amazing. It's like he's a magical unicorn. You know the man who checks every last one of my boxes. The one who I can give my all to and I'm never depleted."

"That's called being loved by a grown ass man. I don't think anything ever tops that feeling."

"You ain't lying. When I'm with him I feel like even when I have nothing left, I'll still have everything I need because he replenishes me. Whatever I'm lacking, he's providing. When I'm at my lowest, he's propping me up. He's just everything to me."

Phoenix dabbed at her eyes with the sleeve of her cardigan. Crying tears of joy felt so much better than sobbing with sorrow. For the first time in a long time, she was overcome with genuine happiness. She finally saw just how blessed she was and just how life happened the second she wasn't expecting it.

Just a year ago she was battling the worst flare of her life, praying for a professional breakthrough and wishing she could find some essence of normalcy amid her chronically chaotic life. Her tears were long overdue, but as she stood at her best friend's register watching tears form in her eyes too, she knew it wasn't the time or place. There was a line forming behind her and because Forge only had one checkout counter, she needed to pull it together and move along. They had all afternoon to cry over how amazing their men were.

After Forge helped her last customer, the two left arm-in-arm. Before they could really get to their shopping spree, they had a backseat full of plants to drop off. The plants would be fine for a simple day of shopping, but the women knew they'd need every inch of space to haul all that they planned to purchase. Plus, their day of shopping would carry them into San Francisco, and they were sure to make a few pit stops into tourist spaces like they'd never been before. There was never a dull moment when the two linked up for an unplanned ladies' day. With no concrete plans, they simply allowed the events of the day to carry them wherever it took them.

Forge decided to drive her truck, so she followed Phoenix back to Blaise's house. She'd only been there a few times to oversee her landscape team as they completed the landscaping job he'd hired her nursery to handle and never had a chance to see the inside. Phoenix ran away from him too much for anyone to really get an invite over.

But as she helped Phoenix rehome his new greenery, she took in his space. It was a beautiful home, and she could tell he took pride in its appearance. Peace and comfort were most certainly at the forefront of his mind when he was decorating his home. The color scheme and minimalist feel of the furniture made it airy and spacious. The homely feeling made her want to kick off her shoes and relax her feet instead of spending the day swiping her man's black card.

Laughter followed the women as they bid farewell to Vivian for the day. Stopping in her tracks, Phoenix's smile fell as her eyes landed on her sister. She hadn't spoken to her in weeks, and this was the last place she expected her to be.

As she slowly wobbled down the three porch steps, she took each step deliberately until she was standing in front of Rue. Her blank stare indicated that she was not going to be the one to initiate any dialogue. Her silence caused Rue to shift her weight from one foot to the next before beginning to speak. Her palms slid down her thighs, Phoenix imagined she was nervous and trying to figure out what to say that wouldn't result in her foot in her mouth like every other time they spoke lately.

"Hey," Rue smiled, nervously.

"Hey."

"I invited her. She's your big sister and you're going to need her in your corner," Forge asked.

"Look, Phoenix, I know I haven't done the best with letting you do your own thing and I apologize if you feel like I crowd you, but I only want what's best for you. It's all I've ever wanted. You're grown and I have to learn to accept your decisions even if I don't agree with them. You won't learn from your mistakes if I don't allow you to make them."

Phoenix's face distorted as she listened to her sister's attempt at an apology. It was no secret Rue raised her when their parents died. In many ways, she was more like her mother than she ever was a sister, but her sense of dictatorship over Phoenix was nauseating. It was deeper than just caring about her well-being. She treated Phoenix like she was a fragile egg, in danger of cracking whenever the pressure was applied. Nothing Phoenix accomplished or overcame was ever enough to prove to her older sister that she was capable of making decisions that would put her in a better position than she currently was.

"Rue, do you hear yourself? Even if you don't agree. Learn from my mistakes. You make it seem like I'm some bimbo failure. Let me guess, your mom and I'm Aunt Phaedra in your head right?"

"Phe, that's not what I meant."

"Nothing you ever say is what you meant and that's the damn problem. I'm sorry if my life is too chaotic for you, but it's mine and I'm going to live it how I see fit."

"I know that. I just want you to consider shit more before making hasty decisions like an unplanned pregnancy when you have a chronic illness and choosing to be a damn single mother when the father is more than capable of helping you."

Forge sucked in her breath as she saw the fire in Phoenix's eyes. This was not at all what she had planned when she invited Rue to join them for their ladies' day out. But now that they were in the thick of it she weighed her options. She could step in and stop the conversation before it went any further. Or she could stand back and let the sisters hash this out.

They'd been in a silent war for weeks, and she'd never seen them divided like they were. She understood both sisters' perspectives and only hoped they could find a way to see each other's. Choosing the ladder, she took a seat on the second step and allowed them to continue their conversation. While their voices rose an octave, she hadn't classified it as an argument yet. Elevated voices were an indicator of passion in her book, not anger.

"You know what, Rue? Everybody can't have a perfectly planned life like you. With your college sweetheart, two children, and a white picket fence. Shit doesn't happen like that for everyone. My life is my life. The choices I make are mine too. I love you and I appreciate everything you've done for me since mommy and daddy left...died. But I cannot continue to walk in your shadow, staying in the lines and trying to keep it together while I'm dying.

While everyone else has forever, or thinks they have a false sense of forever, I don't have that luxury. No, my pregnancy wasn't planned, but this is most likely the only child I'll ever carry. I know everyone around me likes to overlook the facts, but here they are. I have lupus. I'm in stage four kidney failure. There is no cure, and all any medical professional can do for me is make me comfortable until my body loses the fight against itself. So, excuse me if I act on impulse sometimes. Or if I want to live, even for just a moment, without my disease looming over every decision. One of those decisions being that I'm having a baby by a man that I met less than a year ago and love with all my heart. Those are the facts. This is my life, and if you can't accept that and try to muster up some support, then..."

Phoenix's emotions got the best of her as her tears started falling. She couldn't bring herself to tell her sister that she could walk out of her life. It wasn't at all what she wanted, and it pained her to even think the thought. She'd never argued with her sister like that. Usually they'd exchange a few words, but she had no idea just how unhappy with her sister's judgment she'd been until that moment. She didn't know it had been weighing so heavily on her. She'd been dealing with so much she never even took the time to access her feelings. Everything she'd been suppressing had bubbled over.

"Phoenix, I didn't know you felt like that. You never tell me or anyone else for that matter. I apologize for ever making you feel like I was tiptoeing around you or making you feel like you were inadequate. You matter to me, more than my husband or my children. Hell, in many ways you were my first child, and I would give my life just for you to have more time to accomplish whatever it is you want. I love you with my whole heart, not just a piece of it. And I support you in everything. I always have and always will. I just want you to be more careful. I know sometimes I don't have the right words and sometimes things come out judgey, but everything is from a place of love."

Rue walked closer to Phoenix and pulled her in for a hug. She loved her little sister. Their family wasn't big and were scattered all across the country. Besides their aunt, they were the only two closer than a 4-hour flight. The time they spent not speaking pained her and as much as she wanted to make up, she listened to Trav and waited for an opportunity to present itself.

Phoenix wouldn't have responded to her just showing up trying to make amends. Her stubbornness ran deep just like their grandmother's and aunt's. She stood firm in her emotions, even when she knew that she had no real grounds for being upset. Rue knew what she said to Phoenix wasn't 100 percent off base, and she knew her baby sister knew it too. But for the sake of sisterhood, she apologized for the way she said it and how it made Phoenix feel.

Forge joined in on their hug and joked to them about never putting her in the same position again. She loved them both and knew that with two strong-willed women, it was inevitable that they'd have squabbles. But those squabbles should never result in weeks without communicating. Phoenix and Rue both promised to always keep communication not only open, but also authentic and transparent. They were family and there should be no reason why family couldn't express themselves freely without feeling like someone would judge or attack them for their feelings on any subject.

The three women spent the remainder of the day buying furniture, toys, clothes and anything else they felt that baby Love Jones would need once they were six months old. It was a day full of love, light and all the side-splitting laughter their bodies could stand. Phoenix was exhausted by the time she ventured home and was overjoyed that Blaise had beat her there. She wanted a foot rub and fluffy pillow. Every limb from her waist down was sore and she felt bad having to cancel their date. It would be a while before they'd get the opportunity again with Blaise leaving for a conference the following week.

The smell of garlic greeted her before she could fully open the door. Her smile widened as she entered the house completely. Vivian was in the living room with her feet up continuing her streaming binge of *How to Get Away with Murder.* She'd mentioned countless times that Viola Davis was her favorite actress next to Cicely Tyson. That meant Blaise was cooking his famous stuffed garlic mushrooms.

Her stomach growled as she followed her nose to the kitchen. Creeping up behind him as he bobbed his head to the music blaring through his earbuds, she snaked her arms around his waist from the side. Her belly put too much distance between them for her liking, so she opted to remain sideways as he stared down at her. His smile caused his earbud to fall from his ear on to the counter and he turned fully to properly greet her.

A quick survey of his attire let her know he'd been home long enough to workout, shower and prepare dinner. Checking the time on the stove, she realized she'd been out far longer than she'd planned. Her afternoon shopping spree turned into a full-on girl's day thanks to the unplanned reunion of her and Rue. The women spent the ladder of the day sitting on the seventh pier of San Francisco's Embarcadero catching up on everything they'd missed since their big argument.

"How was shopping?" Blaise asked with a kiss to her temple.

"It was interesting, rejuvenating. Therapeutic."

"How so?" he asked, taking his attention away long enough to remove his pan of stuffed mushrooms from the oven."

"I saw Rue today. We talked."

"That's what's up. So, everything is all good with the sisterhood again?"

"You're corny, but yes." She laughed. "Then we blew a few bags in every baby boutique we found from San Francisco to The Junction."

"I swear baby Love Jones is going to think he is the King of the World. Two fully furnished living spaces with two complete wardrobes."

"He has a village that already loves to spoil him."

"Have I told you I loved you?"

"Mmhmm. But I'll never get tired of hearing you say it or seeing you prove it."

"I love you for having my baby. For giving me a real chance to love you."

"And I love you for making me a mother and wanting to love my complicated, difficult ass."

"I mean you put the Mrs. D in Ms. Honey's poem."

"Did I mention you were corny?" Phoenix laughed as she pulled the plates from the cabinet.

Phoenix set the table and prepared to have a light, late dinner with her extended family. She genuinely loved the life she was living and couldn't wait to see what else God had in store for her. This was the life she'd planned for herself, and while it hadn't gone exactly according to plan, it was finally happening. Her career was back on track, she had her man, and her family was officially in the making. There was nothing else she could possibly want.

CHAPTER EIGHTEEN

PHOENIX FUMBLED WITH THE BUTTONS ON HER BLOUSE AS SHE TRIED TO quiet the voices of chaos that clouded her mind. No matter how many times she tried to turn each negative thought into a positive one, the pessimism didn't let up. As she redressed, she replayed Dr. Ruiz's words over and over again in her head. This was what she had dreaded. There was no shock in finding out that her pregnancy was about to get a lot harder, in fact, it was exactly what she expected. But what she didn't expect was the drastic changes she needed to make immediately. Intermittent bed rest was something she expected further down the line, not at 28 weeks.

Rue and Forge both sat, taking in what the doctor had just explained. They didn't know how to comfort Phoenix. Her facial expressions were non-existent as she redressed in silence. Both women knew that she was trying to fully process everything that had transpired in the last forty-five minutes. The realization hadn't yet set in, and they both prepared themselves for the reclusive tactics Phoenix would employ once she fully understood what Dr. Ruiz had just told them.

Opting to feel something new, Phoenix sat down in the empty

chair in the corner of the spacious examination room. She couldn't stand to feel the scratchy covering on the examination table against her flesh any longer. Truthfully, she wanted to run and hide until it was time for her to give birth, but that wouldn't change the present circumstances surrounding her child's pending arrival. Placenta previa. Preterm labor. These were terms she'd only read in the many books she'd downloaded from Kindle the second she decided to carry her baby to term. Now, she was learning these things weren't just textbook case studies anymore, they were her reality. All she wanted to do was run into Blaise's arms and cry, but it would do no good. She'd fill a thousand oceans with tears, and it wouldn't change the fact that she was in the fight for her baby's life.

"Okay, Ms. Colleville, I need to get some blood from you and then you can set up your next appointment. Dr. Ruiz is finalizing your care instructions now, so it'll be at the receptionist's desk once you get up there."

Phoenix didn't register a thing the nurse said. Over and over, Dr. Ruiz's words echoed in her brain. She wondered how they never caught it before. She tried to think back to see if she missed any signs. Questions of whether the outcome could have been predicted or prevented plagued her as the world around her kept moving. She was exorcized from reality as she retreated into her mind. No words could soothe the agony she felt or assuage the guilt that formed in her gut. Was this all her fault? What could she have done differently? Why didn't she listen to Blaise when he told her to take it even easier than she already had been?

Realizing that Phoenix was not going to move from her seated position, Rue did the only thing she thought would comfort her baby sister. After sending out a distressed text to Blaise, her phone dinged alerting her that he had stepped away from the conference and was about to call. Pressing her phone to Phoenix's ear, she watched as the tears silently rolled down her cheeks. There was no word to describe the somber mood that cloaked the atmosphere of the examination room. Everyone hurt for Phoenix. No one had the words to make her feel any better than she did because they hurt.

Rue stood, holding the phone as Phoenix had a one-sided conversation with Blaise. It was unknown to both Rue and Forge what words he used to comfort her, but whatever it was seemed to work. Phoenix took a tissue from the box on the counter and dabbed at her eyes and nose before pulling her jacket over her shoulders. The bohemian farm girl outfit she donned accentuated her seven-month baby bump. Even with the uncertainty of the remainder of her pregnancy, her glow didn't seem dull despite the crushing weight of her circumstance. There was a light that shined, emitting from her being. The warm, fuzzy feeling it brought passersby was magnetizing. It was impossible to see her and not feel joy. But what she felt inside was anything but joy.

After Phoenix had composed herself, the women exited the examination room and made their way to the receptionist counter. Dr. Ruiz was due to leave the country for a conference but assured her that everything would be fine if she followed the care plan they'd devised. Being still didn't come natural to Phoenix, but more and more she was learning that stillness was the portion God had planned for her. In just two years, he'd given her new variations of the same lessons. Whenever she felt like life was beginning to happen for her, she sat down again. She thought this would be different. She thought motherhood would be her chance to finally experience life without the hurdles.

"Alright, Ms. Colleville, Let's get you scheduled for your IUTs. Dr. Ruiz wants you to do two sessions to start and then we'll retest your little one's blood before scheduling out anymore. She wants you in as soon as possible, so can you do September 5th at 10 a.m.?"

"What's the procedure like? I mean, will I need to have transportation or can I drive myself? His father isn't due back until the 7th."

"We recommend having someone with you in the event you're

too fatigued to drive yourself. But in your case, Dr. Ruiz has a note here that you should have transportation."

"She'll have it," Forge butted in.

"But you're supposed to leave on the 5th."

"I can postpone my flight. Fly out in the evening. Onyx will understand."

"Okay, I guess the 5th works then."

"Alright. I have you scheduled for September 5th at 10 a.m. with Dr. Ruiz. Do you want to schedule your second transfusion, or wait until the 5th?"

"I'll wait until the 5th so I can correlate with his schedule."

Phoenix was tired. She wanted to get this visit over with so she could eat and get some sleep. Dr. Ruiz wanted fasting blood work during this visit, so she hadn't eaten anything all morning. It was now late afternoon, and her head was pounding. The events of the day had drained her not only mentally and emotionally, but also physically. Exhaustion had quickly set in, and her lack of fuel had her feeling weak from all the blood that had been drawn from her body. She was grateful that Rue went to get the car from the garage while she and Forge finished up her check-out.

"Alright, you are all set. I've already sent your standing blood work orders down to the lab. You'll be able to go in every Tuesday for your glucose testing. Dr. Ruiz wants you to call if your bleeding worsens or you begin to show any signs of labor."

"Thank you, Bev. I'll see you on the 5th," Phoenix responded, forcing a smile.

Taking the papers, she turned to Rue and Forge and weakly smiled as she let them know she was ready. The walk to the car was uneventful as each woman processed the last hour. While they all thought they were coming in for a 3D ultrasound and routine check-up, things had shaped up to be far more than any of them could have expected. Unable to take the silence any longer, Phoenix sighed loudly, filling the space in the hallway with her frustration.

"I'm okay. I know I haven't said much of anything since she told me everything, but really, I am okay. Y'all don't have to worry. Blaise comes home in three days, and Mama Jones is home with me. We are going to be fine," Phoenix told them.

"Phoenix," Rue started.

"We're going to be fine," Phoenix's voice cracked as she looked into Rue's face. ""We're going to be fine, right?"

The tears came as her confidence in the statement she spoke shattered. The truth was Phoenix had no idea what was going to happen. She had enough faith to know that God would never give her more than she could bear, but she didn't have faith in herself to know that she could bear it. Losing the child that she and Blaise already loved so much would crush her. She knew she couldn't survive that reality. Her mental state was already fragile and that would just send her over the edge.

As Rue and Forge stopped walking and hugged her, she made a note to call Triumph. She hadn't needed a session on his couch since meeting Blaise, but even he knew he couldn't be her remedy. On the phone he reassured her that both she and their baby would be fine but encouraged her to make an appointment.

"Yes. You're a fighter. It's in your DNA, so it's in theirs too. You both will be more than fine, you'll be healthy. You are going to carry them to term, and everything will be okay," Forge told her.

From the hospital, Rue and Forge drove Phoenix to her house. She asked Mama Jones to meet her there. If she were going to be on bed rest for the next few weeks, she wanted to be in her own home. More precisely, she wanted to be in her parlor, surrounded by the essence of life. Her plants were her source of calming energy. The soothing aura she curated there was just what she needed for maximum comfort and reduced stress. For the next three days she'd be laid up in there, thinking happy thoughts and envisioning the day her legs were up and Blaise was yelling 'push.'

After filling Mama Jones in and going over the visit summary in Phoenix's patient portal they made sure she was settled into her temporary living quarters and bid her farewell and left her with her thoughts. Surprisingly, the words of encouragement from Blaise, Rue and Forge were enough to help her relax. She devoured the salad and sandwich Mama Jones had prepared for her and retreated to the pull-out bed in her parlor. Stripping down to her bra and panties, she climbed under the oversized sherpa blanket and let her head fall to the memory foam pillow. She was exhausted without having exerted much energy. Emotionally she was spent and the ease at which her body sunk into the bed was a clear indicator. Within a matter of minutes she was asleep and dreaming of a world where she was healthy, successful and coming home to Blaise every day.

Sweet kisses to her belly woke her from her peaceful slumber as the first genuine smile in two days graced the lower region of her face. Since leaving the hospital she spent every moment in her bed, journaling and binge-watching black sitcoms that hadn't been on air since her teen years. Mama Jones fed and bathed her, and while she'd normally fuss about all the assistance, she welcomed it because her mind could only focus on how she was going to make it through the rest of her pregnancy.

Softly, Phoenix palmed the sides of Blaise's head as he talked to their baby. His reassurance to their little one helped her breathe a little easier. Doing this alone would have killed her by now, she was grateful that he never let up on her when she tried to distance herself from him. He made everything right in her world and she never wanted to know wrong again.

"Hey, you," he smiled, finally giving her his undivided attention.

"You came home early?"

"You needed me. Y'all needed me," he corrected, touching her stomach again, "There wasn't no way I was having you go anywhere else without me."

"I love you," Phoenix pronounced as she leaned forward and kissed his lips.

"I love you too. How are you feeling?"

"Exhausted. The intermittent bleeding really snatches my

energy. But other than that, I'm okay. Especially now that you're home."

"So, what are we in for during this last trimester? I looked over your results in the patient portal on the ride from the airport, but what do you think? It's your body and you know it better than any of us."

"I had been spotting a few days before my appointment, but the morning of my appointment it was really heavy. Dr. Ruiz said I have placenta previa. I'm sure you know what it is, so I won't go into it. She did some tests and said that my body is attacking Love Jones. And it's restricting his blood flow or something. I can't remember exactly what she said, because by then I had sort of tuned everything out, but she wants me to get an intrauterine blood transfusion. Two to start. Blaise, I'm so scared. I put on a brave face for everyone because I don't want them to worry, but I am terrified and I am really trying not to freak out," Phoenix admitted as tears welled in her eyes.

"You are a fighter and I know that it's hard, but we're going to get through this together. You and me. I'm not going anywhere. And when we make it to the other side of this, I am going to shower your fine ass with whatever your heart desires," Blaise affirmed as he leaned up and delicately kissed away her tears before latching on to her lips.

"Did I mention how much I love you?"

"You did, but I'll never complain about you saying it too much," he laughed as he stood.

Reaching out his hand, he waited for her to place her palm in his. With his assistance, she rose from the bed she'd called home for the last two days. Hoisting herself up on the balls of her feet, she wrapped her arms around his neck, palming the back of his head. Lovingly, she looked into his eyes, and all that looked back was love and admiration. She knew he loved her and would do anything to make sure she was as comfortable as possible for the remainder of her pregnancy.

The couple walked hand-in-hand into the office accompanied by

Mama Jones. She'd decided that from now until her grandchild's birthday, she would be at every appointment. Phoenix squeezed tightly as they approached the counter. For once, she allowed someone else to take the reins of her care. Silently, she gripped Blaise's hand with both hers as Mama Jones talked to the receptionist to get her checked in for her procedure.

Within seconds, they were whisked to a cozy room in the back. A recliner was in the corner and a heating blanket sat in the middle of the examination table. Phoenix stood still as Blaise undressed her. She held in her breath as he pulled her dress over her head. For a brief moment, she looked in his face, searching for an inkling of fear, but all that stared back at her was hope. Her breathing returned to normal as she fed off his energy. After Dr. Ruiz entered the room with her team, she felt secure, like everyone there had her best interest in mind as they walked her through the coming series of events.

"First, we're going to draw some blood from Baby Love Jones to see if my suspicion is correct. If so, then we'll start the transfusion. The procedure should take about 30 minutes, 45 tops," Dr. Ruiz reassured Phoenix as the technicians prepped all the equipment and supplies.

"Oh. Ah. Ahhhhh!"

Phoenix's cries commanded the attention of everyone in the room. She doubled over as she hugged her belly. Tears streamed down her face as the fear sat in. In waves, the pain came one after the other. She didn't have time to compose herself in between the contractions. Her deepest fear was coming true. She was inadequate, unable to carry her baby to term.

Before she tuned out the world, her eyes focused on the worry plastered across Blaise's as the staff around him sprang into action. They'd prepared for an intrauterine blood transfusion, but Baby Love Jones had other plans. He or she was coming, and they needed to make sure they did everything in their power to see to it that he survived.

Phoenix felt like a fish out of water as she was rushed to the OR.

It was too late for any efforts that might have delayed her labor, which meant she and Blaise were about to meet their baby twelve weeks early. With her placenta partially blocking her cervix, an emergency C-section was the only safe way to ensure their baby arrived with less complications. All hands were on deck as they strapped monitors to her arms and inserted tubes into her nose. She winces with pain at the insertion of the catheter.

Blaise briefly left her side to scrub in with the rest of the staff. Though he wasn't a member of her medical care team, he wanted to ensure their baby was born into the most sterile room on the unit. Within minutes, he was back at her side.

As machines were connected and the anesthesiologist explained what would happen next, Phoenix maintained her grip on Blaise's hand. His presence is what kept her anxiety at bay throughout the fast-paced transition from exam room to operating table.

Softly, Blaise sang *This Very Moment* by K-Ci & JoJo to calm her nerves. Though she was heavily medicated, he could feel that she was afraid of what was happening. She was worried for their child; the vice grip on his fingers and the wild wandering of her gaze proved his notion.

"You're doing great, babe, just a few more seconds and we'll be meeting Baby Love Jones in the flesh," Blaise assured her with sweet kisses to her temple, forehead and lips.

"Babe, I'm cold. I don't think I'm gonna make it," Phoenix whispered into his lips as he kissed her.

"Yes, you are. You're strong and resilient. Protected and safe. Just hold on for a little while longer, and Dr. Ruiz is going to get you all closed up.

Forty-five minutes after her initial outcry, Phoenix was greeted by Blaise's gentle kisses to her temple again. Tears streamed down her face as she took in the scene. It was chaotic as health professionals moved around her, completing various tasks to ensure the health and safety of her and her baby.

"Congratulations Mommy and Daddy! You have a beautiful, baby girl," Dr. Ruiz said as she placed her on the warmer. With a big smile, she handed Blaise the clamp for the umbilical cord. Baby Love Jones' weak cries filled the room shortly after as the nurse cleared her air passages. It was the last sound Phoenix heard before her world went dark

CHAPTER NINETEEN

Blaise sat holding his daughter. He studied her closed lids as her eyes moved slowly behind them. He listened to the suckling as she drank up her mother's breast milk from the tiny slow flow nipple on the bottle he held to her mouth. Life for him had drastically changed overnight and ten days later he still didn't have a handle on things. The only person keeping him going was the beautiful baby girl he cradled in his arms. Her homecoming was finally upon them, and it should have been a joyous moment, but sadness overshadowed the happy occasion.

Ten days. That's how much time had passed since he heard the angelic voice of his dream girl. The trauma surrounding the birth of their daughter sent her body crashing and recovery for her hadn't been as progressive as it had been for their little one. While Baby Love Jones was making strides to know a life outside of the neonatal care unit, her mother was in a constant battle that for the last nearly three weeks knew no end.

The slowing of the suckling alerted Blaise that Baby Love Jones was done with her feeding. The wrinkling of her nose and kicking of her toes against his chest let him know she'd had enough of his arms and desired the soft comfort of her blanket. Placing her back in the crib, he kissed her ten little fingers before rubbing her head full of hair, jet black loose curls. She was the perfect combination of Blaise and Phoenix.

The squinting of her eyes as she cut them in his direction made him smile as he recalled her mother giving him the same look whenever he said or did something she didn't like. He loved how in tune with his routine his baby girl had become. She knew when he was preparing to leave her presence, her fussiness commenced every time. As much as he wished he could sit with her forever, he had a few errands to run before he returned later in the day to take her home.

"Daddy will be back in a few hours to rescue you from this place, fat mama. Your Grammy is coming to take my place, so you won't be alone." Blaise spoke in the voice he'd reserved only for his princess. She stirred up something in him he never knew was in him. Baby talk was something he swore he'd never give in to, but here he was softening his voice and taking it up a few octaves to create a unique voice curated just to communicate with her. He looked up just as his mother walked into the room.

"Hey, Ma. I'm going to check-in on Phoenix before I run to the house to change," Blaise announced as he gave her a kiss to the cheek.

"Okay, son, love you."

Blaise greeted the staff at the nurses' station on Phoenix's floor. Even though he never engaged with many of them before this, he'd become quite acquainted over the past few weeks. They made sure he was always briefed on any changes to Phoenix's condition. Since the day their daughter was born, she'd been lost to him and everyone else. Elevated blood pressure from the event surrounding labor caused hemorrhaging. She'd been in a medically induced coma ever since. It was the only way doctors could stop the worsening of her condition. He hadn't laid eyes on her since they hooked her up to the machines that kept her alive that first week in a half.

"Hi, Dr. Jones, how's baby girl doing," the head nurse asked.

"Hi. She's doing great. Finally getting to come home today. How's mama bear doing today? Anything new?"

"The doctors came by this morning. She's stable, but there hasn't been any changes to her condition. Give her some time. She's been through a lot and her body needs time to recoup. I'm optimistic, she's a fighter."

"Thanks. That's what everyone keeps saying."

"Are you going to sit for a while today?"

"No, I have a few more things to do before I bring baby girl home this evening. Call me if anything changes or she wakes up?"

"Okay. Oh, and Dr. Jones, a woman called today asking to be updated and to be put on the visitor's list. She said she's family to Ms. Colleville, a Tracy Peppers."

"Yea, that's her best friend who lives in Dubai. Please add her. I think she's coming into town, but not sure how soon, given the travel."

Blaise left the hospital with only two things on his agenda, shower and sleep. Life had come at him faster than he could ever have prepared for. He'd had no down time since Baby Love Jones made her debut. He went from his appointments to his daughter's bedside. In between, he found time to get updates on Phoenix's status and hop on virtual meetings with medical care teams he consulted with.

There was hardly any time to catch his breath let alone get adequate sleep or food. From the moment his feet crossed the threshold of his door, the stillness calmed him. He was depleted of what little energy he had left, and he knew he was not prepared for parenting without Phoenix. A tear left his eye as he fell on the sofa in the living room.

The curtains were drawn as was his mother's morning custom, and the sun shone down on him. The warmth of the sun's rays radiating off the window soothed his aching limbs. Pulling Phoenix's throw over his body, he turned on his side and decided to forego the shower. Sleep was much more pressing than anything giving the reality that sleep would be something he would know even less of once Baby Love Jones came home that evening.

Back at the hospital, Mama Jones softly hummed Whitney Houston's 'I didn't know my own strength' while she finished cleaning out the breast pump. She'd served as Phoenix lactation consultant, making sure Baby Love Jones had an ample supply of her mother's liquid gold to sustain her until her mama bear decided to wake up. After storing the final pouch of milk in the rolling cooler she had beside her feet, she pulled out the medium sized cosmetic bag from her oversized tote bag.

Removing her brush, she gently brushed Phoenix's hair. She'd washed and detangled it the night before while her, Rue and Forge visited. She loved how it had grown out during her pregnancy. The short cut shaped her face and showed the artistry of her features, but the new length matured her. Now, shoulder length with the purple being only at the tips, Mama Jones thought she'd look regal with mini two-strand twists.

As she sat at her side, pillows propped under Phoenix' neck to make it easier to part her hair, she reminded Phoenix of all the reasons she had to keep fighting. As a cancer survivor, she was no stranger to wanting to throw in the towel. Even the spot beside the bed was familiar to her as she remembered sitting at her husband's bedside when he slipped into a coma. For seven days, she spoke life into him, until one night his knee tickled her underarm when he woke. He told her his family is what kept him fighting, what helped him find his way back to them and she knew if God did it once he could do it again. But Phoenix had to want to wake up.

Four hours passed before her phone vibrated in her pocket, interrupting the comfortable silence she'd become accustomed to at her bonus daughter's bedside. Letting it go to voicemail, she finished up the last three rows of Phoenix's hair. Whoever was on her phone could wait until she was finished with the task at hand. Persistence was surely a trait of the caller as her phone rang two more times. Sighing, she stopped to pull the phone from her pocket and rolled her eyes at the caller.

"Yes, son. What's so urgent you blowing up my line like this," Mama Jones answered, irritation dripping from every word.

"I'm all done checking out Baby Love Jones. Was wondering if you'd be at the house by the time I get back there?"

"I just got done Phoenix's hair, so I should be there around the same time as you. Anything else?"

Blaise noted his mother's shortness with him and wanted to question it, but they had all evening to get into that, "Nothing else I need to ask over the phone."

Mama Jones hung up before he could get out anything else. Blaise had tap danced on every last one of her nerve endings with the way he was handling himself. To say she was disappointed in him would be an understatement. When his father fell ill, she stood beside him and fought until he decided he'd fought all he could. She never gave up on him and she never left him alone. By her observation, she felt like she was the best example of how to care for those you loved, but her son wasn't following the example she set. He hadn't been into Phoenix's hospital room once and she was angry with him because of it.

Just as she finished oiling Phoenix's scalp a beautiful, full-figured woman stood in the doorway. Her hair was pulled back, leaving her big round eyes and pouty lips on full display. She offered a polite yet forced smile as she stepped fully into the room. Sadness shone through her eyes as she tried to keep it together when her gaze fell on her best friend. Tracy slowly walked over to Phoenix and caressed her cheek with her knuckles. Only one tear escaped her eye before she wiped the excess away. Crying would not change this, prayer and strength would.

"Sorry, where are my manners? I'm Tracy, Pegasus' best friend. Sorry, Phoenix. Pegasus is my nickname for her," Tracy announced as she extended her hand to Mama Jones.

Mama Jones walked up to Tracy and pulled her in for a hug. Phoenix talked about Tracy a lot whenever she brought up her college days. It was not easy to fathom being halfway across the world and finding out your best friend was in a hospital bed, fighting for her life. It was probably an indescribable feeling of angst and though she couldn't imagine it, she could lend a bit of comfort.

"It's nice to meet you. Phoenix talks about you all the time. I'm Mama Jones, Blaise's mother."

"Wish we were meeting under different circumstances, but it's still nice to finally meet you. Thank you for easing her fears and making her feel good about giving birth."

"You don't have to thank me for that. I'm going to get out of your hair and give you some privacy with our girl. You take care of her, while I go take care of our other baby girl."

"What's her name?"

"B decided to wait for Phoenix to wake up before naming her, so we're still calling her Baby Love Jones."

Once Mama Jones left the room, Tracy pulled up a chair and sat beside her friend. She cried a river as she thought about the many conversations they'd had over the years. This couldn't be her life, it shouldn't be. Anger built up and she thought about Phoenix lying in that bed for the last fourteen days. This was not what she wanted for her friend, and this was not what her friend wanted for herself.

CHAPTER TWENTY

Tracy paced back and forth before plopping down in the chair by the window. Aimlessly, she gazed out the window, watching the people on the street below her window walk in and out of the shops surrounding Brewer's Bed and Breakfast. The faces blurred as she thought about her friends while she waited for her guests to arrive.

She'd opted to stay at Brewer's bed and breakfast instead of in Phoenix's house. Every day she got dressed, grabbed coffee at Forge's café, and went to the hospital to sit with her friend. She'd kept the same routine for the past 5 days with no variation or deviation. Something had to give, and she realized that it was up to her. She had to make sure that Phoenix had a voice in her care, even though she couldn't speak for herself.

A knock at the door jolted Tracy from her daydream. Wiping away the tears that came, she stood and smoothed out her hair. Her nerves were tightly wound and knotted in her stomach as she tried to gather her emotions. This was a delicate situation, and she wanted to make sure she got her grievances out without succumbing to her emotions. Somehow, she'd managed to keep them in check this long and prayed that God not only gave her the strength, but that He also gave her the words.

Blaise, Rue, and Mama Jones all piled into the room. Blaise had asked Forge to take Baby Love Jones with her to the hospital to see Phoenix. Tracy offered them all a seat as she tried to find the words to say what needed to be said. Throwing caution to the wind, she opened her mouth and hoped that her words expressed her thoughts and feelings.

"I know you're all probably wondering why I asked you here. So, I'm not going to mince words or waste anyone's time. I want to discuss Phoenix's circumstances. What should happen?"

"What do you mean, what should happen?" Blaise asked. He looked at her like she'd grown three additional heads.

"I mean my best friend has been in a medically induced coma for fifteen days and still hasn't woken up. It's been damn near three weeks, and everyone seems to be okay with her current state. Frankly, I'm not."

"Is this bitch forreal? You called us here to suggest what exactly?"

Rue jumped at the base in Blaise's voice. She knew he was taking everything hard and putting on a brave face. He was in a difficult spot, and she was sensitive to his plight. She gave him his space and allowed him all the time he needed, but his outburst proved he was in a bad space, and no one should have left him with his emotions for as long as they had. He was hurting, and it was evident in the way he lashed out at Tracy, whom he never met.

"Aye, now I know we are all in our feelings, but we are not going to sit here and disrespect each other. Blaise I did not raise you to talk to anybody like that. So, calm down and let's talk like adults," Mama Jones instructed as she flexed her elder status.

They could have a discussion, but it needed to be with decorum. Phoenix would never want the people she cared about most arguing and berating each other in her name. She was shocked by her son's tone and choice of words. This entire ordeal revealed her disillusioned thoughts of him she'd never known. It was the parts of them she didn't like, and she would be sure to check him once they made it back to his house.

"I'm not discussing shit. Ma, she's insinuating that we give up on Phoenix, and I'm not going for any of that bullshit she is spitting."

"Giving up? You wanna talk about giving up? How many times have you gone to see her? Sat by her side? Listened to the monitors that let us know her heart's still pumping?"

"Okay, everybody calm down. This is not getting us anywhere," Rue interjected.

She had been discussing this exact topic with Trav. As the only person legally able to make decisions for Phoenix, she questioned what to do every night she came from visiting her little sister. Though the doctors had assured them she was showing improvement, they still hadn't reversed the induced coma. Their options were limited, but she'd been weighing them with her husband.

"So, tell me, what do you propose we do? Huh? Since you've been there for everything and know what's best? Tell us," Blaise mocked.

"Look, I'm sorry for coming off at you like that. I know you're in the toughest spot and I shouldn't have said that. But, I know Phoenix, and she wouldn't want to be laying up in some hospital bed like a damn vegetable."

"She's not. Her brain is functioning. There are signs of cognitive function on her scans. She hasn't shown sufficient enough gains for them to wake her up yet. So, we need to just give her all the time she needs, and she'll come back to us when she's ready. She always does," Rue offered.

Tracy listened as Rue talked. Medically, she knew the facts, but that was as far as it went. But when it came to knowing Phoenix, she felt there was no one more qualified than her. They'd spent the most time together and had the tough conversations. She was the one who sat down with Phoenix and wrote out her living will before she moved to Solace Point. She was the one who talked her out of her taking her own life the same night Darrell left her. There were moments and conversations that Tracy swore she'd never tell a soul. But now all the people in the room wanted a say in how she'd live.

"With all due respect, no one in this room knows Phoenix better than me. We've talked about this often, and she always told me that she'd never want to live like this. She told me to not ever have her laid up in a bed, a shell of her existence."

"You know what, I'm not listening to this bullshit. There is nothing to do but wait for Phoenix to wake up. She's the only person who is going to dictate what happens to her."

Blaise stood and walked to the door. Anger and agitation fueled by sleep deprivation and grief had him ready to explode. He'd been operating out of his element for weeks and nothing seemed to make it better. Phoenix would wake up, and they'd have their life together. He didn't want to get in a screaming match with her best friend, so he took a queue from Phoenix and left the conversation all together.

Once he was gone, the women continued to talk. Tracy was able to fully communicate how she was feeling. Everyone admitted that seeing Phoenix peacefully sleeping made them think it was what she wanted, but they just couldn't be the ones to make that decision. Not when they all felt like she had more living to do.

"Tracy, I know this is hard. It's hard for everybody, but this is our reality right now. It's a waiting game. We are on Phoenix's time," Rue said as she hugged her. Tracy welcomed the hug as her tears came. She missed her friend and thought they had more time.

"Now, baby, please check out of this room and go to Phoenix's. There ain't no point in blowing your bank account the you can stay at her place. Might help ease your mind a bit."

Tracy pulled every blanket from the top of Phoenix's closet. She'd rummaged through every box stuffed into the empty spare room before deciding to check the rest of her house. On her previous visit with her dear friend, a one-sided conversation transported her back to a time where everything was nearly perfect in both of their lives. An impromptu night of club hopping made them stumble upon a man who had easily become their favorite R&B crooner. It was her last night in the states, and she couldn't have asked for a more perfect send-off. The attending nurse told her she could bring in items for Phoenix that would make her space feel more at home.

Yelping in pain, she looked down at the ambrosia box that had toppled from the shelf onto her head. Reaching down, tears welled up in her eyes as she realized what was housed inside. *The letters.* She thought as she slowly reached down and picked up the box. Walking back to the room she'd claimed, she cradled the box like it was her last piece of Phoenix. Though her friend's body was lying in the hospital bed, she knew her spirit followed them everywhere they went. She was always with them. She remembered the day she told her the plan she had to start her solo tradition. It was three years ago, and she'd kept it up.

Tracy twirled the letter between her index and pinky fingers. She contemplated the ramifications of breaking the beautiful, golden wax-seal on the envelope her scripted name adorned. Was it considered an invasion of privacy? Though it was addressed to her, peeking before it was actually given could be seen as such.

In all her years of learning Phoenix in all her seasons, privacy and trust were at the top of her dear friend's list of requirements for her loved ones. There was never a time she ever wanted to break Phoenix's trust or revoke her right to privacy, but she prayed there was something housed behind the elegant fold of the paper that would help her make sense of everything happening around her.

To say she was lost would be an understatement. Just weeks ago, they were laughing together via video call while Phoenix walked through the mall. She'd made plans to come visit once Baby Love Jones was three months old. Never in anything that she every imagined, did she think this would be the first birth story of their friendship.

Now she was grappling with a reality she thought she'd not have to face for at least another fifty years. Even with her diagnosis and all the treatment that followed, she just knew in her heart Phoenix would be with her for a lifetime. Without considering for another moment, Tracy broke the seal on her letter and marveled at her best friend's handwriting on the page. Since they were younger, she teased Phoenix for taking calligraphy seriously in middle school. But as the corners of her mouth met her eyes, she let a tear fall.

My dearest Tracy,

With all the heartache I endured as a child, I'm surprised I even have a childhood friend. You've stayed down even when I went radio silent for years. Thank you for a lifetime of laughs, adventures, secrets and unforgettable memories.

We've prepared for this moment. The one where I'm no longer a call away. Where distance and time no longer matter. Where forever has ended. And even as I pen this the tears are plentiful, so excuse the smudges. They say that I'll no longer know pain where I'm going, and I imagine they could only mean physical because not physically being with you pains me to think about. Honestly, I wish heaven would just wait a little while longer. Not being able to call you up at ungodly hours or go to the same concert in 6 different cities together just seems like our version of hell. I want more time to create more magical moments, but this was it for us.

Please take care of my family. Blaise is an amazing man and I know he'll be an even more amazing father to our little Love Jones, but he'll need you and Rue both. He'll never ask, as protecting and providing is the pinnacle of his existence but keep him covered in prayer and remind him he isn't in it alone. Even though you are across the oceans, I know you will make sure they'll have all the love and support they need to survive without me.

I love you for forever and the 30-day grace period after. Don't cry for me. Don't be sad. I'm with you always. When you're front row at a show or finally bathing in the Dead Sea, I'll be with you. Keep living. Keep traveling.

Until I see you again,
Pegasus

Loud sobs filled the empty room as she clutched the letter to her chest. This was too soon for her. She felt robbed, like God had cheated her out of the time and memories she was supposed to make with her dearest friend. They were supposed to grow old together, hold each other's bouquets at their weddings and plan playdates with their children. Living their dream lives in real time was what they deserved. But somehow it just wasn't what was in store for them, and that reality crushed her more than anything else.

Curiosity plagued her as she glanced at the other letters in the box. Rue, Forge, Blaise and even her Aunt Phae all had letters that were just as beautiful addressed to them. For the next thirty minutes, Tracy poured over the series of letters. With a rag in one hand and the letters in the other, she protected the pages from her salty tears.

Phoenix was selfless, and the words she wrote for Baby Love Jones and Blaise were everything. Reality sunk in as she realized that it was easy for Phoenix to say to let her go if it ever came down to it because she had no one she needed to live for. Phoenix hadn't found love back then. She felt like she had nothing and no one worth fighting that hard for, but now Blaise and Baby Love Jones were here. She knew she'd want to fight for them. She'd want to see her daughter grow up. She'd want to get lost in Blaise's deep, dark eyes for an eternity.

And even if I have nothing left, I'll have all I need. Tracy read that line of the letter she held a million times. It was embedded in her heart and committed to her memory. Phoenix finally found love, the agape kind. The kind of love that made you want to risk it all. The kind of love that made you feel like life was worth living. The kind of love that made you feel like nothing else even mattered. It was a supernatural love. A supernova love, burning bright, fast and bursting into remnants that could sustain the multitude. It was spiritual.

As she cried for her friend, she understood Blaise's pain. He hadn't abandoned her. He loved her enough to keep their world together until she returned. He gave her the one thing she'd asked for more of constantly from everyone who loved her, space and time. Putting all the letters back in their envelopes, she placed the box on the end table and continued her search. Finally, she found the custom PinkSweat$ woven blanket she'd sent her as a gift and returned to the hospital.

This next morning, she rose early. Handling her hygiene in record time, she enjoyed a quick breakfast while she updated Kellz on Phoenix's current status before heading over to Solace General. Thinking about everything Kellz had said to her, she hugged the blanket as she exited the elevator on Phoenix's floor. As she neared the hallway, she saw Blaise talking to one of the doctors. Wanting to avoid the awkwardness of forced pleasantries, she proceeded past him. But he stopped her in her tracks.

"Tracy, I want to apologize for the way I acted yesterday. I could give a million reasons about why it was so easy for me to lash out at you, but none would be sufficient. I'm too old and have been taught how to communicate my feelings in a manner that doesn't demean, belittle, or dismiss the feelings of others. So, please forgive me for my boisterous attitude and harsh words."

"No need to apologize. I should have been more sensitive with my approach. We are all processing this differently, and your feelings are valid. I have no doubt that you love her unconditionally and would give the world to have her back."

To say she was taken aback by his accountability, would have been useless. The dumbfounded look on her face before she accepted his apology was enough evidence. A hug and brief update followed before she continued her stroll to Phoenix's room.

Mama Jones greeted her as she continued her daily lactation routine. For an hour she sat and talked with Blaise's mother, and she silently prayed to God for him to not only give Phoenix back to them, but to restore the time that they all lost. God could restore it all and she prayed the full weight of her faith for him to make all things new for Phoenix.

As she covered Phoenix with the blanket from the waist down, she pressed play on her phone, allowing Pink Sweat$, *Pink City* filled the space around them. It was one of Phoenix's favorite songs. The first song she'd ever heard by him and one that held special meaning. Softly, she laid her head on her friends shoulder and sang the chorus. Phoenix had built a home in her head, but she wanted to remind her there was a home waiting for her.

CHAPTER TWENTY-ONE

DANDELIONS TICKLED THE TIP OF HER NOSE AS SHE HELD HER BABY GIRL close to her chest. The warmth of the sun coupled with the chill of the breeze coming off the water centered her. Faintly, she swayed back and forth in her armchair as she soothed the sleepy little human nestled in her arms. Laughter consumed her as she reengaged with the conversation happening among the women in her family. For the first time in forever, she was surrounded by her mother, favorite aunt and sister. It seemed like the birth of new life was the only way to get her parents and aunt to fly clear across the country and she was overcome with joy that everyone was together to celebrate the arrival of her beautiful baby girl.

Sundays were her favorite day of the week. She got to reset her energy and replenish the joy, passion and love she disseminated to her audience during the week. Spending hours surrounded by her family was the peace she couldn't find anywhere else in the world. They grounded her in purpose and showered her with enough love to cleanse the multitude.

"Phoenix! You're daydreaming again," Phae laughed as she took Baby Love Jones from her arms.

"No, I'm not. I'm breathing in the moment; you should try it sometimes. Instead of filling every moment with your voice."

"Ard now, you two. Play nice," Phoenix's mother interjected.

Phoenix leaned over to pour herself a glass of wine. Quickly, she glanced over her shoulder to find her adoring husband. A sigh of relief left her slightly ajar mouth as she saw him and her father busy themselves with getting the fire going. She took that as a chance to get in a few sips of the wine her mother had been raving about for weeks. He took breastfeeding serious, and even though her doctor told her dry red was fine, he threw a conniption every time she mentioned wanting a glass.

On any other day, she would oblige his concerns, but this was a special Sunday because it was the last one of the season. With a new season came new possibilities for the future and new opportunities to make moments worth reminiscing. Her family had adopted her burning ceremony and made it a family affair. Every season they cast into the fire all the thoughts, feelings and instances where their faith was shattered by limiting beliefs. She wanted to toast the occasion with her favorite women.

Life has been going better than she expected. Everyone in her life seemed to be thriving in their own right. Her health has been in a steady incline, and she anticipated freedom. A tear slid down her face as she listened to the sweet sound of her mother and aunt's laughter. She prayed she'd have more years with them. Both women meant the world to her. Their impact was the most profound, shaping much of how she chose to live her life and raise her daughter. Even with their mistakes, she'd always choose them to emulate how she chose to live and care for her family. With a bond like Debbie and Phylicia, they were the epitome of sisterhood and she and Rue always swore to be just as close.

Phaedra ran her hand through Phoenix's twists as she sat by her bedside. A quaint smile teased the corner of Phoenix's mouth as she slept. Phaedra wanted to alert the doctor, but she joined her niece in the moment. She imagined her ranting about how they let her new growth get so uncontrolled. It was amazing to see her natural beauty shine through even with tubes coming from her nose and mouth.

The monitor's beeping served as the only noise in the room as she listened to the rhythmic beating of her niece's heart monitor. So much time had passed. So many words went unspoken. So much love unrequited. And now as she stared down at the woman who once followed behind her like a shadow, she hated herself for never truly fighting for her niece's forgiveness.

Phoenix made her proud. Both her nieces did, but it was the fight in Phoenix that made her poke out her chest every time she talked about her. Though Phoenix had albeit damned her to hell after the death of her sister and brother-in-law she never stopped keeping tabs on her. Rue made sure she knew every move Phoenix made and got to celebrate her wins from a distance. Sitting there, watching Phoenix sleep, she knew that not another second of time would be wasted. Though she wouldn't force Phoenix to forgive her, she would finally speak her peace.

"I know I am probably the last voice you want to hear, but Rue thought I needed to see you. She thinks you're wrestling with something that you don't want to face when you wake, but I know that the reality you're experiencing behind your lids is a euphoria you don't want to depart. Tell my big sister I said hi if you're with her.

Niece, I know I let you down and I apologize. I wish I could take it back and I think about it every night I lay my head down. Please come back to us, to Blaise, to Baby Love Jones. You've remained my pride and joy even through distance and time. Time is something I know we can never get back, but it is something we can maximize by being willing to be present. Come back, Phoenix. I know you're probably experiencing your version of heaven, but honestly heaven can wait, your daughter can't. Heaven is forever and this life is not. Wake up and live in love with the beautiful family you're making with Blaise. He's a catch by the way. Good job locking him down. I miss you. I love you. But the most important thing to know is I'm waiting for you."

Phaedra kissed her nieces forehead again before leaning her head to her shoulder. With Phoenix's hand still clasped between her palms, she rested in the eerie silence of the room. The monitors beeped and she felt her niece's shoulders rise and fall with each breath. Phoenix's eyes moved faintly behind her lids as she looked up into her face. She knew she was fighting her way back. There was much to muddle through physically and emotionally, but she knew Phoenix was strong enough to endure it all.

After resting in Phoenix's presence, humming 'Count on Me' by Whitney Houston and CeCe Winans, she released her hand. Wiping her damp cheeks, she pulled out the letter that Tracy had given her when she first arrived. Everything in her wanted to reseal the envelope and tuck it back in the box. She knew Phoenix was not gone to them forever. She was just taking a much-needed break from the climatic life she'd lived the last three years.

My Dearest Auntie Phae,

There are a million things I wish I would have said to you. Now as I sit here on the edge of my existence, I know the time I spent angry with you is time we'll never get back.

For much of my childhood, it was you who I wanted to emulate. You were confident, unapologetic and free. Your spirit radiated with joy, and it was contagious. That zeal, that fervor with which you chose to live your life was invigorating. Awe-inspiring. Though I never made it known, I was always thinking Aunt Phae taught me whenever someone complimented how I chose to move through life.

My heart aches for the years we lost because of my stubbornness. It aches more for the ones we won't get in the future. The memories we shared, I've carried in my heart and recalled them often when I felt I needed your presence. You were always on my mind. You were always in my heart. And though you thought your apologies fell on deaf ears, I heard it. I accept it. And above all, I forgive you.

I know you hate long and mushy, so I'll keep it short. Don't cry for me. Don't be sad. Know that even with all my rage, I never stopped loving you. Take care of Rue, she'll blame herself for my departure and it's on you to make sure she knows she did all she could for me. Keep living wild and free, dance on a few more tables...or dicks because I know how you still get down with the get down. Until we meet again.

Love always,
Your Phe, Phi, Phae

"Thank you for forgiving me. I love you, Phe, Phi, Phae."

Phaedra sat by her niece's bedside for a little while longer as she tried to come to grips with everything Phoenix revealed in her letter. Though these words were intended to stamp the ending of her presence with her family, there was a sense of belonging that just continued to persist. As a woman who hated to be viewed as a strong black woman, she was also well-aware of her niece's impenetrable strength and persistent nature to fight through anything. To her, this was no different. Phoenix would find a way to make it back to the people she held dear, Tracy prematurely calling her life did not dull that fight nor erase the fact that Phoenix was indeed a world-champion when it came to fighting obstacles.

CHAPTER TWENTY-TWO

Weariness covered every feature on Rue's body as she entered the nursery. It had been nearly a month since she saw her sister's bright eyes or heard her sweet, squeaky laughter. Life had been hard managing her children and husband all while trying to keep her composure. But it had become too much, so she sought solace with the one person who knew Phoenix better than she.

Forge dropped the ribbon and scissors once she saw the sadness in Rue's eyes. Rushing to her friend, she pulled her into her bosom. Rue sighed before breaking their hug several minutes later. As they sat on the stools in the garden studio, she unpacked all her feelings. There was no moment to exhale as she went from one role to the next, and she hadn't realized she was holding on to so much. With her head in her hands, Rue let everything she'd been holding spill from her heart.

Allowing her to cleanse the anguish she was sure Rue held since her sister went unresponsive, she wrapped her in her arms. It was only a few years ago she'd dealt with something similar, and she understood all too well how Rue felt. Being the person responsible for someone else's fate came with an insurmountable weight. Love wanted you to hold on, but that same love compelled you to find a way to muddle through the selfishness and release them from their pain. Her grandmother was different because she'd lived a full life, while Phoenix hadn't even reached her prime yet. Letting go would be hard for everyone, but extremely difficult for Rue as she was not only her sister, but her maternal figure and caregiver.

"Her letter said that we all reach a moment in our lives where we aren't meant to get better. Forge, she wants to go, but something is keeping her here. I feel like she's fighting a battle that's deeper than lupus, and I can't help her through it if she doesn't wake up. It's like she's surrendering to something or someone. I just can't figure it out. My journals are full. My mind is overloaded, and nothing seems to be changing. *She* doesn't seem to be changing."

"Because it's not something you are meant to help her with. Have you ever stopped to assess her life these last, what, ten months or so? She may not be surrendering; she may be surveying. It's something she has to fight on her own and she's doing that. Phoenix is going to come back to us. She just needs time and peace. Even though no one mentions what's been going on between us and our indecisiveness about her fate. She can sense it. Our energy is off, and we all need to just let her be. And she needs to know her man hasn't given up on her. Rue, he needs to go see her, not just see about her."

Rue hadn't considered that. Her mind had been so focused on finding legal avenues to give Phoenix the peace she deserved. Medically, everything was as good as it could be with her condition, so there was no way to pull the plug when plugs weren't necessarily what were keeping her alive. She just wouldn't wake up. But Forge made the most profound realization. Phoenix needed Blaise at her side. She needed to know he hadn't abandoned her. She didn't want to live a life where he wasn't a part of her reality.

The next morning Rue rose two hours early to make sure her family would get through the morning without her. As she drove to Blaise's house, she rehearsed the script she'd wrote out a million times. There was no way for her to understand or even relate to what he was feeling. She prayed that God would give her the strength to say what everyone else had been thinking. He'd been incorrigible since Phoenix blacked out. There was nothing anyone could do or say around him that wouldn't bring on his unsolicited wrath. The situation was delicate, and if she didn't handle it with care, she could lose her sister and niece at the same time.

Pulling up to his door, she stared at the house and said a prayer out loud. The curtains were drawn, but there was no movement in the house. Before talking herself out of it, she cut the engine and stepped out. Slowly, she ascended the stairs and raised her hand to knock, but before she could, the door flew open.

"Good morning, sugah, what brings you here so early?" Mama Jones greeted her as she unlocked the screen with a sleeping Baby Love Jones in her arms.

Rue hugged her before kissing the crown of her niece's head. Stepping inside, she looked around. Noticing Blaise's car keys were gone, she sighed in relief. She knew she needed more time to go over the words she'd planned to say. Two seconds of relief was all she was warranted before she heard his baritone voice greet her.

"What's up, Sis, why you here so early?"

"Why y'all keep asking that?" She laughed nervously. "But, actually, I came to talk to you."

Blaise gave her a confused look as his brows met in the middle and his top lip curled up. His demeanor alone made her recoil and reconsider taking Forge's advice. Mama Jones offered to make breakfast as she excused herself. Her son had been hell to be around, and she knew she needed to stay close just in case she had to referee another verbal altercation.

"What's up?"

Blaise leaned against the wall, his arms folded across his chest. Rue had only been to his house a handful of times and none of them were unannounced. Silence fell between them as he waited for her to speak.

"I wanted to talk to you about Phoenix, I've been thinking..."

"Rue, if you're here on bullshit, you can step, forreal. I'm really not for all that today. It's my first day on leave, and I want to spend it with my daughter. Just one fucking moment of peace," Blaise interrupted. His tone was even, voice barely above a whisper, but Rue got the point.

"Nothing like that. I've been wracking my brain trying to figure out what the doctors can't, and I keep coming up blank. But what if she's waiting for you?"

"Waiting for me?" He asked incredulously. "It's crazy how everyone can so easily part their lips to say this shit is my fault. Maybe if you would have loosened the fucking reins and let her live a little she wouldn't have been safeguarding her symptoms. She would have let me help her."

"No one is blaming you for any of this. I take full responsibility for being an overprotective big sister. This is all on me, but I'm not the person she needs right now, it's you. And you're running around here treating everybody like we put her in that hospital bed. You despise everyone and everything that doesn't have anything to do with that sweet baby girl in there. And that shit isn't helping anybody, not you, not Baby Love Jones and damn sure not Phoenix." Rue paused as she tried to regulate her breathing. Her heart rate increased as her voice elevated. She didn't come there to argue, she came there as a last-ditch effort to pull her sister back to their world before she did the unthinkable, before she decided this world was no longer her home and she completely gave up on life.

"Look, I didn't come here to argue. I came in fucking peace and out of love for my sister. Go see her. And I don't mean look through a damn window. I mean walk your ass into her room, pull up a chair, sit the fuck down, hold her hand and tell her that you're still fucking here. It's time to man the fuck up!" Rue yelled. She stomped her foot as tears streamed down her face. She didn't want to cry, but anger and sadness culminated into an emotional overload she couldn't stop. Her tears burned her cheeks as they fell in fast, large droplets.

Like acid rain, they seared away the resolve that had held her together for the past 24 days.

Blaise dropped his arms to his side. His hardened expression softened as he recognized her pain. She was lashing out just like he was. Misconstruing the truth and mincing words. They were all feeling Phoenix's absence, but no one more than him and her.

"Rue, I can't go in that room. I just can't. I love Phoenix, I want her to wake up probably more than anyone else on this earth. But I can't go in there and see her laid up like some life-sized doll. That won't be what I see last if she really is leaving us. I want to remember the woman who captured my heart the moment she smiled as she took the first sip of the drink I sent over when I first laid eyes on her."

With defeat etched across her face, she nodded her head. She understood his plight. It was once hers. She could never bring herself to enter either of her parents' rooms when they were on life support. She'd made the tough decision to pull the plug on them and left Phoenix to stand watch as they both took their last breaths. It's an act she wished she could take back. Exposing Phoenix to such heartbreak was the catalyst for Phoenix's acceptance of her own fate. She was always comforted by the idea of death and unnaturally wanted it to overtake her in the beginning stages of her illness. With Blaise in her life, she thought Phoenix's relationship with death would have changed, but maybe she was wrong. Her current unwillingness to wake let her know that.

"I get it, I've been where we are before, and I didn't take the opportunity I had to let the ones I love most know how I felt about them in their final moments. I wish I could go back in time and walk in that room. I regret not doing it every day. Don't make the same mistake I did."

Rue wiped the tears that fell from her eyes. Hesitantly, she walked over to where Blaise stood and opened her arms for a hug. His pain radiated from his body, and she knew he was trying to keep it together for his mother and daughter. He welcomed her hug, and she stood rubbing his back as he cried like a baby. Heartache was unkind and relentless. It devoured even the most devoted and loving people, hollowing them out until there was nothing but anger and pain left. She didn't want that for Blaise or anyone else connected to her sister. Feeling eyes on them, she looked up to see Mama Jones smiling at her. Tears threatened to fall as she mouthed thank you.

"She never heard him come in and didn't know how much of her conversation he'd heard, but she knew there was no turning back now. She wanted this moment more than anything; to be in his space, breathing his air, telling her truth, clearing the fog that kept them from seeing each other," Forge read from her iPad.

After slipping her iPad back in her bag and sighed heavily. Forge sat at the foot of Phoenix's bed sipping her tea. Reading to Phoenix every afternoon had become her favorite pastime. Since finding an unopened package of books on her doorstep the week following her daughter's birth, she'd blocked out time each day to read a chapter or two to her friend. Reading was their favorite thing to do together, and she couldn't stand to read alone now that they decided to buddy-read every book.

There was a comforting calm in the room that never seemed to be there any other day. She felt it wrap around her and instantly release the tension in her shoulders. Her friend was waking up soon, she could feel it. There was a shift, a stirring of life happening, and she wanted to leave her alone to do whatever she needed to come back to them, to her family, to the little girl who'd grow to be an extension of her legacy.

Standing to leave, she placed Phoenix's copy of *Bleeding Love* by Harleigh Rae on the table beside her bed. The bookmark had already been placed where she'd stopped her read aloud. A smile crept across her face, as she looked down at her friend. She kissed her forehead and bent down to her ear.

"I know you always say that it was all of us who kept your light shining. It was us who gave you strength, but Sis, you do more than carry the light. You *are* the light. It shines in your eyes and gives all of us the hope to keep pushing, even now. When I close my eyes all I see is a big ball of light and I know that means you're still with us. We're waiting for you and will wait as long as it takes."

Before she could exit the room, Rue and Blaise entered the private suite. Her eyes watered as she realized he abandoned fear and showed up for her. She'd had a lengthy conversation with his mother about his father's death and she understood his hesitation. But like Janie Mae said in Phoenix's favorite book, *love makes your soul crawl out from its hiding place.* Stuffing her hands in her pockets, she resisted the urge to hug him because she wanted him to live in this moment. The moment he let love give him the strength he needed to do the one thing that he'd fought. Instead, she retreated to the entrance like Rue and gave him his time.

Blaise stood at the foot of her bed, watching her chest heave up and down. There was life there, there was love there. His eyes trailed from her chest to her face. It was surreal how at peace she looked during the most chaotic moment in his life. He'd stood where Rue and Forge stood several times, watching as families prayed to God, begged the Universe and wished on falling stars for them to get more time, more moments, more memories. But now that he found himself on the other side of the threshold, he couldn't bring himself to utter those selfish words. As he watched her lying in complete stillness, aside from her chest doing its part to circulate oxygen to her brain, he knew there was only one thing he needed to say to her.

With haste, he sat in the chair beside her and caressed her cheek with his knuckle. His free hand, took hold of her hand as he brought it up to his lips. Sweetly, softly, he planted a kiss in the palm of her hand before pressing it to his heart. Several seconds of silence passed as he listened to the subtle sounds in the room. The faint beeping of the machines, the always inaudible sounds of the nurses outside the door, and the steady thumping of his heart all magnified by the sorrow he felt looking at his heart lying in the bed. As much as he wanted her to wake up, to be fine, he knew that was a selfish thing for him to desire. She needed rest, deserved it even and he wouldn't be the one to stand in her way of knowing it, even if that meant it weren't with him and their daughter.

"You of all people know, I am a man of few words. They aren't my thing, they're yours, so instead of trying to find the perfect words, I'll borrow them from your favorite vampire in your favorite on-screen love scene. Do not be afraid. Do not be selfless. If you're tired, if it's too much, if the pain is too great, then rest my love. Your pain will end. Your heartbreak will mend. You will find peace. You're free to go now where many have gone before you. And where even the rest of us will follow in time. You'll see me again because this love is eternal."

Gently he kissed her lips as he held her hand. Doing what he'd plan to do at their baby shower, he slid the engagement ring he carried in his pocket onto her finger. A wide smile covered his face as he prided himself on guesstimating the ring size.

Rue and Forge both stood with tears streaming down their faces. As they one-armed hugged each other, they listened to the love letter that Blaise serenaded Phoenix. Blaise displayed a strength neither of them never would possess. His selfless acts of love showed them that he truly loved their girl with his entire heart.

Faith was needed to love someone in a way that would transcend space and time. He loved her enough to let her go and if he could then they knew they needed to fall in line. They'd watched Phoenix fight. Rue had watched her die twice and fight to come back. This time, she knew they all needed to release her. Let her know that her baby girl was in good hands, and she was free to leave this world if that was what her soul wanted.

CHAPTER TWENTY-THREE

Rue laughed as her daughters caught their aunt up on everything that had been going on in their lives since she'd been in the hospital. Envy washed over her as she considered how unfazed they appeared to be with her condition. They talked like she was coherent and responded to their inquiries by pausing briefly before continuing the one-sided conversations. To them, she could hear and her responses to their stories struck them right in the heart. They were connected to her in a way only they could decipher.

Their giggles and whispers pulled her out of her morbid thoughts as she sat beside her husband. He and the girls had come to collect her from Phoenix's bedside for their game. Slowly, she'd been trying to maintain a sense of normalcy. Like Blaise, her boat had been a lot less buoyant, and she felt like she was slowly sinking into a dark place. Up until that day, Trav had stepped up in a major way. He handled his tasks and picked up her slack. He'd doubled as a soccer dad and breadwinner for the past few weeks, and she loved him immensely for the care he always showed her and the girls.

For another ten minutes Rue allowed her daughters the time they needed with their aunt. She'd kept them far away from everything that was happening because she felt she should have done the same with Phoenix when they were younger. Protecting their innocence and preserving their happy moments with their favorite auntie were her top priority but they'd persisted for days until she finally gave in. Not wanting to keep them from their teammates any longer, the family of four prepared to head out for the game. Stopping short, Rue allowed her daughters and husband to precede her as she lingered at the threshold. Watching them made her heart melt, God took Phoenix from this world then these would be moments that Blaise and their daughter would never get.

"Hey, Mommy really needs to go hug Baby Love Jones. Is it okay if I skip the game tonight? I promise I'll meet up for the celebratory canna cream at Rose Marie's afterwards."

"Sure Mommy, take all the time you need," Kaleigh permitted, giving her mother a tight hug around the waist.

The drive to Phoenix's house had granted her the stillness she required to process what life fully and finally might look like without her sister. There were no more tears left to cry. Phoenix deserved peace more than anyone she knew. Pulling up beside her baby sister's car, she cut the engine and sat for a little while longer. With a deep, weight-lifting sigh, she weakly pulled on the handle to free herself from the confines of her van.

Mustering up the courage to knock, Rue took several deep breaths. She needed to compost herself before wrapping her beautiful niece in her arms. There was no way in hell she would transfer any of her misery onto such a precious, innocent soul. These were burdened thoughts to bear, and they needed to be exorcized from her body before she even laid eyes on the baby that was at the root of her deepest concern.

After sealing her faintly whispered prayer with the mighty name of Jesus Christ, she raised her fist and pounded on the door, matching the cadence of heart beating inside her chest. Mama Jones greeted her with a warm smile and opened arms as she ushered her into the foyer of her sister's home. Blaise always made sure they stayed at Phoenix's house whenever he had to go into the office, making sure his daughter was in sync at both homes.

For several seconds the two women stood in the foyer engulfed in each other's strength. Rue had reached her breaking point days ago and still somehow managed to keep moving forward. But she was weary of how much longer she could be the one that kept everyone else hopeful, certain of her sister's return to them when she was barely clinging, every other second grasping at some semblance of possibility.

"What brings you this way so early. I thought Kaleigh and Dallas had their games today," Mama Jones asked.

"They did, but I asked them if I could come here instead. I needed to hug Baby Love Jones."

"I just put her down for a nap, but she's fighting it."

"Awww, she's probably just missing her mommy. When is the last time she's been up there?"

"Blaise said he's taking her tonight when his flight lands. He's been gone for two days on a consultation case. He'll be in town in a few hours."

Rue pulled her sweater from her shoulders and hung it on the coat rack before proceeding through the foyer to the den. Mama Jones always allowed BLJ to bask in the warm sun that shone through the bay window while she napped. A smile crept across her face in rhythm with the stride of her steps. Standing over her niece, she gently caressed the soft bed of curls that hugged her tiny little scalp. Phoenix had a baby; a beautiful surprise that warmed the dankness that chilled her aunt when her dear sister slipped away.

Gently, she slid her hands under BLJ's shoulders and butt, scooping her from the plush blanket that brought her comfort. A faint whimper left her being as she felt her body press against her aunt's chest before settling back into her nap. Nestling her little head into her bosom, she breathed easy knowing she was in safe arms, arms of someone who loved and cared for her. Mama Jones stood joined them just as Rue went to sit. Picking up the remote, she pressed play, resuming the episode of Passions she had been watching. Lifting her feet up onto the ottoman, she leaned back and closed her eyes. Caring for her newest grand baby in such a unique capacity had been draining. She hadn't realized just how much went into caring for a baby because she hadn't had to do it in over a decade.

"I never got a chance to thank you for talking to Blaise. I had been trying to get him to open up about everything since she first went under, but he had shut me out."

"You don't ever have to thank me for that. I wish I had someone in my corner when I went through this with my parents. I was right where he was, and I only wish I had his same courage back then."

"Courage in facing the things we don't want to and still moving forward when those things cease to look back. My son is resilient, but sometimes I think his resilience clouds his humanity. He is strong to a fault, never asking or accepting the help others lay at his feet. So, I thank you for never giving up on him during his moment of darkness and for reminding him that his love for your sister is far greater than he can ever truly imagine. Love can do powerful things when we yield to it."

Rue rocked her niece as she considered Mama Jones' last words. Love could do powerful things. Love made Phoenix realize her life was worth living. Love made her commit to Blaise when she'd usually run from any form of intimacy. Love got her aunt to agree to fly clear across the country to see her niece who'd hated her for the last few decades. Love brought every person that Phoenix loved most from their respective corners of the world to a little, black town that most people don't even know existed. Love indeed was powerful, and it would wield enough power to wake her sister up at the exact moment she was supposed to wake.

After she'd gotten sufficient cuddles from her niece, she placed her back in her bassinet and went into her sister's most sacred space. The parlor was Phoenix's place of peace. It was the place in her house where she felt the most at home. Rue needed a sense of home more than anything because lately she'd felt so uprooted, ungrounded and constantly in a state of yearning for emotional nourishment.

For the first time since everything unfolded, she had finally digested everything that had been happening around her the last few weeks. Her daughters were simply killing it in every aspect of their lives. Her sister had been fighting for her life for just as long. She was both proud and perplexed. Navigating this space had become quite the task, and as of lately, she just didn't wanna get up and work at them anymore.

As she sat in the parlor looking at the ashes in the tin. The last remnants of her heart forged on paper and seared from her soul. It was truly cleansing. Her eyes fell to the two elegantly dressed letters sitting on the end table. Slowly, she reached over and pulled them toward her. *My Sweet Baby Love. My Loving Sister.* Her hands ran across the gorgeous foil stamping as she sucked air into her lungs. Tears glistened the brim of her eyes, threatening to fall, but somehow she managed to keep them from ruining the work of art her sister had decided to bless her with. She was sure the words etched on the paper would serenade and soothe her aching heart.

With delicate apprehension, she used the engraved letter opener that sat beside the letters to break the seal on her letter and the one for her niece. Seeing her sister's handwriting on the page caused the floodgates to open. Every little instance caused her to recall the moments she shared with Phoenix so many years ago. First, the day Phoenix picked up her first pencil. She'd sat with Rue as she finished up her homework and decided she wanted to learn to write her name. At only two and half years old, she was determined to perfect the seven letters that would grace their television screen decades later. A smile crept in the corner of her mouth as she remembered just two years ago when Phoenix had to relearn how to write and that same dedication as she penned her signature over and over, filling countless notebooks with calligraphic and print versions of her name until it exceeded her former handwriting.

My Sweet, Sweet Baby Girl,

With all my heart, I want you to know one thing. I love you in this world and the next. I don't know how long you'll have with me, but I want you to know that every moment spent with you from the moment you were conceived has filled me with such joy. As I write this, your dad and I are going through a rough patch, but I know our love is strong enough to withstand whatever storm may come our way.

Lately, I've been feeling this sense of finality, like maybe I won't get to physically see you grow into the beautiful trailblazer I feel in my spirit you will become. But just know that wherever life takes you, I am always with. You are surrounded by more love than life can ever try to snuff out. With everything in me, I will fight to make sure you see this side of life, but even if I can't promise we'll live out this life together, I promise you this, YOU ARE WORTH THE RISK. You are meant to be.

Life won't be easy. It won't be a cake walk. But you're already equipped with all you need to make it through. Love. Family. And the powerful prayers of all the Collevilles and Joneses that came before you. With angels in your corner spanning generations and a father who will fiercely protect and defend, tirelessly provide, and immensely love you, you'll do great things.

Chart your own path. Live your own dreams. And enjoy every moment. Cherish the memories and hold on to this one truth. You are enough. You are worthy. You *matter and you will be all you desire to be and have all you desire to have.*

I love you. Forever, until forever ends.

Eternally yours,

Mommy.

Swiping away at the tears, Rue folded the letter and placed it back in the envelope. Phoenix knew this was coming. She knew long before the signs even showed. She had been preparing to leave this world from the moment she knew she was carrying her child. Whether it was a gut feeling, a dream or even a whisper from God, Phoenix had done all the preparations the leave this world on her own terms. Lupus hadn't stolen anything from them.

Closing her eyes, she pulled her fondest memory of Phoenix from the part of her mind where she kept all favorite moments with her family. It was the day she officially became a big sister. She secured Phoenix's head in the palm of her little six -year-old palm and smiled down at the smaller version of herself. Phoenix was a doll, her perfect little fingers and tiny little toes fascinated Rue as she marveled at the baby sister her parents had finally blessed her with. She only begged them for the last four years to give her a sister and now her wildest dream had been realized. Phoenix opened her eyes and reached for her sister's glasses. Laughter filled the space around them as everything else seemed to disappear into the background. All that remained was Rue, holding her sister and promising to protect her.

"How did we get here?" Rue whispered as she tried to opener letter. Her fingers trembled, as she wondered what she could possibly say to soothe the aching of her heart. Her soul had been in turmoil since Phoenix stopped breathing in the delivery room. Her spirit was in a constant state of unrest, and she prayed ferociously for the powers that be to give her sister back to her, to her family, to her friends, but most importantly to her daughter. No little girl deserved to be motherless. It was a cruel and unusual punishment for her as an adult, so she knew Baby Love Jones would struggle, never evening knowing her mother.

Rue,

Of all the letters I've written over the years, yours always seems to be the hardest. I don't want to leave you alone. I don't want to devastate you like this, ever. The pain I know my absence will cause is too unbearable to even be realized. I try my hardest to fight for you because you've fought with me for so long. Since birth, you've promised to protect me, and I want to thank you for keeping that promise. You shield me from the darkness of this world and your light is all I ever truly see. But I want to relieve you of your duties. I want you to wake up every day and live for you without having that lingering urge to protect me. Your days of guarding, shielding, protecting and serving are over. I relinquish the hold your oath to me has had on your life. You're free. Be free. Be love. Be light. And know that I love you forever and a day, until my last day. This may be my final hour, but it's your encore. Take centerstage in your life and make those big dreams you hold captive in your mind reality. You have two beautiful daughters watching you and an amazing husband cheering you on.

I'll be watching. I'll be waiting. Until we meet again, dear big sister.

All my love,

CHAPTER TWENTY-THREE

Phoenix

Several moments passed before she had composed herself. She needed a good cry, and this seemed like the perfect decided to pick up one her sister's favorite coping mechanisms. She pulled one of the pieces of paper and the beautiful pens from the tray on the window sill. Phoenix believed in the power of writing down words and allowing them to be penned on the heart. Words were powerful whether written or spoken and she made journaling a gift to anyone who entered her home.

Grabbing one of the cute little clipboards from the golden hook on her wall, she plopped down on one of the many throw pillows and poured out her heart. She needed to relinquish her control of the situation to the only person who could change this, Phoenix. She needed to believe her sister was strong enough to withstand the eternal battle and would come out victorious. And so, she wrote. She wrote until her heart was free of anguish. She wrote until there was no more doubt. She wrote until her tears had dried up and the love had been replenished. She wrote until her hope was restored.

"Now, for the final step. Activation," Rue whispered as she walked over the tiny, tin pail.

Tearing her paper into tiny little pieces, she doused them in peppermint, bergamot, and rose oil and placed them inside the pail. Striking one of the long matches, she prayed a final prayer over her journal entry and watched it go up in flames. The flickering of the flame and aromatic soothing of the oils blanketed her spirit with calm. For the first time in weeks, she attached peace and joy to her inhalation. Everything would be okay, she felt it the instant the words kindled in the tin. Love would do everything she couldn't, she just needed to be patient.

Kneeling over the tin until the last ember of the flames' glow burned out, Rue smiled. She stood, turning in circles as she took in the current state of the parlor. Phoenix's plant family had begun to feel the effects of her absence. Their leaves drooped, some were wilted, others were beginning to brown. Her dumb had never been green, but she was sure she could render a bit of aid to them by drawing the curtains that had probably been closed since the day her niece was born and quenching their thirst.

As she watered the plants, she noticed dust on many of the large leaves and looked around for something to clean them with. She never quite knew where Phoenix got her incessant love for plants, but as she looked at how she cared for them, it was evident that Phoenix was a nurturer.

She had been hovering over her for so long, she never stood back and saw her baby sister for who she truly was outside of the roles she'd played in her own life. She'd been the jail bird, the reporter, the sick sister and now the coma patient. But she was indeed so much more. She was a nurturer, a mother, a lover, and overall, the most compassionate woman she'd ever known. Her love extended to all living things, and she made sure to surround herself with the same kind of love she chose to pour into the world.

Finally, she tended to nearly all the plants in the parlor. She lost count at 77 plants but was pretty sure the large space probably housed over 100 varying in size and color. The beautiful fan plant was the last and it commanded attention. She tenderly wipes the dust that has formed between the folds, before misting them with the gold plated, engraved watering can. A golden note clip caught her eye as she placed the can on the sill behind the plant. Pulling the note from the clip, she ran her hand across Blaise's signature. This must have been the plant Forge has told her about after Phoenix finally told her they were dating. A tear dropped as she glanced at the little heart hanging from the letter 'E'.

Some crazy lovebirds told me one time that learning to appreciate nature teaches us to appreciate the love that's standing right in front of us. Thanks for the view.

Rue admired how much Blaise loved her sister. He'd been by her side, holding her down for a long time. When many others would have run for hills, he remained committed to her and dedicated to making their love work.

As much as she told her sister not to, she began comparing and contrasting him with Darrell and seeing that he measured up to be a far better man than Darrell ever had been to Phoenix. She silently thanked God for placing Blaise in Phoenix's life, for allowing her to know love as she did. Their parents always told them love could cover a multitude, but until that very moment she never understood just how much.

Love kept Blaise at her side. Love kept her heart beating and her lungs pushing oxygen through her body. She didn't know what it would take for love to give Phoenix the energy to finally open her eyes, but she was sure it had that energy to give as well. Hope had finally reentered the chat and she was reassuring Rue of all she'd doubted.

CHAPTER TWENTY-FOUR

FILLED WITH SADNESS AND FATIGUE, BLAISE RAN HIS HANDS DOWN HIS FACE as he sat up in bed. The blaring of his alarm had jolted him from the most peaceful sleep he'd had in weeks. Between his patients, his daughter, and his comatose girlfriend he had nothing left to give to anyone. Yet, he still rose every morning, put a smile on his face and served his patients as if the weight of the world wasn't on his back. Not knowing the source of his current feeling of strength, he bowed his head and quickly sent up a genuine thank you. Thank you for the strength to keep going knowing all he wanted to do was sit at Phoenix's bedside until she opened her eyes.

Glancing over at his baby girl laying beside him, a smile forced its way through the solemn expression he'd adorned since her birth. He leaned over and gently planted a kiss to her curly mane. Her chunky body took up most of her mother's favorite pillow and she slept peacefully. Her soft snores melted his heart every morning and gave him all he needed to make it through the day and back to her. Pulling the blanket from his lower extremities, he slid from the bed and commenced his morning routine.

First stop was downstairs to prepare a bottle for the instant his princess woke from her slumber. She was very demanding about her meals and would make sure the entire house heard her wrath if it were even a second late. Returning upstairs he started the bottle warmer and placed the bottle inside to keep it at the perfect temperature.

Next, it was personal hygiene. His wardrobe had become boring since his love was gone from him. He donned khakis and a button-down shirt that was always some shade of purple with a contrasting dark or light blazer. There was no personality to his clothing choices and nearly 3 quarters of his closet went untouched. He hadn't exfoliated in weeks since he was all out of the body scrub Phoenix made him every month. Clippers hadn't met his head or face in the same amount of time. He'd successfully cut his morning time down significantly to make more time to cuddle with his daughter before he had to leave her for work.

Just as he'd fastened the last button on his shirt, he heard her faint cries over the home theater system. His mother was a genius for suggesting they route the baby monitors through it. Taking one last look at himself in the mirror, he grabbed his comb and beard oil and went to spend the next hour with his baby girl before he had to leave her for the next 6 hours.

"Good morning, Daddy's Baby Love. How did you sleep? Did you dream of Mommy like I did," he cooed as he lifted her from the bed.

"Ohhh, somebody packing on the pounds. Your momma is feeding you good, huh."

Blaise continued the one-sided conversation with his daughter as he disrobed her and changed her diaper. It amazed him how much she'd grown over the last few months. She'd inherited his height and covered nearly the entire changing area from head to toe.

Tears lined his lids as he thought about how much of her firsts Phoenix had already missed. She was rolling over and holding her head up and had begun to babble relentlessly throughout the day. She was a miracle, and he had her mother to thank for making sure she made it into the world healthy and strong.

Baby Love Jones pulled diapers from the shelf beside her, bringing him from his thoughts into reality. Laughing at her antics to command his attention, he resnapped her onesie and covered her legs in a pair of leggings. Swooping her into his arms, he grabbed the bottle from the warmer. Like he did every morning, he walked into her almost complete nursery and took a seat in the rocking chair by the window. The clipping from the plant he'd gifted Phoenix the day of their first date sat in the windowsill. It had grown slightly since he'd placed it in the water for rooting a few days ago. He couldn't wait to re-pot it with Baby Love Jones once she turned six months. Finally giving her little heart's immediate desire, he tilted the bottle and smiled as she began suckling before he even placed the nipple to her mouth.

"Slow down before you can't fit any of the clothes your aunties just brought over here."

Blaise was grateful for the friends Phoenix inherited as family. Forge, Tracy, and Kellz had been his saving grace when it came to making sure Baby Love Jones had all her necessities. Though Kellz couldn't get away from her own life, a package arrived nearly every other day with things she thought they would need.

Mama Jones spent so much time caring for them both that she barely had time to shop for anything, but the women of Phoenix's life made sure they had everything they could possibly think to need during this time. They filled in for him and Rue many times when they were both just too overcome with grief to even function properly.

For the next two hours, Blaise and Baby Love Jones played inside her gated play area. Like every morning, they laid on the floor while she crawled on his chest where they watched the sun rise through her nursery window. Her light snores let him know it was safe to place her inside her crib and officially start his work day. No matter what the day brought his way, whenever he was in town, he made it a priority to start and end every day watching the sun rise and set with his baby girl. She held the number one spot in his life, and there wasn't a soul in this life or the next that would ever take her place.

"Daddy loves you. Sweet dreams, tell mommy I love her."

The drive into work felt longer than it had in a long time. The sun peeked less and less through the tree covered route he took to work each day. From nowhere, rain fell. He inhaled and exhaled in sync with the steady dropping of rain on the roof of his truck. Rain always calmed his fears and quieted his thoughts. This time it was no different. He was afraid he'd used up all his time with Phoenix. He was angry with himself for wasting so much of it being stubborn and not granting her his forgiveness when she repeatedly asked for it. He cried, the rain masking his sobs as he continued on the lonely road to work.

"God, I very rarely ever come to you with a request. In fact, lately all I've been doing is extending you gratitude, but today I need you more than ever. I can't do this alone. I can't do parenthood without her. I can't live without her. I can't love without her. Please, please heal her. Fix whatever is broken and bring her back to me. I've given so much to others. I've followed the steps you've charted for my life. And I know I ain't always the best man I can be, but my heart is pure. Though my thoughts, actions, and deeds don't always reflect that, I've done my best to live a life and walk in a way that you can use me as a vessel of love and compassion for others. Now, I'm asking for you to return to me ten-fold the love and compassion I've given selflessly. Bring her back to me, please. Amen."

In the middle of the road, Blaise pleaded with God to give him the one person who he ever loved more than his family. The sun peeked from behind the clouds, and he smiled somberly. God had heard his prayer. He'd finally done what his mother told him to do from the beginning... sandpit it in God's hands. There was no medical reasoning to explain why she hadn't waken up from her coma after they withdrew the medication. Mama Jones had been telling him it was spiritual, but until that very moment he refused to believe there was no medical explanation for her condition.

Halfway through his full day of appointments, he decided to walk across the campus to see Phoenix. He hadn't seen her since the day Rue encouraged him to go in the room. He knew he needed to show her that he was all in with her no matter what obstacles arose, and he had been failing miserably. She could feel his presence, she could sense his support, and he had been inadvertently neglecting her. But that ended at that very moment.

Walking into the room, he smiled seeing his mother retwisted her new growth. He didn't know what she would do with her hair once she was home, but he absolutely loved the way locs looked on her. The small twists framed her face perfectly, making her look even more angelic. Something he thought was impossible because she already had a spiritual glow about her essence.

"Hey, Ma. Hey, Baby Girl," Blaise greeted his mother and daughter.

"Hey, Son. What are you doing over this side? I thought you had a full day of appointments."

"I did, but two canceled, and the next one isn't until 3:15. So I figured I'd come sit with my baby until then. What are y'all doing here so late?"

"Miss Fussy pants over there been whiny all day. I thought she was getting sick, but everything was fine when I did the normal checks, so I figured she was just missing her momma bear."

Blaise nodded before going over and lifting Baby Love Jones from her carrier. She looked up at him with glossy eyes. Her little body went limp the second he pressed her against his chest. Her head fell to his shoulder as she gripped his stethoscope. With his free hand, he pulled the armchair closer to the bed and sat down. Once seated, he grabbed Phoenix's hand and raised it to his lips. Softly he kissed it before pressing it against his cheek. A comfortable silence filled the room as Mama Jones put away her hair care supplies and excused herself.

Baby Love Jones had babbled herself to sleep as Blaise lightly bounced her on his shoulder. The second her breathing mellowed out and her light snores commingled with the serene silence, he laid her in the bed beside her mother. With her head placed directly over Phoenix's heart, she snuggled up to her mother. He watched how the restlessness washed away, and she completely relaxed against her mother's body. He wanted to cry for the longing she must have felt on a daily basis.

For nearly eight months, she shared everything with her mother, and from the moment she was born she'd been detached from that initial source of life, of light, of love. He did all he could to make sure she didn't feel her absence, but nothing could measure up to the bond they'd form while she was in the womb. She needed her mother more than anything else and her angst would only get more intense as the days went on how they were.

"Phoenix, baby, I'm sorry. For abandoning you. For feeling like neither of us were strong enough to endure. For feeling like my love wasn't enough. For not supporting you how you needed. Our baby girl needs you more than any of us care to admit. We want to think we are enough and if you decide that this life is no longer what you want, that we can be all that she needs but we can't. I understand that more than anything. Nothing has been more clearer to me. She needs you. She craves you. She yearns for you. Please, come back to her."

Blaise's pager blared, startling both him and the baby. Her cries pierced the air and assaulted his ears. Every time she cried his heart constricted. His baby girl's cries were his kryptonite and it never mattered why she was crying. After silencing his pager, he rubbed her back until he fell back off to sleep. She was exhausted, he felt it the second he picked her up when he entered the room. He wanted her to get as much sleep with her mother as she possibly could.

Leaving her, he joined his mother and Nurse Carmen in the hallway. They were both laughing into their cups of coffee as he approached them. Blaise loved and appreciated his mother for putting her life on pause to return to being everything to his daughter that he just couldn't seem to be while the love of his life fought for hers. He planned to send her and her best friend away on a long vacation to whatever corner of the earth they wanted whenever she felt like she was ready to leave them.

"Hey Mama, I got her down for a nap, but I don't know how long she'll be out. You may want to go check on her to make sure she doesn't roll. I left her in the bed with Phoenix and wedged the extra blanket on the side with the rail."

"Boy, I don't know who will be the death of me, you or your child. You're a damn doctor doing reckless shit like that. Carmen, let me get in here and make sure this child doesn't end up in y'all's ER. Stop by before you head out today. I knitted a new hat and scarf set for your baby boy."

Blaise kissed his mother's forehead and wrapped up his conversation so he could trek back across the hospital's campus to make it back in time for his last three appointments. It was officially his last day before he was on paternity leave for six-months. As many times as he tried to stay away from work, he couldn't seem to find peace at home, so he ended his time off early. But after having a few off-the-books sessions with Triumph, he accepted that he was using work to distract him from dealing with his own reality.

He needed to really digest the possibility of a reality where Phoenix wasn't there physically. Where he'd have to name his daughter without her and raise her to be a fraction of the woman her mother was. Though he knew he had the village, using them to their full benefit was a struggle. His independence served as a crutch, stopping him from accepting that he might not get his way this time around. Phoenix may have run to the one place he couldn't physically follow her to; heaven.

"Oh, and you don't have to keep her tonight. I asked Carmen to get a crib for the room tonight so we can stay."

"Are you sure? I can stay if you need me to."

"I'm sure. We'll be fine."

CHAPTER TWENTY-FOUR

Blaise breezed through the rest of his appointments before he was finally able to get back to Phoenix and their daughter. She was all he could think about after seeing how soothing her presence was to their baby girl. He realized while everyone else had their time to sit with her, talk with her and just feel a bit of her in their midst, Baby Love Jones hardly ever got that chance. It was rare she accompanied the adults to the hospital. And he was angry with himself for not seeing it earlier.

After bathing and feeding her, he placed her back in the bed with Phoenix and patted her butt until she fell asleep. He'd since swapped out the uncomfortable armchair with one of the recliners from the infusion clinic. Making himself comfortable with his warm blankets and extra pillows, he laid his head on Phoenix's knee and drifted off to sleep.

Morning had come and gone and neither Blaise nor Baby Love Jones were in a rush to wake. Phoenix's eyes slowly scanned the room. Fear sat in as she registered that she was no longer in the labor and delivery room she'd been in before her eyes closed. Panic quickly sat in as she tried to speak, but the dryness of her mouth constricted any sound from forming. Her hands slowly moved, and she felt her way through the darkness. Her hands glided over soft hair before tears welled in her eyes as she registered she was feeling her baby girl's head. With all the strength she could muster, she was determined to lay eyes on her. Finally finding the button to raise the bed, she pressed it three times before she became winded.

With a gasp, she looked down at the tiny human being resting on her bosom. Instantly, her eyes panned down and she got a glimpse of Blaise resting on her leg. Gliding her hands to the rail, she sat up in the bed a little to have better access to him. With the hand closest to him, she traced his brow with her thumb. Slowly he stirred. Her mouth curled into a smile as she watched confusion spread across his face. His eyes scrunched as she checked to see if their daughter was awake. After registering that she was still fast asleep, he moved his head slightly before the tears formed.

"You're awake. God, how I've missed you," he confessed, rushing to her side.

His lips touched every part of exposed skin on her body as the tears continued to fall. He knew he needed to alert the attending staff and call everyone, but he was frozen in place, marveling at the beautiful woman who made his world make sense. Finally, he rushed to his phone to call Rue.

"Rue, she's awake," he whispered in the receiver when he heard her groggy voice on the line.

He was met by the dial tone. He knew that meant she would be at the hospital in a record amount of time, so he quickly got into doctor mode and let the staff come in and assess her abilities. She had been in a coma for two months, and he knew the next few hours were crucial for determining the severity of being under for so long.

Just after the doctors had given him their report, Rue burst into the room with glossy eyes. He knew she probably blasted her praise music all the way over as she prayed to God he got her there in one piece. It was evident that she'd cried the entire drive.

"H-h-how is she?" Rue's voice shook as she asked. Her reservation let him know she was nervous about what she'd hear next.

"She is doing better than we all expected after being in a coma for 50 some odd days. She just drifted back off to sleep. But that's expected."

"So, when can she come home?" Rue asked as she picked up her niece.

"They want to keep her for another week or so, just to monitor her and get some scans and tests done to make sure her lupus is under control. They started her on some IV prednisone to help with the inflammation that is expected once she starts getting mobile again. Her rheumatologist will be down later to do a full work up," Blaise explained, finally taking a seat in the chair.

"Rue, she's awake. She really came back to us," he mumbled as the tears welled up in his eyes again.

Rue shouted as she twirled around with Baby Love Jones in her arms. Her niece's cries added to the chorus of sound bouncing from the walls of her sister's room. Suddenly the tears came like a monsoon, quick and unexpected. They fell steadily in a stream, and she processed what was actually happening. As Phoenix's eyes flickered open again, she rushed to her side, crying as she tried to form the words in her brain.

"Baby Love Jones, meet your mommy," she finally got out as she saw Phoenix begin to cry too. Placing her daughter on her chest, she took Phoenix's arms and clasped them around Baby Love Jones.

"Congratulations baby sis. You have a beautiful baby girl who's waiting for you to name her," she said as she tenderly kissed her sister's forehead.

Blaise came over and stood on the opposite side of Rue. For the first time in a very long time, they both exhaled the breath they'd been holding. Phoenix was awake, alive and fully aware of the world around her. God heard them and answered them. Giving them more time to love on the one who meant the most to them.

CHAPTER TWENTY-FIVE

The intense winter sun blinded Phoenix as she sat up in the hospital bed for the last time. It was the final morning sunrise that she'd watch from the uncomfortable hospital bed. After spending an additional week admitted, she was finally cleared to go home and sleep comfortably and peacefully in her own bed, next to the love of her life and her baby girl.

I'm somebody's momma. The reality of that thought had finally begun to sink into her identity. Searching around the room, she looked for whoever decided to spend the night with her last night. Since she'd awakened, she hadn't spent one night alone. One of her family members always seemed to get left behind when everyone left after she'd fallen asleep for the evening. Her smile broadened as her eyes fell on the man that seemed to drop from heaven and shower her with love she didn't deserve. Blaise looked peaceful, like it was the first real sleep he'd had in months as he slept curled up in the loveseat across from her bed.

Slowly, she pulled the heated blanket from her limbs and swung her feet to the side. Holding on to the rail, she slid from the bed being sure to avoid the nurse's call button. Once to her feet, she stood in awe. It had been a long time since she was able to wake up and practically jump out of the bed. Her legs felt like they weren't her own as she glided across the floor with next to no effort. Nothing ached; there was no pain present in her body. Lifting her head to the sky, she silently thanked God for restoring her mind, body, and soul.

In no time she was standing over Blaise as he slept. As much as she wanted to let him sleep, she wanted to look into his eyes. They hadn't had one moment alone since she woke up. There was always someone else invading their privacy whether it was medical staff or family. Someone was always physically present or on video call with them.

Kneeling down beside him, she caressed his cheek with her knuckles. Her heart smiled as his eyes flickered from the intimate touch. Next, her palm covered his heart as she closed her eyes and synced her breathing to the beat of his heart. Deeply, she inhaled his intoxicating pheromones as she brought her face to his. Her lips softly pressed against his, causing his eyes to fully open.

The rays of sunlight created a soft aura around his frame, causing him to appear dream-like. In her mind, this was a dream, a dream she never wanted to wake from. Where they could forget about the very things that plagued their relationship and sail off into the sunset with their baby girl.

"Hey, you." She smiled as he sat up.

Pulling her down on his lap, he kissed her neck softly and inhaled her hair. She was really awake, and he still couldn't believe how quickly God answered his prayer. He beat himself up every day he selflessly gave her permission to leave them. He knew in his heart it wasn't what he really wanted, even if that's what she needed. He needed her by his side, raising their child, and creating a home where she grew up whole, no parts of her voided. No holes in her heart from suffering such a loss that she'd eventually grow to blame herself for. But God knew his heart. He knew he couldn't survive without her by his side. He heard the cries of his heart and didn't let them fall on deaf ears.

"Hey, my love. How are you feeling?"

"Good. Happy that I'm going home in a few hours. I want a real bath and real food and to sleep in a real bed. And..."

"Nah, you ain't getting none of him no time soon."

Blaise followed her eyes as they trailed down to his dick. He shook his head as she started whined her waist, creating friction that she knew would make him stand at attention. Phoenix had no shame, when she felt the urge to get up on it and ride that thing, she did just that. But this time he wasn't letting her.

"Babe, it's been months. You're being stingy," Phoenix pouted as she whined into his neck. She planted soft kisses along his neck and collarbone, trying to remove his shirt. As good as it felt, he knew he had to stop her before he had her sprawled out in the hospital bed.

"Phoenix, you just went through a very traumatic experience. You've been in a coma for almost two months. How can you even think about my dick right now?"

"How could I not? I'm having dope dick withdrawals." She quipped.

Blaise laughed as he put a little bit of space between them. Phoenix was so damn sexy when she didn't get her way. Her pouty lips and bashful eyes made him want to give her exactly what she asked for, but the fact that any of his colleagues could walk in at any minute deterred him.

"As soon as you're discharged, I will take you home and fuck you seven ways to Sunday if that's what you want, but first you gotta get discharged. Plus, I'm sure our daughter will wake up any moment now. Or Rue or Tracy or Forge. Shit, probably even Mama or Trav or Roddy are going to bust in here any minute now. You want them to see you face down, ass up?"

"I mean, they'll understand. I ain't had no dick since before our baby girl made her unexpected entrance into the world. But I guess I wouldn't want her to be scarred for life like I was after walking in on my parents."

"Whaaaat, you ain't never tell me that one."

"Shit was detrimental. I couldn't even look at a boy after that. Sike, I'm lying, I was sneaking my lil' boyfriend in a week later, while they were on their annual couples' retreat with their friends. But still, I really couldn't even look at porn after that. Still to this day I can't bring myself to watch any type of BDSM porn scene. There were whips and chains, a butt plug and vibrators. Sex toys just laid out on the dresser. Christian Grey ain't have shit on my daddy."

"You saw all that from just walking in," he laughed.

"I was in shock. I walked in and was frozen in place. Couldn't even walk back out. I just kept opening and closing my eyes, hoping the images would fade away, but I was just searing them deeper into my repressed memory. See now you ruined it, taking me down memory lane. Ion't even want no dick no more," she laughed as her body shivered.

"I love you," Blaise laughed as he palmed her face, bringing her lips to his.

Phoenix closed her eyes as his tongue separated her lips. She welcomed his warm, thick tongue as it twirled around her mouth, pulling her into a forbidden tango. Her arms fell loosely around his neck as he gripped her waist. Pulling back, he searched her eyes for any signs that what he was experiencing might be a dream or worse, he'd slipped into a state of catatonia where he was living inside himself while the outside world didn't exist.

"This is real babe," Phoenix assured him.

She could sense that he needed to hear her say it because she needed it too. They'd spent more time apart than they did together, but her love for him wouldn't allow her to just give up. They deserved love and they deserved it with each other. They'd been through too much to be denied the satisfaction of a love that would last.

"I know. Sometimes I still can't believe he answered my prayer. I never prayed harder for anything in my life. God, I'm so grateful you fought for our daughter."

"I fought for you too. For us. Blaise, I'm so sorry for not seeing it before. For trying to explain away my love for you. For thinking I could do this on my own. You're my heart in tangible form and I almost cost us both the purest kind of love."

"We all have our own battles, demons, fears and traumas to conquer. Thank you for realizing you weren't ready for the love I wanted to give you. Thank you for refusing my heart when you knew all you'd do was fumble it. I know I gave you hell about your decisions, but I couldn't even fathom being in your situation and still trying to live fully. I commend you. I don't take your sacrifices lightly and if you'll let me I want to show my appreciation for the rest of your life," Blaise said as he picked up the velvet ring box from the window sill.

Phoenix's hands flew to her mouth to muffle her screams. Tears freely flowed from her eyes in a steady, never-ending flow. Her vision blurred, and her words remained caught in her chest as she tried to control her breathing. The eleven and a half months of her life had been the most tumultuous. She'd endured and overcame so much but looking at the beautiful oval Amethyst stone flanked by two 2-carat diamonds on the 14K gold band tore down the last of the wall she'd built around her heart. Blaise never ceased to take her breath away. He was the only person in the world to quiet the woman with all the words.

"Blaise, tell me this is just a very expensive ass push gift," she finally pushed out breathily.

"Nah. Your expensive ass push gift is waiting in your driveway. This is an expensive ass gesture for the one thing of yours I could never put a price tag on. Your heart. Say you'll be my forever in a day."

"Baby, a day ain't nearly long enough. I'll be your forever in a lifetime," she whispered into his lips before she kissed him, pulling his face to hers and feeding him her tongue.

"Always and forever." Blaise laughed.

"Until forever ends," she giggled.

As much as she wanted to be mad that Blaise had clearly

continued The Originals without her, she loved that he showed her every day her interests, hopes, fears, dreams and nightmares all mattered to him. He truly loved every part of her in a way she never imagined anybody ever would. Unconditional love was something she never thought she'd know before leaving the world, but Blaise proved her wrong. He eradicated every warped thought she had about her life every chance he got. Her future was gloriously bright, and she'd owed it all to his persistence to not let her intransigence stop him from fighting her guardedness for her heart.

"Speaking of forever, our lil' Baby Love Jones has been waiting forever for a name."

"What about Eternal. I kept dreaming about that name. All that time, you were in my dreams and so was she. We were on a vacation or something. The sand was white, the sun was setting, and you called her back to our blanket from where she played at the water's edge. You called her Eternal."

"Eternal. Eternal. Eternal Love Jones."

"Eternal Love Jones. It's perfect," Phoenix said, leaning into Blaise. She cupped his chin between her thumb and index finger, seductively kissing his lips.

"Quit it girl before I have to tell them to restrain you until you're discharged."

Accepting that Blaise was not going to give into her ploys to get some dick before she was discharged, she settled on cuddling in the hospital recliner with him until the attending made their rounds. As they laughed to reruns of Martin, she stole glances at him. He really was the answer to a prayer she never sent up and she was truly grateful for the people who constantly prayed that God sent her a helpmate. Just as she heard him begin to lightly snore like their daughter, there was a light tap on the hospital door. Expecting the doctor, she raised slightly to peek over his shoulder.

"Aunt Phae," She smiled.

"Hey, my sweet baby girl. I know I'm the last person you..."

"You're the first person I wanted to see. Auntie, I've missed you so, so much," she whispered, meeting her in the middle of the room.

Though she was overjoyed to lay eyes on her estranged aunt, she knew Blaise needed his rest. She could only imagine what he went through mentally and emotionally and how that transpired in his physical. His endurance made her love him even more because he so selflessly gave himself to her, even when she felt she didn't deserve it.

"Auntie, I want you to know I never stopped loving you. Tracy told me she gave everyone my letters, and while I absolutely wish she hadn't, I'm glad Rue called you. I'm so happy to have you back in my life and I'm deeply sorry about the blame I placed on you. You are the only piece of mommy I have left, and I shut you out."

"You were young, hurt and alone. And I didn't step up. I ran. I retreated. Out of grief, but moreso out of guilt. I love you my little Phe Phi Phae. I am so glad God kept his hand on your life. I'm elated you're still with us. And when we get you all settled in and you get to bond with your beautiful baby girl and that gorgeous specimen of a man over there, I want all the details."

"Auntie, really. We're bonding and you tryna trade relationship tea."

"Girl, you know I never miss a sip."

As the two women sat on the side of the bed reminiscing and catching up on all they'd missed, Phoenix realized she'd somehow managed to end up with a life better than the one she thought she lost with Darrell. Her parents had always told her that whatever was for her would be for her. She wouldn't have to settle or compromise. She wouldn't have to dim her light or shield her personality. Everything she tried to hide about herself were the things that truly illuminated the best qualities about her. She was so grateful Blaise chose to see her, even when she was drowning in darkness.

"Okay, Mrs. Jones, I know you are ready to bid us all farewell," Nurse Carmen greeted as she entered the room.

"Mrs. Jones?" Aunt Phae quizzed.

"Wait, he did ask you already right? Please don't say I spoiled the proposal?" Carmen asked as panicked spread across her face.

"No. You didn't. He asked me this morning. But just out of curiosity, how long did he have this ring?"

"Maybe a week or so after you were put in a medically-induced coma. He slipped it on your finger a few weeks later when he said his goodbyes. But a few days before you woke, he slid it off and said he just felt you were on your way back."

Phoenix's head swiveled in his direction. He was still fast asleep in the recliner. Tears stained her cheeks as she quickly swiped at them. They were falling faster than her fingers could glide them away. He never stopped amazing her with his dutiful acts of love. She never doubted he loved her, and every story she heard from the people who watched him maneuver through her time away made that even more clear to her. There was no one else on earth for her but him. He was and would forever be her person. Her fortress. Her refuge. Her strength. Though she could find all those things in herself, she no longer had to because he'd assumed the role.

CHAPTER TWENTY-SIX

Lovingly, Phoenix walked slowly behind Blaise as he carried their picnic basket. Eternal cooed as she bounced with each step he took. She loved how he wanted her close to him at all times. Phoenix hardly had to do anything but nurse her baby girl when he was around. The love he showered her with increased exponentially for Eternal. He beamed with pride for his role as a girl dad and she oozed pride watching them together.

Her smile widened as they neared her favorite hiding place. Lavender, lemongrass and sage peaked above some of the rocks as she got closer to where she usually spread their blanket. Her eyes darted around as she noticed how much it mirrored the meadow behind her house. This had to be his and Forge's doing because it was rare anyone else ventured so far off the trails on this side of the town. The ocean could be unforgiving at times, and if you weren't familiar with the area, one slip could land you in the deeper part of the water.

"When did you do this?"

"I started on it about three weeks after you..."

"Slipped into a coma," she finished, seeing the sadness in his eyes.

It had been a month since she'd awoken and been home with him and Eternal, but he still got a bit choked up whenever the topic came up. Unlike before, she was more aware of her words and didn't speak so freely of her leaving them one day. Before, it was something she accepted and felt she'd be ready whenever the time came. But now that she had a fiancé who literally would move the heavens and earth to spend his life with her and a daughter who'd need her guidance, she wanted to have more life.

"Yea. I came out here a lot when I'd leave the hospital after checking on you. It took me weeks to build up the strength to walk in your room. But I'd come here and just sit here for hours or stand out on the edge of the cliff. I felt closer to you when I was out here. Away from our families, away from the noise. I could think and process my emotions. I'm not sure if any of them told you, but I was mean to everyone in the beginning. Coming here helped me recognize what I needed to do to be more supportive of everyone around me."

Phoenix wiped the tears that threatened to spill over her lower lids. It was supposed to be a happy day. They were sharing a piece of their love story with their baby girl. It was their first family outing, and she did not want to spoil it by taking a trip down their not-so-distant memory lane. They were in a happy space. Every appointment since she'd been discharged was better than the one before it. She was doing better than her doctors expected, and none of them had an explanation as to why her health had been on an upswing. But she did. Her circle was full of prayer warriors whose prayers were always answered with 'yes' and 'amen.'

"Did she fall asleep?" Phoenix asked, changing the subject.

"You already know she did. This girl gets enough sleep for all three of us."

"Not too much on my baby. Growing is a full-time gig. She's exhausted."

"You know she never slept this much before. I think she knows you're safe, she can rest easy."

Phoenix unrolled the extra blankets she'd brought along for Eternal's nap. After creating her palette, she fluffed the pillows and sat down. With her hand shielding her eyes from the unrelenting setting sun, she watched Blaise unharness Eternal from the baby carrier. He showered her forehead, cheeks, and little nose with kisses before handing her over to her mother. Phoenix kissed her eyelids and whispered 'sweet dreams' in her ear before laying her down.

Reaching out her hand, she invited Blaise to sit with her. Placing his palm in her petite hand, he sat down between her legs. Phoenix loved to feel the uneven edges of the rocks against her back. The pressure was unmatched. As she leaned back, she pulled him back as well, allowing his head to rest on her thigh. Softly, she played in his hair. During her time in the hospital, he hadn't shaved or cut his hair. Once she was home, she loved his full beard and head full of pillow soft hair. Her request for him not to part ways with his new look was granted. As often as she wanted, she twirled his kinky coils between her fingers. Taking the comb and staple black mama grease from Eternal's diaper bag, she began parting and greasing his scalp, massaging as she worked her hands through his hair.

Silently, they enjoyed time together away from everyone else. As much as she wanted to just exist with her fiancé and daughter, she didn't want to be selfish and tell all the people who'd come to see about her that she just wanted them to go home. There was no way for her to say it and it not seem insensitive to the mental and emotional healing they were all trying to achieve. She knew her complications from childbirth sent all her loved ones down a dark path and she didn't want to shake their already unstable foundation. But while the family all went to cheer on her nieces at their track meet, she took the opportunity to get in some quality time with her family.

As she listened to the light snoring of Blaise and Eternal, she silently thanked God for giving her back to them. She loved waking up to them every morning and spending her days sprawled across the couch with Blaise while their eyes bounced between the television screen and Eternal having tummy time on the floor just a few feet away from them in her play quarters. There were no words that needed to be spoken. Their presence was all she needed to feel at peace and alive. As the sunset over the beautiful family hiding out in their favorite cove, it was as if for a second God was personally watching over them. For that moment, he didn't send an angel to man the post, but he took up arms himself, shielding them, restoring them, refining them for the next leg of their journey together.

The night's chill soon crept into her bones, and she thought it best to wake her family so they could get back to their warm abode. Gently shaking Blaise's shoulder, she woke him so he could get Eternal. She still had yet to wake, and Phoenix beamed with pride. The second Eternal's pediatrician gave her the okay to start giving her food, she put the baby food maker that Forge had given her to good use. Eternal was chunky and wasn't missing any meals. Those hearty meals kept her full and asleep. She barely woke throughout the night anymore and her parents appreciated being able to sleep uninterrupted.

"B, come on, it's getting windy. We should start heading back to the truck before it starts raining."

"Awww, babe, I fell asleep on you. You can't be out here giving massages and shit. I'm just like our daughter, that shit puts me out every time."

"Whatever. That's cap. Your ass falls asleep on me even when there is no massage involved."

"One thing about me, I'm gon' take me a nap."

"Clown."

"You love this clown, tho, don't you," he taunted as he pecked her lips before getting up.

"More than my fat ass loves canna cream," she responded as he helped her stand up.

Hurriedly, they folded their blankets and packed up the toys they thought Eternal would play with at some point. Phoenix stood back and watched as Blaise carefully strapped Eternal to his chest. He was extra gentle with her, trying not to interfere with her sleep.

"Why you standing over there all by yourself for," Blaise sang as he reached out his hand for hers.

"I just love watching you with her. She brings out a softer side of you."

"So do you."

"Yea, but your soulmate softness is a little firmer than your girl daddy softness. Watching you with her is like watching my favorite romance movie on repeat. My heart is just full the whole time."

"Softie. You're such a fucking word girl. Who just thinks of shit like that to just say in real life?"

"What can I say, I'm just a walking, breathing romance movie."

"Girl, your idea of romance is Klaus and Cami."

"You know what, not too much on Klaus."

"Why are we never serious?" Blaise asked as he took her hand.

"Because being serious doesn't keep the romance alive."

The happy, unserious couple walked hand-in-hand back to the truck. As they walked, Phoenix twirled her engagement ring around her finger with her thumb. She'd been engaged for a month, and it was still surreal to her that she was living the life she thought Lupus stole from her.

Since moving to Solace Point, more than just her health had been restored and she was grateful for her sister's persistence. She would have died working toward her goals if she stayed in Atlanta. Her life revolved around meeting deadlines and if she would have continued, she would have flatlined instead. But, as her fiancé opened her door and helped her inside the truck, she realized the importance of sitting still, waiting on God, and accepting the help offered from the ones she loved.

The next morning, Phoenix rose early to sit alone and journal in the parlor. She hadn't picked up a pen since being home and until that morning, she hadn't felt the urge. But as she watched her family, a sense of gratitude and introspection consumed her existence. She needed to unearth the transformative musings that made her the person that she was in this new phase of her life.

Time seemed to pass by without her as she sat in the bay window watching the rain fall. Her pen easily glided across the pages of the brand-new journal that sat waiting for her. She loved Blaise more each day, and it was days like the present one that made her realize just how much he paid attention to her. She'd mentioned needing a new collection of journals because hers were nearly full and throughout all the angst that surrounded their daughter's birth, he remembered. He even had them personalized and numbered, so that she could serialize them afterward.

Without even looking up from her page, her smile widened. His scent was intoxicating and nearly a year later, she couldn't see herself ever tiring of inhaling it. Her eyes closed as he walked up on her and leaned into her ear. With a gentle kiss to the temple, he greeted her, interrupting her moment of solitude.

"Have I told you I love you lately?" she asked as she closed her book and turned around.

Playfully, she tucked her finger in the waistband of his pajamas and pulled him between her knees. With his palms planted on either side of her thighs, he peered down at her. Love stared back at him as he leaned in for a kiss.

A devilish smirk appeared in the corner of her mouth. Since being home, it was rare they were ever alone. There were always at least two other adults in their space. And as much as they both wanted to duck off in a room and get their rocks off, they refrained.

Phoenix's hand cupped his face as she pulled him fully into her space. Gently, she kissed his forehead, eyelids, and nose before making it to his lips. Her breath caught in her throat as she tongued him down. Never coming up for air, she pulled his shirt over his head. In one motion, they were both on their feet, sensually caressing every part of each other's body. Clothes landed on her plant babies, shielding their eyes from the debauchery that was about to take place.

As Blaise lifted her into the air her pussy leaked instantly. Her legs dangled over his shoulders as he blew on her clit. She couldn't wait to feel his tongue on her hot flesh. Seconds later, Phoenix gasped for air as she clawed at his head. With her back pressed against the wall, and her toes curling, she whimpered with pleasure.

Blaise's tongue trailed the path from her clit to her asshole before he French-kissed her pussy. He fucked her with his thick, stiffened tongue as he cupped her left breast. They'd grown even more since she'd given birth and he loved how her triple D's felt against his flesh. Soft and pillowy. Her legs shook and tightened around his neck as he increased the rhythm of his tongue.

"Mmm. Shit, B. Keep it right there. Ssss," Phoenix begged as he replaced his tongue with three fingers.

"Fuck, babe. I'm about to cum, I don't wanna cum yet," she whined.

"Gimme that shit. It's never one and done with me. Let that shit go, babe."

Blaise coached her through her orgasm. Phoenix always tried to hold onto her nut as long as she could, but he encouraged her to get her rocks off as often as it came. Making her bust all over his chin and dick was always the goal. He loved bringing her the pleasure he knew she both desired and needed. When it came to pleasure, hers was always above his own.

His thumb circled her clit as he flicked his tongue over her asshole before inserting his tongue inside. The overstimulation she felt caused her body to convulse. She wanted to tap out as she hung in the balance, unsure of her present state. Searching the space above her head for sound, her eyes slightly rolled to the back of her lids as a rush of liquid splashed all over his face and shoulders.

"Ahhhhh. Fuck B! I'm cumming," Phoenix's passion-fueled cries bounced off the walls as she yelled out in ecstasy.

Blaise smiled as he marveled at the sight before him. Her chest rose and fell in rhythm with her pulsating pussy. His newfound task was to make her squirt like that every time he ate her pussy.

As she rode the high of her orgasm, his kisses rained all over her body. Her hot flesh against his lips was electrifying. From her neck back down to her pussy, his lips intensified her orgasm. Her breathing slowly returned to normal as her eyes fell onto him. A sultry grin rested at the corner of his mouth as he looked at her through low lids. She looked heavenly with her purple locs pressed against her sweat-glazed face.

Taking a step back, he lowered her from his shoulders on her wobbly legs. Realizing that she wouldn't make it a step, he lifted her thighs into the crooks of his arms. Her arms found their home around his neck as she nibbled on the tattoo of her initials just below his collar bone. Pulling the throw blanket from the love seat, he wrapped it around her shoulders as he sat down.

Not wanting to waste another moment with his dick outside her pussy, she lifted up slightly to free him from the pajama pants he still donned. Biting her bottom lip, she placed her bodyweight on her ankles and gave herself room to slide him into his forever home. They sighed in unison as their souls reconnected. Neither realized just how much they both needed the pulse of electricity that coursed through them at the connection of their bodies.

Slowly, Phoenix rode him as she gazed lovingly into his eyes. Her favorite pastime was getting lost inside his dark orbs. They were inviting and provided a warmth she never felt. For once she felt at peace being wrapped up in his love, shielded from the chill of loneliness she always tried to convince herself she didn't know. Everyone commented on how good love and motherhood looked on her, but no one could ever understand just how at home she felt with him. She didn't need to be anyone other than her goofy, irrational, stubborn, vulnerable self, and he loved every part of her.

With intention, she watched him as she increased her speed. She gripped his shoulders, her fingertips piercing his back as he matched her rhythm. His strong arms around her waist slowed her speed until she was no longer in control. Her moans and cries reverberated throughout the room as she felt her next climax building.

"Open your eyes, I wanna see you," Blaise coached as he lifted her from his lap with every thrust.

"Fuck, I caaaan't," she cried as she clinched her eyes tighter shut.

"Yes, you can, now be a good girl, and open them" he praised her as he delivered powerful deep strokes.

Her whimpers were music to his ears. Sweat dripped from her chin onto his chest as she dropped her head. His smile was bright as he admired the sex-spent look on her face. She hadn't opened her eyes as she concentrated on holding in her orgasm. He knew she was fighting hard not to climax, and he was determined to pull it out of her.

"Open your eyes," he demanded as he pulled completely out of her.

"Put him back in," she moaned, as her eyes opened. They were glossy, and low.

"That's my good girl," he smirked as he kissed her lips.

His dick and tongue simultaneously filled their intended holes. The air left her lungs as she felt his dick knocking at her g-spot. He wrapped a hand full of her locs around his fist as he yanked her head back. His tongue trailed the length of her neck, causing her to yell out in ecstasy. In her mind, she didn't deserve the amount of pleasure he was bestowing upon her. Her eyes fluttered as she fought to keep them open, afraid he'd snatch his dick back if she closed them.

Unable to fight it anymore, she tried to drop her chin to her chest. Her eyes rolled in the back of her head briefly before he was demanding her attention again.

"Open your eyes," he coached as he lifted them both up from the couch. He laid her down on the couch and kneeled down until his dick was poking at her center again. Looking into her eyes, he sighed as his dick found its way back home. Slowly, he delivered rhythmic strokes to her, causing her head to raise slightly from the couch.

"You take this dick so well," he said as he pulled all the way out and admired her thick, creamy coating as it covered his shaft.

"And your cum got my dick looking like the latest Yayoi Kusama piece," he sang her praises as he fed her pussy his dick.

"You ready to cum for daddy?"

"Mmmm."

The way he fed her soul with his dick had her unable to form a sentence. Her moans of gratitude were all she could offer as her walls tightened around him. Allowing her the pleasure of busting all over his shit for the second time, he gyrated his hips, causing his dick to paint figure eights on her insides. Her cries compounded with the sloshing of her gushiness as she squirted all over the place.

"Good girl," he said as he kissed her lips. Her body went limp as she basked in the afterglow of her orgasm. His tantalizing kisses let her know she was still among the living after the earth-shattering love making, he'd blessed her with.

Since they had the house to themselves for the day, they decided to lay in each other's comfortable silence. Phoenix locked her legs around his as she traced her initials on his chest. He kissed her forehead as he pulled the throw from the floor and covered their naked bodies.

"Can I buy you a short set," she asked as she kissed his chest.

"You so damn goofy." He laughed as he lifted her chin. "But yes you can buy me a short set, only if it comes with red lobster and a flight on your chopper."

"Now who's the goofy one?" Phoenix laughed.

"I mean I'm just letting you know I want the experience since you treating."

"Let me find out you a lowkey member of the Hive."

"I'm a high-key member. Did you forget I'm J.J's lil brother? She used to have my black ass standing in as her Kelly Rowland every day after school until her weird ass made some friends."

"Dang, she was Hive like that. I thought I was always doing

something by guilt-tripping Rue into getting me tickets to the concerts and begging for all her albums for Christmas."

"Nah, she got you beat. She only learned how to sew because she wanted to be some era of Bey every Halloween and my pops told her he wasn't about to be buying her all them separates for her to make an outfit. She needed to make it herself or just buy a damn costume."

Phoenix and Blaise lounged around for the rest of the morning. This was the first day they didn't have people breathing down their necks. Mama Jones had flown back home the night before and they were relieved. She never let them get a moment alone because she was constantly pining over Phoenix and Eternal. Rue, Forge, and Tracy had taken Eternal off their hands for the weekend, and they planned to spend nearly every moment fucking and sleeping, with meals at some point.

After lunch the couple had finally retreated to the upper level of the house to shower and change. Feeling refreshed they fell into bed and decided on a movie to watch together. With her head on his chest and her left arm draped over his body, Phoenix listened to his resting heartbeat. It was the most soothing sound she'd ever heard, and she closed her eyes to thank God, he granted her more time.

Tears always threatened to fall when she thought about how her independence nearly cost her the opportunity to know and be loved like she'd never known or been before. Nothing on earth compared to how she felt with him. She wanted to experience his love as much as possible for as long as she could.

"Why you get all quiet on me?" Blaise asked, kissing her forehead.

Phoenix sat up, thinking this was her only opportunity to say what was really keeping her silent. She didn't want to ruin the great day they were having, but she needed to share the news she'd been holding in since she read the email two weeks ago. The deadline for her answer was fast-approaching, and she knew she couldn't make the decision without him. They would be married in less than a year and they needed to make every decision together. Hard conversations couldn't be avoided and storming out was not an option.

"Just thinking about my future. What it'll mean for us?"

"What you mean," Blaise sat up too and paused the movie they were watching.

Her body tensed up, thinking about what happened the last time they tried having this exact conversation. She understood where Blaise's reservations came from. She didn't discredit his concerns, but she wanted him to for once see things from her side of the aisle. She worked hard and overcame so much to be where she was. Her dreams were one 'yes' away from being realized and she'd been blindsided by Lupus, by motherhood, by a pending marriage. Though the ladder was in her plans, she always thought they'd come after she had the career she'd always planned to have.

"Simone reached out to me about a two weeks ago with the opportunity of a lifetime. I've been putting off talking to you about it because I really just don't have the words to say. I don't know how to ease your concerns and let you know that I'll be fine. Or that we have nothing to worry about, because honestly, I don't know that any of that is true. But I do know I want this. I want it so bad, but not more than I want to build a family with you. I want an existence outside of the sick girl, the mother, the wife. I want something that is just mine, something that grew from my sacrifices. Something that says everything I overcame was worth it."

"What's the opportunity?"

Blaise wanted to kick himself after listening to Phoenix. The first time she got upset with him he never took the time to realize how everything made her feel. Their whirlwind romance happened fast.

Within eleven months of their first encounter, she'd almost died, gave birth to their daughter and accepted his hand in marriage. She'd turned down the opportunity to host Solace Point's biggest celebration of the year because of his concerns. He never took the time to see that she didn't see it as him saving her life, she saw it as him hindering her success.

"You really want to know?" Phoenix asked with apprehension laced in her tone.

Blaise closed his eyes and hung his head. He immediately felt like someone had drove a wooden stake through his heart. As many times as Phoenix made him binge The Originals, he'd always related to Elijah, but as she asked him for reassurance before telling him about her accomplishment, he realized he was indeed the Klaus of her world. He'd taken away her freedom to dream, to exist, to be all that she wanted to be, just like Klaus did to Cami.

"Babe, I really want to know. I'm sorry for not realizing just how much I'd hindered you when I told you I didn't want you to host. I won't even try to rationalize it because I based my opinion off of fear. I was afraid. I didn't know what would happen, and I should have had more faith in you to take care of yourself, you had been for so long before I met you."

"You were warranted in your fear because I hadn't been doing the best at caring for myself, but you did make me feel like you didn't care about what I wanted. I felt like you were taking away my identity outside of you, and I should have told you that instead of running away.

But this proposition is even better. She wants me to host a new talk show for black women called 'A Black Girl is Talking.' I'll have special guests, other black entertainers, creators and change-makers. Basically, we're taking back the narrative, redefining what journalism looks like for us and having some damn decorum while doing it. It will be a 60-minute time slot at nine. And Babe, guess what my starting salary is."

Blaise couldn't stop beaming with pride. Phoenix lit up as she talked about this opportunity and while his doctor hat was off, he still was apprehensive about how this would affect her health. He'd almost lost her once and he didn't want to meet the same odds a year from now if she leapt at the opportunity. But he knew she had to do this because not doing it would kill her slowly, painfully. It would make her battle mean a little less. And he never wanted to be the cause of her unhappiness.

"What is it," he asked, matching her excitement.

"The starting salary is $15 million a year for five years, with a $1 million signing bonus before I even start taping next summer."

"Get the fuck outta here. Babe, are you serious?"

"Dead ass. Simone sent over the contracts last week. I want J.J to look at them before I officially sign. I asked her to represent me last week. I figured after Eternal's first birthday I would start actively looking for a network home and would need an agent. I talked to her last week about it but didn't want to send the contract over until I talked to you first."

"Phoenix, I am so fucking proud of you. Send J.J the contracts. You're accepting that offer."

"Seriously? You're not going to give me one of your, 'Phoenix, your kidneys are fucking failing' lectures?" Phoenix mocked as she puffed out her chest, deepening her voice and furrowing her brow.

"Nah, a milder lecture on taking t easy and always putting you first is definitely coming at some point. But I don't want you not making your dreams a reality because you're sick. I realize it never stopped you before you met me, and I shouldn't stop you either. I love you and all I ever want to be to you is your peace, your joy, and your biggest fucking supporter."

"Really, B? You mean it?"

"I mean it. I've heard you and I see you. Your happiness is important to me and I know living out your dreams is a part of that happiness."

"You'll never fully understand just how much that means to me."

"It's the least I could do for the woman who holds my heart in her hands. You've mastered survival, now it's time to master living. And as long as there is breath in these lungs, I'm going to make sure you do," Blaise promised.

Phoenix jumped into his lap, raining kisses all over his face. Her tears streamed freely as reality sat in. Blaise had truly changed the trajectory of her life with one cup of tea. She made a mental note to have Forge mint the recipe for that blend because she wanted to be the owner of that NFT. Love had been all she'd known since she took that first sip.

"It really is us against the world," Phoenix said as she pulled him down onto the pillow.

"For eternity."

EPILOGUE

TWO YEARS LATER

PHOENIX SAT PERCHED ON THE BENCH AS SHE WATCHED ETERNAL AND HER big cousins chase their fathers around the yard. The party goers had all trickled out, leaving just her immediate family left to cap off the celebration of her baby girl's two years on earth. The day had been exhausting but the smile that remained plastered on her face since she first ran to the door was worth it. A smile pressed against her lips as she watched her blood sister and the five sisters she'd collected throughout life, Tracy, Kellz, Forge, J.J and Simone, over the rim of her glass. With a slow, intentional sip, she drank in the scene, thanking God for allowing her a second chance at life. So far, she'd done it right.

Her left palm circled her 5-month-old baby bump as she thought about all the moments she had made with her family since she woke from her coma. Her daughter's birthdays, her wedding to the love of her life, her career as a talk show host and co-host of the number one syndicated podcast with Simone.

For once, she sat with nothing on her plate that didn't serve her. No deadline requiring her attention anymore. No column needing her unique skill of searching through thousands of stock images for fitting black representation. Everything required of her was intentional and necessary for the goals she'd set for herself.

"Hey, Auntieee!" Kaleigh mimicked Erik Killmonger as she plopped down beside Phoenix on the bench.

"Hey Kaleigh, girl."

"Are you coming to the lake? Daddy and Uncle B are about to light the bonfire."

"It's time already," she smiled as she patted Kaleigh's hand that was on her knee.

"Yup, and you have to make the first wish, since this is your bloody tradition."

Phoenix laughed at her as they walked hand-in-hand to the edge of the lake where the rest of their family waited for them. A warm and fuzzy feeling engulfed her as she took each step. This was what realized dreams looked like. This was what answered prayers whispered in the night look like. This is what the manifestation of persistence and perseverance looked like.

She was living not just her ancestors' wildest dreams, but her own. She'd somehow overcome every roadblock placed in her way. And as she looked around and saw the love she felt for each person looking back at her reciprocated, she understood the power of love and loyalty.

Tears welled in her eyes as she looked at them all. Their gazes hadn't left her as they all waited for her to kick off their second annual family bonfire. Though she usually held her personal one on New Year's Eve, they'd elected the third Saturday in November as their family bonfire. Instead of burning old things that they'd want anew as she did, they burned wishes for each other.

A laugh tickled the back of her throat as she recalled the night she and Blaise planned the first bonfire. She wanted to go back to the night she introduced him to The Originals because, ever since she had, he found any instance to drop a Klaus quote or adopt some principle or tradition the Mikaelson family shared.

For the next hour, the family and friends took turns burning the wishes they'd made for each other and praying they came to fruition. Love and laughter flowed as free as the water that met them at the shore. The full moon glowed behind them as the stars filled the clear sky. The sky in Solace Point was unmatched, and she took every chance she could to marvel at its beauty.

From the corner of her eyes, tiny flickers of blue and orange flames caught her gaze. She turned to see her entire family enclosing her into a circle. Blaise assisted Eternal as she held a small cake adorned with a 'congrats' candle.

"I know that we are here to celebrate the second year of our beloved Eternal, but we could not let today go by without giving you your flowers. You've been a testament of faith, resilience and love for us all. Tonight, we celebrate the woman who as of 11:59 p.m. tonight became the host of the No. 1 ranked late show across both the network and syndicate," Simone announced.

"Wait, what. Are you serious?"

"Yes, girl! Your 100th episode put you literally on top of the world. You're a household name, sis. Three million viewers tuned in to hear you talk about love and Lupus. You've not only commandeered your treatment, but you've also captivated the hearts of millions of strangers."

Blaise lifted her into the air as she let out a joyful cry. Everything she'd asked for had been given. Everything she'd lost had been found. Everything she'd sacrificed had been restored. Everything she'd sowed had been returned tenfold. Life and love found her at the edge of herself and pulled her from the edge.

"Thank you for loving me back to life. I love you," she whispered into Blaise's mouth as she kissed him with the sound of their family and friends cheering and clapping.

"With me, you'll never perish. I'll always make sure you fly before you fall."

"Like a parachute," they whispered in unison.

ACKNOWLEDGMENTS

From Harleigh, with love:

As a self-published author, I'm only as good as the amazing black women who assisted me with presenting a love story that encompasses the stuff that black love thrives on. Mercy B. (Studio M), Cyn A. (Cynful Monarch), Jasemine K. (SheKnowles Editing), and Qiana H. (Hopeful Heartbreakers) without the services y'all provide to the Black indie author industry *Parachute* would have never saw this side of publishing.

There was much to unpack while writing. So many times, I tucked this story away, too triggered, too consumed, too preoccupied with what the words housed between the cover meant to a woman like me, a woman just like Phoenix. It's because of friends like Rhaniyah, who never left me on read when I sent back-to-back audio messages in the wee hours of the morning because I wanted to throw in the pen on this one so many times. But she reminded me this story needed to be written, not just for me, but for the black women out there also navigating life, love and lupus. It's because of OG Raevins like Jaleesa, Syretta, Nikki, and Crystal who reassured me that *Parachute* was indeed a love story worth telling. Sorry y'all, I didn't listen, and I touched this book just a little after y'all read it. But the added scenes were comical, right lol. Thank you, ladies, because without y'all Blaise and Phoenix would still be on draft number fifty-leven instead of on y'all's shelves.

To the advanced readers, thank you for reading *Parachute*. I first imagined the concept for this book back in 2015, after an extensive conversation about navigating love while battling with lupus. It was conversation I expounded on every fourth Thursday with my fellow lupus warrior women while we sat in the infusion clinic getting the necessary treatment to keep up going until the next time we saw each other. But even with the idea lingering on my heart for so long, it wasn't until 2020 that I fleshed out the idea and penned the first of six rewrites.

To the Raevins, y'all already know how I'm stepping about y'all. On some Lil' Bow Wow shit, there legit would be no me without y'all and I don't ever take the support y'all give lightly. Whether this is your first or seventeenth Harleigh Rae read, your support is felt the same. If you've reached this page, I hope Blaise and Phoenix's journey have touched your heart in some way. Please consider taking a moment or two to let me know what you thought of *Parachute* in the form of a review. Book ratings and reviews do a world of good for indie authors, they are to us what rain is to flowers. Plus, they let me know what's working and what's not. I love hearing what you'd like to see from me and even what you never want to read again.

If you liked (or loved) this book, please share it with a friend and let me know too. I'm pretty much on the main social media platforms, @xoharleighrae and love kicking it virtually (and a events) with those who read my work.

That about wraps this baby up, remember black love is real, is ours, and always matter.

Love always,

BOOK DISCUSSION QUESTIONS

ON CHARACTERS

1. Which character did you relate to the most, and what was it about them that you connected with?
2. How did the characters change throughout the story? How did your opinion of them change?
3. Are there any characters you'd like to deliver a lecture to? If so, who? What would you say?
4. If the book were made into a movie, who would play each of the lead characters?
5. Were there times you disagreed with a character's actions? What would you have done differently?

ON SETTING/PLOT

1. What scene would you point out as the pivotal moment in the narrative? How did it make you feel?

2. What scene resonated with you most on a personal level? (Why? How did it make you feel?)
3. What was your favorite chapter and why?
4. What (if any) questions do you still have about the plot?
5. How did you feel about the ending? What did you like, what did you not like, and what do you wish had been different?

ON THEMES/MESSAGES

1. What do you think the author's purpose was in writing this book? What ideas was he or she trying to get across?
2. What were the main themes of the book? How were those themes brought to life?
3. Did you notice any symbolism?
4. Do you have a new perspective as a result of reading this book?
5. Did you learn something you didn't know before?

ON ROMANCE

1. Did you like the "heat" level of the book?
2. Was the couple's connection believable? If so, at what point did they click for you?
3. Would you fall for either of the leads?
4. Were you rooting for the couple to get together all along? Why or why not?
5. Did the plot make sense or were there some gaps/liberties taken to help get the couple together (or keep them apart)?

GENERAL

1. What was your favorite part of the book? What was your least favorite?
2. What did you think of the writing? Are there any standout sentences?
3. What other books by this author have you read? How did they compare to this book?
4. What surprised you most about the book?
5. If you could ask the author anything, what would it be?
6. How does the book's title work in relation to the book's contents? If you could give the book a new title, what would it be?
7. Are there lingering questions from the book you're still thinking about?
8. Did the book strike you as original?
9. What did you think of the book's length? If it's too long, what would you cut? If too short, what would you add?
10. What songs does this book make you think of? Create a book group playlist together!

OTHER BOOKS BY HARLEIGH RAE

Noëlle & Ezra Saga

The First Noëlle

The Second Song

Serenade Me

Extended Play

A Graham Rhapsody

Big City Bliss Series

Ready. Set. Love.

Ready. Set. Lose.

Ready. Set. Live.

High Stake Love Series

Waiting Game

When We Were Flowers Series

A Rose Is Still A Rose

With A Dozen Roses

With A Winter Rose

The Singles

Love After Loss

If You Were My Best Friend

Coffee in the Noon

Bleeding Love

www.ingramcontent.com/pod-product-compliance
Lightning Source LLC
Chambersburg PA
CBHW020457310726

48979CB00016B/2695/J
9798987738504